"First Prize Is Nothing"

THE MARION INCIDENT

By: Jim Kitker

PublishAmerica
Baltimore

ISBN: 1-4241-7933-5 (softcover)
ISBN: 978-1-61582-260-7 (hardcover)
PUBLISHED BY PUBLISHAMERICA, LLLP
www.publishamerica.com
Baltimore

Printed in the United States of America

4/9/11
Best Wishes

Jim
1/23/2014
Frank ~ any friend~
of Mr. Pete Cowboy is
a friend of mine!
Mike Craig
(aka Kerry Gentry)

For the true Warriors of all the world...guardians of our sacred peace.

Acknowledgments

I am indebted to a dear old friend, who cogently explained to me the engineering, tactical and strategic elements of a nuclear submarine. He is a Warrior in the purest sense, whose request for anonymity shall be forever honored. I also want to express my profound gratitude to my children Patrick and Kara, for their unwavering support, friendship and, most of all, their love.

Special thanks are also due to Ana Alosco, Susan Ciboldi, George Comolli, John DiStasio, Kathy Gruner, Mike Kelleher, Bob Levitt, Marita Murray, Al Seifert and Sylvia Stedman for their countless hours of editing and constructive comments that always challenged me to reach for more than the stars. Who was it that said, "A friend in need is a pest?"

All descriptions of life aboard the *Marion*, a U.S. Fleet Ballistic Submarine (FBM), are factual and accurate. Its operations, equipment, tactics and the portrayal of its operating environment at sea in the 1970s at the height of the Cold War, are also factual and accurate—as are the landmarks referenced in London, St. Petersburg and Moscow.

While the ship and its characters' names are fictional, all major elements of the *Marion's* patrol and its aftermath are authentic and have been drawn from actual events, publicly revealed here for the first time.

Introduction

"First Prize is nothing.
Second Prize is a kick in the ass"
Hyman G. Rickover's first rule of positive leadership

A submarine, with all its crew and sophisticated technical being, serves, in the final analysis, to implement the will of one man—its commanding officer. To a remarkable degree, the effectiveness of the ship in her operations and her safety are determined by the strength of that will and the wisdom underlying it. No other single factor is as critical to a submarine's fortunes as the competence and leadership of her skipper.

One would expect, therefore, that prospective commanding officers would be subject to the most intense and sophisticated evaluation process to ensure their aptitude for command. To be sure, by the end of World War II, the scrutiny of senior officers and battle-tested peers effectively provided just such screening. But by the 1970s, the old Warriors of World War II were gone and, with them, many of their time-honored values. A new criteria had been initiated, by which submarine officers' potential was judged and by which their success in command were measured. This criteria placed more emphasis on engineering skills than on tactical competence, on academic performance rather than demonstrated leadership; and finally, on a willingness to follow rather than strength of character. Many of the old Warriors knew then that the new criteria were a dark portent for the future of submarine command.

What happens when a man is chosen for command for the wrong reasons, and as the governing will of his ship, loses touch with reality? What does it mean for the world at large? Little, perhaps, if the ship is a rowboat. But, what if the ship has the capability of pushing an already tottering world on the brink of nuclear confrontation over the edge to Armageddon?

Armageddon

"Can we ordain ourselves to the awful majesty of God...
to decide what cities and villages are to be destroyed,
who will live and who will die, and who will join
the refugees wandering in a desert of our own creation?"

Robert F. Kennedy

Since the end of the Korean War there have been three or four major instances when the world stood at the brink of a nuclear holocaust.

The first and best known was in October 1962 and occurred when the United States discovered that the Soviet Union had installed nuclear missiles in Fidel Castro's Cuba. After a standoff from October fifteenth to the twenty-eighth, that included a naval blockade of the island, Soviet Premier Nikita Khrushchev acceded to President John F. Kennedy's demands that the missiles be withdrawn. At the time of the crisis, the U.S. was unsure whether or not nuclear warheads for the missiles were actually on site in Cuba. The world did not learn until 1998, from Fidel Castro himself, that at the time of the missile crisis in 1962, Cuba had indeed warehoused 168 nuclear warheads on the island. And he said that he had also recommended to Khrushchev a pre-emptive nuclear attack on the U.S., despite the full knowledge that such an attack meant the total annihilation of the Cuban people.

Fortunately, Khrushchev realized such a preemptive attack also would bring the destruction of most, if not all, of Russia. The Soviets agreed to a quick withdrawal of the missiles in Cuba and the crisis ended.

The next incident of importance occurred on November 9, 1977, when the computers of three U.S. command posts indicated that the Soviets had launched an enormous nuclear missile strike toward the United States. Fortunately, ground-based radar stations indicated there were, in fact, no incoming missiles. Good judgment prevailed, and no counterattack was launched. Eventually, it was discovered that a training tape simulating a Soviet missile attack on the United States was mistakenly placed into the Pentagon's computer system.

The third and most documented incident, next to the Cuban Missile Crisis, occurred on September 26, 1983. Lt. Colonel Stanislav Petrov was in command of over two-hundred technicians and military officers in a vast secret underground bunker on the outskirts of Moscow. Shortly after midnight on that day, a new Soviet satellite system known as Oko, flashed a warning that five U.S. Minuteman nuclear missiles had been launched toward Moscow. Petrov had written the protocol for just such an event, which required immediate notification to superiors in Moscow. Thankfully, the clear-headed Petrov realized that the scenario he then faced was flawed. If the U.S. were going to launch a preemptive strike against the Soviets, it would not be with only five nuclear missiles. Petrov advised his superiors he thought it was a false alarm, though he was not totally confident of his reasoning. The next fifteen minutes were filled with the worst heart-pounding terror anyone in the bunker had ever experienced—waiting to see if Petrov's instincts were wrong—that the incoming missiles would actually strike Moscow. Gratefully, for millions of Americans and the rest of the world, Petrov's reasoning and judgment were right and, consequently, no Soviet nuclear counter-attack was launched.

Soon after that incident, a Soviet investigation disclosed serious glitches in its Oko satellite system. In 1984, Petrov "retired" from the military, scorned by the senior military and political leadership of the Soviets. Ironically, when his wife died in the early '90s, he had to borrow money to pay for her funeral. The world, at large, will never be able to pay its debt of gratitude to Petrov.

There are a number of other incidents where nuclear confrontations have been averted by responsible decision-making and, perhaps, the intervention of fate. All such incidents have given the world time to pause, but they did not rise to the level of sheer apprehension and incomprehensible fear that a nuclear conflagration was imminent.

This is the story about a fourth incident, that could have brought us all so perilously close to a nuclear Armageddon.

Washington, D.C.

October, 1970

Prologue

I stood at the entrance to the long second floor hallway of the Central Intelligence headquarters building in Langley, Virginia, admiring the portraits of former CIA Directors. I studied with curiosity the portrait of Major General "Wild Bill" Donovan, the acknowledged "Father" of the CIA. Truly a legend of epic proportions, his World War II-era Office of Strategic Services, known as the OSS, was the precursor to the present day Agency.

You must have been one interesting character from what I've learned... wish I had known you.

I had a few minutes before my scheduled briefing was to start and I turned to examine the photo exhibit of the missile sites taken at the time of the Cuban Missile Crisis. The sun's rays darting off the pictures made it difficult to concentrate or see. As I moved to a better viewing angle, I caught sight of my good friend, Lt. General John A. Mallove. Had I not seen who was approaching, I would have known it was him. The brisk cadence of his highly polished cordovan leather shoes clicking against the marble floors was unmistakable.

The "General" as everyone called him, was trim and obviously fit. A few inches over six feet tall, he was a handsome, energetic person with a ready smile. The smile reflected his friendly demeanor and sometimes masked the inner toughness of the man. The rugged square jaw, set in a face that seemed to be immune to nature's natural aging process, also hinted of that strength. A sharp dresser, he typically wore dark blue suits with flashy ties that complimented his cool blue eyes and neatly groomed medium-length light brown hair. The eyes were striking, always calm, but imbued with a unique vibrant intensity of focus—the eyes of a supremely confident man. His total countenance was that of an ageless Olympic warrior. I often thought his persona matched that of a flamboyant entrepreneur, or a Greek hero, more than that of a Deputy Director of the CIA. It was easy to understand why he was so universally liked and admired by those who knew him.

The General was a multi-lingual West Point honors graduate and war hero, highly respected for his personal association with and analysis of the crucial events of the Cold War. I knew that one of the principal reasons I was here for these briefings was the close friendship we had developed during the three years I had spent working at the State Department.

It seemed like only yesterday that I had graduated from Princeton with degrees in Russian language and history, with dreams of a career in the Diplomatic Corps. After graduation, to better my chances of reaching that goal, I entered Georgetown Law School to study international law. It was in my last year of law school that one of my professors introduced me to the General. Some inexplicable chemistry of personality must have taken place in that meeting. Maybe he thought, in time, I might become the son he never had. For whatever reason, he became my patron, and our relationship became extremely close—in a real sense, paternal. He and his wife had opened their home to me like I was a member of their family, and I cherished the relationship.

A year after completing my law degree, and with, I'm sure, the General's influence, I found myself one of the State Department's Russian analysts, and now I was its Chief Analyst in the area of Russian political and cultural affairs. My principal area of expertise was in assessing the everyday dynamics and motives behind the activities of the individuals overseeing the Communist Party, its senior military leadership and, most importantly, the Politburo.

We shook hands, he with his other hand on my left shoulder. Both of us simply stood smiling for a moment before he spoke.

"Patrick, I know we're scheduled for dinner tonight at 8:00 p.m. at the Capitol Grill. I forgot that I'm giving a lecture late this afternoon at 4:00 p.m. to first year foreign relations majors at Georgetown. Why don't you meet me at the lecture and we'll go to dinner from there?"

"That's fine with me, General," I replied. "I should have plenty of time to change and meet you."

"By the way, Patrick, your previously scheduled briefing here has been changed. In a few minutes Kevin Spicer will join us and you will both meet with George St. Pierre, our Director of Operations. George has been responsible for our clandestine collection of foreign intelligence for some time. He's very interesting and quite savvy. You'll like him. I've already cleared the meeting with your boss over at State, and he's approved your involvement. I'm running late, so I can't explain what this is about right now. But we'll talk tonight."

"Certainly, General," I replied. *What could this be all about?*

* * * * *

I found Kevin, a CIA specialist on all aspects of missile technology, waiting for me in St. Pierre's office. Kevin had a Ph.D. in both engineering and physics from M.I.T. and had been with the agency for over four years. Articulate, humorous, and a low handicap golfer, he was the antithesis of the popular stereotype of a technical analyst.

The large hulk of George St. Pierre completely filled his high back mahogany chair. He was, as the General promised, a fascinating character. His windowless office was tastefully decorated with artwork and pictures of family and friends. One could not help but notice that all his books, papers and other assorted items were meticulously stacked or set in place. St. Pierre obviously paid attention to every detail, and I surmised was not a man to waste time. As soon as our brief introductory pleasantries were over, he went right to the point of the meeting.

"Gentlemen, you both have just been appointed formal members of the SALT negotiating team. I appreciate your 'volunteering.' Effective immediately, and for the duration of this assignment, you both work for and will report directly to me. Questions?"

Kevin and I exchanged glances. If either of us had a question, neither was about to raise it.

St. Pierre continued. "One of the key supporting players on the Soviet side of the current arms limitation negotiations is a Colonel Nikolai Pesarik. He's a former nuclear submarine commander, and is presently on the staff of Fleet Admiral Gorshikov, which serves as his cover as a KGB colonel.

"He is closely allied with a number of influential members of the Politburo and Kremlin insiders who are pushing Brezhnev to make significant reductions in the arms race with us via the Strategic Arms Limitation Treaty negotiations.

"In spite of the fact that he is ten or twelve years older than either of you, he is your counterpart on the Soviet team. We have reason to believe that he will not be hostile to either of you on a personal basis. Our hope is that, through your professional and social contacts with Colonel Pesarik, one of you will develop a personal and confidential relationship with him such that you can, in effect, become a behind the scenes conduit for position information normally not presented up front at the negotiating table.

"Pesarik is already aware, Kevin, that you're CIA, and that Patrick's from State. He also knows that you're both on the primary negotiating team, and that you both speak fluent Russian. The colonel is the Kremlin's primary discreet conduit to their negotiating team.

"This part of your mission and the Agency's involvement will remain classified indefinitely. Understood! Any questions?"

Kevin and I again exchanged glances and mutely shook our heads. We were too stupefied to think of the hundred or so questions we should have asked.

St. Pierre was anxious to move on.

"Good luck, gentlemen. Your plane departs from Dulles tomorrow at 4:30 p.m. My secretary will give you directions to the Agency hanger from which you will depart. Be there no later then 3:00 p.m. for clearance procedures and routine processing. I suggest you pack for at least a twelve-day stay. I'll see you both upon your return."

* * * * *

It was now close to 4:00 p.m. and the General's lecture was about to begin. The theater was filled to capacity, but I found a seat near the back. I was curious to hear what he would have to say to this body of students. Over time I had had many private conversations with the General about various aspects of the Cold War. Each was unique and I knew, based on that experience, that I would learn something new from this one, too.

One of my former law professors, John O'Meara, gave a concise biographical sketch and introduction for the General. Even so, the General seemed anxious to be finished with the accolades and was quick to take the podium. Typically, the General spent little time on his preamble.

"Good afternoon, ladies and gentlemen. I have personally and closely observed all the events that fan the fires of the present day Cold War. No one could have imagined the incredible sequence of events that have brought the Soviets and the Americans to the daily edge of mutual annihilation. For a few minutes, let me review certain historical aspects of the Cold War that have brought us to this point. It may help your understanding of the present day mentality and posturing of the Russians."

For the next hour or so the General chronicled the history of the Cold War. He began with the origin of communism after the 1917 Bolshevik Revolution in Russia, then described significant post-World War II events; the division of Berlin and Germany and the creation of the Iron Curtain across Eastern Europe by Stalin; the 1948 blockade of West Berlin; the defeat of the pro-West Nationalists in China by Mao Tse-Tung's communists in 1949, a defeat that confirmed communist domination over most of the Euro-Asian continent and legitimized concerns of a communist monolithic movement; and then the Korean conflict that began in 1950 and lasted close to three years.

He became terse, and his displeasure evident, as he included in his lecture comments relative to the despicable witch-hunts of Senator Joseph McCarthy here in America—the era of "Red hysteria"—that attempted to destroy all who had any fascination or mere association with the communist philosophy, even academic interest in it.

As the General talked, picture slides depicting various aspects of each historical event appeared on a large screen off to his right. All in all, quite impressive I thought. The General ended the first segment of his lecture with the Soviet erection of the Berlin Wall in 1961, noting that it had become a chief symbol of the Cold War's cruelty and Europe's division. The next slide was that of a mushroom cloud of a hydrogen bomb detonation.

The General paused a minute to clean his glasses and check his watch. No one stirred. The effect of this picture assured everyone's attention.

The General then continued. "After much reflection, I now believe that, in addition to the cultural and political schism between East and West, the primary driving forces behind the Cold War are the fears and miscalculations, by both sides, associated with the advent of the 'Nuclear Age.'

"As you know, on August 6, 1945, the United States dropped the first atomic bomb on Hiroshima, then three days later, on Nagasaki. Japan quickly surrendered and World War II ended. But the war fought to end unspeakable brutality closed by giving birth to the dawn and specter of the Nuclear Age—and with it, the inherent fears, tensions and suspicions from which the Cold War eventually bloomed. A Cold War fueled by the contagious distrust of two superpowers with irreconcilable ideological differences…the Soviet Union's version of communism vs. Western democracy.

"Soviet spies, having stolen American nuclear secrets, allowed the Soviet Union to detonate its first atomic bomb in 1949, years ahead of schedule, and the nuclear arms race escalated to heights that were previously unthinkable, and indeed now almost inconceivable.

"In 1952, the United States detonated the first hydrogen bomb, then, in 1954, the Soviet's did the same. The Hiroshima bomb, which killed eighty thousand souls in less than fifteen minutes, is $1/700^{th}$ as powerful as a one hundred megaton hydrogen bomb. In 1957, Soviet scientists tested the world's first intercontinental ballistic missile, and on October 4, 1957, shocked the world by launching Sputnik, the world's first satellite.

"One of the reasons the winds of the Cold War swirl so viciously today involves the seldom-understood interrelationship of certain significant events.

"For some time in the fifties, each superpower used every propaganda means at their disposal to claim nuclear superiority, but, in fact, by 1960 the United States overtook the Soviets in missile/satellite technology. Many in the United States mistakenly believed that the Soviets were still in the lead. The myth of the 'missile gap' endured despite evidences to the contrary—a result of Premier Khrushchev's colossal bluff of bluffs.

"And then the birth of Fidel Castro's communist government in Cuba, in 1959, significantly heightened Cold War tension. Khrushchev and Castro embraced each other by early 1960.

"In a daring move, Khrushchev, emboldened by the youthful President Kennedy's Bay of Pigs humiliation, secretly introduced intercontinental ballistic missiles into Cuba, and thereafter, the "'Thirteen Days of the Cuban Missile Crisis' ignited the closest nuclear confrontation between the two superpowers—each on the brink of total nuclear war. The world's survival literally hung in the balance.

"Kennedy, resolute in his belief that we had nuclear superiority over the Russians, ordered a naval blockade of Cuba. On October 28, Khrushchev blinked and withdrew all missiles from Cuba.

"A relieved world sighed, as nuclear annihilation, which had been only a hairbreadth away, was averted. Averted, because Khrushchev knew that America's superior nuclear firepower meant the Soviet Union would be completely destroyed. I now believe the peaceful resolution of the Cuban missile crisis by Kennedy may someday be seen as the first building block in the tortured process of ending the insane madness of this Cold War.

"But, as a result of the Cuban crisis, the entire world now knows that the possibility of a thermonuclear war is a very credible reality. Each side has enough nuclear missile capacity to destroy the world ten-fold, yet the sheer madness and insanity of the arms race continues.

"Finally, I'm sure you need little reminding of recent events that have affected the ever-shifting balance of power.

"Vietnam from 1954 to 1964, was divided by the communists in the North, who are supported by the Soviets and Chinese, and the non-communists in the South supported by the United States. President Johnson, in 1964, committed American ground troops, naval and air support to Vietnam in a showdown with the communists to stop their Asian expansion.

"This long tragic war has torn not only Vietnam apart, but also the very fabric of America. I have no doubt that its effects, social and political, will result in profound distrust of government and its institutions for many years.

"With Cold War tensions heightening in the 1960s, the two superpowers escalated the arms race. The Submarine Launched Ballistic Missile or SLBM was born in 1959. Married to the nuclear powered submarine, it became the linchpin to the nuclear paradox 'Mutually Assured Destruction.' For the concept of MAD to succeed, each side needed to be able to swiftly retaliate with annihilatory force within minutes of being warned of a surprise attack…and so nuclear submarines carrying ballistic missiles have become the king maker because of their invulnerability.

"Détente soon eludes what strategic sanity is left when the Soviets developed anti-ballistic missiles, or ABM's, that could destroy our missiles in flight, thus threatening the viability of MAD. American scientists countered by developing "MIRVS," Multiple Independently Targeted Re-Entry Vehicles, to defeat Soviet defenses by saturation. One single missile can now carry ten separate warheads, each independently aimed and capable of destroying multiple different targets.

"As of last year, the Soviet Union and the United States are each spending fifty million dollars a day on nuclear armaments. It is an engulfing financial and social burden I believe both sides will soon find intolerable.

"Today, the seas of world politics are, perhaps, the most treacherous in history. We are still embroiled in a "hot" war in Southeast Asia and a "cold" war worldwide, a Cold War that has continued unabated since 1945. Insurgent, revolutionary movements are active on every continent, most of which are presumed to be Moscow motivated and communist inspired. The Cold War has not ebbed, and nowhere are the spear points closer to touching than at sea.

"Nuclear submarines are where the decisive strategic balance rests. Each side plays cat and mouse games in a near war atmosphere that challenges the technology and wit of both sides. Soviet and American submarine fleets are now routinely operating with the nuclear strike capability of initiating global nuclear war within a time frame of just under fifteen minutes. Clearly, the critical theater of the Cold War has moved to the realm of the submarine.

"Nuclear stockpiles remain at absurdly high levels as the world's two superpowers maintain a wary eye on each other in the global arena. Our military forces are in a constant 'alert' status ready to go nuclear.

"This is why the pursuit of a Strategic Arms Limitation Treaty is so important. I'm convinced it's another essential building block in the process of reducing tensions and the risks of a nuclear exchange. The proposed treaty would impose a five-year freeze on the testing and deployment of ICBM's and SLBM's. Hopefully, it can also achieve an agreement reducing the total number of offensive nuclear weapons. SALT is the first real diplomatic effort to curb the insanity of the arms race.

"Thank you for this invitation to speak to you, and good luck during your tenure here at Georgetown. I have a few minutes left to answer any questions you may have."

The General deftly answered questions for over twenty minutes, then politely acknowledged the audiences' standing ovation and long applause. I knew he would be anxious for a Dewars.

* * * * *

It was a short drive to the Capitol Grill where a secluded table in the rear of the dining room was reserved for us. The General ordered a fish special and I, the steak au poivre. We both loved good food and soon agreed that our dinners were exceptional. This being my last night in D.C. for some time, we moved to the two armchairs in the far corner of the now dimly lit lounge-bar area and lingered longer than normal over coffee and a few cordials.

"Patrick, the SALT negotiations hinge for both sides on the offices of good honorable men and the issue of verification of each's respective missile levels. Colonel Pesarik is extremely bright, his English is quite good, and I believe he can be trusted. Remember, that despite the public posturing, the Russian's are as desperate as we are for an agreement. I think you'll both like each other."

"General, let's hope so," I replied.

"It's starting to snow and I know you have a full day tomorrow before your flight, Patrick. We should leave soon."

"I think you're right General."

As we finished our coffees, I ordered our cars from the valet service. Outside we exchanged "God speed, good luck" words followed by the typical bear-hug embrace.

It was unusually cold for this time of year in Washington, and I wished I had the foresight to have brought a trench coat with me. The falling snow was thick in the now gusting winds. Late tomorrow afternoon I had an overnight flight to Geneva with other members of the negotiating team, where the first round of private talks was scheduled. My ride home was uneventful, and I found myself thinking about the General's Cold War lecture.

What the General and I didn't know, and couldn't have suspected this night, was that the most significant Cold War event of 1970 was one that had just recently occurred—suppressed by a few senior military officers who had decided on their own not to reveal it to anyone.

My inadvertent and unknowing journey to discover it would be a fascinating one. It would take almost half a lifetime.

Connecticut

July, 2001

1

The Ghost of the *Ehime Maru*

The Connecticut landscape was rich with the many green hues of a summer afternoon in mid-July. It was a bright sunny day with a clear blue sky sprinkled with small, lazy cumulus clouds—what aviators typically referred to as "ceiling and visibility unlimited" with a thin scattered layer at seven thousand feet. New England had been under a widespread bubble of high pressure for the last several days, but today's air was still and increasingly heavy with rising humidity. If I had to travel, it was a good day for it, but it would have been much better to enjoy a few more days of the easy summer routine at my beachfront home.

From the back seat of my corporate limo, I leaned over to turn up the air conditioning a notch. I had just finished the last of my "must" calls from the car's built in phone—a last minute check in with the office and goodbyes to the kids—and looked forward to a quick read of the sports page and my customary Red Sox dialogue with Dan, my driver.

Dan was an affable young man of obvious Italian ancestry. He had a head of thick, jet-black hair and a face rounded by soft bulging cheeks. He adored his wife and three children, and, like myself, was cursed from early youth with an insane loyalty to the everyday heartbeat and drama of a Sox pennant race. Despite the fact they were six games behind the dreaded Yankees and looked like they were fading fast, Dan and I kept believing in another miracle stretch run like 1986.

Dan and I were employees of Consultech, Ltd., a multi-national conglomerate specializing in consulting services to the health industry. It was a Fortune 500 company with corporate headquarters just outside Stamford, Connecticut. He was well liked by the executives he chauffeured, mostly for his trait of keeping to himself all that passed by his ears and eyes while in their company. Dan had picked me up at my home in Old Lyme and we were on our way via I-95 South to New Milford to pick up my colleague, Michael Craig.

I had worked with Mike on and off over the last three years. Now in his mid sixties, he was Consultech's top troubleshooter and perhaps one of the brightest men I had ever known. A voracious reader, with an unrivaled vocabulary, it seemed to me that he knew something about almost everything—not just something, but exhaustive details on most given subjects.

Like most friendships that grow over time, ours was one based on mutual respect and trust. Mike was happily married with two grown children. He had graduated from Annapolis and had a distinguished Naval career in the submarine service, eventually given command of two different nuclear submarines. For reasons never shared with me, he had retired early at the rank of Commander after only twenty years of Naval service. He was widely published in his fields of expertise and was a respected authority on the art of managing large technical programs.

He seldom, if ever, talked about his military days, preferring in our social time to focus on the various nuances of whatever Consultech project had brought us together. And each time I worked and traveled with him I came to like and respect him more.

On the surface, he seemed to be a straightforward, simple study—the "what you see is what you get" type of guy. At times he could be dictatorial, an obvious carryover from his days as a commander, but typically he was genial in nature and well liked by his peers. Although Mike was an avowed atheist, I knew he had his own set of deeply held principles and moral values coupled with a warm streak of compassion for both people and animals.

For reasons I couldn't explain, I also had an intuition or suspicion that there was a "skeleton" lurking in his closet. I thought it might have something to do with the reason he had left early from a promising Navy career. There was something that he kept from the world behind a closed door of silence. He was usually willing to talk freely about his professional experiences during his post Naval career while he invariably turned aside any conversation about his days in uniform. I believed there was some life experience, buried deep in his past that he did not choose to share with me. I sensed it…but I couldn't quite touch it. I wondered if I ever would.

Dan was skillfully negotiating the high-speed heavy traffic on Route 95, on our way to New Milford. Looking in his rearview mirror he said, "Mr. Conley, is your flight to London still at 8:00 p.m.?"

"Yes, Dan. And for the tenth time, please call me Patrick."

Laughing he said, "Mr. Conley, you know I won't do that!"

This was my third trip to London with Michael in the last six months and its novelty had long since worn off. We were there at the behest of Dan Johnson, our corporation's CEO, to audit a venture of our British subsidiary that had incurred the wrath of its biggest customer, the National Health Service.

Mike and I were, in essence, a corporate fire brigade. I was now the corporation's lead litigation attorney and had become an expert on the medical health industry. Mike's job was to look at all aspects of the subsidiaries' technical and management issues with a particular focus on corporate risk. It was my responsibility to look at the contractual and political issues and, much like the maestro of a large symphony, find and eliminate the sources of disharmony in the business ballet between Consultech and its client.

I had left the State Department once the SALT negotiations had concluded, in May of 1972, to return to my home in Connecticut to practice law. For over twenty years, prior to coming to Consultech, I had been a reasonably successful civil trial attorney in New England's Federal Courts. By the end of that time, I desperately needed a change of pace. I was keenly aware that my success had not been due to any great intellectual capacity or rare courtroom talent, but more so to a God given gift of conveying sincerity when communicating with people and an innate ability to quickly discern and understand their motives, emotions and biases.

Now in my early fifties, with two grown children, I was still single after being divorced for over nine years. Working in the international corporate world had provided the refreshing venue I needed for my personal and professional energies. The money was good, but traveling the world first-class and meeting a wide spectrum of personalities in challenging situations had sold me on my new adventure.

We were getting close to Mike's house, and Dan blurted out, "The Sox are starting an important West Coast swing tonight, but don't put any action on them. They never do well out there. Texas and the Angels always have their number at home."

"Dan, I wouldn't bet on the Red Sox even when they play at Boston. My heart couldn't take it. And you should stop too—you have kids to educate."

After we pulled into Mike's driveway, Dan jumped out to load the luggage neatly stacked on the front steps. A medium sized dark-blue suitcase and a matching garment bag. Not much, as Mike was always a light traveler. I went to the front door to say hello to Mike's wife Meaghan. Still slim and pert, Meaghan looked much younger than her years. Pomp and social position failed completely to impress her, but she returned the warmth of real friendship many times over. I had come to sincerely like and admire Meaghan very much.

Mike was waiting at the door, so after quick hellos and hugs she shooed us out the door and we crunched our way across the pea gravel of the driveway to the limo. Mike and I settled into the back seat for the balance of the ride to JFK. We occupied ourselves with casual conversation, some laughs and good-natured needling. The status of my present love life became the prime target of barbs from both Mike and Dan. I didn't mistake their harassment for jealousy. Both of them knew I missed having a family around me.

Our check-in at JFK was routine and we headed for the American Airlines private lounge. Mike and I both favored scotch—Glenlivet for Mike, Johnnie Walker Red for me. We had an hour to kill before boarding, so we both sat down in lounge chairs to watch the nightly news.

ABC's Peter Jennings opened the broadcast with the findings of a U.S. Naval Court of Inquiry that detailed the reasons for the collision of an American submarine, the *USS Greenville*, with a Japanese research vessel, the *Ehime Maru*. I looked over at Mike, who was sitting calmly. He knew I was checking his "pulse" and he shrugged without comment, his face showing no emotion.

The mask of a great poker player?

Though nearly five and a half months had passed, my memory reeled back to the night of February ninth of this year like it was only moments ago. Then, as now, I was with Mike waiting for our flight to London and we were sitting in the same lounge chairs to watch the nightly news…

* * * * *

That night we both watched in dismay as Jennings detailed the breaking news of how an American nuclear fast attack submarine, the *USS Greenville*, had just sunk a Japanese fisheries training vessel about ten miles off the coast of Hawaii. The submarine had executed something known as an "Emergency Main Ballast Blow" which shot the submarine to the surface like a rocket. The Greenville's rudder ripped open the hull of the *Ehime Maru*, at the stern, where the engine room was located. Electrical power was lost and the Japanese captain was unable to radio for help. The *Ehime Maru* sank in ten minutes and early reports indicated there were only a few survivors.

Jennings went on to say that normal procedures required the crew to use sonar and a periscope to scan the surface of the ocean before such an unusual exercise was ordered. It was implied the submarine's commander may have been "showboating" to impress some visiting dignitaries on board.

I was shocked. *You have got to be kidding me. How could that possibly happen given the well-known high level of training and technical sophistication in our nuclear submarines?*

I turned to Mike. I was surprised by what I saw in his eyes. It wasn't just horror at the loss of life, it was grim, smoldering anger. His graying hair and white collared shirt clearly framed the anger that was so evident in his face. The *Ehime Maru* incident had touched some nerve in him in a way I had never seen before. I waited a moment. "Mike, how can something like that happen?"

He never raised his voice, but the heat in his reply was withering. "It only happens when the captain is tactically incompetent. In short, there are NO excuses."

A bit stunned, I still wasn't satisfied. "But, how could the captain have been so incompetent? Submariners are supposed to be the elite of the Navy?"

His look of anger was replaced by one of scorn mixed with resignation. "Elite engineers, yes—but sometimes, incompetent seamen. In ways you could never know, Hyman G. Rickover should get a lot of the credit for this tragedy. He made an enormous contribution to the creation of the nuclear submarine force, but he also did great harm in ways the public was never allowed to see. His distorted view of what makes a good submarine commanding officer is directly responsible for more submarine disasters and near disasters than you can imagine."

Now I was disbelieving. "But, Rickover is a national hero. He's known as the father of the nuclear powered submarine. And, he's dead! How the hell can he be connected with this?"

"Look, Patrick, there is an awful lot that you and the rest of the general public don't know—have never known—about the Navy, the nuclear submarine force and the men who lead it, including its 'Father.' You are right about those officers being an elite group. You just wouldn't recognize it as a cult and, if you did, you couldn't fathom the culture." With that, Mike stood, finished his drink in a single swallow and left for the gate.

I stood looking at his back as he walked away. *How the hell could the ghost of the Ehime Maru stir up those comments?* I knew he was upset and thought it best to let things settle, but his comment about a "cult" caught my attention. *What cult? He must be mishugana.*

I wanted to talk to him about what he had just said, but thought it would be best to wait until we were airborne. Mike's mood improved only slightly as we began the process of boarding. His thoughts were clearly elsewhere, concentrated on some distant place or time. I let him be.

Once settled in first class, our flight attendant brought us a round of scotches. She was very pleasant, and I remembered her from one of our earlier flights to London. She would make sure our heated nut dish would never be empty.

Mike had finally put aside his thoughts and returned to reality. I would wait for the meal service to start before attempting to talk to him about his earlier comments.

We decided to share a bottle of fine red Australian Shiraz for dinner. I gulped down my salad and a surprisingly good chicken dish. Mike was hungry also and finished his steak dinner quickly, ordering a cup of coffee to wash down the last roll.

Finally, I turned to Mike and said, "What's all that bullshit about a cult that still survives in the Navy?"

He looked at me with that half grin, half poker faced stare of his, that from past experience told me I had better buckle up.

"Order your Rusty Nail and I'll have an Amaretto. Are you ready for a serious discussion about the Navy?"

"Sure," I said.

"Do you know who Hyman G. Rickover is?"

"Of course. He's the father of the nuclear Navy. A legend of sorts."

"Let me suggest we both get doubles so we're not interrupted for the next half hour."

I was not a hard sell. There were empty seats near us so we could talk privately in normal tones. The drinks arrived and Mike turned in his seat to face me.

"Patrick, for a variety of reasons you and I have become great friends, and I trust you like the brother I never had, but there has never been any reason for me to dispel you of any of your romantic notions about the Navy. That period of my life is buried deep in the past for me and not relevant to what I do now."

32

Disabuse? The use of that word made me even more curious. *There must be much more to this than I can imagine at the moment.* I nodded a few times in quiet assent.

Mike settled back in his seat. "Look, Patrick, I'll give you my version of how the *Ehime Maru* incident happened, but I'll have to go back a long way and kill some sacred cows for you to really understand. You comfortable with that?"

"Sure," I said. "It's a long flight." *Was this going to be one of Mike's esoteric philosophical lectures or a lesson in unrevealed history?* I soon found out.

Mike went on. "In all ships, but especially in a submarine, safety and success are vested ultimately in the overall competence of the Commander. The ship exists, in a sense, as an extension of its captain's will. Ultimately, the ship and its crew reflect his traits. His intellect, judgment and leadership are implemented by his crew. Even a crew's attention to detail is governed by the focus of their captain. Conversely, it is true that the ship and its crew become as vulnerable as its captain."

"So, what does that have to do with the *Ehime Maru?*" I asked.

"Everything."

"I remember well your reaction to the first reports of the *Ehime Maru's* sinking this past February and your stoic one tonight. What could the *Ehime Maru* possibly have to do with you?"

Mike shook his head. "Nothing. Nothing any more."

I wasn't going to let go that easily. "Mike, there's more to this for you than you're telling me. What is it?"

Mike was threatening to shut down on me, but he reconsidered, and added, "Patrick, you know better than most that public perception is a manufactured commodity. The reality behind most public figures, be they national heroes or Hollywood stars is one thing. What you see publicly is often another."

What had Mike experienced during his career in the Navy? What did that cryptic remark about a "cult" mean and how could a dead Admiral have anything to do with the Ehime Maru disaster? Whatever it was, I was going to have to be a patient listener to find out.

The flight attendant passed with a smile, making the rounds of her passengers. When she had passed, Mike continued. "You have to know a little history of the U.S. Navy Submarine Force to understand what is happening today."

He paused for a moment, apparently collecting his thoughts and began. "The submariners that emerged from the penumbra of World War Two were an elite group of professional naval warriors by any standard. Their philosophy honored, above all, the skillful use of the submarine as a weapon. Beginning in 1954, though, they, along with their philosophy and values were progressively replaced by an officer corps that subscribed to a more political and, somewhat, superficial definition of professional competence."

I interrupted. "Why did that happen? And, what do you mean by political?

"Be patient and hear me out. By 1970, the Cold War was at its peak and the warriors were almost gone. The few that were left were like the last dinosaurs. There was no place left for them in the new world. At the same time, the influence of the Submarine Force was growing rapidly within the Department of Defense. Because its stealth made it the one strategic force that could not be preemptively neutralized, the fleet ballistic missile submarines, the SSBN's, were the force that assured ultimate, inescapable destruction of any would be attacker. Attack submarines, the SSN's, were yeoman intelligence gatherers and, in turn, our first line of defense against the Soviet's SSBN's. However, by this time, the Submarine Force belonged to a new and far different generation of officers…the NUC's. Their values were not those of the warrior, but came from their mentor, who had been the driving force behind their transmutation—Admiral Hyman G. Rickover."

Mike stopped for a sip of his drink, then continued. "The metamorphosis of the submarine force officers from a clan of keenly honed warriors into an elitist band of technologists came about gradually. It was a process that perhaps was never generally recognized, much less understood, by those whose professional values and integrity were molded by the sacrifices of war. It left the submarine force with an officer cadre that was compromised by the division of their loyalty between their strategic mission and the demanding dogma of Hyman Rickover, the head of Naval Reactors."

Mike's view seemed almost heretical to me. "Why should there be a conflict, any compromise?"

"Patrick, since the advent of nuclear power, submarine officers have been molded by a unique combination of conflicting professional and ethical pressures. First, there are the ethical pressures that arise from their responsibility for the performance and safety of their crews and the sheer magnitude of the awesome destructive power in their charge. Then, there are the professional pressures, sometimes more immediate and, perhaps, more influential, that are imposed by the rules of fealty to their fraternity."

"Fraternity?" I questioned.

"The fraternity was that of the nuclear trained officers, commonly known as the "NUC's." Membership was, and is, indispensable to professional success in the nuclear submarine force."

"So," I asked, "how did this fraternity—I think you earlier called it a cult—come to be? How could the 'warriors,' as you called them, be pushed aside so easily?"

"It wouldn't have been so easy," Mike replied, "if part of their fundamental character had been more political. A good warrior is not instinctively self-serving. He is apolitical by nature. His virtues are dedication to his mission, to his profession, and to his integrity. His Achille's heel is his tendency to assume those qualities are present in everyone that wears the same uniform."

"Then how did this transformation come about?"

Mike motioned the flight attendant over and asked for another drink. After it was served, he started talking again. "The metamorphic mechanism was simple, yet insidious. Admiral Rickover demanded and was granted total, unchallenged power to accept or reject any candidate for nuclear power training. No procedure existed to appeal his rejections and, more importantly, no higher authority in the Navy was willing or able to call Rickover to account for his selections. Or, for that matter, any other decisions he made. He, therefore, had unfettered power to mold his officer corps—the nuclear trained officers."

I had heard stories about Rickover, but they were always positive tributes to the man and his persona. A few had hinted that he had amusing idiosyncrasies, but I had always discounted them as exaggerations. *Where does the truth about the man lay?* "You say he molded 'his' officer corps. Did you mean to use the word 'his?'"

"Yes," said Mike. "My use of 'his' was intended. As I just said, Rickover interviewed and personally approved each officer candidate for nuclear power training. He started this process with the selection of the initial crew of the Nautilus prototype powerplant—in Navy parlance, the S-1-W."

I was in danger of getting lost in the acronyms. "S-1-W? What does that mean?

"Just like the military designates airplanes, the first letter represents the type of vehicle, the number is a sequential model number for the supplying manufacturer, and the last letter identifies that manufacturer. In this case, "S" means submarine, "1" stands for the first model of shipboard nuclear powerplant, and "W" represents the manufacturer, Westinghouse."

Mike was always good for a short tutorial. At least I now knew how the Navy labeled things, but I was more intrigued with Rickover's interview process. "You mean he interviewed and personally selected the first few crews?"

Mike laughed. "No. I meant what I said. He interviewed every officer candidate until he was forced into retirement nearly thirty years after that first crew."

I remembered reading, over the years, general praise of Rickover's personal dedication to the selection of his officers and said as much to Mike.

He went on. "You have to understand his real reason for doing that and the kind of officers that he chose. Probably more out of ego than conscious design, Rickover chose officers who were willing to sacrifice much to follow him as a kind of Messiah. Rickover was an EDO, an Engineering Duty Only officer, who, like all others of his support specialty, provided engineering support to the Navy Department ashore and was neither trained nor eligible for command at sea. He, therefore, had no experience in submarine command at sea.

"His personality was such that he looked down on those who did. In his eyes, academic performance outweighed demonstrated leadership in operational fleet assignments. He sought individuals who would subordinate themselves, their personal lives and their professional judgment to him. In short, he sought bright, zealously ambitious men who were willing to compromise their personal independence for a place in his favor."

By now both of us needed a comfort break. When we returned to our seat, I was still digesting what I had heard. Disturbing, but not shocking. *This still hasn't explained the Ehime Maru.*

Mike seemed to sense my impatience. "The *Ehime Maru.* We'll get there. Just keep following what I'm telling you."

I smiled to myself. *There's that damned Commander again!*

Mike continued. "In his interview, Rickover invariably forced the candidate to demonstrate willingness to submit to his will. This almost always took the form of Rickover demanding that the candidate give up something of personal value that had no intrinsic value to Rickover himself. In some cases, it actually was a demand that the candidate stop seeing a girlfriend, or give up a favorite hobby…like golf—or something like that. Once the candidate submitted to Rickover's will by surrendering to him something that he had no legitimate right to demand, the fealty relationship was, in the great majority of cases, permanently established. Psychologically, this relationship was no different than the oath of absolute allegiance Hitler demanded of the Wehrmacht—the infamous 'Wehrmacht Oath.' They promised him fealty. He promised them professional success."

I began to understand what Mike was driving at and was becoming disturbed by it. Still, I had reservations. "But, Mike, why didn't those guys just quit the club after they got in? They didn't have to keep showing up for church, so to speak."

"You couldn't quit. By the 1970s, the senior officers in the Submarine Force chain of command were loyal Rickover disciples. Whatever their subsequent misgivings, once the candidate committed to Rickover, there was no escape from the cult. For the rest of an officer's career, or, at least as long as he was a NUC, Rickover and pressure from his chain of command would keep him from open dissent. Whatever their other qualifications, candidates whose strength of character or will were found by Rickover to be insurmountable were routinely and summarily rejected."

Mike frowned at his glass. "Let me assure you that having the courage of one's convictions was never an asset in dealing with Rickover. As his disciples moved into positions of power throughout the submarine force, the popularity of that virtue dwindled."

Mike paused and took another sip of his drink. "Are you with me so far?"

I nodded my head. "Yes. You're claiming that Rickover built a cult around his own personality that dominated the U.S. Submarine Force. But, why?"

"Rickover's ego fed on and was sustained by power. He became, in the purest sense, a prodigious egomaniac. To his last breath, Rickover denied the existence of the infamous "HGR Checklist," used by submarine crews to prepare for his visits. But, I have one that I had to use, and I have seen other versions of it that ran to over six single spaced typewritten pages. When we get home, I can show you my copy. You'll be amazed at the demands it encompasses."

This was all too much at odds with the public image of Rickover that I was, in a general way, aware of. I was having trouble accepting some of what I was hearing. "But, how could the public perception of the man be so different?"

His answer was simple. "Rickover was a masterful politician. Equally, he was a master at creating and manipulating his own public image. He stands alone, a giant among men, the 'Father of Nuclear Power,' right?"

I agreed. That was the image I had before this conversation started.

The edge was back in Mike's voice and I could see that cold, hard look coming back into his eyes.

He really despises Rickover.

"Patrick, contrary to carefully created popular belief, Hyman Rickover was not the only one to possess the intuitive brilliance and force of will to create the nuclear submarine. In fairness, give him his due. Certainly, as the steward of the program, he is entitled to be known as the "Father" of nuclear power and, surely, his extraordinary influence in the halls of Congress made him its most effective proponent. But…I would like to make the point that no mere captain in the United States Navy ever had the sole authority to initiate a program on the scale of the naval nuclear power program without the supporting approval of the Navy's military and civilian hierarchy. You have never heard of the people who gave him the job and the funding, have you?"

I had to admit he was right. So far as I knew, Rickover had never shared his billing with anyone. But, I still didn't see how this was connected with the *Ehime Maru.* "Mike, I understand what you have just told me, but there is a big gap between that and this recent maritime disaster."

Mike's eyebrows furrowed. "I know that. I'm going to fill that gap now. Hopefully, you now understand the environment that produces submarine commanding officers, but now you need to understand their role and responsibilities. When I finish, I think you'll see the connection."

Satisfied he hadn't wandered off course in his dissertation on Rickover, I nodded agreement.

"In any command at sea, the safety and success of the ship are ultimately vested in the overall competence of the commanding officer. The ship exists, in a very real sense, as an extension of his will."

"Mike," I interrupted, "you explained that to me a few minutes ago."

"Patrick, I know that. I wanted to reinforce that concept before I went on" He continued. "It's important that you understand that there is no equivalent anywhere else in the military to the responsibility of the submarine commanding officer, particularly if his ship carries strategic weapons. Even in my day, an FBM commanding officer had the capability of destroying one hundred forty eight Soviet population centers in a single four minute ripple launch.

"The Strategic Triad is composed of sea based ballistic missiles, land based ICBM's and bombers. The two legs belonging to the Strategic Air Command, that is, the ICBM's and the bombers, employed a two-way communication link, called a "permissive action link" that allowed higher command to physically control the release of nuclear weapons. Submarines are different. Since any type of communication transmission could compromise the security of the mission by disclosing the ship's location, the submarine must observe strict communications silence to preserve its stealth and survivability. This precluded the use of the permissive action links that acted as safeguards in the other two legs of the triad.

"Every submarine captain must perform his assigned mission while insuring that his platform survives all tactical threats. However, unlike the Army or Air Force, where a commander is in constant communication with his boss, with all the backup support and direction that implies, the submarine captain is on his own.

"Submarine command is unique in that the captain has no two-way communication with his superior command structure. There is no comforting safeguard for his decision-making, no one to back up his judgment. He must, without external supervision, ensure that peacetime safety is maintained and, when ordered by the appropriate National Command Authority, strike targets accurately and reliably. He is utterly alone in his responsibility. He alone has the final responsibility for his ship and for properly safeguarding and employing the weapons—nuclear or conventional—in his custody.

"No other military force requires one man to bear such a weight of responsibility in isolation from his chain of command. It is the ultimate extension of the ancient law of the sea that a captain's authority and responsibility are absolute."

I thought about that. "No wiggle room for the Captain of the Greenville, is there?"

"Let me finish with this," Mike said. "By 1970, Rickover's political power placed him beyond the influence of any authority within the Navy Department. His imperious, narrowly focused demand for absolute control within the nuclear powered submarine force was widely supported by a chain of command and governing officer body, who were, for the most part, his cult followers.

"The very real result of this absolute power was a perilous hypocrisy. In the submarine force of the 1970s, a commanding officer's career was likely to suffer far more severe penalty, even serious jeopardy, from relatively minor issues in engineering than from major and critical errors affecting the ship's weapons or navigation systems. Errors that could have, in the event of a nuclear exchange, annihilated hundreds of thousands of innocent civilians, were professionally deemed less significant than invoking the ire of Rickover.

"Many commanding officers, at least the ones who were more independent than ambitious, recognized the true weight of responsibility thrust upon them by their missions. Unfortunately, for many of the others, such was the depth of their indoctrination into the dogma of Rickover and his followers that few saw or, having seen, would admit a distortion of values when they accepted one standard of performance for operating and maintaining the nuclear propulsion system and a lesser standard for all else."

The connection with the *Ehime Maru* incident was becoming clearer to me, but Mike was painting a pretty dark picture of our submarine force. *How objective is he being? Is he so embittered about something that his views are distorted? Maybe too cynical?* I again wondered what the "skeleton" was that he still wasn't sharing with me?

"Patrick, there was a moral collision in the submarine force of my day between the focus required for a successful career and the priorities of a truly professional warrior. There were really three major vectors of pressure that every captain had to deal with. First came the dictum that a commander's attention not be diverted from the nuclear engineering focus so necessary to enjoy the approval of Rickover and the Submarine Force chain of command. In yielding to this dictate, a commander could easily become guilty of failing to meet the second, that is the silent but sacred expectations of a wider world, that he be the competent keeper of his store of strategic weapons. Failing that charge could light the fires of Armageddon. Third, every ship's captain worthy of the position always bore a more ancient burden, his responsibility for the safety of his ship and crew."

Mike paused for a moment, obviously waiting to see if I had absorbed what he had just said. Apparently satisfied that I understood the significance of his words, he was emphatic as he finished. "Unfortunately, in the world of the NUC, the holy grail came to be nuclear power. All else was secondary."

"And you believe that is still true?" I asked.

"Operational incompetence and misjudgment certainly played a role in the loss of the Thresher, the *Ehime Maru*, maybe the Scorpion, and a half dozen other unreported incidents that I can't tell you about. Christ may be dead, but the Church lives."

Mike was finished as he turned away and said he was going to stretch his legs on a trip to the bathroom.

Mike, you never cease to amaze me!

Before he left I looked deeply into his eyes, the windows to his soul, and knew I'd been given a glimpse of only a portion of the story. Somehow, he felt personally touched by the *Ehime Maru* incident—or threatened. I couldn't tell which.

His dissertation had been typically Mike. It came out so effortlessly, succinct and cutting right to the mark that I knew he had thought it through long before tonight. Thought provoking, yes, but much more. Never in my wildest dreams would I have thought the sinking of the *Ehime Maru* would lead to this serious a conversation. I then understood the emotions Mike had exhibited on first learning the news and his detachment thereafter. *The Ehime Maru reopened something sacrosanct in Mike. Whatever it was, it wasn't public knowledge and he intended to keep it that way.*

* * * * *

Close to six months had passed since that night and Mike and I had never returned to that conversation. Tonight's news broadcast made it all fresh again, but he showed no inclination to discuss it.

Mike was exhausted from many days of long hard work and, to some extent, the rekindling of the *Greenville/Ehime Maru* incident. He ordered one more scotch and soon nodded off to sleep. I read some position papers, sipped another drink and fell to sleep as well. We both came awake on the glide path to touchdown in London.

2
London

When we finally landed, it was early morning on a warm sunny day and London was stifling—as only London can be—with temperatures just a little above eighty-five degrees. Britain was enjoying a reasonable surge in tourism after a couple of down years due to the public fright over Mad Cow disease.

Long accustomed to the slow march that was our penance for not being denizens of the European Union, we waited, tired and sweating from the humid heat in one of Heathrow's immigration areas. Ahead of us, at least three hundred fellow arrivals from various destinations also waited to have their passports checked and stamped. The British civil servants were even more leisurely this day than usual. It was, I suspected, another "slow down," a favored tactic of Her Majesty's Civil Service to force concessions from the government during their frequent labor disputes. We were not in London for recreation though, and the slow shuffle through Immigration was frustrating.

At the moment, our thoughts were fixed on getting to our hotel so we could clean up and nurse our jet lag. White's Hotel, a small five-star hotel facing Hyde Park just a block from the Lancaster Gate tube station had long since become our home away from home on these trips. It was friendly, convenient and exquisitely Victorian in its appointments and service. Our suites adjoined each other and were very spacious, with separate sitting rooms and work areas that had great views of the park. By now, Mike and I were on a first name basis with most of the hotel's staff and just about all of the staff at the nearby pubs and restaurants that we frequented.

I wasn't paying much attention to our surroundings, just shuffling ahead a step or two at a time as the line moved. I was entertaining myself, as I often did, by speculating on some aspect of a female that caught my eye. Mike nudged me out of my somnolence, nodded in the direction of a queue two removed from ours and asked, "Interesting looking tall black man there.

Maasai, do you suppose? As I recall, you knew an African diplomat from that tribe some years ago."

I looked in the direction Mike was pointing. The man he had singled out was indeed very tall. His back was to me, but I could see close-cropped graying hair above the physique of someone who could well have been a retired professional basketball player. He was more than a full head taller than the surrounding crowd. As I idly studied him, I noted the impeccable fit of his conservative, but obviously expensive dark suit. *Whoever he is, the cliché "regal bearing" certainly fits.* A moment later, he moved forward a step or two; turning to follow the queue and Mike saw his face.

"My God! Patrick, hold my place in line. I'll be right back. That's no African diplomat. That is Linc Mann!" With that, Mike ducked under the cloth rail lining the path for our queue and, without regard to the annoyed looks from the crowd, pushed his way through to the tall black man.

As Mike made his way through the crowd, he also collected a few stares from the Immigration officials. Coming up, unseen, behind the tall man, I heard Mike say, "Linc. Lincoln Julius Mann!"

The man spun around, surprised. Halting for only a few seconds, he replied, "Mike! Good Lord…is that you? What's the last dinosaur doing in London?"

The crowd around them must have been a little bemused at the sight of their reunion. It was a hugging, back slapping, laughing disregard for the British tradition of reserve.

"Linc, what brings you here? Where are you staying?"

He answered. "I'm on my way to a conference on international law at the Hague. I'm spending a few nights here in London working with our embassy staff, then catching the Dover ferry across to Calais on Wednesday. I'll be at the Columbia House, a little hotel that I like in Chelsea. What about you?"

"I'm over for a review of some business issues with our local subsidiary. The guy over there waving is Patrick Conley, our corporate attorney and a good friend. We're staying at White's on Lancaster Gate."

"Jesus, what a surprise! It's good to see you again!" Have you got any plans for this evening?" Linc asked.

"Absolutely. Dinner with you tonight at White's. It's been too long since we shared a bottle of wine!"

"I'll look forward to it, Mike. But I have to stop at the Embassy before I check into the hotel, so I can't make it much before seven."

Linc's line was beginning to move again and Mike had to get back to ours. "Linc, call me as soon as you get settled. It's White's on Lancaster Gate, just about a block from the Tube station. We'll have dinner when it's convenient for you."

When Mike got back to me, grinning from ear to ear, my curiosity was obvious. A very controlled person, he rarely allowed himself the kind of public exuberance that I had just witnessed. I was mildly astonished at what I had just seen. Lincoln Mann was not just another lawyer. He was an icon in my profession and he and Mike were obviously old friends.

"Where do you know him from?"

Mike replied with a laugh. "From another world that I haven't visited in a long, long time. I hope you don't mind, but I invited him to dinner tonight."

"Of course not, but what is he doing here?"

Mike laughed again. "Don't try to talk shop with him. He may be the Senior Judge on the Missouri Supreme Court, but I believe you know his reputation as an authority on international law."

My mind had already raced back over what I knew of Lincoln Mann. From time to time during my career, I had heard or read about an African-American who was the first of his race to be seated on the Missouri Supreme Court. Just as quickly, I also remembered that, I had occasion to read one or two treatises written by Judge Mann on various aspects of international law when traveling for Consultech.

My curiosity about Mike now took another leap. I would never have suspected a connection between him and a man like Lincoln Mann. This guy suddenly appears out of Mike's past and they greet each other like long lost brothers. *What could that phrase about a "world I haven't visited in a long time" and the remark about "the last dinosaur" possibly refer to?*

With Mike's dissertation on Rickover and the responsibilities of a ship's captain still fresh in my mind, I began to suspect that whatever it was in his past that he was so reticent about was not trivial. And, most certainly, his friend Judge Mann was not a trivial acquaintance.

I grinned and shook my head. Going straight to the heart of my curiosity, I asked. "How the hell do you know a Missouri Supreme Court Judge?"

Mike grinned thoughtfully and was about to say something when he changed gears and, in a matter of fact voice, replied, "We're old friends and I look forward to your meeting him. I think you'll like him a lot." Clearly for the moment, that was all I was going to get out of him.

After clearing Immigration, we taxied directly to the White's Hotel to check in and get some rest. Mike had grabbed the *London Times* for the taxi ride to the hotel. Its bold headlines reported that the Court of Inquiry findings damned the U.S. Navy commander for the *Ehime Maru* sinking. Mike's reaction, as he read bits of the article to me, was restrained, but quite evident in his voice was a simmering aggravation. In fact, over the last six months, in a curious way, I too had become indignant about these events. After hearing Mike's comments at the time of the incident, I was now more emotionally involved than I cared to admit.

After a long hot shower I jumped into bed, asleep before I finished three pages of my new book. Four hours later the phone rang. It was Mike with a wake up call advising he had ordered us a light lunch that room service would deliver to his suite in twenty minutes. Though we came from different worlds and had very different characteristics and traits, there was one thing we both were slaves to—punctuality.

I cleaned up, threw on shorts, a recently purchased loose fitting "Beatle's" tee shirt and a pair of flip-flops, then knocked on Mike's door. Room service arrived minutes later.

Over the next hour we did an exhaustive review of our agenda for the next four days and agreed on specific areas of responsibility. In a very short period at the beginning of our professional relationship, Mike and I had developed a routine that allowed plenty of room for our personal styles, yet was unusually singular in its overall purpose and goal. On the job, we were like a couple that had been married twenty or thirty years—we didn't need to verbally communicate to each other to know what the other was thinking—a glance or gesture conveyed all that was needed to be said. This was a huge advantage for us when we were confronting the usually somewhat hostile local management team with our findings and recommendations. Nobody likes visiting firemen, particularly when they are right and the time has come to shoulder responsibility for the fire they have just put out.

It was 5:00 p.m. London time by the time we finished our preparation for the next day at the office. As I started to return to my room, Mike said, "Patrick, Linc called. We're meeting him for cocktails and dinner here at the White at 6:30 p.m

"I'll look forward to meeting the Judge. I'll come over 6:15 p.m. or so."

"Roger. Don't be late."

I laughed out loud. *There's that damn commander thing again.*

Mike must have read my thoughts, as he said, "Patrick, I'm sorry if I preempted your evening. If you want to do something else, go ahead and it's not a problem. I want to spend as much time with Linc as I can while he's here, and I'd be extremely happy if you joined us—you're no intruder. You know that."

"I completely understand, Mike—I look forward to being with you and Linc. I can't imagine many things in London that would be more interesting than an evening with Judge Mann."

Lincoln Julius Mann, what is your connection to Mike Craig? The question kept rolling through my mind as I walked the short distance to my room to shower and change. In my wildest dreams I could never have guessed the answer.

* * * * *

That evening, just before 6:30 p.m., Lincoln Julius Mann made his way into Whites. Typical of the man, he had found his way from Chelsea to Lancaster Gate on the Underground rather than taking a cab. Aloof and remote on the bench, in reality, he liked being among people. Financially secure beyond any need for pecuniary concerns, he simply liked a certain quality in life, but disliked ostentation. He enjoyed mixing with the crowd on the "tube" and feeling the pulse of London's streets.

Climbing the half dozen steps from the minuscule parking area between the hotel and the street, he paused for a moment in the richly paneled foyer, then turned left into a bar that looked and felt like the lounge of an expensive men's club. Except for the bartender, it was deserted. As he approached the bar, the man behind it spoke. "Good evening, sir. And what may I serve you?"

"Whiskey. And, give my best regards to Mac."

The bartender's expression never changed, but Linc didn't miss the passing twinkle in the man's eyes. He stooped and rummaged briefly beneath the bar. When he straightened up, he was holding a slightly dusty bottle of fifty-year-old MacCallan whiskey. Without a word, he poured a generous double and handed it to him. "Compliments of Mr. Craig, sir. I will let Mr. Craig know the gentleman is waiting here in the lounge."

The bartender picked up the phone and dialed. "Mr. Craig" he said, "Davey here. The gentleman has arrived." He then chuckled. "Yes, sir. I believe he and Mac are warming to each other."

Turning back to Linc, Davey smiled. "Mr. Craig keeps a bit of private stock here. When others are with him, and he does not care to indulge them, he simply tells me to give his regards to Mac. You must be a very special friend for him to have granted you the code."

Linc laughed. "We are indeed very old friends."

Davey answered. "Then, sir, you will always be most welcome here."

A few minutes later, Mike and I arrived. After Davey had, without instruction, set out a round of drinks, Mike spoke to him. "Davey, please tell Humphrey that we will be in for dinner in a few minutes."

Then Mike introduced me to Mann. We exchanged friendly handshakes, and I said, "Nice to meet you, sir." My formality, despite my years, was a habit nurtured and fostered by my late dad that bore me well over the years.

Linc grinned and said, "Patrick, I assume we're all friends here and my friends call me Linc."

I replied, "Yes, SIR!" and all three of us erupted in laughter.

* * * * *

By the time we had finished our "starters" and half the accompanying bottle of Pouilly-Fusee, it was obvious to me that an amazingly strong bond existed between Mike and Linc. A bond that seemed incongruous, with what appeared to be their infrequent contact over a thirty-year period. Linc talked about Meaghan and Mike's kids as if they were family. And, Mike spoke warmly of Linc's family, but didn't seem quite so closely connected to them. It took no great deduction for me to conclude they had been very close during Mike's days in the Navy.

Somehow, these guys are both part of something...

We were about to order dinner when Linc turned to Mike and said, "Mike, can you believe what happened in Hawaii?"

Mike replied, "No. I thought by now the cult would have pretty much burned itself out. It brought back a lot of bad memories."

"For me too," Linc said.

Mike replied, "Hell, nothing has changed."

Linc responded resignedly, "Mike, you knew it wouldn't. The last dinosaur can't breed more of his kind."

Dinosaurs again—this can't be about another Jurassic Park! I looked directly at them, and said, "What in the hell are you two talking about?"

Mike responded, "A reality that you and most of the world may not be ready for, even today."

Finally! He's going to open up! My curiosity was by now at its zenith and I didn't try to hide it.

"Reality?" I said, "About what? The sinking of the *Ehime Maru*? It's pretty obvious from the reports that the submarine's commander failed to follow proper procedures and was showboating for some dignitaries." Exasperated, I continued. "The reality? Better still, what about the truth! I'd like to know what the Ehime Maru's sinking has to do with you two…and why you both appear to be so fixated by it? And what's this about 'the last dinosaur?'"

Linc was a fascinating person and I knew Mike was brilliant man, who at times could be playful with other people's minds. I briefly wondered if they were playing a "fool's game" with me. An unseen scrutinizing look at the two of them and I instantly knew that was not the case. They were serious men who shared something even more serious.

Dinner arrived. Venison for Linc, Dover sole for me, and the typical steak for Mike.

No one would ever accuse Mike of having an exotic palate.

After Humphrey had withdrawn to his discreet watch stand in the rear of the dining room, Mike looked at Linc and said, "Maybe it's time for at least one citizen and taxpayer to finally know the long concealed truth of what happened on the *Marion* thirty years ago. What do you think, Linc?"

Linc answered, "I agree with you, Mike. Perhaps it will be good for both of us. Enough is enough—the world should have known about the *Marion* a long time ago. There's really no need to be silent any more."

Linc took another drink from his glass, and holding my eyes with an intense look, said, "Your friend here, Mike, is, in fact, the last dinosaur. Mike, do you want to tell him why?"

Mike finished chewing the piece of steak he had just taken, then washed it down with a sip of his wine. A good Medoc now. "This will take awhile, Patrick. Are you sure you want to sit through a long and not very funny old sea story?"

Hell, yes. By now, I was like a kid out of school—like when Lois first met Superman—and I couldn't read minds. I was eager to hear what they'd say, especially Linc. What could possibly keep a secret hostage for over thirty years by men who had the stature and intellect of these two?

Linc interrupted my thoughts and said, "How much do you know about the Cold War Era?"

Much more than I can disclose, Linc! "I have a general knowledge, I know about Jack and Bobby Kennedy and the Cuban missile crisis, that the good guys won, that communism in Russia is just about dead. But, first, what's the bit about Mike being the last dinosaur."

Mike laughed before he turned serious again. "I think it just means that you are the last of your kind and there is no place left in the world for you."

Obviously logical, but it still didn't answer my question. "But how are you that dinosaur?"

Mike tolerantly waved his glass at me. "Listen to our story and you'll understand. The world looked quite different to those of us at sea in the 1970s. We knew we were nose to nose with the Soviets and the sense that our confrontation was hostile and dangerous was profound—and accurate. We viewed the Soviets as the most dangerous of adversaries, though we were confident that if WW III erupted we would win. At that time, in 1970, I was a submariner and served as the Executive Officer on board the *USS Francis Marion*, a Fleet Ballistic Missile Submarine. Those were fine ships."

Having read quite a few submarine novels, I was distracted by a bit of trivia. "Ships? I thought submarines were called 'boats.'"

Mike laughed. "So they were, in the past. It is pretty difficult to call something that weighs eight thousand tons a 'boat.' The correct reference to submarines is now 'ship.' Submariners often use the term 'boat' conversationally or affectionately, but in official correspondence, it is a ship."

I nodded, my impulse of curiosity satisfied.

"So, 1970 was a very different time and I was the Exec of the *Marion*..."

I was single then and with the State Department, the SALT negotiations were ongoing—but I couldn't remember one significant event that occurred in 1970. I was about to find out that it would be one that the world never knew occurred...an event that may well have been the most significant of the time.

Rota, Spain

March, 1970

3
Back to the Ship

Craig stood on the 01 Level of the submarine tender, the *USS Canopus*, looking out over Rota Harbor. Through his fatigue and general depression, the question again came to his mind…why do gray ships always look golden in the sunlight? Twelve years at sea and he had never ceased to marvel at the ability of the sun to transform a cold gray sea into a blue canvas painted with golden ships. *Small recompense*, he thought, *for the isolation from all the good things of life that are found only ashore.*

Lieutenant Commander Michael Craig had more than his usual handful of reasons for being tired and a little morose on this particular brilliant Spanish morning. He was the Executive Officer, or XO, of the Gold Crew of the *USS Francis Marion*, SSBN 623, a "Lafayette" class Fleet Ballistic Missile Submarine, commonly called an "FBM." He had arrived with his crew the night before to relieve the Blue Crew upon their return from patrol, and this was the first of only twenty-eight days they would have to refit the ship before taking it to sea on its next patrol. The jet lag from their trans-Atlantic flight accounted for his fatigue. The source of his depression was a little more complex.

Part of it came from the sudden separation from home and family, some from the prospect of being confined aboard ship for the next three months, but this time, some of his malaise was a niggling uncertainty and worry about an incident during their departure from the Submarine Base at Groton, Connecticut. The incident didn't concern him, but the Old Man's reaction to it did. Craig had delayed the crew flight departure for twenty-four hours without checking with the Old Man. Why hadn't he torn a stripe off him like any other captain would have done? He was bemused, but the day would have enough problems to solve without obsessing on that one.

He pulled himself up and turned away from the rail and headed toward the ship's wardroom where the other officers would be having breakfast. *Time to put on the happy face,* he thought. As second in command, he couldn't display his wilted spirits to the rest of the crew.

* * * * *

It had begun the day they left Groton for the *Marion* Gold Crew's 18th Fleet Ballistic Missile Patrol. The crew mustered at 1700 on Easter Sunday, March 29, 1970, in front of Building 439 at the Submarine Base.

Against the background of a dark, late afternoon sky filled with water laden clouds, the red buds of soon to be leaves were just beginning to show the fresh mint green of spring as they made ready to unfold their new crop of leaves on the many old oak trees that surrounded the parking lot. The forecast had a fluke spring snowstorm moving up the East coast.

The Chief of the Boat, "COB" to one and all, was, if not happy, at least satisfied. No one was missing or late for the muster. A large, trim man, he had the flattened face and broken nose of a boxer and a scowl that struck fear in young sailors. Less obtrusively, like most submarine sailors, he was exceptionally intelligent and a true professional in his trade. After a last look up and down the wavering line of sailors to be sure there were no drunks or other potential problems, he turned to the Executive Officer, smartly saluted, and reported, "All present and accounted for, sir."

Craig returned his salute with a quiet, "Aye aye, Chief."

Before the Exec turned to report to the Commanding Officer, his eyes and mind quickly reviewed the crew. Musters express something fundamental to the Navy and its traditions, like the dark navy-blue uniforms, which to the entire outside world, looked black. The enlisted men standing at attention, wearing the traditional soft white sailor hats, jersey v-neck tops with collar flaps outlined in a white stripe, neatly tied neckerchiefs and bell-bottom pants. Few civilians would ever recognize a properly rolled and tied neckerchief. Proud sailors took great pains to get it right.

The chiefs and officers were dressed in service Dress Blue, a double-breasted navy blue suit, white shirt, dark-navy tie, and a visored cap. Somehow, it was a uniform that lacked the élan of the sailors. The officers' uniform, with six brass buttons and embroidered gold stripes to signify one's rank, carried on the tradition of "brass." As the "Exec" or "XO," Craig was a "Two and a Half Striper," and the captain was a "Three Striper." The stripes represented another vestige of Navy tradition and law. The more stripes, the more privilege…and the more responsibility. And so it went.

The Exec's eye caught two baby-faced sailors exchanging somewhat devilish grins in the front rank of the crew. McJimsey and Kane had reported aboard together about a month earlier. They were brand-new graduates of the Navy's Basic Submarine School and would be making their first patrol. Like nearly a quarter of the men at muster, they wore no "Dolphin," or "Patrol Pins." The silver Patrol Pin, in the shape of an FBM, would come after they completed their first patrol. Tiny stars were added underneath the pin's submarine to signify the number of patrols one had made. Some of the older chiefs wore Patrol Pins with stars for as many as fourteen patrols.

Unlike a pilot's wings, Dolphins weren't awarded until after completion of a year-long process of "Qualifying in Submarines." Gold for officers and silver for Chief Petty Officers and enlisted men, they were awarded only when the man had proven himself at sea. Most, but not all, made the grade. Those who didn't were unceremoniously returned to the surface Navy to serve out their enlistments. The pin was another slightly anachronistic connection with the past. In the insignia, the two dolphins face each across the bow of an ancient "R Class" submarine. Sort of a "Wooden ships and Iron men" reminder. Graduation from submarine school wasn't enough to gain membership into this club. It would take the rookies a full year and two patrols of hard work and study on board to earn the "Dolphins." By then, their Patrol Pins would have had the first star added along the bottom. Like all people, sailors value some things more than others, but the "Dolphins" were universally prized for the membership they represented in one of the Navy's most elite societies.

There was nothing unusual in McJimsey or Kane's service records. But the Exec noted their excitement and his intuition told him to be a little wary of those two. Even for young sailors they seemed to have a little extra ration of piss and vinegar.

Satisfied that the crew was ready to embark on the buses that would take them to the airport, Craig made his way to where the Captain stood talking quietly to his wife. When he caught his attention, he saluted and said "All present and accounted for, sir."

The Captain, a tall, slightly overweight man turned and returned the salute. The voice that filtered through his blond mustache was surprisingly thin and reedy. "Thank you, XO, let's go!"

The three waiting buses were the same ones that had brought the crew home from Quonset Point Naval Air Station three months earlier. During those three months, the Blue Crew had been deployed to the ship while the Gold Crew rested and trained in Groton as the "Off Crew." Now it was their turn, in the inexorable rotation, to fly back to the U.S. Naval Air Station at Rota, Spain, relieve the Blue Crew, refit the ship and take her on her 18th Patrol. The bus drivers had seen a lot of tears hauling these crews back and forth. Some were tears of joy…many more of anguish.

The first large fluffy snowflakes, carried along by an uneasy wind, swirled around and through the crowd as the crew broke ranks to board the buses for the ride to the Naval Air Station in Rhode Island. Those with families or lovers present let the bachelors board first while they grabbed a last few words or embraces with their loved ones. The ride to the Naval Air Station in Rhode Island would be a short one, an hour at most. Still enough time for most to wrestle their personal emotions into the background of their thoughts. Suddenly, home lay in one world and their thoughts and attention would be focused on another—the ship and their shipmates.

As usual, the younger sailors were excited and boisterous, while the veterans were generally subdued and quiet. A few in both groups were still half drunk, but none so badly as to require official notice. As the buses were loading, the Exec, like most of the other married men in the crew, found his way through the crowd to where his wife stood waiting. Meaghan Craig stood near their old green Buick where she would wait until the buses were out of sight. She was a striking, dark-haired woman whose petite size and youthful beauty belied her inner strength—and, her two children and thirty-five years.

Unlike many of the other women present, Meaghan would shed no tears until she could give private vent to her emotions. As much as did her husband, she understood her public role as an example to the other members of their small community. For the sake of the others, she would be strong even though her dread of the patrol was, perhaps, greater than theirs. Mike and Meaghan shared a relationship so close that it was, at times, almost telepathic and the separation of a patrol was privately excruciating to both. Each hated the prolonged hiatus that a patrol brought to their lives.

Where goodbyes were concerned, they had long since learned the wisdom of Cassius who, when dealing with the unpleasant duty of murdering Caesar said, "If it must be done, let it be done quickly." They didn't prolong their partings. They embraced and clung fiercely together for a moment.

Mike gently touched her soft, dark hair. "Take care of yourself and give the kids a hug when you get home. I'll call as soon as I can after we get to Rota…I love you."

Meaghan nodded and hugged him a little tighter, then stepped back. She didn't speak, afraid of breaking the fragile emotional dam that held back her tears. Craig turned and, not looking back, resolutely walked away from Meaghan toward the buses.

Across the parking lot, the Captain was standing alongside his family's tan Ford station wagon. After a few last words with his wife, he got into a waiting staff car and was driven to a position at the head of the short convoy of buses for the drive to Quonset Point.

The ride was uneventful, but by the time the buses passed through the gate at Quonset Point, the wind was whipping snow that had intensified to near blizzard conditions. A Texas International DC-8, a "Stretch Eight," chartered for the Trans-Atlantic flight was already there waiting. The buses drove directly onto the terminal apron alongside the aircraft and the crew immediately began their embarkation. The baggage and cruise boxes had arrived ahead of them with an assigned working party, drawn largely from the most junior members of the crew, and had already been loaded onto the plane.

As the sailors filed from the buses to the plane, the snow was accumulating rapidly. Quonset Operations watched the rate at which the snow was deepening with increasing concern, anxious to see the *Marion* crew flight on its way before runway conditions became unsatisfactory for takeoff. Runway clearance operations were losing ground to the storm. Before the crew members were settled into their seats, a party of sailors with squeegees clambered onto the wings of the aircraft and, aided by a pumper truck spraying deicing fluid, began to remove the snow accumulation.

The snowstorm continued to intensify. After an hour, the cleaners were losing ground in removing snow from the plane and several more inches had accumulated on the runway. The Exec got up and walked to the front of the plane where the Captain was sitting.

"Captain," he said, "I'm going to Operations and see what our problem is in getting out of here."

The Captain was reading a book entitled, *Science and Health with Key to the Scriptures* written in 1875 by Mary Baker Eddy, founder of the Christian Science Movement. At the Exec's comment, he quickly looked up, said, "Okay, XO," with apparent disinterest and went back to his reading.

The Exec found the Duty Operations Officer talking to two Warrant Officers on the apron beneath the wings of the plane. All three were swaddled in the Navy's heavy A-1 arctic foul weather gear and none of the three looked happy.

"Lieutenant, what's up?" Craig asked. "Are we going out of here tonight?"

"We haven't made a decision yet," the Lieutenant replied.

"What's the decision waiting on?" asked Craig.

One of the Warrant Officers spoke up. "We've run out of deicing fluid and by the time the truck can reload and get back here the runways will be closed."

Craig felt the stirring of annoyance. It was not in his nature to suffer fools gladly and, avoiding an obvious decision was, to him, the mark of a fool. "How long will it take you to plow the runway and de-ice the plane once the snow stops?"

The lieutenant looked uncomfortable. "About three or four hours, I reckon."

"Then why in the hell am I and my crew still sitting here freezing our butts in this plane?" The exasperation in the Exec's question was unmistakable.

Sensing that his night was about to become even less pleasant, the Operations Officer's face began to redden. "Because if I cancel or delay departure while the runway is open, the Military Aircraft Command down at McGuire Air Force Base gets charged a hell of a contract penalty and McGuire Operations will crawl all over me."

The buses were still there. Routinely they stayed until the plane had left.

Taking out his pocket notebook, the Exec wrote his home phone number on a blank page and ripped it free of the binder. "Here," he said, handing the Lieutenant the page, "call me when the snow stops. I'll have my crew here by the time the aircraft is ready to take off."

The Lieutenant was agitated. "You can't do that. MAC rules say you wait."

The Exec had had enough. MAC's contract penalty and the ass chewing the lieutenant stood to get did not concern him in the least. His crew was his concern. "Lieutenant," he said, "why don't you and MAC go to Hell. We'll be back within four hours, right after you call me."

Leaving the lieutenant fuming behind his back, the Exec climbed back up the stairs to the door of the aircraft, still simmering and was met by the Chief of the Boat. "What's happening, XO?" the COB asked.

"COB, get the troops back on the buses. We're going home for the night. Set up an ironclad recall system to get people back. We'll have three hours to recall, muster and get back here."

As the first sailors poured off the airplane, racing for the buses and a short reprieve, the Exec made his way to where the Captain, Commander John Holcomb, sat. Holcomb was putting his book back into his briefcase. Seeing the approaching Exec, he asked, "Who authorized us to go back to Groton?"

"I did," replied Craig.

The Old Man just shrugged and, without a word gathered up his coat and suitcase and headed up the isle toward the aircraft exit. The Exec stared after him. His temper had cooled enough for him to consider how far he had overstepped his authority by failing to consult with the Captain before telling Quonset Ops to go to Hell. Although Holcomb was a man of quiet manner, his passive, unquestioning behavior surprised and slightly unsettled Craig. Any other commanding officer would have skinned his Executive Officer alive for not consulting with him on a decision that might delay the crew's arrival at the refit site. As the Exec watched the Captain leave the plane, he wondered briefly when he would face the private reprimand that he knew he deserved. It wasn't a question he would dwell upon. Spending an unexpected bonus night at home with Meaghan and the kids was worth any ass chewing the Old Man could deliver.

In less than twenty minutes, the crew was off the plane, on the buses and on their way home to their families. Just before the buses rolled off the airport apron, the Exec went in search of the Captain to brief him on the arrangements he had made for recalling the crew. He was surprised and baffled to find the Staff car bearing the Captain had already left Quonset Point. Craig was not concerned about his ability to manage the recall, but the Captain's behavior, once again, had certainly been odd.

What the hell kind of a Captain would leave his crew here without a word? Craig quickly dismissed the thought. Meaghan was all he wanted to think about now.

4
Rota

The lieutenant's call came shortly after 0600 the next morning. The recall went like clockwork and at 0930 the Gold Crew was airborne from Quonset. They were twelve hours behind their normal time schedule, but after an uneventful flight, the Stretch-8 still arrived the evening before the ship was due to return from the Blue patrol. After the short bus ride to our submarine tender, the *USS Canopus*, the crew turned in to their assigned bunks for the night.

The officers were less fortunate. Before they could rest, they had to look through the "arrival package" given to the Exec by the Squadron Duty officer. Their short officers' meeting included a review of the Quick Look Report and Refit Repair items in preparation for the next morning's activities. That done, and eager for what little sleep remained to them this night, they all went straight to their assigned staterooms and turned in.

* * * * *

The next morning the Gold Crew was suddenly on Zulu, or Greenwich Mean Time, the local time zone in Rota and the standard reference time throughout the military. Once underway on the submarine, the clocks were never moved ahead or back since day and night were artificial. Today, however, the shift in time zones, along with the effects of jet lag was another significant adjustment for the men of the crew. The transition from home to refit and patrol was always jarring. Yesterday, they had been at home in a blizzard. Today, they were in nearly tropical Spain with their biological clocks struggling to catch up.

By 0600Z, as he made his way down the deck to the Wardroom, the Exec could already feel the coming heat of the day. The entire sky was a cloudless blue and it would be a warm day in the high eighties, a welcome change from New England's cold spring, but the crew would feel the unaccustomed heat.

The tender itself was enormous, close to five hundred feet in length and filled with its own crew of nearly a thousand men. It served as the forward based repair ship to refit the submarine and also house their respective crews during the turnover period.

A large amphibious vessel, an LPD, was tied to the quay wall directly across the basin from the tender's mooring. Beyond, the scruffy low-lying buildings of Rota's Naval Air Station seemed to shrink in the light of the quickly rising brilliant sun. Soft winds gently rippled the warm blue-green waters of the basin.

The Exec shrugged, hunching his shoulders as if feeling the bite of a cold wind. It was a private symbolic gesture...shrugging off his bleak state of mind and turning to the affairs of the day. If he wanted to eat, he would have to be quick about it.

Officer's call on this first day of the refit was scheduled for 0700Z, earlier than usual, to allow time to muster the boarding party and embark on a tugboat by 0730Z. The *Marion*, now returning from her 17th Patrol, was due to arrive at the Rota sea buoy at 0900Z. All the Gold Crew officers and leading petty officers would ride out on the tug to meet her. Then, on the way into the harbor, they would observe the operational condition of the ship's systems and equipment. It was the first step in a tightly choreographed four-day process during which the Gold Crew would relieve the Blue Crew, as a unit, and commence readying the ship for its next patrol.

As the ship's officers straggled into the tender wardroom, breakfast was being served by the Gold Crew's own white coated Steward's Mates. Craig caught sight of Morales, a slender, dark-haired Filipino who was the leading Steward's Mate. He was standing near a table on the port side of the tender's large wardroom. *That would be the table reserved for us.* As he crossed to the table, he saw that several of his officers were already seated and in various stages of eating their meal. The commanding officer's place at the head of the table was vacant. Waving a good morning to those present, the Exec took his customary seat next to and to the right of the CO's empty chair. The Engineer, a somewhat horse-faced man of generally morose demeanor, sat across from him, dejectedly picking at a pair of colorless eggs. They were fried to that neutral state of taste and texture only a slightly hostile U.S. Navy Steward could achieve. The Engineer spoke first, "Don't have the eggs. They're old."

His assessment came as no surprise. Craig wasn't very hungry and, in any case, he had long since learned the ways of a tender's Wardroom mess.

A few minutes later, the Steward brought V8 juice and coffee to the table and set it before the Exec. Morales nodded good morning and departed toward the pantry. After draining the glass of V8 Craig, studied the Engineer for a few moments. "Eng, you look so damned jolly I can hardly believe my eyes. Your jet lag terminal this time?"

The Engineer pushed back the congealed remains of his eggs and picked up his coffee. Before he could answer, the Navigator, who was just rising to leave the table, interrupted, "Hey, don't go picking on the Eng, he was up late last night."

The comment aroused the Exec's curiosity. "What in the hell did you find to do that was worth staying up late for?" he asked.

The Engineer ran his fingers through his uncombed blond hair. He was a chain smoking workaholic with a permanent disheveled Scandinavian appearance. After gulping the last of his coffee, the Engineer fumbled for a cigarette before replying. "The Captain came around and rousted me out around 2200. He wanted to go over my turnover checklists and the refit work package again."

The puzzlement showed on the Exec's face. "We went over those last night after we got in. I know we have quite a few annual Preventive Maintenance Actions due this refit, and the 'Quick Look report' had a couple of leaking primary valves in it, but is there something else? Did I miss something?"

"No, sir. He just wanted to go back over everything. He's concerned about being ready for the ORSE."

"Oh? What time did you break up?"

"About 0030Z."

When Craig looked around, all the officers had finished eating and were making their way out of the wardroom. Officer's Call would be held in the Captain's stateroom in ten minutes. He asked if anyone had seen the Old Man up and around. No one had. Turning to the Steward he, asked. "Morales, did the Captain get his call?"

"Oh, yes, sir. He just called and asked for some coffee."

Satisfied that the Captain would be ready to receive them, the Exec said, "Okay. See you guys in five minutes."

Twenty minutes later, Officer Call completed, they were on our way to the pier where the COB and a cluster of twenty or so other senior enlisted men waited. The other officers were trailing along behind the Captain and the Exec.

The Old Man had been in a jovial humor during Officer's Call, showing little of the jet lag fatigue that plagued most of the others.

As they approached the group, the COB detached himself and came to meet them, saluting and crisply offering his "Good Morning, Captain, XO." Senior Chief Petty Officer George Bailey was a deceptive figure. Well over six feet tall, he was powerfully built with a shaved head and flattened nose. He looked every bit like a caricature of a Marine First Sergeant. The COB was a man imbued with exceptional loyalty and integrity. Along with his keen intellect, he possessed a high degree of technical and military professionalism and was the ranking enlisted man on board. The COB was the Exec's right hand, his deputy in general administrative and housekeeping matters with the crew. Senior enlisted men of his type have been the backbone of every military force since the days of the Roman Legions.

The Exec returned his salute. "Good Morning, COB. Did you find everybody at Muster on Station?"

"Yes, sir."

"Any problems settling our people in last night?"

"No, sir. McJimsey and Kane tried to sneak off in civvies, but the Chief of the Watch on the quarterdeck spotted them and called me."

McJimsey and Kane were the two new seamen in the crew Craig had noticed at the muster in Groton. It hadn't taken long for them to confirm his intuition that they might be problem children.

"And?"

"The Chief Boatswain on the tender thought we ought to titivate the cage where we store our baggage and cruise boxes. I figured McJimsey and Kane could take care of that today after working hours."

The image of two lonely souls sweating long into the night, stacking and restacking piles of bags, boxes and obsolete files in the dingy recesses of the tender's most remote storerooms came to the Exec's mind. With a grin, he nodded to the COB. "Good housekeeping is a virtue, COB. All hands here for the tug ride?"

"Yes, sir. Can't wait."

* * * * *

By the time the tug had cleared the inner breakwater of the harbor, the Captain and the Exec could see the incoming submarine. From their vantage point in the pilot house, the first thing visible was a great cross protruding above the horizon. Seen from bow on, the sail of the submarine, with its protruding, wing-like fairwater planes has undoubtedly caused more than one superstitious fisherman to cross himself. Sitting low in the water, like an iceberg, her sleek hull, with its flat missile deck came into view fifteen minutes later. Twenty minutes after that, the tug was maneuvering into position alongside to transfer its passengers to the ship.

As many times as he had seen it, coming alongside an FBM underway still made an impression on Craig. The ship was huge and sleek. At eight thousand two hundred fifty tons submerged displacement and four hundred twenty-five feet long, it very nearly could have surfaced with a World War II diesel submarine resting on the great long flat expanse of deck that covered the sixteen missile tubes. In spite of its size, it moved through the water like a porpoise, the sea sliding around its streamlined form with hardly a ripple. Nothing protruded from the above water parts of the hull to break the streamlining of the blended curves and, the Exec knew, the underwater body was just as smooth, all the way down to the keel, thirty-two feet below the surface.

All in all, the ship projected an eerie aura of a living creature, something more than the sum of the HY80 steel hull and the one hundred and forty or so humans that lived within. Too sleek and comfortable in the sea for a mechanical thing, the USS Francis Marion (SSBN 623) was a true leviathan of the deep. It also now smelled like something alive.

With waves and broad grins from the Blue crew, the tug approached the starboard side of the ship. Two men scurried topside from the engine room hatch and raised the starboard number two cleat from its streamlined storage position just forward of the sail. The ship slowed as the tug took its position alongside and passed a line from its bullnose to the submarine. Put down on the cleat, the submarine's thrust against the line caused the tug to stream securely alongside and the personnel transfer began.

The Old Man was first across the brow where he was met by the waiting Blue Crew Commanding Officer, whose grin flashed through the lush growth of a newly cultivated beard. First the salute, then the handshake, then the ritual welcome back. Holcomb spoke briefly to the Blue Commander, then the two parted, the Blue Crew Commander clambering up the side of the sail to the bridge of the ship. Holcomb immediately dropped below through the nearby engine room hatch.

At the foot of the ladder, Holcomb paused outside the Maneuvering Room, then after a moment of seeming indecision, turned aft, made his way slowly back to the shaft alley, crossed to the starboard side and clambered down the short ladder to the lower level. From there he methodically worked his way forward, reemerging outside the Maneuvering Room where he peered in for a few minutes, then went forward through the watertight door to the Auxiliary Machinery Room and continued his inspection.

The Exec followed his captain onto the ship and found his counterpart waiting on deck just aft of the sail. As Craig walked forward, the characteristic odor of a recently surfaced submarine rose around him. The thin film of marine slime and small barnacles that grows on everything not covered by antifouling paint had already begun to putrefy, no more than two hours since being hoisted out of the depths.

It smells like a whale with bad breath.

The odor is unforgettable and it evoked a visceral recoil in the Exec, a physical reminder that he was about to spend another three months of his life in the belly of the beast.

As was to be expected of a man coming back to the real world from months of isolation, the Blue XO's good humor was barely constrained.

Craig suppressed his revulsion at the scent of the beast and greeted him. "Hello, Bill, welcome home."

The Blue XO laughed and thrust his hand forward. "Mike, glad to see you could make it."

"Good run?" *Must have been, judging from Bill's exuberance.*

"Yeah, very quiet. The weather was pretty bad for several weeks around the middle of the patrol. We lost three trailing wires and were sure sweating the last one out, but it went all the way and is on the reel now. Other than that, nothing special."

"Any surprises for refit?"

"Couple of primary leakers and number two turbine generator governor is acting up. No real problems in Weapons and Navigation."

"Okay, I'll be around the wardroom or our stateroom. Wake me up when we get alongside."

With that, the Blue Exec was off to tend to the remaining preparations for entering port. Craig went straight below decks to the wardroom where he poured himself a mug of coffee, then sat down to wait out the one-hour ride to the tender. There was little for him to do. Several Blue Crew officers spoke briefly to him as they passed by the wardroom door. Mostly, Craig concentrated on forcing himself to relax.

The next few days would be a frenzy as both crews rushed through the script of the crew exchange. The worst part would be the lack of a place, however small, to call his own. A submarine is barely able to house one crew. During crew exchange, when both crews are on board, no place could be found for even a moment of peace. However much he dreaded the isolation of patrol, Craig would be vastly relieved when the Bluies departed and the ship belonged to the Gold Crew. Elsewhere throughout the ship, the rest of the boarding party turned to finding their counterparts and watching as the Blue Crew demonstrated the operation and condition of systems, equipment, etc., the bits and pieces of the ship.

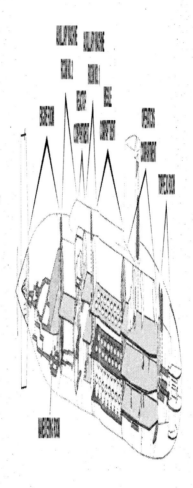

Marion's Below Decks Arrangement

5
Refit

It was a typical first day of refit. Mooring the *Marion* alongside the submarine tender was uneventful, as was the subsequent round of arrival conferences. The Commodore, Commander Submarine Squadron Sixteen, had been pleased with the Blue Captain's debrief of his patrol. It had been a model of the successful FBM patrol…uneventful and ready…with no tactical encounters of interest. Patrol statistics were good, meaning very little down time had been accumulated for the Strategic Weapons System. Having obtained an excellent mark on his Operational Reactor Safety Examination, or ORSE, during the previous refit, the Blue Commander basked in his current role of "favored son."

Craig, knowing from past experience that the Blue CO was an adroit manager of his image when he was before his seniors, suspected that "no significant encounters" equated to lethargic watch standing in Sonar, but said nothing. In view of the good numbers they had turned in, no one would probe for, nor report the haphazard way in which preventive maintenance had been carried out in many non-nuclear areas of the ship. The Bluies had their First Quarter ORSE ranking and had gotten through their patrol without incident. That, he knew, was the current Submarine Force recipe for professional success. Do well in engineering and avoid embarrassment elsewhere.

Craig's reverie was interrupted when, after the last briefing slide, the lights were turned on and the Commodore spoke to the two Commanding Officers. "George," he said, turning to the Blue CO, "Congratulations. You've had a magnificent patrol. After your ORSE, I would have expected nothing less than an outstanding run, and that's what you delivered. I consider that to be a direct reflection of your personal performance. Well done!"

Turning in his seat to face Holcomb, he continued, "John, George has set a high mark for you to shoot at. Judging by your last ORSE, you have your work cut out for you!"

The Old Man blanched slightly and for a moment said nothing. Finally, almost inaudibly, he replied, "Yes, sir."

As the Commodore rose to leave he said, "George, when you finish going over the refit work package with the tender and my staff, stop by my office for a cup of coffee." With that he was gone.

The Squadron Chief of Staff, a gaunt, acerbic Four/Striper, spoke as soon as the conference room door had swung shut.

"Each of you know the Commodore's policy is that there is to be no liberty outside the gate until turnover is complete and Change of Command has taken place. That policy needs no defense. You're here to work, not play, and we want your crews concentrating on a good turnover instead of bars and women. For the information of you both, we've recently had a series of incidents. Submarine sailors have been going outside the gate during crew exchange and their CO's have let them get away with it. I'm telling you right now, don't let it happen with your crews. If it does, either you bust the offender's ass or you'll read about it. The Commodore is pissed and I am pissed about this lack of support from our Commanding Officers. Do you both understand?"

Both CO's nodded their heads in assent.

"Good. Now, let's get the tender Repair Officer in here and get on with the work package. Where's the Squadron Engineer?"

The Squadron Engineer came in seconds later and the conference began.

The work package review was unremarkable. As with almost every patrol the BRA-8 communications buoy, a subsurface communications buoy that the submarine could tow ten to fifteen feet below the ocean's surface, had been lost and finding a replacement was the currently recognized refit cliffhanger. Then again, something else would certainly emerge to displace it as the number one crisis. Refitting the most complex, sophisticated submarine ever built to "100% in Commission" status during a twenty-eight day refit period always had at least one or two surprises… almost invariably all bad.

* * * * *

Much later, after a full work day and a light evening meal, the Exec again stood, relaxing for a while on the tender's 01 deck outside the Wardroom, surveying the harbor scene. It was his habit to wear wash khakis during turnover, although most of the crew shifted immediately to the blue "poopy suits" that they would wear on patrol. It was another manifestation of his reluctance to leave the shore where all the good things of life were to be found. Symbolically, the shift to a poopy suit marked his step through the looking glass…a step from the real world of off crew back to the surreal world of patrol. Craig briefly thought about the veal cutlets and instant potatoes he had just confronted. Very early in his naval career he had learned to hate instant mashed potatoes. At home Meaghan had completely given up and always left the potatoes slightly lumpy to avoid any resemblance to the ersatz product.

As the Exec stood surveying the harbor scene, the COB appeared on the ladder from the tender main deck and caught his eye, approaching in the company of the Chief Navigation Electronics Technician. On the rare occasions when the COB went ashore, his companion was usually Ed Brown, the Chief NAVET. Chief Brown was the epitome of an old sea dog. Tall and thin, he appreciated the arts and classical music. His dark brown hair and luxuriant full beard accentuated his flamboyant personality. He was fluent in Spanish and enjoyed a remarkable rapport with the local bartenders and merchants. He was always calm and thoughtful—yet very quick and cool in a crisis. Both Brown and the COB were closet intellectuals. On board, the two were careful to avoid being seen as a clique, but they were close friends. Both men were seasoned enough in the art of living in a highly confined and structured society to avoid the paths that lead to friction and alienation. It did not escape the Exec's notice that tonight they were obviously on some sort of mission—probably one of which he would prefer to remain ignorant. He hailed them before they could speak.

"Now where are you two liberty risks headed?"

The COB grinned. "The Chief's Club. Everything is pretty well under control, so we thought we'd have a beer with the Blue Chiefs."

"Okay, but before you go, I want you to make sure the word is out. No one, and I mean no one, is to go outside the fence. I want a sea daddy watching everyone."

The COB's good humor was unaffected. "Aye, aye, XO. No problem."

The Exec wasn't through. "COB, I don't want any problems in the Greenhouse either. Make sure a couple of old hands spend the evening up there. With the Squadron's policy on town liberty, the Bluies are going to release a good deal of pent-up steam tonight and that's where it'll come out. I don't want any Goldies in trouble. There's also the Dedalo and those Spanish patrol craft moored at the head of the pier. We don't need any international incidents either, okay?"

The American submarine tender, with its refitting submarine alongside, was moored "Chinese" style, stern to the end of the pier. Approximately one-third of the long pier was segregated from the landward balance by a sturdy chain link fence and the standard ration of intensely focused U.S. Marine guards. The Spanish Navy utilized the remaining pier space and, at the moment, their sole aircraft carrier, the Dedalo, was present, along with several small patrol craft. American submarine sailors returning from the Greenhouse full of beer could be relied upon to interact with any available Spaniard…with unpredictable results.

The Greenhouse was situated in a building bordering a sports field just beyond the pier. It had served the Luftwaffe when the sports field had hosted the ME 109's and JU52's of the Condor Legion. Now, its beer bar served a crowd of dungaree and poopysuit clad sailors. It regularly discharged its daily quota of drunken souls to run the Spanish gauntlet of the pier, back to the security of the fence and the tender quarterdeck. Actual incidents were few, but not unheard of, and, with the mood the Chief of Staff had displayed, the Exec preferred to take no chances.

The COB and Chief Brown nodded their heads in assent. Both said, "Aye, Aye, XO," and hastily departed on their night's mission. Craig knew they would be thorough in following his orders, despite the fact that the Blue crew CPO's already had a half hour head start at the club.

After the Chiefs had left, he turned back to the railing and pondered the question of the moment, to go or not to go to the O Club for a couple of drinks? He was undecided and in no particular hurry to make up my mind. On the one hand, he was restless, feeling newly caged, but on the other hand, going would entail changing out of his working uniform, then making his way across the base by foot. That seemed more trouble than the evening's entertainment would warrant. Craig was wrestling with near terminal ennui.

Several minutes later, having finally decided the trip was not worthwhile, he turned from the railing and made his way to his stateroom. Inside, he kicked off his shoes, stripped off his uniform and tossed his outer clothing onto the unused top bunk. Wearing only boxer shorts, Craig sat in the only chair, flipped on the light wired into the metal desk and began a letter to Meaghan. With every patrol he found the daily letter more difficult to compose. Less and less of what went on seemed interesting enough to warrant description to a woman who, he knew, was having her own difficulty in keeping up her faithful flow of daily letters. For both of them it was a lonely life.

He was halfway through his letter when he was interrupted by a knock on the door. The Exec opened it to find the Old Man standing in the passageway. Scarcely waiting to be invited, he came in and sprawled half reclining, across the bunk. Craig dropped back into his seat at the desk.

"Writing home already?" asked the Captain.

"Yeah, my wife and I have never gotten to the point where these separations are really easy."

"No, not for us either."

The Captain paused for a few moments. He was a fairly large man with a newly adopted mustache. Somehow, even in a poopysuit, one could see small town Arkansas in him. He went on. "I miss the farm. You know, my father and two brothers are still back there. They're all elders in the Church now. Their lives are simple and fruitful. They aren't rich in material things, but they don't have to make compromises with their principles."

Craig had no ready rejoinder. After a moment, he offered, somewhat awkwardly, "I guess 'back home' always has an idyllic appeal, but usually we can't stay in that world."

"You're right," replied the Captain in a drifty soft tone.

The Captain abruptly changed the subject. "It looks like the ship came back in pretty good shape. That's a break for us. We can put more time into training for the ORSE."

"Captain, I hate to count chickens prematurely. Murphy's law says something will surface that the Bluies didn't notice, or something will break during the next two weeks."

"XO, I know something can always emerge, but maybe God will give us an easy refit this time. Anyway, I have given a lot of thought to how best we can prepare for this ORSE, and I've made a decision. I want you to assume command responsibility for all aspects of getting the ship ready for patrol. You act in my stead in everything except preparations for the ORSE. I want to be absolutely free from all distractions. Okay?"

Craig's mind raced. He was absolutely confident of his own abilities. If the Old Man was willing to give him de facto command of the ship, his ego clamored for him to grasp it, but what about the risks? *Bad idea. If we're not careful, it'll usurp the Captain's position with the crew.* Ego won. *To hell with it! You can't hide from the crew anyway.*

Craig's hesitation in replying was barely discernible. "Yes, sir, if that's your decision."

The Captain stood up and said, "Thanks, XO" and quickly left. The Exec stared at the door, troubled by what had just transpired. He thought back to Quonset Point and his presumption there in unloading the men from the aircraft. Twice now the Old Man had yielded command authority in a way he had never seen before. Every other Commanding Officer he had known would have savaged him in the first instance and been horrified at the thought of the second. He settled uneasily back in his chair.

I hope I didn't just make a mistake that we can't recover from. I don't understand Holcomb's behavior. Is there something else behind his request that I'm going to have to worry about?

It promised to be an interesting patrol.

6
Change of Command

The turnover period struggled its way to its inevitable conclusion on the morning of the fourth day of the refit. After three days of jostling cohabitation with the jubilant, homeward-bound Blue Crew, their dour Gold counterparts were ready to take over the ship and change of command was at hand. All of the multitudinous inspections, inventories, audits, and changes of custody had been done—or at least attested to by an "I swear to God" signature. The voluminous, time-tested checklists were complete. The cruise boxes had been swung aboard, emptied of the Gold crew's possessions, and immediately repacked by the Bluies. Holcomb and his men were now installed on the ship as the "on" crew. The official ceremony marking the exchange of command was scheduled for 1000Z. By 1030Z the Bluies would be gone. By 1700Z, the Gold Crew liberty party would be hotfooting it across the brow for their first taste of Rota's nightlife.

Both Executive Officers lounged in what was now Craig's stateroom, waiting to go topside for the change of command ceremony. Craig now sat in "his" desk chair and the Blue Exec took the visitor's seat on the bench that converted into a bunk. Both were satisfied. The turnover had gone smoothly without the squabbles that occasionally arise between crews. Even the communications officers, whose task it was to audit and inventory, page by page and item by item, the ship's huge volume of classified material, had finished on time and without discrepancies. It was one of the smoothest turnovers either had experienced.

Craig was in a generous mood. In spite of his reservations about some of the Blue CO's claims in his patrol debrief, the Blue XO had done a good job preparing for the turnover. "Bill," he said, "thanks for the turnover. You and your troops did a good job getting ready for us."

"We tried," Bill replied. "Anything else to talk about before we go topside?"

Stone, the Gold Crew Supply Officer, had come to him the previous day about the coffee problem, but, in the press of events, Craig had nearly forgotten. As the Supply and Executive Officers of both crew's knew, they had three quarters of a ton of bootleg coffee on board. It had been mysteriously acquired while the ship was in the shipyard during its last overhaul…how; no current member of either crew seemed to know. Neither crew's XO nor Supply Officer had ever been so foolish as to look the gift horse in the mouth.

The coffee wasn't accounted for on any inventory and, therefore, it could serve two very valuable purposes. First, coffee grounds were the medium of exchange for cumshaw work on the tender. "Cumshaw" was the time-honored practice of rewarding tender or shipyard personnel with unofficial gifts in exchange for equally unofficial extra bits of work or material and a twenty-pound can of coffee has been the currency of cumshaw forever in the United States Navy. Secondly, because of its high value, the crews could afford to spend more than their legal dollar allowance for rations on each patrol. They just fed the required few hundred pounds of free coffee back into inventory to offset any dollar value shortage. Sweet deal until now.

"Coffee. Let's talk about the coffee stash," Craig said. "Stone was on the tender yesterday and the Squadron Supply Officer told him we're going to convert to freeze-dried coffee machines during your next refit."

Bill's eyebrows rose at that one. "Freeze-dried coffee?"

It didn't sound good to Craig either. Personally, he viewed any form of instant coffee with disgust. The problem, however, was more serious than his coffee preferences.

"You heard me right. We have a Ship Alteration scheduled to remove the urns in the crew's mess and install those new push-button machines that run on instant coffee. Some dumb bastard in NavShips probably got himself a medal for saving us a few cubic feet of storage space. Never mind that he won't have to drink that shit…now, what do you want to do with your half of the approximately one thousand six hundred and forty pounds of bootleg coffee we have stashed in the Lower Level Missile Compartment frame bays?"

The Blue Crew Exec stared back in stunned disbelief. He didn't have any better idea what to do with the coffee than Craig or Stone. He blurted out the obvious. "We won't be able to drink it and, after this patrol, we can't use it to pad the inventory. We sure as hell can't turn it in." Both Captains had been signing their commissary inventories in blissful good faith for patrol after patrol, never wondering how it was they enjoyed steaks so often.

Craig looked on for a while as Bill chewed his lip, saying nothing. "By the way," he said, "our standard commissary load-out for this patrol will have the usual four hundred pounds of grounds in it. We can't even turn that down without drawing attention."

Bill wasn't much help. He shrugged helplessly. "Dump it on the tender for cumshaw IOUs?"

Craig shook his head. "Too obvious and, besides,, it would devalue the whole market. We can hang on to some of it for future cumshaw, but as for the rest, I'm going to paint every other can blue and leave it for you. I'll get rid of my half. Okay?"

Bill didn't look relieved. "Okay."

It's getting harder and harder to live graciously on these damned patrols.

Before they went topside, Craig had one other question he wanted to ask. It had nagged at him ever since the Blue Captain had debriefed their patrol on day one. "Just out of curiosity, you didn't log many sonar contacts on this patrol, even though you were in normally busy areas. Why were things so quiet? Is there anything I should give an extra shake in Sonar?"

The Blue Exec's good humor was persistent. "Nope," he said, "it was just a quiet patrol."

Craig kept after him. "Why?"

"Oh hell, how should I know? I'm going topside to make sure the Squadron Sixteen letters of commendation are on the podium for the Commodore to read to our troops. We got eight out of him for this patrol, you know."

As they rose to leave the stateroom, a cynical thought occurred to Craig. *And your Chief Sonarman is gonna get one.*

He would soon find out. Along with about two-thirds of his crew, he would stand on deck at parade rest and listen to the Commodore read each one of the letters. The Execs wrote them for their people on the way in from patrol, gave them to the Squadron Secretary who framed them, then listened while the Commodore read them as if they were his own words. That's how it always worked.

After the Blue Crew had left, racing across the brow to a chorus of hoots and yells with their Chief Sonarman clutching his new commendation, the Gold Crew formation broke up into small groups. Watching their counterparts scurry for the buses waiting to take them directly to the charter flight home brought into sharp focus the depth of the isolation that loomed before them. The Blue Crew would be home in about eight or nine hours. It would be about two months before even the anticipation of going home would become a palpable daily sensation for the men of the Gold Crew. On the other hand, there was some hollow consolation. The Bluies would feel the first cold breeze of dread, the first thoughts of their next patrol in about two months also, just about the same time Craig would start thinking about going home.

7
The Refit Begins

Rakowski, the Main Propulsion Assistant, or MPA, stood with the Medical Officer and Stone, the Supply Officer on the number three missile hatch. The flat surface of the huge hatch constituted approximately three square yards of the *Marion*'s afterdeck.

The red-headed Rakowski was stocky, and with his ruddy complexion looked more Irish than Polish. He often affected an air of mild amazement when treated to the most ordinary of conversational revelations. That and his slow, self-deprecating, sense of humor often caused people to underestimate him. In fact, as a young seaman, Rak's agile intelligence and driving ambition had won him a place in the Naval Academy Preparatory School. Later, his high class standing at graduation from the Naval Academy became his ticket into the Submarine Nuclear Power Program. At the Academy, Rak had finished twenty-third in a class of almost nine hundred without breaking a sweat. The sailors who worked for him soon saw through his facade and learned to respect him as a hard, fair taskmaster. Many of his fellow officers were slower to perceive the tough, streetwise core of the man. Rak was mischievous and, at heart, a born instigator. He was also unflappable under stress.

Stone, or "Stores" as he and every other Supply Officer were known by one and all, was a laconic ex-farm boy from Oklahoma, with a distinctly mid-Western twang and a dry sense of humor. As he approached the trio, the Exec noticed that Stone was chewing, as he habitually did, on a toothpick, looking every bit like he had just come to town from the farm. The Exec was well aware that Stone and Rak were mischievous and, not infrequently, co-conspirators in wardroom hijinks.

Rak and Stone intended to liven up their first night of liberty in Rota and the unsuspecting doctor was central to their plans. As such, he was a natural target. The doctor, or "Quack," as he was already generally known, had, to a remarkable degree, avoided the worldliness his years and medical training should have brought him. His baby face and wavy brown hair gave him an image of innocence…and gullibility.

It was an interesting dichotomy that both the doctor and the Old Man held passionately to their religious beliefs and tended to praise God in harmony during religious services. Meanwhile, with equal conviction they subscribed to precisely opposite beliefs regarding medicine. The Old Man was a devout Christian Scientist who rejected all concepts of healing except by the intervention of faith. The doctor followed the path of a hard-shell conservative, Southern Baptist who didn't drink or swear, but considered modern medicine to be God's greatest gift to man. The captain and the doctor had yet to confront their respective philosophical differences, as this was the doctor's first patrol. Commissioned barely two months earlier, he stood trustingly in the midst of a new world. Except for their language, the shipmates around him were as alien as the Spaniards he would meet that night outside the base gate. His self-appointed tutors, Rak and Stone, viewed their rookie pupil with intense expectations. To Craig's suspicious eye, they looked like a pair of coyotes considering a cornered rabbit.

"Want to go over tonight?" Rak asked Stone. The doctor listened, eyes bright.

"Sure. You want to eat on board or go over early and eat in town?" Stone knew the script. The doctor said nothing.

Rak appeared to think for a moment. "Let's go early. If we cut out at 1700, we can get into town before the shops close. We could show Doc around town a little, then get a good dinner."

By now the doctor was as attentive as an expectant puppy. Stone picked up where Rak left off. "Okay. Good! I want to stop at that little lace shop just off the main drag to get something for Sandy. After dinner, maybe we'll have a drink on the way back? Sound okay to you, Doc? They'll have soft drinks and other stuff wherever we stop."

It was obviously okay with the doctor. He wanted to be included, but had worried that Rak and Stone would want to go to a bar. But their proposition seemed all right. He accepted eagerly. They then split up and went their separate ways to finish the workday.

* * * * *

Virgin sailors McJimsey and Kane had begun to lose faith in the recruiting posters that had led them to this elite service. Having titivated the *Marion*'s storage cage on the tender for most of their first day of refit, they had spent long hours on days two and three cleaning the crew's temporary berthing space. Their only respite from scrubbing decks and toilets had been the "all hands" working parties called to manhandle large quantities of material on or off the submarine. Now, sweating in white trousers and tee shirts behind grimy aprons, McJimsey was struggling to finish the last of the midday meal dishes in the scullery. Kane was on his hands and knees scouring the deck in the crew's dinette, the "crew's mess."

The duty cook had already fired the first haranguing barrage. They had to speed up. When cleanup was completed, they were to break out the stores he needed to prepare for evening meal, set up for the meal, serve the meal, then start the cleanup again. They were "mess cooks," the lowliest station in life aboard a submarine, and the initiation rite of nearly every young sailor into the fraternity of seagoing men.

As they raced past each other, both dripping with sweat, one with a scullery basket filled with pots to be scrubbed, the other with his arms filled with canned beans soon to soil a just-scrubbed pan, McJimsey and Kane paused for a moment.

"You going to hit the beach tonight?" asked Kane.

"You fuckin-A, I'm going to," replied McJimsey who looked haggard, but determined.

"By the time we finish cleanup it'll be 2100. We gotta be back up at 0430," Kane pointed out.

"I don't give a shit! I'd kill for a beer right now. I'm going to the Greenhouse as soon as we get off. You coming or not?"

Kane didn't relish misery without company. He knew he'd go. "Yeah, okay."

They had by now caught the cook's eye. The cook, having duty on the first liberty night, was none to happy to begin with, and reacted promptly. "You two! Get your asses in gear!"

They were off running. Two harried, sweating fugitives with a vile-tempered cook nipping at their heels.

* * * * *

The Exec had gone below directly after the change of command ceremony. Lunch was a pleasantly quiet affair without the crowding bustle of the Blue Crew's presence. He again saw Rak, Stone and the doctor huddled together, and his suspicion grew that some sort of mischief was afoot. He wondered, with quiet amusement, what they were up to, but didn't pry. The Doc was a "Little Lord Fauntleroy" if ever he had seen one. Soaking wet behind the ears. The doctor was not yet aware that Rak and Stone were a pair of treacherous urchins, but, in the Exec's opinion, Doc would soon find this out.

After lunch, Craig settled down to stowing his gear in his stateroom. The first thing he did was rig the settee back into a bunk. Visitors could sit on it when it was rigged as a bench seat, but Craig liked having the space to spread out his paperwork. He didn't much care if someone sat on the bunk or had to stand up until they left, as he didn't view his tiny bit of personal space as a reception room. A one and a half by two-foot desk just couldn't hold the sea of paper that a Fleet Ballistic Missile Submarine floats on.

He was still sorting through the stacks of paperwork brought along from off-crew, organizing his desk and lockers for the next three months, when the Captain came in. Holcomb had been doing the same thing in his stateroom and had come over looking for extra coat hangers. After the Exec handed him the few spare hangers from his gear locker, the Captain perched on the edge of the already littered bunk and asked, "XO, what do you have planned for training this evening?"

"Section Emergency drills," Craig answered. "Duty section Fire and Flooding drills. Also, I want to station the Maneuvering Watch before we put liberty down."

Prudence dictates a quick series of basic drills as soon as possible after a crew change. Stationing the Maneuvering Watch mans the stations required to get the ship underway and maneuver it in the confined waters of a harbor. The exercise of setting it as a drill ensures that everyone knows his assignment and that all the necessary equipment is located, tested and ready. Section emergency drills are more examples of the same common sense. In the event of a real emergency, the Exec wanted to be sure the personnel available on board could deal with it.

A section, in the *Marion*'s case, was half the crew. Because of the amount of work to be done, SSBN's generally ran port and starboard duty sections during refit. Allowing half the crew to take a few hours off during the evening while the other half kept on with the testing and maintenance was all the relaxation the demanding refit schedule would tolerate if the ship was to return to sea with all systems fully in commission.

Again, the Captain nodded. "Good. That's fine. I'll want to be onboard for the drills tomorrow night. Tonight everything is up forward. Right?"

"Yes, sir," the Exec replied.

Holcomb went on, "After we secure the Maneuvering Watch, the Duty Officer can handle the drills tonight, can't he?"

"Yes, sir. The Navigator has the duty forward and the Engineer aft, so we'll have plenty of coverage."

"Good! Good!" said the Captain, rising as he spoke. "Let's you and I go up to the Officer's Club for dinner. It'll be awhile before we'll have another chance for a meal off the ship."

"Okay," Craig replied, hoping to hell that the captain's "we" was the royal 'we.'" He had no intention of staying on board every one of the remaining twenty-five nights before going to sea for two months. "What time do you want to leave the ship?"

"Around 1900Z, okay?"

"Yes, sir." Craig wasn't all that happy. The Captain, like every man, once in a while needed companionship and he was stuck with providing it. Holcomb was a gentle person with extraordinarily simplistic moral and religious convictions. Craig liked him well enough, but didn't really care to go on liberty with him. From his perspective, it was certain to be like a night out with the family pastor.

Holcomb went back to his stateroom, never suspecting how profoundly different he and the Exec really were.

8

The First Drills

The Exec picked up the 1MC microphone and announced, "Station the Section Maneuvering Watch" over the ship's general announcing system at 1630Z. As usual, the first time was a fiasco. The Quartermasters couldn't find grease pencils or the harbor chart. The seamen on deck could only find one "heavey," a length of cotton clothes line with a "monkey fist" knot at the end of it, that is thrown from the ship to the pier and then is used to haul across the mooring lines. On the first practice throw with the only heavey on board, McJimsey forgot to hold on to the bitter end and consigned it to the briny deep, thus reducing the inventory of heaveys to zero.

The bridge "suitcase," a plug-in box carried to the bridge of the ship during surface operations that contained the speakers, telephone connections and ship control instrumentation necessary for communicating with the rest of the ship's control stations, didn't work. A headset on a long extension cord was routinely passed up to the bridge from the control room as a backup. This time, the Quartermaster, checking the operation of the bridge hatch, slammed the hatch on the cord and cut it, leaving the Exec and Duty Officer isolated on the bridge to helplessly fulminate with no one to hear. Effectively, they were on the other side of the moon from the rabble scurrying around below decks. And so it went.

Finally, after an interminable fifty-four minutes, at 1724Z, all stations were manned and had reported that they were ready to get underway. The suitcase switches had been aligned properly and the world was alive with clear communications. The Exec's good humor had departed with the last heavey. He nodded to the Duty Officer to secure the drill and went below to change. Not a happy man, he reckoned that after the Chinese fire drill he had just witnessed, even a pious dinner with the Captain would be a relief.

Elsewhere, Rak, Stone and the Doc were scrambling into civvies. McJimsey and his friend Kane, were discovering the sympathy sailors have for new mess cooks who throw away heaveys. It was like a flock of chickens with only one June bug to peck.

* * * * *

Craig knocked on the Captain's door at exactly 1900Z. He was dressed in civvies, as was Holcomb, and they wasted no time in leaving the ship. The watch section drills were due to start at anytime. By custom, had they been aboard when the alarm for the drill sounded, they would have participated until its completion. Neither of them wanted to be caught by the drills. Time enough for that later.

The two wound their way from the brow through the tender's machine shops, up the long ladder to her main deck, then aft to the quarterdeck on her stern and down to the pier. They walked on toward the head of the pier, passing the high fence and Marine guard that isolated the American controlled third of the pier from the Spanish occupied remainder. Being in no hurry, they stopped for a while alongside the *Dedalo.* Like two tourists, they stood and gawked at her.

The Dedalo was an ex U.S. Navy CVL, a light aircraft carrier built on a cruiser hull. Small for an aircraft carrier, it was nonetheless a large ship. It was too small to operate modern high-performance aircraft, but had an assigned composite squadron of anti-submarine helicopters and fixed wing aircraft. The inadequacy of her flight deck was irrelevant in her present political climate. She rarely, if ever, moved from her moorings. Based on animosities surviving from the Spanish Civil War, the Spanish Air Force refused to let the Spanish Navy embark their small squadron of fixed wing Grumman S-2-F aircraft on the carrier, threatening most convincingly to shoot them out of the air if they tried. The best the intimidated Navy could manage was to keep their showboat spruced up and occasionally conduct a few desultory helicopter operations from her deck. The Captain and Exec surveyed the huge bulk with its obsolescent radars, but their attention focused on the way she had grown to the pier.

"XO," said the Captain, "look at those wire mooring lines. They look like they never expect to move them."

He was right. The ship was moored entirely with wire rope. You don't do that for a short stay. It's too hard to handle. Besides, the brow from the pier to the Dedalo's quarterdeck and the sentry box at its foot were semi-permanent installations. Craig was reminded of the station ship at Annapolis when he was there as a midshipman. The *Reina Mercedes*, a Victorian Spanish battleship, had been taken as a prize in the Spanish American War and promptly immobilized as a barracks ship at Annapolis. By 1958 her mooring had looked exactly like this.

"Actually," the Exec observed, "I'm more intrigued by the stores stacked there by the brow." He pointed to the cases of empty wine bottles stacked head high, waiting to be hauled off. Both men laughed and moved on.

"There's the real Spanish navy," the Exec said, pointing to a pair of small craft tied up between the carrier's bow and the basin wall. They were fifty foot launches that had been decked over and armed with a pair of Browning M2 .50 cal. heavy machine guns in "scarf ring" mounts. The M2's had probably been cannibalized from a Spanish Army personnel carrier.

"I guess they still worry about people sneaking across the beach," said the Captain.

They saw the base shuttle bus approaching in the distance and hurried to catch it.

* * * * *

The Officer's Club was a low modern building on a slight rise wrapped in expansive glass windows. The dining room looked out over the harbor basin. At one end was a small stage and dance floor. Three or four nights per week some unknown local or USO-sponsored group performed before a group of lukewarm observers whose limited interest barely exceeded their non-existent entertainment options.

Like all Navy O' Clubs, the menu stressed plain dishes at reasonable prices. That was okay so far as Craig was concerned, as he rarely deviated from steak and potatoes. He did enjoy good wine and decided he had earned a decent bottle for the meal…French, not Spanish. Craig never much cared for French politics, nor Spanish Riojas. To his surprise, the Captain, who generally never drank, accepted a glass, though only one.

They finished dinner, and over the Captain's coffee and the Exec's wine, the Captain started to talk. As Holcomb talked, Craig listened with growing discomfort. He didn't consider himself a close friend or confident of the

Captain, and had little inclination to hold his hand while he unburdened himself. Holcomb appeared to be caught up in some kind of paroxysm of self-pity. He said he had never wanted this path in life. He had lacked a personal vision in his youth and had followed his father's bidding, first by going to a seminary, then to the Naval Academy. He had been a junior officer before he truly found God. After much prayer, he believed God had told him to go on with his career, and so he had done "His" bidding. It wasn't easy for him, he said, being responsible for so many souls. He longed for a simpler task in life, but God had set his course. The Exec listened silently.

If God is so smart, I wonder why he picked Holcomb to hold the keys to seventeen megatons of weaponry. Craig was not one to relish the company of a weak leader. His mind flew back to Holcomb's behavior during the crew flight and the agreement to delegate so much command responsibility during this refit. What had been a malaise was now a focused concern about Holcomb's competence. Somewhat fascinated by the insight into his Captain's motivations, Craig let his curiosity supercede prudence and, choosing his words carefully, asked him, "Captain, you are describing a pretty humanitarian view of the world. How do you deal with Rickover's philosophy of leadership?"

He had observed for some time that the Captain was a fanatical NUC and a great admirer of Admiral Rickover, and wondered how he reconciled those notions with what he had just heard.

Holcomb fingered his moustache with his index finger as he answered. "Admiral Rickover is the greatest man alive today. He made possible these ships that keep the world free from war. He teaches us to strive for perfection and honesty. He holds himself personally responsible for all of our mistakes. We don't always understand him because we lack his wisdom."

The Exec was appalled. The Captain had said a mouthful that he considered to be beyond ridiculous. Craig had been uncomfortable with the conversation from the beginning, and, now, was struggling to keep his reaction from showing. He had his own views of Rickover, whom he considered to be a self-serving old political son of a bitch. Then he quickly reminded himself that he also had nearly a full tour ahead of him serving with this Captain. *God and Rickover! Is he confusing the two?*

Craig didn't believe in either. He wasn't one to argue with any man about his God, but having met the Admiral three times, he was absolutely sure Rickover was no deity.

Luckily, the Captain quickly retreated from further discussion about Rickover and God and shifted abruptly to light banter about the band that was filtering into the room. Relieved that he had been spared the risk of further exposing his own feelings on God and Rickover, the Exec briefly wondered if he had let something show in his expression. He quickly decided not to worry about it. He and the Captain were what they were and both would have to submerge their differences if they were going to work together.

After a while, the Captain questioned if they should stay for the show. Craig demurred on the excuse of getting back to the ship to write a letter home. The Captain willingly went along with an early return and, a half hour later they were back on board the ship. That night sleep did not come easily to the Exec. He intuitively didn't trust people who look for someone else, be it God or man, to blame for their decisions, or lack thereof, in life.

The Old Man and I are developing a strange and dangerous relationship.

9

The Greenhouse

At about the time the Captain and the Exec were sitting down to their dinner, McJimsey and Kane had finished their day's work and headed for the Greenhouse. They exchanged their grubby whites for clean poopysuits. Neither had the energy to bother with civvies and an excursion outside the gate. Once inside the Greenhouse, they surveyed the Spartan interior with its bare tables and fiberglass chairs. Everything had been prudently selected to be either expendable or sailor proof. Beer and soft drinks were available in cans only. Bottles were prohibited. Cans can make bruises, but are rarely lethal. The base authorities had suffered long and painfully to learn how to most safely mix sailors and beer.

McJimsey and Kane were oblivious to the functional beauty of the place. They found a table near the rear wall, cleared it by dumping the empties into a battered thirty-two gallon garbage can that contributed its part to the place's decor and set about walling themselves off from the world. Each brick of their wall was a just-emptied Budweiser can.

The wall had only begun to achieve architectural significance when Sonarman Third Class Schroeder walked in. STS3 Schroeder had gone into town early. After sampling the local Fundador brandy in more bars than he could recall, he found himself back at the main gate. From there, he wandered across the base, drawn by instinct to the Greenhouse.

A sociable drunk by nature, he was delighted to spot McJimsey and Kane arguing about the inclusion of a door and window in their wall. In turn, the two young seamen were flattered by the camaraderie of a qualified sonarman. To them, the young Third Class Petty Officer looked like an old salt of the sea. Besides, he appreciated the elegance of their project and eagerly fell to the task of raising the wall.

An hour later, three very drunken young sailors, expelled at closing time from behind their nearly completed wall, steered their course back toward the pier.

In a more sober state, they might have noticed the brilliance of the stars in the clear Rota night sky. As it was, they steered as best they could toward the constellation of lights at the end of the pier. Crossing onto the pier, Kane was seized by the urgent need to urinate. Standing on the edge of the pier, he drained away his accumulated beer into the darkness and was rewarded with a howl of indignation from somewhere below. As Kane continued, McJimsey and Schroeder wove over to his side.

Schroeder surveyed the situation and, with considerable gravity, advised Kane "You're pissing on somebody." Kane giggled and humped forward to project the stream farther out from the pier. The unintelligible oaths were louder and now coming from more than one voice.

McJimsey peered into the night. With the tide out, the Spanish launches were nearly thirty feet directly below Kane. Two furious, gesticulating Spaniards were sheltering under the hatch of the inboard launch.

McJimsey retreated a step or two. "You're pissing that fuckin' little boat full!"

Kane struggled to close his fly. All three were giggling hysterically and staggering from the effects of the alcohol. A large wrench whistled by Schroeder and Kane's head. It was rapidly followed by two wine bottles. Surprised by the sudden counterattack, the three miscreants retreated from the edge of the pier and took stock.

Kane was incensed. "They threw a fuckin' wrench at me!" he yelled. "I just took a piss in their fuckin' ocean and they threw a fuckin' wrench at me!"

After some brief but deliberate consideration, Schroeder and McJimsey concluded that Kane was rightfully aggrieved. They felt aggrieved as well, for reasons of shipmate loyalty and national pride. The Spaniards had attacked one of their own just because he had taken a little piss off their pier. Patriotism rose like a Phoenix from their breasts.

Hell, them assholes just threw wine bottles at three American servicemen.

It was the wiry McJimsey that saw the rock first. It took the strength of all three of them to pick up the two hundred pound piece of stone rip rap from the basin wall and stagger, still giggling, the hundred and fifty feet to where Kane had stood urinating.

Kane screamed, "Banzai mother fucker!" The three launched the rock, then turned and raced for the tender.

The two hundred pound stone had attained a free fall velocity of only about seventy-five feet per second when it struck the stern well deck of the inboard launch. That was enough. The slight resistance barely slowed the stone as it passed through the hull on its way to its watery grave.

By the time the Spanish crew swam to the pier and clambered up, McJimsey, Kane and Schroeder were lost in the bowels of the tender. As expected, the Marine guard at the pier fence spoke no Spanish and performed admirably. He did not flinch in the face of the furious charge by two wet, hysterical Spaniards. He shut the gate on their approach and stood his ground.

10
The Morning After

Craig was at breakfast in the wardroom the next morning when the Navigator came in. It was the fifth day of the refit and the Bluies had been gone less than twenty-four hours. Already he had psychologically settled back into the routine of shipboard life. At home, he never bothered with breakfast, but on the ship he rarely missed the morning meal. Another one of those dichotomies that separated his two worlds.

Usually a somewhat wooden-faced character, this morning the Navigator wore a quizzical expression.

"Good morning, Gator. What's up?"

"Good morning, XO. I don't know. There is a hell of a flap at the head of the pier. Every Four Striper around here, American and Spanish, is up there looking over the side. I heard that one of those Spanish launches sank last night."

It didn't seem important. The Exec changed the subject. "Any problems with the liberty party last night?"

The Navigator grinned. "No, but I wouldn't look for much out of the doctor this morning."

"Oh? Why is that?"

Again the grin. "I'd ask Rak or Stone. They took him out on the town."

"And?"

"I understand he conducted a free street corner clinic for all the whores in Rota."

Craig was incredulous. "Doc?"

"Yeah, Rak and Stone told all the women out at the "Congrejo Arojo" that Doc was a specialist in breast cancer, so they all lined up to let him examine their breasts."

The whole scene of a drunken Doc conducting public breast examinations at a bar called the "Red Crab" was almost too mindboggling to imagine.

"Navigator, tell Rak and Stone that I know what they did. I just don't know how they did it. If they've messed up the Quack's mind, I'll have their asses!"

The Navigator stirred his coffee. "You know," he said, "I would have thought that that was impossible. When they came back aboard, the doctor had this little lace thing over his head. We finally had to let him wear it to bed. I thought he was a teetotaler."

"He was!"

The wardroom door started to open. The Exec got a quick look at Rak's mask of innocence before he said, "Oh, excuse me, XO" and quickly disappeared, leaving the speechless Exec no remaining doubt that the Dodtor was going to be a troubled man when he woke up.

Craig shook his head and looked at the Navigator. "Sometimes it's kind of like being the keeper at the 'Animal House.' God, I hope they haven't ruined that kid for life."

The telephone in the wardroom rang about 0745Z. It was the outside line to the tender switchboard. The voice on the other end was the Squadron Secretary saying there was to be a meeting of all Commanding Officers in the Commodore's office at 0800Z.

The meeting was brief and apparently intense. By 0815Z, the Captain was back on board and had called for the Executive Officer and the Chief of the Boat. As they met outside his stateroom, they exchanged quizzical glances, then knocked and went in.

Holcomb was a little pale and visibly upset. "The Commodore told us that someone from this tender or the submarines alongside sank one of those Spanish launches last night…with a rock! The divers are down there now trying to raise the launch and recover the rock. They say the whole stern is bashed off!"

The Exec was amazed. "I guess that's what the crowd this morning at the head of the pier was all about."

The Captain gave him an apprehensive look and continued. "The Commodore thinks the people who did it were submarine sailors. I have never seen him so angry. He wants them caught and caught now. He's beside himself."

Then the Captain, in a curious half whisper, asked, "Do you believe any of our sailors would do such a thing?"

The COB remained determinedly silent. Finally the Exec said, "No, sir. I really don't believe so."

The Captain was obviously not convinced. "I'm telling you, the Commodore won't quit hounding us till somebody hangs. There are only two submarines alongside. If the guilty party is in our crew, I want them found. I'm telling you, the Commodore is out of his mind! Do you both understand?"

The COB's breathing had gone irregular. Craig was certain he knew something.

The Captain cut in before he could ask the COB anything. "I want a sworn statement from every man in this crew that he had nothing to do with this!"

The COB had nearly reached the limit of his self-control, but continued his mute performance.

The Exec spoke up. "Captain, I don't think we should do that. I don't like that approach. It never catches the guilty and it offends the innocent. We have to trust the troops and they have to trust us. Let the COB and me just quietly ask around."

He wasn't happy with that, but he bought it. Then, in a somewhat haunted stare, he asked, "How am I ever going to prove anything to the Commodore?"

"Captain, I think you should suggest to the Commodore that he focus his inquiry on the tender Quarterdeck Watch that let the bad guys slip by them. We'll let you know if we find anything."

Outside the Captain's stateroom Craig turned on the COB. "Okay, now what the hell are you choking about? Do you know something?"

COB looked at him, tears of laughter rolling down his cheeks. "No, I don't, and I know it shouldn't be funny, but it is. XO, can't you see the headlines? *Drunken Yank Sailors Sink Spanish Warship with a Rock!* I can just imagine the scene up at the Squadron!"

The story did have a humorous side. But a very serious one, too. Fortunately, there had been no injuries.

"COB," the Exec demanded, "I want to know. Did we have anyone over last night that might have done it?"

The COB sobered up and thought for a minute. "No, sir, the only ones it could possibly have been were McJimsey and Kane, and they came back with Schroeder. They were all too drunk to walk, let alone carry a rock that size."

The Exec dropped it there. He was still more worried about the doctor.

* * * * *

Two patrols later, at his retirement ceremony, the COB fingered McJimsey and Kane. The Navy never did.

11
Getting Ready

After the first night of liberty, the crew had pretty much settled down to the routine of the refit. It was now the ninth day of the refit and only nineteen days remained before the start of the patrol. With an Operational Reactor Safeguards Examination scheduled during the refit sea trials, there was a strong undercurrent of apprehension as they began to ready the ship for its next patrol. An ORSE is the most feared, most traumatic experience deliberately visited upon the crew of a nuclear submarine. At that time, it was customary for ORSE's to be given during the sea trials period about two thirds of the way through refit. That left little time after change of command for an oncoming crew to refresh their training, groom the ship and thoroughly review its myriad records.

Eventually a few years later, someone finally realized the folly that was created by having the ORSE during the sea trial period and it was shifted to the end of patrol. The change was made, not in consideration of the crews, but to avoid a publicly awkward situation if a crew failed their exam. In that event, a political conundrum would occur in that two cherished tenets of the nuclear powered submarine force would collide in mutual exclusivity. One was the highly touted, absolute reliability expected of the SSBN and its crew in meeting its strategic deterrent patrol commitment. The other was that no ship's reactor was ever to be operated by a crew that did not meet Naval Reactors' "standards."

Since some ORSE results were politically manipulated by Rickover through "guidance" from Naval Reactors Command, the potential existed for a real public relations disaster. Letting the crew make the patrol first, then raising hell with them at the end of their deployment eliminated the possibility of an embarrassment that a "failure" would produce, one which couldn't be hidden from the rest of the Navy—and the competing Air Force strategic forces.

Rickover's public image, as a dedicated guarantor of the nation's safety, was thereby protected from scrutiny. The crews, particularly, their Captains and Engineers, were so grateful for a more reasonable opportunity to prepare for this most difficult and capricious of tests that they didn't care about the reasons for the change.

The Navy Technical Proficiency Inspection that verified the crew's standards of training and performance in handling the nuclear weapons in their custody was just as demanding of perfection as the ORSE—perhaps more so. That inspection was professionally administered and, also, was always held during the refit. However, the NTPI was never attended by the same atmosphere of intimidation as the ORSE and never inspired the dread that preceded the Nuclear Power Examining Board's visits. The NTPI was tough, but fair, and never had any agenda except the honorable purpose of insuring safety and reliability in handling and employing the nuclear weapons. It was conducted by officers who were, in many cases, "Rickover Rejects." That is, they had been refused acceptance into the Nuclear Power Training Program.

However, for Holcomb and the crew of the *Marion*, the enlightened day of the end-of-patrol ORSE had not yet come. So, during this refit, their preoccupation was with passing it on the first day of sea trials. They had just fourteen days to get ready.

Fitting everything that had to be done into two weeks required some luck, a fair bit of planning, and many long hours for the crew. Fortunately, the basic structure of a refit had become so practiced and methodical that the officers and Chief Petty Officers could plan accurately in allocating time and resources between ORSE preparations and the work of turning the ship around. The night before change of command, the Exec had gathered the Department Heads together to draw up a large wall chart, a PERT activity/dependency network, for the refit.

By getting every task that had to be done signposted on a single huge sheet of paper, they built a roadmap of all the activities for the refit and their interdependencies. Every day had time allocated for engineering training and all major paths on the planning chart converged on "Reactor Startup" four days before sea trials. The planning for the refit allowed each engineering watch section one four-hour session of casualty drills with the reactor critical before they had to face the ORSE. Not much to build confidence on, but it was all that could be squeezed into the available time.

Prior to reactor startup, other, more limited training could be undertaken, but ORSE graduation required a critical reactor and live steam. The plan was based on pushing the troops hard. They would work a full day shift every day on refit work, then, after an early evening meal, spend another four hours training. After that, half would be allowed to go ashore on liberty…if they still had the energy. All in all, Craig was satisfied that his planning gave the Captain as much opportunity to train his NUC's as was humanly possible. Holcomb had made it clear to Craig that he would decide how the time set aside for ORSE preparations would be used.

The crew settled onto the refit treadmill with no more than the usual amount of bitching. Fortunately, they were spared the common experience of a major equipment failure during refit, the kind that blows away any pre-existing plans. Consequently, by the third or fourth day, the routine was already becoming a blur of fatigue and efficiency.

The Captain and Engineer were always aft in the engineering spaces. Things were going well in Navigation, Weapons, and Supply and the Exec was content in his assigned role as "Captain" of the front end of the ship. Certainly, not all things went smoothly. During the first simulated radioactive spill drill, the Engineering Laboratory Technician dumped a small bottle of pure water, representing reactor coolant, on the deck in the middle level of the Missile Compartment and laid down in the puddle pretending to have fallen unconscious.

Following his discovery, in less than fifteen minutes five other people, including the Quack, had "contaminated" themselves and were stuck in the "contaminated" area. Within thirty minutes, all three of the ship's low range beta-gamma survey instruments were stuck irretrievably in the "contaminated" area, carried in by blundering sailors who were more possessed of good intentions than common sense.

At the end of one hour and fifteen minutes, the first of the horde who had rushed into the scene were trussed up from head to toe in yellow anti-contamination clothing, and moved to the prepared decontamination areas. Eventually, nine "200 pound yellow canaries" were hauled out of the spill area to be "decontaminated."

At the end of one hour and forty-five minutes, the "unconscious" ELT was stepped on one time too many and lost both his temper and stage presence.

After one hour and fifty-five minutes, the Old Man secured the drill and stormed off to his stateroom. He was visibly upset.

Later, Craig heard Holcomb talking to himself through the thin bulkhead between their staterooms. The Captain was praying...and the words "ORSE" and "Rickover" had great prominence in his prayer.

Maybe the negotiation with God helped. After that, things seemed to go a little better for the NUC's. They did everything the Captain and Engineer could think of that didn't require reactor power. The Captain himself spot-checked the Machinist Mate's re-packing of some small steam valves. All the NUC's crawled into and out of steam suits and oxygen breathing apparatus during simulated floodings and fires and most of the conceivable combinations of both.

The rest of the ship, the Exec included, held the engineers' coats, so to speak. They played supporting roles during the drills, answered the phones as required, and were relieved to remain peripheral to the Engineers' ordeal.

Sometimes the front-enders suffered more than a little emotional trauma as well.

Late one night, Craig walked into the wardroom. The evening drill period was over and everyone who wasn't ashore was turning in for the night. The Navigator was sitting at the table, elbows on either side of his coffee mug, head cupped in his hands. The Navigator was normally a placid, almost bovine sort of personality. This night his dark fuming eyes made him look like a bull with a very foul disposition.

"Your ears are red, Gator. Problems?"

The Navigator looked at the Exec sullenly for a long moment.

Craig waited, not doubting for an instant that the Navigator was going to let go with both barrels as soon as he found the words. He suspected that he knew what the problem was, but it was better to be sure.

When the Navigator answered, he started calmly, his voice rose with his emotions to a shout, then scaled back down to despondent resignation. "XO," he said, "the Engineers just dropped both SINS on me. We were within two or three hours of finishing both calibration runs when they ran that fire drill and tripped both 5KW motor generator sets. They just turned the fucking lights out in the Nav Center with their ORSE drills tonight! I just lost thirty-six hours worth of Goddamned cal runs!"

The Exec was greatly concerned, too. A Ship's Inertial Navigation System is one of the world's most delicate instruments. Kill the power to one and the odds are that something, usually one of the gyros or accelerometers, will require replacement. Being dropped to cold iron, i.e. completely shut down, without going through a proper shutdown sequence, is a potentially severe trauma to a SINS.

"Okay," Craig said. "You've lost the cal runs. Have you got both systems coming back up?"

"Yeah. So far we don't see any hard failures, but we don't know how stable the inertial components are until we get back into calibration. Goddammit, XO, those systems were both settling out beautifully! At best I'm gonna be two days behind going into Land Station Tracking with the TYPE 11! If I have to shut down to change a gyro we'll have lost another day all because the NUC's couldn't keep their hands off the 5KW's!"

The Navigator was steaming. The 5KW's were small motor generators dedicated as power supplies to the SINS. He had put the SINS on them, rather than the larger primary power supply to minimize the chances of precisely this occurrence. Craig understood his anguish. SINS are such sophisticated and subtle machines that even when all the individual components are within specification, they can show a collective mechanical malaise that results in a lower quality of performance. Before the shutdown, the Navigator had two robust healthy systems. What he now had might never be as good. Besides, the alignment and calibration of the Type 11 Star Tracking Periscope was a lengthy and, often, frustrating procedure that required the support of theodolites ashore. If Land Station Tracking was delayed, there would be precious little slack left in the Navigator's schedule.

"Did you tell the Engineer which power supplies you were on?" the Exec asked.

"Yes, sir. I had also reminded the Captain this morning because I heard they were planning to run electrical casualty drills tonight. Sure enough, they decided to do a zero-ground-on-the-battery drill and neither the Captain nor the Engineer stopped them from isolating all the DC busses while chasing the ground. They just turned the fuckin' lights off on us!"

"Did you talk to the Captain about this?"

"Yeah, he said it was too bad, but ORSE training took priority. I'll bet he'll rethink his fucking priorities if we have to get underway on two shaky SINS and a screwed up Type 11!"

The Navigator finally had vented his frustration and was cooling down. All Craig could think to say were platitudes, so he kept his mouth shut and went off to bed. The bottom line was that they were risking reduced accuracy of their missiles, at least during the early stages of the patrol, rather than curtail ever so slightly the Captain's training for the ORSE.

This is real crap when we risk our mission for a Goddamned drill.

* * * * *

The next afternoon Stone and the Exec were alone in the wardroom. As a Supply Officer, Stone had received very little technical training, but he was a smart, level-headed officer who had qualified on his first patrol as Officer of the Deck Underway. A keen observer, he quickly mastered the technical and tactical skills necessary to stand the top watch at sea. He was one of the Exec's favorites because Craig knew that he was one of the people he could rely on when things got dirty or dangerous. Of the officers in the crew, Stone and Rakowski were the two he would have wanted alongside in a firefight. Today, he sensed that Stone had something on his mind.

"Got a minute, XO?"

"Sure, Stone, what about?"

"Last night the Engineers blew Navigation away. The Old Man doesn't seem to be bothered about it. Is the ORSE that important?"

Craig thought for a second about how to answer Stone. "Yes, it is. If we don't pass the ORSE, we don't go to sea and our mission won't get carried out."

Stone queried on, "If we do go to sea and can't keep the Nav system up, then we can't launch the missiles. How is one thing more important than the other?"

"Stone, listen to me. What happens when a crew fails an ORSE?"

"Hell to pay! The Old Man catches it, and the crew gets beat up by all the visiting firemen in the Atlantic Fleet. They work the crew's ass off round the clock for days, then pronounce them cured. One patrol later, the Old Man is gone."

I replied, "A very correct scenario. Now, what happens when a ship makes a mistake in Weapons? Let's say, for example, they spend two weeks with all sixteen missiles aimed at Poland instead of the Russians because of sloppy maintenance or because the Old Man never verified the targeting tapes? Or whatever."

"I never heard of such a case."

Craig let it sink in for a few minutes. "No, you never did, did you?"

"Has that ever happened?"

"Stores, you know I have always been a 'Goldie.' On my last patrol before I came here, when we met the Blue Crew coming in, we found the PEAC's, the photoelectric auto collimators, loose on their foundations. They had never been bolted down at the end of the previous refit when they brought them back from the calibration lab on the tender. One whole patrol with one hundred forty eight warheads cocked and primed and nobody did the weekly preventive maintenance checks to make sure they knew where they were pointed. God knows where those birds would have gone if they had launched. We reported it to Squadron, but the CO still got his kiss in the ear at the end of patrol. He had had a good ORSE before they went to sea."

Stone was pretty serious by now. He understood the point. "Why the difference?"

"Because Hyman G. Rickover doesn't give a damn about our strategic weapons, or where they are pointed, and, unfortunately, the Submarine Force chain of command basically only cares about what Rickover tells them to care about."

"I still don't understand," said Stone, examining his ever-present, well-chewed toothpick with a perplexed frown. "How do you explain Admiral Rickover's concern for public safety in the operation of the propulsion plant and your suggestion that he doesn't care about the strategic weapons?"

"Look," Craig said, "performance in both areas could be kept secret. Right? By publicly exposing his dedication to powerplant safety, Rickover's public image and political power are enhanced. Right? Expose weapons performance problems to public view and the Air Force lobby cuts into our ship building funds...therefore, fewer propulsion plants and less power base for Naval Reactors. For Christ's sake, don't you see that some people would rather ignore problems in the weapons area than expose incompetence? One way Rickover and his clones gain, the other way they lose. It's that simple."

It really wasn't simple at all. The disproportionate emphasis on Engineering was due to a complex set of motives on the part of the NUC's. Some were good, some were self-serving and bad, and others were simply misguided. The NUC's, from Ensigns to Admirals, had one universal constraint on their professional motives, they all revered Rickover and at the same time lived in mortal fear of his wrath.

Craig was beginning to feel a bit uncomfortable with his unguarded remarks.

I'm saying too much. I should have broken the conversation off, but Stone is a good man. He'll make up his own mind about people and politics.

Stone pressed on. "So, what about Rickover? How can you question the motives of a man who has accomplished what he has? How can he possibly influence ComSubLant? The senior officers in the Submarine Force are damned smart guys. They have minds of their own. How can you suggest Rickover controls them?"

Craig took a deep breath and plunged in, "Stone, sit down. This will take awhile. First of all, H. G. Rickover IS a smart guy! He also has an extremely forceful, aggressive personality…and he's a master politician. You know his name, but have you ever heard of the unknown Admiral in NAVSHIPS that supported the idea of building a nuclear powered submarine and assigned Rickover as the Project Officer? Rickover, quite astute in those days, saw the future importance of nuclear power very clearly, and as soon as he could, proclaimed himself the "Father" of it. Certainly, he also saw nuclear power as a vehicle to carry him to a position of unique influence and power in the Navy."

Craig paused to pour himself and Stone another cup of coffee, then continued. "I suspect that in the early days Rickover himself never realized how powerful he would become. As soon as he started selecting officers for training in this newborn project of nuclear propulsion, he must have realized that he could have payback in spades for every slight his ego had ever felt. Every officer that he let into his program was, in some fashion, going to acknowledge his subordination by letting Rickover take something from him— or he just wasn't going to get in. Whatever it was, it always meant the officer psychologically bowed before Rickover and handed over to him a significant piece of his soul."

Stone turned that over in his mind. "Sounds like the old concept of making a deal with the devil."

"It was very much like that, because the moment they granted Rickover that psychological dominance they surrendered their moral ascendancy and became damned unlikely to ever wrestle it back from him. After that, the only way the NUC's could restore their own pride was to deify the old son of a bitch so they didn't have to admit to themselves they had been put down by a mortal man."

Stone nodded his understanding with a sardonic half grin. "But, in the beginning, he must have had to take some fairly senior people off the diesel boats. Why would they go along with him?"

"Don't forget what kind of people those early NUC's were, the ones who are the Admirals and Four Stripers today. They were the ones who were ambitious enough to make a deal with Rickover. I knew most of those guys when I was a fresh caught junior officer on a diesel boat. Almost without exception, those first NUC's, including one named Jimmy Carter, were people the rest of us didn't want to go on liberty with…or to war with! They were bright as hell, but most were ambitious to a fault. I also knew of some really good submariners who were requested to appear for interviews with Rickover that sized him up, told him off, and came back to the diesel Navy."

"Look, Stores, what I'm telling you is that the Submarine Force may be run by the brightest, but certainly not the best or most competent officers. They are officers whose egos have forced them to be Rickover disciples. They don't just do his bidding, they have blind faith in what they believe or think are his philosophy and teachings. The result is that today, a prospective Commanding Officer will have spent about ten years in Engineering and about four weeks learning tactics. He will have done five hundred SCRAM drills and shot maybe five torpedoes."

Craig paused for a breath and a couple of swigs of coffee.

Stone asked, "Okay, I hear all that, but what about Rickover? Have you dealt with him directly?"

Craig was ready to finish his comments. "Yes. Twice during my interviews, and once when he visited my first SSN, the Skipjack."

"What do you mean about two interviews?"

I expected him to pick up on that.

"You see, I may be nuclear-trained, but I'm not a NUC because I refused to join Rickover's cult. The first time I interviewed with Rickover was early in my first diesel boat tour. I didn't like him and when I refused to cut a deal with him, he didn't like me. It was a fairly noisy scene. Two years later, the NUCS were desperate for sea-experienced lieutenants and I got ordered back for evaluation as a non-volunteer.

"That time, my interview got so bad with Rickover that he knocked everything off his desk and danced around his office screaming and throwing things. I walked out on him, slammed the door, and the next thing I knew I was at Nuclear Power School. I don't know to this day how it happened. Maybe someone just screwed up and I fell through the cracks. Anyway, the next time I saw him was when he came aboard our ship. By that time I was through his

103

school and had qualified on board as Engineering Officer of the Watch. He threw a public fit when he saw me, but I guess he figured getting rid of me then would be too embarrassing."

Stone prodded again, "I've heard guys talk about his visits to their boat, but I was never quite sure how much to believe. What were they really like?"

Craig looked up at the clock. Time enough for one more cup of coffee and the last revelation.

"A Rickover visit definitely established the falsehood of his public image. For starters, several days before his visit the drills and cleanup begin. Normally, you would expect that. What is less public are the preparations required by the Rickover Checklist. That document mysteriously appears about a week before he arrives. I have seen examples that ran to seven single-spaced typed pages. It contains a multitude of prerequisites for his visit.

"We had to have five pounds of seedless white grapes, two pounds of S.S. Pierce lemon drops, no substitutes permitted, pencils and pens laid out in specified order on his desk, arrangements made for him to have his hair cut on board by one of the stewards, a special selection of movies, should he fancy one...and so on for five pages. The kicker is the uniforms and jackets. On every visit he demanded two complete sets of washed khakis and a brand-new foul weather jacket with his name on it. When he left, they disappeared with him. We had to borrow uniforms from the smallest officer on board, then take up a collection to replace them. Rickover must have a warehouse full of other people's clothes by now."

Stone's mouth was slightly agape. "Why does he do that?"

Craig answered, "It isn't the money. It's the symbolic paying of tribute. Largess, whether in the form of knives or jewelry elicited from Electric Boat or the infamous 'H.G.R. Checklist' was important to him, but only as a demonstration or symbol of his imperial power to exact tribute."

"What did he do while he was on board?"

"Nothing much. Mostly he stayed locked up in the Captain's stateroom. He made sure he got his picture taken inspecting the ship. The steward was scared shitless and just about scalped him cutting his hair. He pretended to watch one SCRAM drill. I seriously doubt if he could have taken charge of it, but he snorted and threw himself around a little."

Stone had one last question, "What did he say when he left?"

"He chewed the Captain out in front of half the crew for not maintaining high enough standards of training back aft and left. We had been deployed two hundred eighty four days out of the previous three hundred sixty five without missing a single commitment, but he just bitched and left. It was a perfect example of the Rickover rule of positive leadership: 'First prize is nothing, second prize is a kick in the ass.'"

Their coffee was done. Craig abruptly broke off the discussion and they went their separate ways.

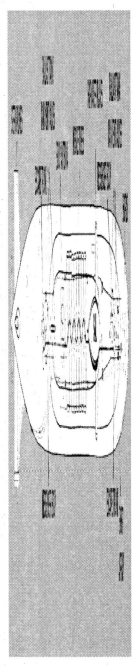

Marion's Top Side Arrangement

12
The Refit Continues

The next few days of the refit were remarkable only because the crew got a few breaks from lady luck. The primary system work, involving cutting out and replacing two valves, went smoothly and the final hydrostatic leak tests were successful. That, plus a lot of hard work on preventive maintenance cleared the way to start pre-critical valve lineup checks on refit day thirteen.

The Navigator's luck held as well, and both SINS showed no evidence of harm from their inadvertent shutdown. The SINS were now out of their calibration runs and were settled "navigating," as the Navigator and his technicians prepared for the calibration of the TYPE 11 Optical Star Tracking periscope. Calibration required hundreds of sights to be taken of land-based theodolites through the periscope, then a lengthy analysis of the data to precisely establish the periscope's errors at all points of the azimuth. It was a difficult, error-prone task and the chances were good that the Navigator would spend several long nights riding on the TYPE 11's uncomfortable operator's seat. Barring some disaster, navigation would have no problem being ready for sea trials.

The new BRA-8 Buoy had arrived and was nestled in its cradle under the main deck aft of the missile tubes. Tomorrow a crane from the tender would swing over a Rube Goldberg apparatus that would allow the buoy's control circuits to be tested by "flying" it in the air above the ship. Its buoyancy in seawater would be replaced by a weight and pulley arrangement. Buoys always flew fine in the air, but in seawater they were another story. No one had ever found a better way to test them though.

On one of his walks through the ship, the Exec stepped into the Sonar Room to look around and chat with whomever might be there. The Chief Sonarman was standing in front of the workbench with a Sonarman First Class, named Jim Franzei, who had reported aboard during the off crew. An experienced man with an excellent service record, Franzei was making his first patrol on the *Marion*. The tall, rail thin, blond-haired Franzei looked gangly alongside the shorter, more rotund Chief. The round rims of his glasses gave him the appearance of a quiet thinker. The Chief and Franzei had before them a long row of electronic plug in modules, more than a dozen. Craig recognized them immediately as pre-amplifiers from the BQR-7, the huge conformal array sonar that wrapped around the outer skin of the forward third of the ship. It was the ship's biggest ear.

The Chief and the ST 1 were in earnest discussion when the Exec walked in.

"What's with all the pre-amps?" he asked.

"XO," the Chief replied, "I put Jim onto the BQR-7 to do a thorough grooming. I thought, like you, that the Bluies just didn't report enough contacts. These pre-amps are part of the problem he's found."

That was a lot of pre-amps to change in one refit. Usually, you would expect three or four, but not a dozen. Craig whistled. "That's a bunch. Were they concentrated in any one sector?"

"No, sir. Jim also has meggared all the hydrophones. We have low grounds on eight or ten. We're also getting some losses through the compensating switches and we want to do a careful alignment on the amplifiers and filters."

"You're telling me that the Seven was a sick beast," Craig said.

"Yes, sir. I expect overall it was down six to eight decibels. Six db is a hell of a lot down. Eight db is twice as bad."

The Blue crew was probably getting no more than a third of the effective range they should have had. The Exec was relieved to know that the Chief and Franzei had found the problem. As is often the case, there didn't appear to be any one big failure, just the compound effect of many small ones.

Craig grinned at the two of them. "Chief, you've restored my faith in Sonarmen. Franzei, you must really know your way around that Seven. Nothing you've described sounds too hard to remedy except the low grounds. Are they in the hull fittings or the hydrophones themselves?"

The ever-logical Franzei spoke up. "I don't know yet. If we're lucky, half of them at least will be condensation in the hull connectors. If we have to go out with three or four hydrophones down, we'd never know the difference. Also, we can replace hydrophones waterborne if the divers are available. I'll know by tomorrow morning what we need to do."

"You guys have made my day! I've been suspicious that old dog wasn't hunting ever since the Bluies brought it home."

As Craig was leaving, the Chief followed him out of the door and spoke quietly. "XO, I'd appreciate it if you'd personally thank Franzei. He's worked his ass off and is a hell of a technician. He hasn't been on the beach even once yet."

The Exec was more than happy to accommodate the request. He knew sailors like Franzei are the reason ships like these make it out on patrol and successfully back. *Gotta wonder how Franzei does it without a Reactor Plant Manual to guide him! Smart, dedicated—you don't motivate people like that with a kick in the ass.*

While the Engineers were struggling to fix all the minor steam and hydraulic leaks, replace noisy bearings here and there, titivate their spaces and train for the ORSE, the Weaponeers rolled along through their refit routine of preventive maintenance like a well-greased automatic elevator. Smooth, no frenzy, everything done with a deliberate haste that seemed almost casual. Compared to the Engineers' world where the man with a pencil reigned supreme, the Weaponeers had automatic test equipment and, even in that early day, the beginnings of automated data processing to support their equally excellent standardized procedures. By Rickover's dictate, there would be no automated aids in engineering for years to come.

* * * * *

Also, by day thirteen, as the Engineers were just commencing their pre-critical valve lineups, the Weapons Officer reported his department fully ready for refresher training on sea trials. They had checked every circuit and function from the navigation data input to the fire control computers to the launchers themselves.

Every missile's electronic and flight control system had been checked, as well as the spare electronic assemblies and gyro assemblies. Finally, they had offloaded two of the tactical missiles and about half of the war shot torpedoes, then taken on exercise units in their place. All this activity had required little more from the Exec than a daily notation of the Weaponeer's "on schedule" progress. Craig, with his warrior mentality, viewed the weapons exercises as the centerpiece of their refresher training. Often, and in his view, unfortunately, they were the first events to be cancelled because of bad weather or preemption of their schedule by something deemed by the Captain or the Squadron Commander to be of a higher priority.

The exercise units substituted for the "tactical," war shot missiles were nothing more than concrete sabots. These cylinders, duplicating the diameter and mass of the real missiles, were fired to definitively test the missile tubes' launch function. The missile tube had two functions. First, it stored the missile in a controlled, benign environment and provided electrical connection of the missile to the fire control system. Second, each tube was a huge pneumatic cannon. When the tube was fired, a modified rocket motor at the base of the tube was ignited. The exhaust from the rocket motor was directed into a water reservoir where the intense heat caused the rapid generation of huge volumes of steam. The steam pressure under the base of the missile then ejected the missile from the tube like a huge bullet from an air gun. The momentum was enough to carry the missile clear of the sea surface where the rocket motors then ignited in the air. Ignition of the missile's rocket motor inside the missile tube would have caused the instant destruction of the ship.

The sabots were, quite literally, dumb as a rock, but firing one tested most of the missile launcher electronic functions without an actual launch. Testing the launcher required pulling the trigger on a "blank." But, it was also a hell of a lot of work for the crew. Not only did they have to off and on-load two missiles, but the fired tubes had to be meticulously cleaned of residue and salt water. Umbilical connections had to be checked and restored, and the exhausted gas generator replaced. In all, the half-second jolts that accompanied "Missile Away" cost a couple of days' hard manual labor for the crew. In the Exec's view, the cost was acceptable. He believed a fighting man was much more confident if he had the chance to pull the trigger on his weapon every now and again. Unfortunately, in later years, sabot firing was dropped as not worth the cost and time involved.

As Main Propulsion Assistant, responsibility for the pre-critical valve lineups fell to Rak. The "primary" systems contained the water that circulated first through the reactor core, then to the steam generators. There, giving up its heat across the walls of the boiler tubes, the "primary" water turned the "secondary" water to steam for use in the ship's turbines. The system kept all radioactive coolant water within the shielded volume of the reactor compartment. It also created two complex piping systems each containing hundreds of valves.

Rak and his men had been checking that every valve in both systems was positioned correctly for critical reactor operation. In fact, as the rules required, they were checking each valve twice with Rak then checking the "checkers." It was late. Rak was perched on the Engineering Officer of the Watch's chair in the Maneuvering Room. He looked surly and was. He had had the Engineering Duty the night before and had been called out several times in the middle of the night. Tonight he would be up until the valve lineup checklists were done and had gotten their final sign-off. He settled back, cradling himself against the EOOW's desk under his left elbow.

The Dial-X phone rang. Rak answered. The Chief reported that the valve lineup team was clearing the reactor compartment. Rak was relieved. The secondary lineup would be done by morning. After he had inspected the Reactor Compartment and locked the door to it, he would inspect the last primary system checklists and turn in. The Reactor Plant Electronics Technicians, the Reactor Operators, could start their "long form" pre-critical alignment and test of the nuclear instrumentation and control circuits at 0400. The ORSE was now four days away and everything was still on schedule.

* * * * *

During all this time, the Exec barely saw the Captain except at meals. Holcomb seldom inquired about the rest of the ship. As the ORSE drew nearer, he got more and more intense, more and more irascible. Mostly, he took his bad humor out on the stewards. Faced with his daily tirades, they turned blank-faced and stony.

Craig watched and wondered. *How many Englishmen have seen that expression under the noonday sun?*

One day the Captain blasted the Communications Officer across the length of the wardroom table when he overheard the expletive "Jesus Christ!"

After the meal, Craig followed him to his stateroom. "Captain," he said, "I don't mean to butt in, but you seem to be a little touchy lately. I know you're putting in a lot of hours. Are you getting enough rest? I know you're probably getting pretty tight about the ORSE. We all are. But seriously, are you getting enough sleep? I can arrange a stateroom on the tender for you if you would like. It's quieter up there."

Holcomb glared back at the Exec. "The need for sleep is the manifestation of an imperfect mind. We only need sleep because we lack faith. I'm getting more than enough."

That ended that. Craig backed out and went to his quarters. He sat down and wrote a letter to Meaghan. Not for the first time, he shared with her his unease with the Captain's behavior. They had both found him odd since first meeting him. Craig had thought it was due to his religious obsession. Meaghan hadn't been so sure. In retrospect, he wondered if her feminine intuition sensed something that he couldn't see. Somehow, sharing those thoughts with his best friend eased his mind. After writing the letter he went straight to sleep.

I'm sleepy as hell. My mind must be pretty imperfect.

* * * * *

The crew's good luck held right through reactor startup and the final three days of pre-ORSE training. The startup went smoothly. The engineers heated the plant up and, as always, as the water expanded in the primary system, they discharged it to retention tanks sitting on deck topside. A person could have drunk it without harm, but U.S. submarines do not discharge anything potentially radioactive into the harbors of the world.

Startup and heat-up done, the engineering watch brought steam back into the engine room, lit off the turbine generators and the *Marion* was self-sustaining, independent of power from the tender. Again, they were lucky. There was the usual rash of small steam leaks, but nothing that couldn't be cured by taking up on the valve stem packing glands. Number 2 Turbine Generator ran fine for a while, and then started surging. The problem was fluctuating control oil pressure, but that too was soon fixed. All in all, they were still on track with three days left until the ORSE.

* * * * *

By day seventeen, the ship was as ready as the crew could make it. There remained one more drill period that night to tie up loose ends, but no one except the Captain had much heart for it. The crew's mood was a combination of tension, apprehension, and resignation. The team of ORSE inspectors had been spotted on the tender, but they had not as yet come aboard the ship.

Craig knew the Chief Inspector well. As one of the first of Rickover's enforcers in the U.S. Atlantic Fleet, he made his own Admiral's Star by being harsher than his master. With a natural talent, he adopted the same arrogant egocentricity of his mentor. He was a snide, self-serving despot of a man, very smug in his powerful role. He could, with a word, tie up any nuclear-powered ship in the Fleet, destroy the career of any Commanding Officer, or wreak havoc on any Engineer. He was "Head NUC" in the Atlantic Fleet.

Early in the afternoon, as he passed the closed door of the Captain's stateroom, Craig mused, *The Old Man has a right to be scared shitless. He has a lot of the qualities of a NUC, but one thing he could never be is mean. This Chief Inspector will eat him alive.*

That evening, after the final drill session, Craig went topside to stand on the fairwater planes and relax for a few minutes in the fresh air. To his surprise, he found the Captain already there. Holcomb was standing near the lifelines looking out across the harbor.

"Captain! Mind if I join you?"

He turned slowly, "Oh, hi, XO."

They stood quietly for a few minutes. Neither was anxious to break the silence.

Finally Craig said, "How do you feel about tomorrow?" Holcomb knew he meant "ORSE," but somehow the euphemism had come more easily to his tongue.

The Captain replied, simply, "Scared."

Craig knew that he was, but he was quite surprised at the tone in which it was said…or even that the Old Man would say it. Suddenly, he felt a deep compassion for him. Holcomb tried so hard to be what he was expected to be, and yet his religion and humanity strongly tempered his efforts. His professional perspective and his religion were both equally difficult for Craig to accept, but Holcomb believed in them and tried his damnedest to live up to the standards that he so believed in.

A good man, just a lousy warrior.

Craig tried to reassure him, "Captain, you've done everything you can to be ready for the ORSE. Eng thinks the troops look pretty good on drills. There's only so much you can do."

He shook his head. "XO, you don't understand!"

"Captain, I know that after we've done the very best we can to get ready, a lot of things can cause us to fail. Among those are luck or a decision by NR to make an example of the next ship inspected. It might have no more to do with us than the old Greek adage, 'Kill an Admiral from time to time to give the others courage.'"

Again, he shook his head. "No, XO. If we fail, it means I haven't lived up to Admiral Rickover's standards. If you live up to what he expects of you, you'll be all right, even when he does things you can't understand."

"Look," Craig said, "you sound like you're convinced we're going to fail. I sincerely doubt it. Anyway, what if we do? You've done your best. I've never heard of a CO working any harder than you have to get ready for an ORSE."

He didn't answer for a while. The Exec was about to leave and go below when Holcomb started talking again.

"XO, when I was an Engineer I had a visit from Admiral Rickover. We were in new construction and he came to inspect us before we did our initial startup. I was really cocky in those days and I thought I had done a good job all the way through the yard, test program and all. Admiral Rickover took me back into the Engineering spaces on a tour and inside of a couple of hours, he made me see how inadequate we had been...I had been. I understood something that day. He was angry with us for not being as good as he knew we could be. We could have tried harder to keep good records. We could have studied harder during our training. We could have pushed the shipyard harder."

Craig stood, silently thinking. *His eyes are misting up.*

"Every mistake I made was because I hadn't done what I had been taught. He yelled, and yelled, and most of the sailors refused to understand. I could see it in their faces. But, I understood. Do you know what happened? When we got back to the Engine Room, just outside maneuvering, he was trying to talk to the Shutdown Maneuvering Area Watch and the outside telephone started ringing. He kept getting interrupted by it. He turned to me and asked why the phone was allowed in there. Didn't I have sense enough to see it was a dangerous distraction? He was right. He always is. I had been careless. I finally couldn't stand it any longer and broke down completely and started crying. I left and went forward to the reactor tunnel steps and sat down...crying! I could see his point. I was a danger to the whole Nuclear Power Program. I hadn't been intelligent enough to realize how weak I had been. I sat there, thinking about resigning. Do you know what happened next?"

Craig was both fascinated and appalled. He had never seen a man, much less a commanding officer, lay his soul so bare before.

"No, sir. What happened?"

"Admiral Rickover came up and found me there. He sat down beside me and talked to me just like we're talking now. He made me see that because I had overcome my pride and realized my weaknesses he would give me another chance. He pulled me back together. He saved me."

Craig didn't fancy himself a psychiatrist, but the whole dissertation again sounded to him like the Captain was getting the Bible and the Reactor Plant Manual confused.

Stress does strange things to people.

"Captain," he said, "I suspect you saved yourself. Anyway, tomorrow's the ORSE and it isn't HGR we have to face, it's his CINCLANT FLEET hatchet man."

The Captain looked at the Exec. His eyes still clouded. "XO, if we fail the ORSE, I'll know in my heart that Admiral Rickover was right the first time. I can't ask him for a third chance."

The Exec had started trying to inch himself away and already had his hand on the ladder. "We won't fail, Captain. It'll be all right. Good night."

Craig scurried off. He couldn't handle one religion and this guy had at least two, with Gods and Devils in both. Then, with profound empathy, he also wondered. *What will happen if we do fail...to him, to all of us?*

13
The Orse

Reveille came early the next morning. The ship was scheduled to get underway at 0830Z so the Engineers latched control rods at 0530Z and started withdrawing them to reach reactor criticality. By 0730Z they were self-sustaining with the shore power cables disconnected. The seamen commenced rigging topside for dive as the Captain, Exec and Engineer waited for the guests to arrive. The Captain paced uneasily about the Control Room as they waited.

Finally, just as the Exec stationed the Maneuvering Watch, the ORSE team arrived and he hurried topside to meet them at the brow. The senior member, Captain Earl E. Farley, came across first.

Craig saluted him and said "Good Morning."

The corpulent Four Striper, forced by habit and military courtesy, saluted back. Without a word he brushed past the Exec and headed below. His cortege of three Lieutenant Commanders followed him across. Craig spoke briefly to them and led the pack below. One of the three was a classmate from his company at the Naval Academy. That did not make Craig glad to see him. His presence on the team meant he was an up and coming member of the cult. His classmates' patronizing manner told Craig what the man had become—and would be.

Below decks, in the wardroom, the Captain, the Engineer and the Exec sat down with the ORSE team. While their official title was the Nuclear Power Examining Board, they were usually referred to by the crew as "NPEEB's " with an emphasis on the "pee." The Four-Striper didn't waste any effort on courtesy. He was pompous and arrogant as he told them what the crew would do to facilitate his inspection. He quoted his authority and charter, told them what drills the inspecting team wished to observe and which inspector would review certain records. Captain Farley let it be known that he would personally review the doctor's radiation health records on the way out to sea. The Exec asked if he preferred to review the records in Sick Bay where they were kept or have the doctor bring everything to him in the wardroom. His response conveyed only arrogance: "You're the Exec. Try making a decision. I'll find the same number of errors in either place."

Craig bit his tongue. *You asshole! I remember helping drag your drunken ass out of the O-club in Pearl Harbor the night you passed out and puked all over the whore you had brought with you.*

A particularly lousy, sick sort of egomaniac thinks he is absolved of courtesy if he's the senior officer. This one was already fat and his obvious obesity accentuated the large sweat areas spreading on his shirt. Anyway, he wouldn't have cared about Craig's contempt. The answer was to take a lesson from the stewards. *Give him a blank face and a flat "Yes, sir," then get out of his way before you lose your temper.*

As the ship got underway, the Exec stayed below to organize the records for inspection. Naval tradition required the Captain to be on the bridge of the ship. Fifteen minutes after getting underway, the doctor was already sweating profusely as he tried to return civil, courteous answers to the Senior Inspector's abusive questioning. Frontier justice took on a strong emotional appeal as Craig wondered how the Captain's nerves were holding up.

About an hour later, Craig heard the order "Ahead Flank." The lights dimmed briefly as Maneuvering shifted the reactor's main coolant pumps to fast speed and gradually, as speed built up, the feel of the ship changed. There was a slight vibration; a change in the way the ship met the sea. He could tell by the feel that they were settling out at their top speed. The Maneuvering Watch had long since been secured and the normal steaming watch set. It was time for the first ORSE drill. The Exec informed the inspectors that the ship was ready to commence drills and all four headed aft to take their positions to observe the drill. As universally known as the sobriquet "NPEEB" was, so was their self styled badge of office, a steno notebook stuck under their belt at the small of their back. They were highly stylized, like Geishas with their little pillows.

The drill was to be a "Back Emergency from Ahead Flank" with a failure of the throttle linkage thrown in. The Engineer had been directed to sneak up to the back of the Steam Plant Control Board through which the big chromed main turbine throttle wheels operated. Once there, he was to open the back of the panel and carefully disconnect the throttle wheels from their linkages. That done, at a prearranged signal, the Captain would order "All Back Emergency." An NPEEB would start a stopwatch and success would be measured by how fast the crew figured out the throttle failure, shifted to local control and stopped the ship. The Exec hoped the Engineer would have sense enough to wiggle the linkage a little as he disconnected. An alert throttle man would recognize the setup immediately. Eng was so unimaginative that Craig doubted he would do anything to compromise the suckers, but he could hope.

Since there was nothing he could do to influence the drill, the Exec went to the bridge. The Captain had headed aft with the senior NPEEB to watch the drill through the Maneuvering Room door. The Officer of the Deck got the high sign that everything was ready and ordered "Back Emergency."

Properly done, it is an impressive drill. Water flies, the ship shakes, and eight thousand tons of submarine stops in about twice its own length. This time was different. The turns had just started to build up in answer to the backing bell when the Engineering Officer of the Watch yelled over the 7MC announcing circuit: "Bridge—Maneuvering, we've got a complete loss of vacuum, port side!"

The noise level in the background was high. This was not part of the drill.

Before the OOD could reply, the Exec ordered "All Stop!"

Quickly, the message came: "Bridge—Maneuvering, the port main condenser boot has ruptured. Port Root valve is shut."

The boot was a huge rubber ring, something like a truck tire that connected the port main condenser with the turbine. That meant the port main propulsion turbine was windmilling and number two turbine generator was unavailable. Half the steam system was down.

"Maneuvering—Bridge, very well. Answer bells on one main engine. Shift to slow speed pumps. Have you suffered any further casualties?"

"Bridge—Maneuvering. Not so far as we can tell."

Then shortly: "Bridge—Maneuvering. Answering bells one main engine."

The Exec turned to the Officer of the Deck. "Go ahead one third. Reverse course and head back to port while we sort this out."

Craig went below, thinking to himself, *I don't know how Rak would have done on his drills, but he did fine with the real thing.*

This was a non-trivial casualty. Replacing the boot would take days. No one on board the *Marion* had ever before heard of one failing.

As the Exec walked into the Wardroom, he could see that the Captain and the NPEB team were already there. He heard the NPEB Four Striper saying to the Captain, "Return to port for repairs. We obviously can't continue with your examination. We'll meet you on your way in from patrol or we'll be back during your next refit."

The Captain looked like he'd had a stay of execution. Craig made a mental note that nobody bothered to tell Rak and his section that they had done a pretty damn good job...with turbines, feed pumps and main coolant pumps coming down around their ears at 100% reactor power. Once again, First Prize Was Nothing!

Craig interrupted the meeting to tell the Captain that he would get a message off to Squadron to let them know what had happened, then withdrew immediately. He didn't bother to mention that he had already put the ship on course to return to port. The Navigator had the message drafted and ready for him to release when Craig arrived in the Control Room.

The Exec could feel the crew's spirit lift. Such was the impact of an ORSE.

14

Justice

As the ship turned to retrace its track back into port, Stone, the Engineer and the Exec met in the Control Room for a quick conference. They had already put the NPEB team and the ORSE out of mind and were completely focused on the real problem—how to restore the crippled propulsion plant without delaying the ship's departure on patrol. There would be time enough later to celebrate their deliverance. The Engineer was almost cheerful, lighting up a cigarette as they set about sorting out the problems ahead.

By the time they could get back alongside the tender and shut down the steam plant, day eighteen of the refit would be gone. That left only nine days to make repairs, conduct an abbreviated set of trials at sea, load out the ship and be ready to depart on patrol.

The key question, of course, was whether a spare boot was available in Rota. Stone already had in hand the Federal Stock Number of the boot. He was headed for the supply office to check the Coordinated Ship's Allowance List to find out where the Navy supply system stocked main turbine boots.

"Stone," the Exec said, "let's get a MILSTRIP requisition message off as soon as we tie up. Eng thinks it'll take about a day and a half to rip out all the interference and remove the old boot. If the tender doesn't have a replacement in stock and we have to wait for delivery from stateside, we're looking at a best case of two days or more for delivery. Even if all goes well on the rip out, that'll cost us at least another day for sure."

The Engineer chipped in, "Rak is down in the condensate bay with the Chief. They're checking to see what piping has to be removed to get at the boot. I told him to make a list of every gasket that has to be disturbed. Better stock check those, too. I don't want to be held up for a $1.98 gasket."

"Good idea, Eng. Better check on tools, too. Make sure that if any special tools are required, we have them."

"Yeah, okay." Stone hurried off.

The Engineer started to turn away, but Craig stopped him. "Eng, how long do you figure before you can be ready for steam on the port side?"

He thought for a moment. "If the boot is in stock locally, I'd say five days. A day and a half to rip out interference and the old boot, two days to put in the new boot and reinstall interference. One day for hydrostatic and vacuum drop tests. That's four and a half days. Add another half day for something to go wrong. Five days. Six if we have to go to the states for parts."

"Okay, that sounds about right. That puts us at the end of day twenty-three. If we get underway on day twenty-four for a forty eight hour sea trial, that leaves three days for final load-out. No sweat, huh?"

"That's if everything works on sea trials and nothing breaks."

"Right. Not enough allowance for contingencies in that schedule. So, I want you to lay out a work plan that gets the job done in four days. Push your troops to make it happen."

"But I just told you that I think we'll need five days!"

The Exec grinned at the Engineer. "I know, and five days is okay. We can't afford six though, so I want you to aim for four."

The Engineer looked a little perplexed, but he said, "Aye, Aye" and left.

The Exec found the Captain in his stateroom and started to report on the discussion he had just had with the Engineer. The Old Man looked relaxed, almost sleepy. He had abandoned the wardroom to the NPEEB's. The NPEEB Four Striper was too much, even for him. Craig had just finished telling the Captain how he saw the schedule when Stone popped his head in wearing a big grin. "We got one of those suckers on board!" he chortled.

Craig shook his head in amazement and laughed out loud. An SSBN carries upwards of fifty thousand line items of repair parts on board, as compared to about eight thousand catalog items for all of Sears Roebuck, and obviously the logisticians who made up the list were no slouches. Time and again, he had seen it happen. A ship might run out of paper clips, garbage weights and flexatallic gaskets, but when something breaks that never in a million years should, you look around and there in some locker is the part you need. No one on board would ever have suspected the need for a spare boot, but right there in a lower level missile compartment supply locker, they had one.

As he left the Captain's stateroom, Craig stopped for a moment at the door. "Captain, we should be setting the Maneuvering Watch in about forty five minutes."

"Okay, XO, thanks."

"Do you think you're ready for another steak at the O'Club tonight?"

The Captain smiled and leaned back in his chair, putting his feet up on his bunk. "No thanks, XO, I think I'll turn in early."

The Exec realized he had forgotten something that he had meant to speak to Stone about earlier, so he hurried after him. Catching him just as he started to open the door to the wardroom, Craig pulled him aside and signaled him into the nearest stateroom.

"Stores, make sure you serve lunch in the wardroom before we get in."

"Okay, we will, but the only people who'll be in there are the Quack and the NPEEB's."

"If you don't serve our guests here, they'll miss lunch on the tender."

Stone didn't much care whether the NPEEB's starved or not and said as much.

"Feed them, then make sure you collect for the meal."

"Charge them?" Stone was incredulous. It was normal to extend the ship's hospitality to guests aboard for only a day or two.

Craig felt his day continuing to improve. "Absolutely. Fifty-five cents apiece for what I hope will be a lousy meal?"

Stone didn't miss the glint of malicious humor in Craig's expression. He laughed and replied. "You got it, XO."

"Stores, make sure they actually pay, or I'll have your ass."

It thoroughly pissed off the fat bastard and his team, but they each paid as required by Navy regulations.

Craig thought it was a nice two-dollar lesson in naval democracy. His ship and its crew might have to suffer the bloated bastard's condescending arrogance, but they wouldn't kowtow to him.

Later, after the ship had moored alongside the tender, the Exec was standing topside watching the electricians wrestle the shore power cables into their connectors in the Engine Room escape trunk. As soon as shore power was available to supply the ship's hotel loads, they could shut down number one turbine generator, then shut down the reactor. The Enginemen were already beginning to strip away deck plates and sheet metal interference on the port side of the engine room to get at the boot.

The Weapons Officer and the Chief Missile Technician appeared alongside him. Joe Wolfman, the Weapons Officer, was slim, dark-haired, bespectacled, and very intense. "Weaps" to his fellow officers and "Mr. Wolfman" to the crew, he was almost painfully diligent in maintaining a reserved and correct relationship with the world around him. He was a highly competent Jewish officer who Rickover had personally rejected for training as a NUC without the condescension of an explanation. Weaps was a careful planner with an almost pathologically low tolerance for uncertainty, and he was already fretting about the change to his well-ordered plans for the rest of the refit.

Wolfman bored right in. "XO, we need to tell Squadron and the tender weapons shop what our plans are for the sabots and exercise units. If we're going to offload them, they'll want them back as soon as they can get them."

The Exec was not surprised by Joe's request for guidance. In fact, he had been expecting him ever since the boot had blown. He was privately slightly amused by the Weapon's Officer's fidgeting. "Gator is up at Squadron Ops now checking on target services for sea trials. When he gets back, we'll know what to do about the exercise units."

The Exec knew full well that as soon as the ship was moored and the brow to the tender was in place, the Navigator, in his role as Operations Officer, had gone immediately to Squadron Operations with the new plan for a two day sea trial on days twenty-four and twenty-five. There he would find out if target and recovery services would be available for torpedo firing exercises.

Wolfman pressed on, still hoping for some immediate bit of direction. "What about the sabots? It'll save a lot of work for the Missile Techs if we pull them."

The Exec wasn't about to give up firing the sabots unless the schedule made it impossible.

"That's true. Any problem cleaning the tubes and reloading them in three days?"

Craig knew there would not be. Things could get a little tight during the short days of winter because they weren't allowed to handle missiles after sunset. This was late spring, though, and the days were longer.

Weaps, as the wardroom arch conservative, wanted to get comfortably ahead of his schedule, but knew a losing argument when he saw one. He resignedly acknowledged what the Exec already knew.

"No problem unless we have bad weather or a tender crane craps out. Then it could get tight."

"Okay, let's go talk to the Captain, but I'm in favor of unloading everything we can through the muzzle."

The Captain wasn't too concerned either way and the target services were available, so the Exec's views prevailed.

Besides, Craig was curious. The crew had not conducted a torpedo exercise during their previous refit, so he had never seen this Captain actually shoot a torpedo. In the training sessions in the Submarine School simulators, where they did their off-crew training, Holcomb had seemed a very stilted, pedestrian Approach Officer. He also had shoved the Exec in as the Approach Officer on most runs, passing it off as training.

Torpedo firing at sea is always much more difficult than in the trainer. There's a hell of a lot more to keep track of. For one thing, buildings don't have depth control problems.

* * * * *

The next few days were almost pleasant. The crew of the *Marion* was left pretty much alone by the Squadron and since, except for the Enginemen, everyone was ready for sea. The Exec was able to relax the usual liberty policy, allowing the crew a little more time ashore.

The Exec got to witness the Quack's Kangaroo Clinic in action. The doctor had by now been institutionalized in Rota's El Matador Bar with a permanently reserved table. His newly gained respect for the local Carlos Primero Spanish brandy seemed now to be about equal to his passion for prayer. The nightly presentation of bare breasts for the doctor's palpitation had awesomely boosted trade at the Matador. It was, Craig thought, a marvelous example of symbiotic relationships.

The repair work moved along, keeping to schedule, and by day twenty-two the Captain and Exec were confident of the ship's ability to get underway on day twenty-four. The refresher training plan included shooting the sabots shortly after arrival in the assigned operating area so that, after firing, the missile technicians could pump down the tubes and fill them with detergent and fresh water. That way, the sloshing of the solution over the next twenty-four hours would do much of the required cleaning. The sabot shoot being completed by noon would allow the crew to fire the exercise torpedoes during the afternoon. After that, the rest of the time underway would be spent cruising slowly to and fro testing systems and equipment.

Life was beginning to look almost good.

15
Rota Cowboy

Refit day twenty-four was nearly over and the Exec was tired but content. The new condenser boot had gone in without a hitch and the ship was ready for sea trials. He had set reveille for the next morning at 0600Z to allow the Maneuvering Watch to be stationed at 0715Z and, in expectation of an early start and a long day, planned to turn in early. The Engineers in the duty section had even earlier calls so that they could start up the reactor and be self-sustaining on the turbine generators by 0700Z.

A knock at his stateroom door interrupted the Exec as he was clearing the day's accumulation of paperwork off his bunk in preparation for turning in. It was Lieutenant (Junior Grade) Zenias Hill, dressed for liberty, including cowboy boots. If McJimsey and Kane were the Exec's cross to bear among the troops, Hill was the wayward child in the wardroom. Hill was the Auxiliary Division Officer. He was on his first patrol and was one of the biggest hayseeds ever wrapped in a blue coat with brass buttons. He tried hard and did a good job on board, but he was so close to his West Texas roots that he wasn't altogether ready for release into general society.

Short, wiry and bowlegged, Hill's most prized possession was a pair of ancient blue jeans to which he applied the bladder contents of every coyote he killed and steadfastly refused to wash lest he lose the advantage of their olfactory camouflage. With considerable justification, Craig suspected Hill's idea of a big Saturday night back home was to jacklight some rabbits, drink a lot of Bud and throw the empties at Mexicans. Like the parent of a teenager, he always worried a little when Hill went ashore.

Tonight, Hill was in high spirits. His area of responsibility included the ship's plumbing, high-pressure air, atmosphere control systems and, as the Chief of the Boat had said earlier in the day, "Everything that's supposed to suck, blow, gurgle or stink."

"Permission to go ashore, XO?"

Craig studied him warily for a moment before answering. "Early reveille tomorrow and a couple of hard days coming on sea trials. Are you sure you don't want to call it an evening?"

"Naw, XO. We're ready to go. Since I don't have the duty tonight, I just want to grab the chance to have a couple of beers before we go dry."

"Who are you going over with?"

"Nobody. Just me. Everybody else either has a watch or is turning in early."

That was what the Exec feared. *Christ, this is like letting a teenager loose with a sports car. He's not a teenager, though, and you gotta trust them sometime.*

"OK, but keep a lid on it and don't stay out so late that you're no fucking good tomorrow."

Lieutenant Hill gave the Exec a cheery "Roger, Boss." and was gone. He then went straight to the Club Matador. He knew he would find the doctor there, holding his nightly clinic along with most of the *Marion* liberty party.

A sizable contingent of the crew were indeed gathered in the Matador, and Hill arrived just as the doctor solemnly called the first "patient" forward for examination. Before he could order a beer, two sailors from "A Gang" were only too pleased to offer their Divison Officer a glass of Fundador brandy from the liter bottle hidden under their table. Several brandies later, Kane, McJimsey and Schroeder joined the party.

As the party wound down, Hill found himself and those three, the last of the *Marion* crew left in the bar. His original companions had finished their bottle and left with the doctor to return to the ship. It was, by Hill's reckoning, still early, but he and his new circle of drinking mates considered that the Matador was now too quiet for their taste.

Hill said it first. "Hey, this place has died. Anybody know someplace else to go?"

Schroeder knew. "Yeah. Ever been to the Congreyo Oroyo?"

None of the others had. Kane asked. "Where's that?"

"It's a place about a mile outside town where all the Brit tourists stay when they come down here on vacation. They got little cabana type houses that they stay in and a big bar with a dance hall. Lotta women."

McJimsey was skeptical. "Can we get in?"

Schroeder reveled in his role of experienced guide to the younger sailors, and especially to an officer. "No problem. Only thing is, we may have to walk to get there. Taxis are hard to get at this time of night."

Nobody minded the idea of a half hour walk if it led to more brandy and women. First things first, however, and willing women were at the top of the list. Not one of the three considered how they would get back at the end of the night. They set off in high spirits with Hill in the lead and Schroeder navigating.

* * * * *

Shortly before midnight the Exec was awakened by an urgent knock at his stateroom door.

It was the Below Decks Watch. "Sorry to wake you, XO, but the Shore Patrol Office called and they want you to call them right back!"

"Couldn't the Duty Officer have taken the call?"

"No, sir. They said they had to talk to you personally."

Muttering to himself about the impossibility of getting any Goddamned rest, Craig got out of his warm bunk and dressed. The outside telephone was thirty feet away in the Control Room.

What in the hell is going on? This is bound to be something that I don't want to know about.

The Shore Patrol's insistence on speaking to him directly was very foreboding. As he made his way up the ladder and into the Control Room to the shore phone, Craig had visions of riots with sailors dead at the hands of Franco's ubiquitous and ruthless police, the Guardia Civil. His apprehension mounted rapidly.

When he finally got through the cranky tender switchboard operator, the duty Shore Patrol Officer answered, "Shore Patrol, Lieutenant Donovan speaking."

"Hi, I'm the *Marion* XO returning your call."

"Yes, sir. Thanks for calling back. We have one of your officers up here."

"Oh, Christ! Who is it and what has he done?"

"It's a Lieutenant Junior Grade Hill."

The Exec's heart sank. *I knew I shouldn't have let him loose tonight.* "What's he charged with?"

"Oh, nothing, sir. He's been in an accident."

The Exec's concern flashed to relief and back to concern. *At least it isn't drunk and disorderly or some other criminal charge.*

"How bad is he hurt? Why didn't you take him to the dispensary?"

"Easy, sir. He's okay. He got a knock on the head and a few scratches. He looks like hell, but he's okay. We've already had him to the dispensary."

Now the Exec was puzzled. Relieved…but puzzled. *What in the hell…*

"Well, if he's okay, and he hasn't been charged with anything, why don't you send him back to the ship?"

"He won't go, sir."

"What?"

"He won't go. He refuses to move off the bench he's laying on unless his XO comes and gets him."

"What!"

"He won't leave unless you come get him."

"Horseshit! Throw him out!"

"XO, he's got a death grip on that damned bench and we've had enough problems with this guy already. Please don't give us any more trouble. Just come get him, okay? If he tells me one more time how he used to put coyote piss on his Levis, I'm either going to hit him or charge him."

The Shore Patrol Officer hung up, leaving the Exec with a dead phone in his hand.

Craig went down to his stateroom for his cap and foul weather jacket. *When I get there, if Hill isn't severely injured, I'm probably going to kill him myself!*

The Quack wasn't easy to wake up after his "clinic" hours, but the insistent Exec grabbed him and together they headed off into the night to collect Hill.

When they got to the Shore Patrol Office, they found the scrawny Hill stretched out on his back on a wooden bench. He looked like everything that could be whipped and torn had been whipped and torn. He was holding an ice bag against a sizable knot on his left forehead while the sole of one shoe flapped loosely, more or less at right angles to his foot.

Everyone present was carefully ignoring him.

Craig stared at him. *This is almost worth getting up in the middle of the night to see.*

There was no sympathy in the Exec's greeting. "Hill, the doctor is here, either to help you make it back to the ship or to perform euthanasia. What he does depends on your explanation of why I'm here."

The body didn't stir.

"Hill! I want to know what happened. NOW!"

"I been illegally arrested!"

"He is not under arrest," the Shore Patrol Officer muttered, obviously weary of repeating himself.

"Am too! Didn't want to come back yet. They put me in a squad car and made me come back. They arrested me! I wanted you to see that they arrested me."

Craig's curiosity was overtaking his sorely tried patience. "Hill, you're not under arrest! Let's forget that for a moment. What the hell happened to you?"

"XO, I went out to the 'Mat' to watch Doc do his clinic. After I had been there for a while, just about everybody left. I got to talkin' to some of our sailors and they told me about this place out south of town called the 'Red Crab.' It's a beach club. Anyway, we couldn't find a cab so we all started walkin'. I was tellin 'em about how I used to bulldog steers. They were city guys from back East and didn't believe me, so when this motorcycle comes along, I said, 'Here, I'll show you.' That's the last thing I remember before these assholes arrested me."

The Shore Patrol Officer, wearing a look of strained forbearance, walked over and handed the Exec an accident report.

"The driver of the 'motorcycle' was of the opinion he was operating a Volkswagen car. He was also sober. This recumbent turkey tried to bulldog a Goddamned Volkswagen! He's lucky to be alive and luckier that nobody is pressing charges."

From beneath the ice bag came a muffled, "It was a Goddamned motorcycle!"

Craig turned to the doctor who, upon mention of his clinic, had become deeply interested in a bulletin board on the far side of the room. "Doc, use whatever painful instrument comes to hand, but get this idiot back to the ship by 0100. I'm going back to bed."

The Exec turned to the Shore Patrol Officer. "Thanks, Donovan. By the way, did he damage the VW?"

"No, but he damn near put it in the ditch. Fortunately, it was another sailor driving it, not a Spanish National."

Craig turned for a last shot before he stalked out into the night. "Hill, can you hear me?"

"Yes, sir."

"If you are not back on board the ship within thirty minutes, you will never know another day of liberty in this lifetime! Do you understand me?"

"Yes, sir."

When he got back to his stateroom, Craig had trouble getting back to sleep. *Crap! When time is running out, the more you try to force yourself to sleep, the more you stay awake.*

16
Refresher Training

The next day was indeed a long day, but Craig had had worse. With no one from Squadron looking over their shoulder, the underway went smoothly. Two and a half hours after they twisted 180 degrees in the basin and rang up "Ahead two thirds," the ship was in its assigned operating area.

The Exec went up to the Control Room to watch the first dive. SSBN's are so large and dive so slowly that the changes to their trim caused by weight changes in the refit usually have little effect. They are easily compensated through the trim system, which permits ballast water to be added to, removed from or moved about the submarine. Besides, with the nuclear powerplant, the ship had the power to overcome massive out-of-trim conditions with brute force and hydrodynamic lift.

His concern for the first dive was a habit from his days on diesel submarines. On the much smaller, less powerful diesels, a few thousand pounds of uncompensated weight addition could produce a harrowing experience.

This time the dive went without a hitch and they were soon at a satisfactory, neutral buoyancy trim at "Ahead one third," the criteria for a properly ballasted ship. After a half hour of random maneuvers to settle in the ship control party, the Captain passed the word on the general announcing system, "Man Battle Stations, Missile," for the first Weapon System Readiness Test. The WSRT culminated in the salvo of the two sabots from the missile tubes. The exciting part was the loud thump, and the jolt as the ship absorbed the recoil from the thirty thousand pound "bullet."

What the Exec watched with the keenest interest was the response of the ship's automatic compensating system. Since a missile tube full of sea water weighs more than a sabot, as each sabot was fired and its tube flooded, the compensating system had to expel a mass of sea water ballast to keep the ship in a proper state of neutral buoyancy. It did. The system worked great.

Torpedo firing exercises filled the afternoon. The Captain shot three and let the Exec shoot one. Holcomb was no John Wayne. On the periscope approach to shoot an old MK 14 steam torpedo, he was awkward with his periscope technique. He put up too much pole, took far too long on each observation, repeatedly forgot what course, depth or speed he had ordered and fiddled through his optimum firing point.

Finally, the target tug zigged just before he intended to shoot and he had to throw a desperation shot up the tug's kilt. Based on a single, hasty and poorly executed periscope observation, the shot went wildly astray. The Sonar approaches to fire MK 37 electric homing weapons were scarcely better. He made the same novice's mistake on both firings of concentrating so hard on obtaining a perfect fire control solution that the target almost ran over the *Marion* before he fired.

In submarine vs. submarine warfare, this is a tactic that guarantees an extremely short life expectancy. Survival goes to the guy who can put his weapon on target before his enemy gets close enough to counter detect and fire. Victory is hollow if you get killed achieving it.

On the second run, the Captain also forgot to slow the ship down before he fired and the excess speed held the torpedo in the tube. When he realized his mistake and slowed down, the unit swam itself out and headed for what was called on the farm "the North 40." The tug, unfortunately, had passed overhead and was by then to the south. It took a hell of a long time for the tug to find that torpedo.

Finally, in a race against the waning daylight, it was the Exec's turn. His weapon was an exercise version of the old MK 45 nuclear-tipped torpedo. They were good, reliable vehicles, but a tactical abortion. If they killed the target, they were likely to cripple the ship that fired them. After radioing "Comex," the commence exercise point, to start the tug inbound from its initial position fourteen thousand yards away, Craig let the target close to its closest point of approach and go by, and then shot him as he was going away. Perfectly executed as per doctrine and the exercise instructions for the weapon, it was the only "hit" of the day.

Clearly a weapon designed by ordnance engineers that knew little of submarine vs. submarine warfare, the MK 45 was a tactical pariah. For the firing ship to be safe, the weapon had to be detonated at a greater range than the then existing sensors and fire control systems could localize the target. As a result, the only way to use it was to let the target go by, then shoot it out in front of him at extreme range. If the bad guy didn't shoot or run over you on the way by, you got to shoot at him with a weapon that was bound to pop every circuit breaker on board, not to mention breaking all the coffee cups.

The Exec took some silent and personal satisfaction in showing up the Captain on the periscope. The WW II vets who had trained him in tactics had insisted on a high degree of skill with the periscope, and Craig was one of the last of their breed still shooting torpedoes.

Properly done, the Approach Officer's sequence of good periscope operation was: Up scope in low power. Find the target. Shift to high power. "Mark Bearing." Note the telemeter marks. Set the Stadimeter. Concurrently, note the targets angle on the bow, bow wave, sensors, guns, smoke and behavior. Snap the scope handles up and, as it slithered down, "Range Mark." The periscope assistant would read the range dial as it disappeared down the periscope well. Finally, the Approach Officer announced, "Angle on the Bow Port/Starboard xxx degrees," then briefed the fire control party on the tactical picture he had just observed.

Done properly, the above sequence required the periscope to be exposed a mere five to seven seconds. Craig normally ran pretty close to that. Holcomb rarely came in under twenty seconds.

On this day, the MK45 ran hot, straight and normal, and was close alongside the tug at the end of its run. It was a beautiful, simple, reliably vehicle built for a tactically stupid mission.

As soon as the MK45 exercise unit had been picked up by the tug, the Captain thanked its skipper, and released him to return to Rota. The *Marion* then settled down to a quiet night of submerged operations. Since "VLCCs," the acronym for Very Large Crude Carriers that are the two hundred thousand ton plus behemoths of the oil trade, often passed through the Rota operating areas en route to and from Gibraltar, Holcomb ordered the ship down to one hundred eighty feet for night steaming. That's the really cozy place in an SSBN's world. Shallow enough to be in the safest part of the ship's submerged performance envelope and deep enough so no one can hit you. Surface weather has to be pretty extreme to feel anything at that depth. The crew quietly went about their equipment checks. So far, no one had uncovered any major problems.

In the quiet of the evening watch, the Exec stopped by Sonar. He was curious about the BQR-7. Luckily, Franzei was on watch.

"Franzei! How does your Seven look?"

Franzei looked up and smiled. "Okay, XO, it's good. I want to tweak the recorder again, but that's nothing."

"Are you getting good ranges?"

"Excellent. Coming out, running on the surface, we were tracking contacts out to 20K. Down here we can't confirm our ranges, but they should be pretty good."

Craig whistled. With all the flow noise on the surface, some people would consider twenty thousand yards unbelievable. *Franzei is one hell of a Sonarman. We're lucky to have him.*

"Okay. Sounds like the Seven is great. What about the BQS-4?"

"It's fine, too, XO. We're going to run a full set of transmission checks with the Fire Control Technicians on the midwatch, then tomorrow we'll use a target of opportunity to compare sonar and periscope bearings. Sensitivity is good, though."

Craig was much relieved. The movie was ready to start in the wardroom, so he headed below, satisfied that Sonar was now ready for patrol.

The rest of sea trials and the refit passed uneventfully, or at least nearly so.

17
Shots

The day after the ship returned to Rota from sea trials for its final two days of provisioning before departure on patrol, Craig got another one of those hints of things to come. Puzzled at the time, he would later wish he had thought more deeply about it. While at lunch, on this the twenty-sixth day of the refit, the doctor's meal was interrupted by a call on the outside telephone line. He excused himself from the table and went up to Control. A few minutes later he was back. As he settled into his chair he commented that the call had come from the Squadron doctor. A sailor on the tender had been found to have hepatitis.

"What does that mean?" asked the Captain.

"Not much, probably. Squadron will probably want everyone on site to get a gamma globulin shot."

"Why?" The Old Man seemed a bit hostile.

Sensing a confrontation with no apparent cause, the Exec jumped in. "Captain, I'm sure Squadron would rather give us all a shot than risk having to MEDEVAC one of our sailors or, worse yet, have to abort a patrol because of an epidemic on board."

The Captain didn't reply.

The Doctor, as yet, didn't have definite instructions to inoculate the whole crew, so all three let the subject drop.

But, a couple of hours later the doctor showed up at the Exec's stateroom with the expected news that all members of the submarine crews were to get prophylactic shots of gamma globulin.

The doctor went off to find the hospital corpsman and dispatch him to the tender to pick up the gamma globulin. He reckoned he would need a half hour for the two of them to load syringes before they started running the crew through.

Craig crossed the narrow hall and knocked on the Captain's stateroom door to let him know what was going on.

"Captain," he said, "the doctor is back from the tender sick bay. We're going to have to dose the crew with gamma globulin."

Holcomb looked up from his desk. He was obviously deeply engrossed, working over the Engineer's draft of his personal letter to Rickover that was required at the end of each refit.

"Oh, okay, XO."

"We'll pass the word in about a half hour for all hands to lay to sick bay. Doc will bring your shot up here."

"No!"

"Sir?"

"No shot for me!"

"Captain, everybody is supposed to have a shot of GG. You're the last man on board that the Squadron would make an exception for."

"I don't need shots. I don't take them."

Craig was perplexed.

What the hell is going on? Why is he digging his heels in?

The best interest of the ship and crew required Holcomb to take the damned shot, and Craig was stubborn enough to refuse to walk away. He had no intention of asking the doctor to cover for the Captain.

"Captain, I'm trying to understand. Why can't you take the shot? Do needles bother you?"

Holcomb looked scornfully at the Exec. "No, XO, I'm not afraid of needles. I do not accept inoculations because they serve no purpose. Illness exists only in the mind. It is only cured by faith, faith in God, not faith in a drug. Illness doesn't exist for me because of my faith in God."

"You believe in faith healing and that all sickness is psychosomatic. Is that what you're saying?"

"I am a Christian Scientist. To accept medication is a denial of my faith."

Craig's disbelief was giving way to frustration. "Let me get this straight," he said. "Do you believe a person can be ill?"

"The body can only be ill if the soul perceives it to be. Sickness exists only in our minds. It is a figment of our imagination, allowed there by our imperfect faith."

I'm in over my head trying to deal with this. He has to take the damned shot. Maybe I ought to let him argue it out with the Commodore. Craig tried again. "Captain, I can't agree with you. I'm not trying to challenge your religious beliefs, but you have to take the shot or we won't be allowed to get underway. Can't you just take the shot to avoid a flap?"

He pulled himself up, shoulders back. "Where principle is involved, be deaf to expediency!"

"Huh? Is that yes or no?"

Holcomb looked a little annoyed. Craig was being a slow pupil.

"I said, 'Where principle is involved, be deaf to expediency.' It means that I cannot compromise my faith just to avoid a confrontation!"

The Exec's current tack of appealing to Holcomb's respect for military discipline was proving unproductive. The Captain's position hadn't shifted one iota, and he was now beginning to sound too damned evangelical.

The Exec was looking for any argument that would lead them out of the impasse. He tried a different approach. "Captain, if the effects of illness are purely a creation of the mind or imaginary, the same could be said for the effect of medicine, couldn't it?"

A note of suspicion lurked in Holcomb's voice when he answered, "Maybe."

The Exec pressed on. *He felt a little softer on that one.* "If that's true, then far from being a denial of your faith, the fact that you don't care whether or not you get the shot is a demonstration of faith. If your mind can make an illness not exist, then it can dismiss the medication. One has no more reality than the other. Right? So, why not take the shot and let's get the hell out of here. There's absolutely no principle involved." Craig held his breath and watched Holcomb's face.

Finally Holcomb said, "I'll think about it," and went back to his desk.

Dismissed and unable to think of any further useful arguments, the Exec returned to his own stateroom.

About an hour and a half later he heard the doctor knock on the Captain's door. The Quack went in and told the Captain he was ready to give him his shot. A couple of minutes later he left. They hadn't had time enough for an argument. Holcomb had taken the shot. Craig let out a sigh of relief.

As a child, his grandfather had always told him that another man's religion was something to be respected, but one should never attempt to change it. Still, he was a little bemused by the Captain's belief that things like illness and medicinal effects could be willed in or out of existence. None of it seemed very rational to him.

What the hell, as a practicing well-intentioned atheist, being tolerant of other people's religion was nothing new. One religion was about as illogical as the other.

Mediterranean Sea

April, 1970

Marion's Track

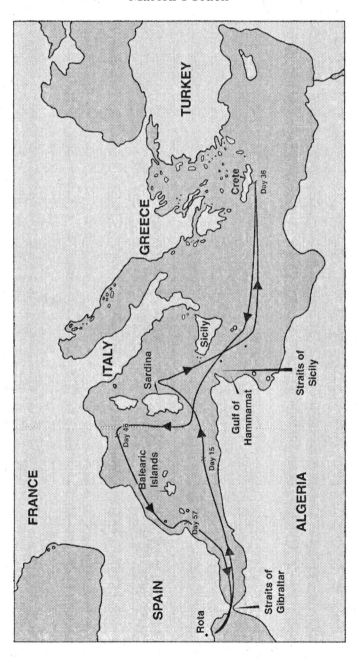

18
Underway

This would be their last day in port as the twenty-eight day refit was over except for last minute personal business. Most of the crew, including the Exec, were finishing off their last letters home and making the final run to the tender's Ship's Store for razor blades, cigarettes, toothpaste or whatever else one deemed to be essential to survive the patrol's sixty-three days.

Underway was planned for 1800Z. As a standard practice, boats getting under way for patrol used the cover of darkness to try to slip by the Soviet AGI that was a permanent fixture in the Rota operation areas. The AGI was a surface intelligence vessel built on a large trawler hull and loaded with electronic eavesdropping equipment. Once on station outside an FBM operating base, they stayed there for several months, steaming back and forth, just watching and waiting and listening. It must have been boring as hell for the Soviet crews.

Occasionally, the American sailors would toss a watertight container of old porno magazines over the side when the Russians were watching. Invariably, the AGI would speed to the package and hoist it aboard. No one was ever sure whether that helped or hurt their morale, but, since they had women on board, the Americans always assumed it would, at least, raise tensions a bit.

There was only one major work party scheduled for the day. Movies had to be loaded. The Motion Picture Petty Officer had, by the Exec's direction, invested forty pounds of coffee, innumerable beers at the Greenhouse and a lot of personal charm in the staff of the Navy Motion Picture Exchange. With sixty-three days at sea to look forward to, the object, of course, was to ensure that a good set of flicks were reserved for the *Marion* crew. It worked. The MPPO returned with seventy films, including a high percentage of "R" rated ones and a healthy sprinkling of new releases. For good measure, the NMPX threw in sixteen episodes of "Star Trek" and eight half-hour reels of National

Football League highlights. By 1100Z the movies were all aboard and stowed, and the now idle crew settled back to wait for 1715Z when the maneuvering watch would be stationed.

The Engineer planned to commence reactor startup at 1300Z. At 1400Z the Captain, the Exec, and the Navigator were scheduled to troop up to Squadron Ops for their departure briefing from the Staff Intelligence Officer.

All hands were marking time now, glad to have the frenzy of the refit over, but dreading giving up their connection with the shore and the real world it represented…all except the Engineer, that is. Around 1000Z, Craig was walking toward his stateroom from the wardroom when the Engineer burst out of the Captain's stateroom. Eng was frowning at a thin sheaf of papers he carried and almost collided with the Exec as he rushed toward the stateroom he shared with Rakowski and the doctor.

"Whoa, Eng. What's up?"

The Engineer quickly braked himself to a halt. "The Captain wants the Incident Report on CS-6 redone."

CS-6 is a small coolant sampling system valve. It was one of the primary valves they had replaced early in the refit. Every time anything, component or people, malfunctioned or had to be replaced in the propulsion plant, the Captain was required to send an "Incident Report" to Naval Reactors detailing the cause, effect and fix. When determining cause, woe betide the Captain who cited "material failure" if, in NR's opinion the material failed because of a personnel error.

Hyman G. Rickover could, and on occasion did, call personally to explain to errant CO's that their own lack of personal involvement in training or supervision of the technicians was the cause of failure. After such calls, most CO's were quick to identify personnel error as the cause of incidents. "Mea Culpa" became a refuge. Absolution came with confession. It was virtually unheard of for a CO to be criticized for proclaiming his own guilt.

In the case of the primary valves they had replaced, the Incident Reports had seemed straightforward to Craig. It was not obvious to him why there should be a last minute flap.

"What's wrong with the CS-6 Incident Report?"

"The Captain has decided the cause is 'personnel.'"

"Why? After a few hundred times of being operated, a valve may leak. What's so unusual about that?"

"The Captain asked for the machinery history on CS-6. It was replaced three patrols ago. He says it shouldn't require replacement again so soon, therefore, a "personnel problem.""

"I agree it seems like a pretty short life. Likely some Engineering Laboratory Technician got heavy-handed. Also, though, maybe the seat was soft."

The Engineer shrugged.

Anybody who has written Incident Reports knows they have a section for "Corrective Action." If they have been marked "personnel," then the fix is going to be a pain in somebody's ass.

"What's the corrective action going to be?"

"An hour of training in primary valve operation for all officers and all engineers."

"Over a hundred man hours because some turkey in the Blue Crew may have over-torqued one little Goddamned valve, perhaps just once?"

"Yes, sir."

No use fighting it. NR would be content."Okay, Eng. You had better get to writing. I'll tell the Yeoman to stand by his typewriter. Last mail will go off at 1600."

The intelligence briefing didn't amount to much. A couple of "Foxtrot" class diesel submarines were coming down from the Soviet NORTHFLEET to INCHOP into the Mediterranean, but they were way up north, west of the U.K. "CHOP," or Change of Operational command, from the North Fleet to the Mediterranean Fleet, occurred for the Russians when they came through the Straits. Hence INCHOP for Soviet units entering the Med and OUTCHOP for units departing. These boats were still days away from INCHOP.

The AGI was on his normal patrol station about twenty miles west of the Rota breakwater. An E-II, a Soviet nuclear attack submarine, a couple of Foxtrot class diesel boats and a half dozen Soviet surface units were operating in the Alboran basin of the western Mediterranean. Nothing unusual. The *Marion* team listened; exchanged handshakes with the briefers, and left.

Getting underway for patrol was the epitome of anticlimax.

At the appointed hour, the tugs moved in alongside and, under the Captain's watchful eye, Rak, as Officer of the Deck, ordered the ship's mooring lines taken in and maneuvered the *Marion* out of the harbor. Nobody came to the rail of the tender to see them off. The Squadron Staff and tender crew had already turned their attention to the next arrival. Once she was underway, the *Marion* was out of their minds.

The Exec stood topside watching the line handlers as the tugs snorted alongside, spinning the ship in place just off the tender. Once turned, end for end, Rak would simply go Ahead One-Third, then Ahead Two-Thirds speed until topside had been rigged for dive. As he stood there, Craig felt the old familiar sense of depression wash over him. *God, I always hate to leave the shore. Everything that makes life worthwhile is found there.* The feeling would lift in a few days, just as it had when he had first arrived for the refit.

The Weapons Officer caught his eye. Joe was jumping up and down vigorously on the forward marker buoy. The marker buoys are located adjacent to the escape hatches. They are the size of a large home heating oil tank and are designed to float free if the ships sinks. Theoretically, they would float on the surface to help rescuers find the ship, then their tether would lead the rescuers to the escape trunk. Nice theory if you're in salvageable water only a few hundred feet deep. U.S. submarines spent virtually all their time underway in water far too deep for the 600-foot tethers, so they welded the buoys down whenever they were going on an operation where stealth was a serious concern. That way they couldn't be streamed inadvertently. There is nothing very stealthy about a mechanical whale towing a huge floating garbage can.

Weaps wasn't happy about something. It turned out that the buoy wobbled a bit beneath his feet. That meant that it would probably rattle in the water flow at high-submerged speeds. One of the seamen scurried below for wooden wedges and a heavy hammer. By the time all the lines had been struck down into their superstructure lockers, the buoy was securely wedged.

Satisfied that Weaps was making a thorough job of securing topside, Craig took his small gray cloud of personal despair below.

Arriving in the Control Room, he made his way to the forward starboard corner to watch the Navigation party. The Navigator was spinning around on number one periscope, taking a round of bearings on navigational landmarks. Close to land they had to use the age-old technique of "piloting" instead of relying on the Ships Inertial Navigation Systems. The reason was that, although the SINS knew precisely where they were, the surveyors, who in an earlier day had created the charts of harbors and shorelines, were much less accurate. A half-mile or more discrepancy between charted and geodetically precise positions was not uncommon. The Exec had seen errors as great as five miles in the open ocean.

A messenger brought up coffee and the Exec settled down to watch the Control Room scene. Throughout the ship, the crew was busy rigging for dive. If they pressed straight on to it, their planned diving point was only a two hour run away. The Officer of the Deck, or OOD as he was commonly known, would soon pass the word from the Bridge to secure the Maneuvering Watch.

A moment later the Captain dropped down the ladder from the Bridge. Stopping at the foot of the ladder to strip his binoculars off over his head, he turned to starboard and handed them to the waiting Quartermaster. Seeing the Exec, he asked, "How's Rig for Dive going, XO?"

"Pretty good. We're waiting on the Torpedo Room and Maneuvering to report rigged. Nobody has reported in 'checked by an officer' yet. The compensation is in."

"How long do you figure before you're finished?"

"I'd guess forty-five minutes to an hour."

Holcomb stood looking at the chart spread on the glass surface of the MK 19 plotter. Craig moved over to his side.

"Captain, if the AGI has been moving in since the P-3 had a visual on him this afternoon he could be coming over the hill anytime now."

When a submarine was deploying on patrol, the local Patrol Air Wing routinely sent a P-3-C Maritime Patrol Aircraft out to locate the AGI and see what he was doing. Today, he had been steaming slowly back and forth in his usual location. The P-3 had snapped a couple of pictures of the waving Russians and come home.

Both the Captain and the Exec assumed the Skipper of the AGI could surely count to twenty-eight and would be expecting them to come out today. No doubt, he also probably knew from coast watchers in Rota exactly when they had cleared the breakwater. Around Rota, the AGI's seldom bothered the U.S. ships very much. Mostly, they just tried to get close and take pictures, illuminate the Americans with searchlights, and pick up whatever was thrown over the side. On rare occasions Ivan would get pushy and play chicken, but usually he just liked to cozy up.

Not being sure exactly what he was up to, the FBM crews naturally preferred to avoid any close approach. In spite of that, Holcomb's intention on this sortie was to simply head for the nearest corner of their assigned Rota Op area, then submerge as quickly as possible. To the Exec, that seemed likely to take them right into the arms of the waiting Ivan. Tactically, Craig didn't like to give Ivan—or any one else—anything for free.

"Captain, don't you think we ought to make Ivan work a little for his dinner?"

"So what are you suggesting, XO?"

"We have these areas all night. Why don't we change our diving point up to the northeast corner of the area?"

"But we're going southwest. We're supposed to clear the local op areas to the southwest, then run to the Straits."

"Yes, sir. It'll be dark in another half-hour. Why don't we slow to Ahead One-Third now and hope the AGI doesn't show up before dark. If he's waiting, we won't close him as fast at one third. After dark, let's flood down to decks awash and turn out the stern light so only the sail is obvious. That way we'll look like a fishing boat and give about the right radar return."

The Captain looked interested. "And?"

"We then run north, inside the Twelve Mile Limit, to within a couple of miles of our new diving point. If we run at an odd, slow speed, Ivan may not make us. If he's out of position to the south, we run ten minutes outside the hundred fathom curve, dive and run like hell for a ways. It'll take us three hours to get up there at, say, 7.5 knots. Submerged, even at two thirds, we can be down in the southwest corner of our areas by 0900Z. We aren't due out until 1200Z. Plenty of time."

"That's pretty good, XO. Let's do it."

"Yes, sir. Do you want to tell the OOD to slow down?"

Holcomb called the OOD on the 7MC, the announcing system that connected the primary ship control stations, and told him to slow to "Ahead One-Third."

Craig went to his stateroom, satisfied.

Maybe all that effort to be cute will be wasted, but I don't believe in making things any easier for Ivan than they have to be.

They never knew whether the plan worked or whether the AGI just wasn't interested that night, because they never saw him. But, about a half-hour before the *Marion* submerged, the electronic countermeasures gear detected a few weak sweeps of the AGI's NEPTUNE radar, the standard Soviet shipboard surface search radar. And, the next day the P-3 aircraft found him steadily circling just about where he had been the day before.

It was after 2200Z when the *Marion* reached her diving point and finally submerged. After getting a good trim, the Captain ordered the ship down to a safe depth and commenced the transit back to the southwest. The Navigator, with the Exec looking on had laid out a slightly circuitous course to avoid the areas where the AGI was most likely to be. To keep the SINS updated, they would track two or three Navigation Satellite passes during the night but otherwise nothing was planned that would disturb the tranquility of the transit. All hands, from the Captain to the mess cooks were happy to make that first night as undemanding as possible. Although the feelings remained unspoken, many of the souls on board felt the same depression the Exec endured when first leaving the shore behind.

Along with the shore, the crew left behind the practice of reveille for all hands. From now until the end of patrol, they would only hold reveille for the weekly field day. That period of detailed house cleaning was always preceded by "Up all hands" and breakfast. The rest of the time, the watch would simply send a messenger to wake their reliefs so as to avoid unnecessarily disturbing their sleeping shipmates. Just about everyone on board, except the Captain, the XO and the doctor would be on shift work, one watch in three, for the duration of the patrol. Standing four hours on and eight hours off, those who had come off duty only four hours before didn't take kindly to an unnecessary "wake up." Naturally, emergencies and all hands drills brought everyone out of their bunks, but unnecessary wake ups were always avoided. During routine steaming watches, life goes on in a quiet, almost artificially subdued way. Even the occasional announcement on the MC systems is cryptic and calm.

Before turning in, the Exec took a tour of the ship and, in a departure from habit, he started aft, in the engineering spaces. Tonight nothing seemed to disturb the tranquility as the watch standers went about their business. The Upper Level Engine Room watch stood between the gray humped backs of the main engines taking readings from the Steam Plant Gauge Board. He jotted readings on the log sheet held by a clipboard in his left hand. Craig passed without his notice.

Moving forward, he stopped outside the door to the Maneuvering Room. Rak was on watch, slumped back in the Engineering Officer of the Watch's chair looking ahead and down at the row of three operators before him. The one nearest the door, the Throttleman, had turned from his panel to the salinity cell-monitoring panel behind him to check the reading on one of the condensate streams.

The Reactor Operator next to him had just finished taking his hourly log readings and was calculating the previous hour's EFPH, the Effective Full Power Hour, a measure of the consumption of the reactor core. The Electrical Plant Operator sat back, eyes flickering from meter to meter on his panel. Craig was tempted to move on without disturbing them, but, as the Throttleman turned back to his panel, he saw the Exec and spoke, "Evening, XO."

"Evening. Everything hot, straight and normal?"

Rak stood up and moved toward the door.

"Hi, XO. Yeah, all quiet."

"I see you have the 8000 GPD lit off. Is that what that salinity cell alarm was on?" *These kids have no idea what a luxury it is to be able to make eight thousand gallons of pure water per day. On the diesel boats, we struggled for three hundred per day and took showers every two weeks.*

"Yes, sir. We just started making water. We're dumping to the bilge until the alarm clears."

The water they were dumping was more pure than most laboratory reagent grade, but even very low levels of chlorides do bad things very rapidly to stainless steel piping at high temperatures. By a distillation and ion exchange process, the *Marion* could supply the powerplant and showers with thousands of gallons of water more pure than the best available for laboratory use a generation earlier.

"Okay. How's number one TG doing?" Number One turbine generator's governor had been a little erratic when the Blue Crew had returned from patrol. The refit repairs had fixed the problem.

"Fine. No problem. Steady as a rock."

"Okay. Goodnight."

A chorus of "Goodnight, XO," and Craig headed on forward to continue his tour.

The scene throughout the rest of the ship was much the same. The technicians in the Navigation Center were quietly monitoring their charges and a quick look at their plots of the SINS propagations suggested nothing more to the Exec's practiced eye than the daily wandering of a well-settled inertial navigator.

The Control Room was quiet. As was standard, the inboard Plainsman had control of the fairwater planes and was doing most of the work keeping the ship on depth. The Stern Plainsman was doing little more than nurse the rudder a few degrees right or left to maintain course. They would not be allowed to use automatic depth or course control for a few days until their manual skills had been sharpened.

Radio had copied the 2200Z schedule. Craig flipped through the clipboard holding the message traffic, but there was little of interest. Mostly just Family Grams to other boats and Administrative traffic. One Family Gram message caught his eye. "Need bracer, thoughts baser." He chuckled. The lady who wrote that would probably be shocked to realize that her words were celebrated Submarine Force-wide before her husband even saw them.

Sonar was the last stop. Here again, the watch was quiet. Two operators were swinging the BQS-4 and BQR-7 back and forth in advancing sector searches, pausing now and then to run back and forth over a bearing that held some sound of interest. Stanzei was the Watch Supervisor.

"How's your Seven, Stanzei?"

"Outstanding, XO. I really have never heard a better one. Look at all the traces on that recorder. We're getting contacts way the hell out."

The Exec agreed. No doubt about it. The strip recorder showed a dozen or more traces. Most were the straight nearly vertical lines typical of long-range contacts.

"Good. Once we get inside the Med that recorder is going to look like a nest of worms!"

"True, true, XO."

"Goodnight."

"Goodnight."

In his cellar-like hole at the bottom of the Ops Compartment, the duty Auxiliaryman was bringing on line the O2 Generators that would supply oxygen to the ship's atmosphere and the CO2 Scrubbers and CO-H2 Burners that would scavenge the carbon monoxide and carbon dioxide. Combined with the electrostatic precipitators and charcoal filters, the result would be a ship's atmosphere more pure than one could sniff on the highest mountain top—with one exception. CO2 levels would always hover just under one per cent of the atmosphere. Although not hazardous in the short run, the Navy never did conclude exactly what the long-term effect of twenty years exposure to an elevated CO2 level might be. It definitely influenced the PH of the submariners' blood, but to what, if any, effect, was unknown. Elevated CO2 levels were a fact of life and the Exec gave it no thought.

As he turned into officer country, he could hear a movie going in the Crew's Mess.

19

Gibralter

A day later, at 1734Z, the *Marion* was approaching the Straits of Gibraltar. The western approaches to Gibraltar are a busy place. In addition to the maritime traffic to and from the Mediterranean, the North-South traffic between Europe and the west coast of Africa crisscrosses in this area. As a result of the heavy traffic, the ambient noise level in the sea is very high. The acoustic signature of an American FBM, one of the quietest ships ever built, is overwhelmed by such noise. Thermal scars abound from the passing merchant ships, as does flotsam that confuses the radar picture. It is a wonderful hiding place for a well-run, stealthy submarine.

It is also a very tight choke point for intercepting ships entering the Mediterranean. So, the Captain loitered there for the better part of a day watching and listening as a precaution before entering the Straits. Once into the Straits, there is damned little sea room for evading contact with the British, Ivan, the Spaniards, or whoever else may be snooping about.

While they were waiting to commence the transit of the Straits, the Exec was struggling with the detested pile of paperwork that, in port or at sea, poured onto his desk. He looked up in surprise when the Captain pushed through his door with an accompanying knock.

"XO, what's your previous experience in the Med? Didn't you operate in here during your last tour?"

"Yes, sir. Three patrols as Navigator." *Now, what in the hell is he fishing for?*

"This is my first Med run."

Realization dawned on Craig. Their one patrol together had been in the Atlantic. The Captain hadn't been through the Straits before.

Craig laughed. "Well, try to get some sleep. You may not have another chance. The Med is a miserable, crowded little pond characterized at times by the lousiest sonar conditions in the world. The good side of the bad sonar conditions is that you'll only know about a few thousand of the contacts that are out there trying to run over us. If you could hear as well as you can in the Atlantic, it'd scare the hell out of you. We'll often hear submarines better than surface ships because of the 'afternoon effect,' a massive, negative thermoclime near the surface on hot Med afternoons. I guarantee we'll probably lose a couple of trailing wire antennas to merchants that we don't hear until they have chewed on our tail."

The captain looked unhappy. "What's the best way to get in?"

He's nervous! "Getting in is easy, Captain. There's a standing current both ways in the Straits. In shallow, out deep. To get in, we just rig for ultra quiet, go Ahead One-Third at about a hundred twenty feet keel depth and let the current do the rest. If we get an echo ranging contact, come to all stop, kill our way and hover. There's all kinds of reverberations in there from the steep walls. If we hover, we kill the doppler on our echo. Damned little chance the other guy will be able to sort us out. As far as passive detection is concerned, don't worry so long as we're slow and quiet." Craig pointed to the surface. "This is a morgue compared to the Straits. Remember those reverberations."

"Okay. Thanks, XO."

"One other thing."

"What's that?"

"Ivan won't be waiting for us close up in the Straits."

"No?"

"No, sir. He'll be at the western edge of the Alboran. Just about where the coast of Spain turns north. It's fairly narrow and quiet there. He knows he can't sort us out in trash like this."

"So what do you suggest?"

"Try not to get there when he expects us. He knows exactly when we left. Odds are he'll estimate that we are making about six knots speed of advance from Rota."

"What else can we do?"

"We'll think of something, Captain. Ivan really isn't all that slick. One final thing, though."

"Yes."

"Make sure Gator gets at least three good NAVSAT passes just before we start through. We want to be sure those SINS are walkin' the line. Make sure he puts them in 'Free Inertial' mode right after the last pass. The currents in the Straits are strong enough and variable enough to cause the stable platforms to Schuler, and the sea room is tight enough for a good Schuler oscillation to get us in trouble."

A guy named Schuler had been first to describe short period oscillations of the SINS stable platforms that could be caused by, among other things, the reference signal being taken from the ship's electromagnetic log in areas of high ocean currents.

"You've been around quite a bit, haven't you, XO?"

"Yes, sir. I've spent my time driving submarines instead of chasing neutrons. I never had to take time out for a tour as Engineer, remember?"

* * * * *

Gibraltar was broad on the port bow when the phone rang in the Exec's stateroom. It was the Captain.

"XO, this is the Captain. I'm in CONN. We have an echo ranger. Could you come up here?"

"Yes, sir. I'll be right there."

As he entered the Control Room, Craig looked around. The ship was at one-third speed and 150 feet keel depth. Over the sonar speakers he could hear the familiar squeaky click of an active sonar. To his ear, the frequency sounded pretty high and the pulses pretty short, not the characteristics of long-range sonar.

Craig swung up on the periscope stand beside the Captain and waited for Sonar's next report. It came shortly.

"Conn—Sonar. Echo ranging now bears 046 degrees and appears to be closing."

The Captain held down the AN/WIC box "press to talk" switch and replied, "Sonar—Conn, Aye. What's the bearing rate now?"

"Conn—Sonar. We estimate true bearing rate to be right point six."

The Captain swung around to the Exec. "What do you think, XO?"

"Has Sonar classified the emitter?"

"No."

"Ask them to check the frequency for an old QHBA sonar. The Spanish and the British both run destroyers back and forth here on an anti-submarine patrol station. The frequency sounds too high for the British."

"Sonar—Conn. Does the echo ranger's frequency match an old U.S. QHBA sonar?"

After a few moments. "Conn—Sonar, the emitter appears to be a QHBA sonar. Now bears 049 degrees T."

The Captain looked at the RO-136 sonar contact recorder where an increasingly solid trace was developing at 049 degrees.

"So he's probably a Spaniard running a North-South barrier patrol just west of Gibraltar?"

"That's my guess, Captain. Why don't we go up for a look and be sure?"

"How far do you think he is?"

"Well, Captain, you're just now beginning to hold his platform noise. That fits, assuming he's running just about due south, or within twenty degrees of it. At twelve knots his bearing rate would put him out around twelve kilo yards. I'd say we ought to try to get a good tracking solution on him at periscope depth, then skirt him to the south after he turns onto his northbound leg."

The Captain was slow to react. Craig was just about to prod him to do something when he turned in the Exec's direction again. "XO, you know what you have in mind. Take the Conn and go ahead and do it."

"Aye, Aye, Captain."

Craig was relieved, but carefully masked his feelings.

There are some drivers I just can't ride with in a car, and I'm starting to get the same feeling here.

The Exec immediately cleared baffles, turning the ship forty-five degrees each side of the course they had been maintaining to listen astern. Assured no one would run up their back, he then ordered the ship up to periscope depth. There, hull down on the periscope's limited horizon, right where it should be, was an old Fletcher class destroyer with a starboard fifty-degree angle on the bow. The Exec maneuvered the *Marion* to the right and slowed to minimum turns to move in closer to the African Coast and avoid closing the Spanish DD.

After twenty minutes of intermittent quick looks, Craig finally caught the destroyer in the process of reversing course. By that time, range had closed to around six thousand yards. He watched the Spaniard for a few more minutes, then ordered the ship back down to one hundred fifty foot keel depth and commenced the transit toward the Straits. At the closest point of approach, the two vessels were no closer than forty-five hundred yards apart. The destroyer's old QHBA sonar was unlikely to be good for more than a fourth of that range.

After the ship was clear of the Spanish destroyer, the Captain and the Exec left the Navigator tending the Navigation and Ship Control parties and trooped off to Holcomb's stateroom. He seemed a little agitated. Craig figured he had embarrassed him by taking over in Conn and, when the door was shut, spoke first.

"Captain, I apologize if I created an uncomfortable situation over that DD. I didn't mean to give the impression that I wanted to take over."

Holcomb was hasty in his reassurance, "No, no, XO. I wasn't bothered. I asked you to come to Conn for your advice. What I want to talk to you about now is how you and I organize ourselves for the patrol."

"How so?"

"I need to concentrate on the ORSE. When they come back, they're going to look at us much more closely than they would have before the delay. I can see you have all the expertise necessary to direct the ship operationally, so I want you to do that. We'll split the Command Duty port and starboard, but you do all the operational planning and direction."

"Captain, I'm happy to split the Command Duty. What about Standing Orders? Night Orders? Targeting changes? ACIP keys?"

"You write the Night Orders. I'll sign them. I'll sign off targeting changes. ACIP keys and all Emergency Action Procedures remain my responsibility."

One last confirmation seemed to be in order.

"Captain, your responsibility for the safety of the ship and crew is absolute, as is your responsibility for our mission performance. Are you sure you're comfortable delegating tactical direction to me?"

"XO, from what I've seen, you have a lot more experience in tactics than I do. I'll always be there if you need me, but I must concentrate on the Engineers. You have to mind the front end for me while I make sure we're ready for the ORSE."

"Aye, Aye, Captain. Now if you'll excuse me, I'll get back up to Conn."

As he climbed the ladder back up to the Control Room, Craig went over the conversation in his mind. His conclusion was that the Captain was obsessed with fear of failing the ORSE and lacked confidence in himself as a tactician. He was happy enough to take over the ship driving, but his misgivings about that aspect of Holcomb's behavior were back.

I wonder how he reconciles his responsibility for the ship, it's crew and it's 17.6 megatons of warheads with the decision to bury himself back aft.

It was a disturbing situation, but the Exec had the ship to run now, and he intended to turn all his attention to just that.

* * * * *

The transit through the Straights was uneventful.

Four hours after their conversation, the Captain was resting in his stateroom and the Exec was in the Control Room studying a large chart of the western Mediterranean. They were through the Straights of Gibraltar and their sea room was expanding rapidly as they pressed on eastward. *Marion* was scheduled to assume Mod Alert status at midnight and the Exec wanted to be well away from the Straits by then. Mod-Alert was the short transitional phase between the Non-Alert of refit and the full war-footing ALERT of patrol.

The ship slowed and went up to periscope depth for a NAVSAT pass at 2134Z. The Navigator was happy. His SINS had ridden through the swirling currents of the Straits with little perturbation and were still well settled.

At 2300Z, sailors in the mess decks heard the line-wiper in the bridge access trunk start its grinding and moaning as the Radiomen streamed the trailing wire antenna. From now on, to the end of the patrol, the ship would be in continuous receipt of radio communications. Silent, never transmitting, but always listening.

At 2400Z, the Captain gave the Weapons Officer permission to commence arming weapons and to enter the first "package" of targets in the fire control computers.

At 0001Z, the *USS Marion* was Mod-Alert, "covering" low priority, long response targets. It would take the Weaponeers the rest of the day to arm and close out all sixteen missiles, but from now on the ship was available and responsible to National Command Authority for striking targets when and as directed.

Whereas, on ALERT, the ship would be responsible for reacting immediately to a launch order, on Mod-Alert it might be hours before the missiles were away. Some strategic thinkers argued that the Navy should never have bothered with the ALERT status since the real strength of the SSBN as a deterrent was its certainty, not its speed.

Since he couldn't find and destroy American submarine launch platforms, Ivan knew retribution was sure to come if he attempted anything pre-emptive.

It might have taken hours, days, or weeks, but sooner or later he would have lost eighty percent of his population to the FBM. The fact that a Nuclear Winter would then have taken care of the remaining twenty percent, as well as almost all other life on the planet, was not, at the time, a recognized strategic constraint.

Promptly at midnight, the Navigator and the Exec knocked on the Captain's door to reposition the keys to the strategic weapon system. As he handed them his ACIP keys, the ones that closed the final switch in the permission-to-fire loop, the Navigator asked him, "Captain, how does it feel to hold the keys to millions of lives?"

"Frightening!"

"Do you ever think about making a mistake?"

"Never!" he snapped. The Navigator had touched a nerve.

As procedure required, they took his keys up to the Radio Room and locked them in a double safe. Two teams of two men each had the combinations. No single officer had the combination to both safe doors. Only the Engineer and the Exec could open the inner door.

As the Missile Technicians set about readying the missiles, the Torpedomen began installing exploders in their fish. By the end of the day, all missiles and torpedoes were armed and fully ready. The Exec ordered "Patrol Quiet" and the ship waited in final readiness for the appointed hour to go "ALERT."

The patrol was about to begin.

20
Alert

At 2359Z, on the fourth day of patrol, the ship went to 2SQ, as ALERT status is designated in the obscure language of military acronyms. The only things that changed were the Target Package the missiles were covering and the finer points of some procedures. But the difference was a palpable one for the crew. ALERT is conducted on a war footing and the mood of the crew shifts subtly with the transition to 2SQ.

Maybe it was the very real confrontation at sea between East and West, which loitered near the brink of open hostilities, that gnawed on the crew's mood. Perhaps the realization that the thermonuclear weapons were armed and aimed gave Armageddon a reality to the crew that most people never confronted. Whatever the cause, a slight undercurrent of tension ran through a crew on ALERT. From skipper to seaman, focus is heightened and more concentrated. The tension is so pervasive, yet subtle, that some men only recognize it in the sense of relief that comes with stepping back down to 3SQ, or ModAlert status.

The crew took the *Marion* smoothly from 3SQ to 2SQ by conducting a Weapon System Readiness Test or "WSRT" as it was universally spoken. By spinning up all the birds in WSRT Mode, they verified and recorded for the analysts at John Hopkin's Applied Physics Laboratory that all missile and fire control systems were in good working order. With the order to "Man Battle Stations, Missile" the clock started running on the ALERT phase of the patrol.

From that moment on, any lapse in communications coverage, any failure of a missile, launcher, or fire control component would incur "downtime" until a recorded test proved complete restoration of proper operation. Every FBM's goal was nothing less than 100% readiness of all sixteen missiles for every minute of their ALERT period. It had been done...and most patrols came very close.

For the next few days, the Navigator was forced to rely exclusively on NAVSAT passes to keep his SINS updated. The ship was moving through the fringes of the Mediterranean's western Loran C chain's coverage, but the weak signals still did not provide the fix accuracy the SINS required. That meant more trips to periscope depth and, therefore, more tactical exposures than the Exec liked, but nothing could be done about it. The SINS had to be kept within the accuracy required by the missile fire control system. Most trips "up" were uneventful, but not all.

In dividing the Command Duty day, the Captain and the Exec had agreed that the Captain would be on duty from 0800 to 2000 and the Exec would be up at night and rest during daylight hours. Holcomb had insisted on the arrangement so engineering drills, almost always held during the morning or afternoon watches would be held during his waking hours.

Two days later, early in the afternoon, the sleeping Exec was awakened and nearly catapulted out of his bunk by a violent roll of the ship. The feeling of the ship's motion was as familiar to him as an old shoe. He listened for a moment to the splintering crashes and cursing that echoed through the ship, then to the colossal bang and shudder as a wave rolled up under the sailplane and slammed into the exposed sail. They were broached on the surface, with decks awash and the whole sail exposed.

The weather had been deteriorating when he had turned over the watch to the Captain six or seven hours before. Now it was rough as hell. The Captain must have come up to periscope depth broadside to the sea and the ship had been sucked up to the surface by the venturi forces of the heavy swells sweeping across the flat expanse of the missile deck.

Craig chuckled to himself as he struggled to keep his footing on the lurching deck and get dressed. From all the screaming and shouting echoing down from Control he suspected the Diving Officer was having a character-building experience. Nothing stows a ship for sea quite as well as the first really big roll!

A minute later he was in Control, marveling at the scene. The *Marion* was wallowing about, decks awash in broad daylight, held to the surface by the same venturi action that had brought her up, out of control, from periscope depth. The Captain, eyes flaming and mustache bristling, was yelling at the Engineer who, as OOD, was periodically turning away to yell at the Diving Officer to "Get her down, Goddammit! Get her down!" Lieutenant Junior Grade Hill, on watch as the Diving Officer, looked like he'd rather be bulldogging another Volkswagen.

Slightly amazed and barely able to control his mirth, Craig heard the Captain screaming to the Engineer, "—you stood there looking at it through the scope and put left full rudder on and cut it! You cut the wire while you were standing there looking at it!"

The situation was clear. The seas on the port beam had carried the trailing wire off to starboard. When the Engineer had put on left rudder, he had swung the stern across the wire and the screw had cut it.

The captain wasn't through. "Get us down!" he yelled at the Engineer.

Between furious exhortations to the Diving Officer to "Get her down!" the cornered Engineer came the closest the Exec had ever witnessed to fighting back. "Captain," he said acidly, "YOU told me to come left into the sea!"

Meanwhile, lacking any other seemingly good ideas, Hill was continuing to flood water into the variable ballast tanks as rapidly as possible, attempting to gain enough weight to overcome the forces holding the ship on the surface.

Craig heard the Chief of the Watch report "Flooding Number One, 80,000 lbs. in." He noted the bow and stern planes were on full dive. As he stood, head shaking at the scene before him, he heard a giggle and, turning, found Stone standing behind him nearly collapsed with hilarity.

"XO, maybe you ought to tell Hill to try jumping up and down on the deck. Maybe he could pound her down."

The Exec broke up. *I can't fucking believe this!* As quickly as he could contain himself, he caught Hill's eye. "You had better ask for more speed. When you break through the surface effect, you're gonna go down like a rock. You'll need Standard speed to catch it."

On his third request for more speed, Hill got the attention of the fulminating CO and Engineer. Just as the additional RPM's were coming on, the ship started down. As the Exec had expected, the ship went to three hundred feet before the speed built up enough to carry all the extra weight. As the stern planesman, having experienced the event at firsthand, confided later to Kane, "Man, we fell through our own asshole. I thought we never would stop going down!"

On his way back to his stateroom, the Exec met the Chief of the Boat, who was coming aft from the crew's mess.

"Well, COB, I guess we're stowed for sea now."

The COB shook his head.

"You oughta see that galley. The roll spilled grease on the deck. Kane fell and busted his ass in the grease and slid into McJimsey and knocked him down too. McJimsey was carrying a tray of cups. We're down forty-eight cups and two sore-assed mess cooks."

"Marvelous."

Later, when he came off watch, the Exec sought out Hill.

"Educational watch, huh?"

"Miserable is more like it."

"Next time you have to come up in this kind of sea, put about 50K in auxiliaries on the way up. That way, you run with an up bubble to carry the extra weight. The stern is deeper, the venturi forces are weaker, and you have 50,000 pounds of water offsetting the lift."

"Coming up in the trough didn't help either."

"No. Just count it as part of your continuing education. Goodnight."

21
The First PDC's

By 2000Z, when Craig relieved the Captain of the Command Duty, the weather had begun to abate. The Loran signal was improving rapidly as they moved farther East and was now almost usable for the SINS. Sporadic distant hydrographic operations to the south were the only thing of tactical interest. Ocean survey and oil exploration seismic operations often use small explosive charges as sound sources. For convenience, submariners referred to all small explosive noises as PDC's, a habit derived from the surface fleet's use of hand grenades as practice depth charges. Twenty or thirty of the small explosions had been heard by sonar during the afternoon watch.

It was now the seventh day of the patrol, and shortly after taking the watch from the Captain, the Exec walked into Sonar. The Chief Sonarman was there, having just stopped by to check on the watchstanders. While they were there, both heard the faint crash of a distant explosion. Shortly it was followed by another. Then another. Craig was mildly curious. PDC's were a common enough feature of the acoustic environment, but they were usually heard in small numbers and in short trains.

It was a good conversational point, and Craig habitually made it a point to exchange a few words with the watchstanders as he walked through the boat.

"Still picking up PDC's I see."

The Chief Sonarman grunted. "Yeah, we've had 'em off and on all day. Sounds like seismic survey down along the African coast."

"They must be running one hell of a long survey line to drop that many."

The Chief laughed. "Maybe they're fishing with hand grenades."

So much for the PDC's. The Exec was, in fact, more immediately concerned with sonar conditions.

"Probably. Did you have any afternoon effect today?"

"Not much. The water is still pretty stirred up from that rough weather."

"Chief, make sure your guys are alert as hell when we're going up to periscope depth. Some of our OOD's don't know what this pond can be like."

"Yes, sir. I know. Franzei or I will be here every time we come up."

Craig felt better. Good heads like the Chief and Franzei keep junior officers out of trouble.

The next couple of days were quiet ones. The Captain and the Engineer were getting in stride with the Engineering Department's training. The contact log in sonar filled up rapidly as an endless line of merchant vessels clattered by in the ceaseless bustle of Mediterranean commerce.

* * * * *

Late one evening, well after the end of the Wardroom movie, the Exec had gone to the head. With nowhere to go and nothing to do, he lingered over one of the old magazines that jammed the rack on the back of the stall door. His reading was interrupted by the doctor's voice wafting over the separator from the next stall.

"XO, is that you?"

"Yeah."

"XO, do you know anything about those two subs that were lost in here last year?"

"Yeah."

Two diesel boats had been lost in the Mediterranean. One was French and the other Israeli. No cause was ever known for their loss.

"Do you have any idea what happened to those boats?

"Yeah, what do you want to know?"

Craig didn't actually know a damned thing, but the Doc's mind was always subject to manipulation.

"What sank them?"

The doctor's voice reflected a tinge of apprehension. No doubt his imagination was in high gear. He had never learned enough about submarine operations to dispel his fear of the unknown.

"Giant Squid got 'em. Hauled em down below their crush depth."

"XO, are you kidding me?" The voice was plaintive.

This is unbelievable! Craig stifled his laughter with considerable difficulty while the doctor continued.

"Could it hurt us?"

"Naw. We're too big. Those were small diesel subs."

Quack was quiet for a long time. Craig began to worry that he had hurt his feelings by not taking him seriously. *He can't possibly believe this.*

After the long pause came the question.

"XO, have you ever encountered one of those giant squid?"

Craig choked. Boredom was vanquished and his day made. *He really believes this incredible line of bullshit. Millions of doctors in America and I got the one who believes stories about giant squid!* The Exec answered carefully, "Sure, Doc. Just about every patrol. They live in the deep basins. They never come this far west, but in a day or two we could hear one."

"Hear one? Is that how you know they're there? What do they sound like?"

"Doc, I'll have Sonar call you the first time they get contact on one, okay? Now leave me alone. I want to finish this article."

The voice was plaintive now. "XO, you're not shitting me, are you?"

"Of course not, Doc. Now shut up."

"Okay, XO."

Fifteen minutes later Craig was in Sonar with Franzei making sure the Quack didn't miss the first "Giant Squid" contact of the patrol.

The next night, three NAVSAT passes out of the three they attempted failed to produce fixes. The sea was a little bit rough, but the receiver locked onto the bird's transmission and appeared to collect enough data for a fix. Three times in a row the computer chewed around on what the receiver fed it, then, after a while, gave up and printed out "no fix." Fortunately, the Loran C signal was good enough by now to use for SINS reset calculations. Still, three in a row didn't seem right. The Navigator had the technicians do a complete alignment of the BRN receiver and run a full set of diagnostic routines on the computer. Neither revealed a problem, and on the next pass everything worked fine. Such is life with high technology systems.

After seeing the ship back down to patrol depth and verifying that the NAVSAT fix was good, the Exec again cycled by Sonar. The PDC's were still going off down to the south. The ship hadn't moved very far during the last couple of days as they wandered to and fro in the assigned patrol area. Whoever was conducting the seismic operations seemed to be moving east at about the same rate as the *Marion*. At least the small explosions were still very distant, very faint. The Sonarmen now routinely noted in their log when they started and stopped. They had given up trying to record every one.

After watching and listening for a while, the Exec asked the Sonar Supervisor what he thought about the PDC's.

"I don't know, XO. Just seismic ops, I guess. The only thing is, I never heard seismic ops go on for so long with such a precise interval between explosions. These are at precisely fourteen second intervals whenever we hear them."

He was right. They had been evenly spaced at that interval since the day they had first detected them. Suspicion began to suffuse Craig's routine interest in the PDC's. "That's interesting. How good do you think your bearings are to them?"

"Not very good. Actually, lousy. It's pretty near impossible to get a bearing on an explosion. These are so regular we can train back and forth during a series and get a general direction, mostly by eliminating the sectors where we don't hear them."

Craig pressed him, "Give me a number, plus or minus ninety degrees? Five degrees?

"Plus or minus fifteen degrees probably."

The Exec knew, without looking, that the intelligence chart kept in sonar didn't have anything plotted to the south of them. As intelligence reports came in via the radio broadcast, they were immediately passed over to Sonar where the sonarmen updated the plotted positions of all warships and naval auxiliaries observed to be in the Med. There were no reports of anything to the south between the *Marion* and the African coast.

The Exec left sonar and went on about his business of the moment. *Surely within a day or two we'll leave those PDC's behind.*

22
Giant Squid

Two nights later, on the patrol's tenth day, at 0243Z the ship began its first giant squid encounter. Seated in his stateroom Craig heard the messenger of the watch let himself into officer's country and make his way to the doctor's door.

"Doctor, Doctor."

"Huh. What?"

"Mr. Stone said to wake you up and tell you we are tracking a giant squid on sonar. He said you wanted to get up for it."

Suppressing his laughter, the Exec could hear the doctor's collisions with his desk, chair, and door as he piled out of his bunk and hurriedly dressed. The messenger came next to his door and made the same report.

"Very well, tell Mr. Stone I'll be up in a few minutes. Tell him he had better start tracking it on the MK113 in case it gets too close and we have to make a 'Snapshot.'"

The doctor rushed out. The Exec followed a discreet few minutes later.

When the Exec got to Control, the watch party was tracking the squid with quiet efficiency. Under the red lights, the Quartermaster stood before the MK113 Fire Control System computer, intently watching the solution generate. Occasionally on Stone's direction, he made small corrections to the squid's course, speed or range, then matched the sonar bearing to start another observation period. Sonar already had the BQS-4 in ATF, Automatic Target Following mode, precisely tracking a target.

Craig looked at Stone. "Are you in ATF on the squid?"

"Yes, sir."

"What's the bearing rate?"

"Real low. Almost zero. I'll bet he comes real close."

"They almost always do. Don't maneuver unless I order it."

Craig heard only one quickly suppressed snicker from somewhere out of sight in the Control Room's red gloom before he left for Sonar. There he found the doctor, wide-eyed and tousled, watching the Sonarmen as they went about the business of tracking the Giant Squid. They were calm and precise, a model of watch standing efficiency, as they tracked the squid with the BQS-4 and continued to search for "non-threatening" contacts on the BQR-7.

The squid was a horrible sounding thing. Still very distant, it could be heard as it snuffled along, occasionally emitting a series of almost mechanical groans. Sometimes it ended a groan with a snarling vicious chatter. Obviously it was closing on the *Marion* and hunting.

As the Exec entered Sonar, the doctor looked up at him. Suspicion flared for an instant.

"XO, is this some kind of setup?"

Before Craig could express the depth of the wound such doubt opened in his feelings, Franzei stepped in.

"Doc, listen here. Use these earphones and you can hear what's coming in over the FOUR."

The earphones were plugged into a patch panel between the BQS-4 and the spinning UNQ7 tape recorder. The doctor listened intently, then his face relaxed. A moment later his eyes widened with astonishment. A terrible scream echoed through the depths as if ripped from some leviathan in mortal anguish.

"What was that?" the doctor wanted to know.

The Exec appeared almost nauseous and said, "Probably caught a sperm whale. They eat sperm whales. Turn that speaker down, Franzei. Makes me sick listening to it."

The doctor was pale, earphones clamped to his head with both hands. "Oh my God!"

"Do you believe me now, Doc?"

The doctor's head nodded. The squid was closer now. If one listened carefully, as the doctor was doing, the gory crunching slurping sounds of the beast devouring its prey could be faintly heard.

The Exec turned to Franzei, and asked, "How much has true bearing changed since initial detection?"

"Only two degrees, sir."

The Exec tapped the doctor on the shoulder. Startled, Quack lifted one earphone.

"This one's gonna come real close, Doc. I'm going out to Control. Do you want to stay here?"

The doctor's head again bobbed a frantic affirmative. Craig went out to the periscope stand and ordered a cup of coffee. He and Stone then waited patiently.

At 0321Z, precisely on schedule, the door to Sonar burst open. The doctor, looking slightly demented, stormed through into Control.

"You sons of bitches," he screamed. "You fuckin' assholes are sick!"

With that, he was gone. In the background, over the sonar speaker, a somewhat "squidish" sounding Tiny Tim could be heard tiptoeing through the tulips.

Stone and Craig looked at each other and did a "high five" as Stone observed, "Pecky, ain't he?"

"Yeah. Bad language, too."

Franzei sauntered out of Sonar to join the hysterical laughter in the Control Room. Tears streamed down his cheeks.

"Gawd," he said, "I didn't think I could keep a straight face."

After regaining his composure, the Exec asked, "Franzei, how did you make that tape?"

"XO, we snuck in and taped the Doc's own snoring. After that we added a little hydraulic ram noise and dubbed in a chattering relay. We had to add a little of the Chief Cook's snoring for the grisly part. He's really disgusting, you know. We got the scream by pouring coffee on McJimsey's qual card. After that we just mixed it with an old tape for background noise. The MK113 was driving the BQS-4 in training mode. All very simple!"

Craig shook his head and went below to try to calm the doctor down.

Given a challenge, the inventiveness of sailors is marvelous.

The first bunch of Family Grams came in that morning before the Captain relieved the Exec of the Command Duty. Each sailor was allotted four twenty-word messages from home per patrol. He could distribute his allotted four forms to whomever he pleased, such as his wife, parents, or girlfriend. Eighty came in, grouped in batches of ten per naval message. Most of the officers received one. Craig got one and was glad to see the doctor had one, also. That would help offset his pique at the giant squid setup.

It was amazing how much twenty words could communicate. The gram from Meaghan was timely, and Craig could read between the lines that, so far, the patrol was pretty routine for her. For any sailor, the worst frustration of all on patrol was to know or sense that there were difficulties at home while being aware, with even greater certainty, that they were powerless to help.

One or two words in a gram could tell whether all was well or not. The wives shouldered a hell of a burden. For six and a half months out of twelve, their husbands' absence added to that burden. If nothing else, a little worm of fear for the well-being of her mate probably lived deep in the psyche of every wife. In spite of that, they took care of the home front and sheltered the men from bad news or worry as best they could. Without doubt, a submariner's wife daily faces tasks that are often much tougher than her husband's, and her lot requires just as much courage…if not more.

Reassured that the home front was okay, Craig was in high spirits when he turned the watch over to the Captain. Little did he suspect that this had been the last day of the patrol during which he would enjoy a general sense of well-being.

23
More PDC's

They had reached the thirteenth day of ALERT and most of the crew had found that natural biorhythm that would govern their lives for the remaining forty-five days. The night people and the day people had migrated their sleeping hours to suit their natural proclivities. In this world of artificial light and air, their biological need for a diurnal cycle was generally met. Some white light always could be found and, usually, some spot of eerie, red semi-darkness.

Time was measured in reference to the Greenwich meridian. The rising and setting of the sun was only noted by a few souls who manned the periscopes when the ship briefly ventured near the surface. In their sealed world, detached from the passing sun and the nights' wandering moon, day and night were represented only by "Rig for Red" in the Control Room during hours of natural darkness and "Lights Out" in crew's berthing from 2200Z to 0700Z.

The day people's world and the night people's world coincided during the hours set aside for daily training and weekly field days. It is a magical feature of the modern submarine that the need for training and cleaning is infinite.

At the end of a long patrol, the last drill and the last field day yield approximately the same quantity of ineptitude and dirt as the first. Each is simply scoured from deeper and deeper recesses of that cybernetic organism known as the submarine. Partly due to natural inclination, but primarily because of the Captain's insistent delegation of the Command Duty during the ship's "nighttime" hours, Craig had become a full-fledged night person. This day, as usual, he slept while the Captain and the Engineers trained.

In the afternoon Morales, the Leading Steward's Mate, shoved his empty bowl aside and scraped the remains of his rice and chicken adobo into the garbage can. Preferring their own, more highly spiced dishes to the food served in the crew's mess, he and the other stewards often cooked for themselves on the wardroom hotplate. Today's meal had been adobo, made with a few pieces of chicken pilfered from the frozen stores, and heavily laced with garlic. He had reserved the uneaten portion for the Exec. It was generosity born of an abundance of street smarts.

Months earlier, when the Exec had interrupted one of their suppers, Morales had reacted swiftly. He quickly lost his comprehension of English, smiled to show his cheerful naiveté, and offered Craig a bowl. Any quick-thinking Filipino steward would have done the same. Well knowing the rules of the game, the Exec had accepted the proffered share of their meal and a tacit contract was sealed. Henceforth, stewards could cook their own meals and he could share their table.

Both were satisfied with the exchange, but Morales probably wished the Exec had not noticed the Transactional Analysis textbook open on the pantry counter that day. He saw little advantage in drawing attention to either his Bachelor's Degree in Electrical Engineering or to his correspondence courses in psychology and business.

The short, wiry Morales was a quiet man by nature, but very well spoken with no hint of an accent. He was an extremely intelligent man who carefully guarded his feelings toward the officers and the rest of the crew, most of whom he correctly considered to be his intellectual inferior.

Filipino's came into the Navy as Stewards Mates under a long standing policy, agreed to with the Philippine Government, that allowed their enlistment, much the same as the traditional privilege accorded the Ghurka's by the British Army. In most cases, they were intelligent, well educated young men from middle class backgrounds who saw the U.S. Navy as an opportunity for themselves and their families. Their role aboard ship tended to exacerbate their language and cultural differences with the rest of the crew, and their abilities were often under-appreciated.

Today, nothing had roused the Exec from his stateroom since lunch. He had put in a wake-up call for 1645Z.

The Captain, as usual, had been aft with the Engineers conducting drills for two hours before lunch, then back for another session on the afternoon watch. Morales had rigged the Middle Level Ops Compartment for reduced electrical power four times since clearing away the remains of the noon meal and, consequently, was mildly aggravated. He had barely been able to finish his adobo and knew the repeated power interruptions would make the cooks late serving the evening meal to the oncoming watch. He was not especially concerned if members of the crew were displeased, but he knew the officers would be irritable if they were served late. He hurriedly rinsed the dishes from his meal, walked down the short passageway to the Exec's stateroom and knocked. "Sixteen forty-five, sir."

Craig reached over his head and turned on his bunk light. "Okay, Morales. Thanks. What's for dinner?"

"Hockey pucks." *Crap! Better to get the hockey pucks and lousy movies out of the way early in the patrol.*

Hockey pucks were a gastronomic insult. Somewhere a huge machine squeezes overage cows into endless tubes of meat, which are then sliced into discs and consigned to submarines, bones, gristle and all.

Later, as the patrol wore on, officers and crew alike would need something, almost anything, to look forward to. Still, hockey pucks were a hell of a way to start a day. Besides, Craig had not slept well. Every time the 1MC had blared "Rig for Reduced Electrical" or "Reactor Scram," he had come awake until he had heard enough to be sure it was a drill. Today the 1MC had been busy. If that weren't enough, with every "Rig for Reduced Electrical Power," the downshifted fans had robbed his stateroom of cooling ventilation. Four times he had kicked the covers off, sweating.

"Thrilling. Make sure I have a pair of red goggles when I come in. Okay?"

"Yes, sir."

Morales withdrew and returned to the Wardroom where he quickly cleared the table, replaced the green felt cloth with a white one that was only moderately stained, and commenced to set the table. As with all laundry done on the ship, the white cloth had recently been washed, but had not been ironed.

While the stewards were setting up the Wardroom for the evening meal, Craig showered and pulled on his poopysuit. Shaving could wait another day or two. Once on patrol, isolated from the outside world, most submarine crews relaxed grooming standards and allowed individualism to reign. Craig, as was the Exec's prerogative, endorsed that common sense policy. Throughout the crew, many of the men quickly sprouted beards and mustaches. Personally, his limit was to skip the unrewarding task of shaving for only a couple of days at a time. He had never been able to grow a good beard because of his sparse facial hair and, in reality, had never personally liked them.

Coming out of his stateroom, and seeing that the Captain had still not come forward from the Engineering Spaces, Craig decided on a quick visit to the

Control Room. He surmised the "fuckup" list for the day's drills must be unusually long, but didn't much care so long as he could remain uninvolved. He detested engineering drills as much as he enjoyed directing the ship's tactical systems and operations.

Craig, during moments of introspection, realized that his attitude toward engineering was an exaggerated dislike and that he was rebelling internally against his environment. After giving considerable thought to his feelings, he had decided that it probably meant that his ego was a problem in his ability to deal with the constant badgering the NUC's were forced to endure. He then decided pretty quickly that he really didn't give a damn and had never revisited the question. He considered Nuclear power and Rickover to be a pain in the ass and didn't propose to waste any effort trying to rationalize away his dislike of them.

Craig started up the ladder to Conn, still vaguely annoyed with his world. *You would think that the only reason we're out here is to run engineering drills. The Goddamned missiles are just here so the NUC's have something to push around.*

As he topped the ladder outside the Control Room, the Exec paused and turned, half entering the Sonar Room. The Sonar Supervisor was standing between the two-seated operators, both of whom were listening intently through their earphones. Both sonars, the BQS-4 and the BQR-7, were being trained back and forth over the same sector, waving the focused beams of their sensitive hearing like the antenna of a giant insect. Something had concentrated the watch party's interest.

"Got a contact?" he asked.

At the interruption, the Sonar Supervisor relaxed from his tense position hunched over the operators. "Well, yes and no, sir," he replied. "At 1320 we got more of those PDC's. They have been going off every fourteen seconds for the last three hours and we were just trying to narrow down the bearing to 'em."

"Distant?"

"Yes, sir...very weak. They must be a hydrographic survey, but I never heard so damned many. We had 'em on the last watch and, on the watch before that, they logged a hundred or so of 'em."

The Exec was not surprised. "Yeah, I know. That was just before I turned in. Those seemed to be down to the South. Where are these?"

"Well, sir, you know there's no way to get a good bearing on a PDC, but I'd say they're within plus or minus fifteen degrees of one nine zero true."

"No change in signal strength or interval?"

"No, sir."

"Okay…anything else?" *Time,* he thought, *to change the subject. I don't like these damned things. They don't fit any threat profile, but they sure as hell are peculiar. Nothing justifies a reaction…yet.*

"Naw, just one big assed tanker that scared the shit out of Mr. Rakowski when he came up for that NAVSAT pass right after lunch."

"Oh?"

"Yeah, you know how those big S.O.B.'s cargo of petroleum absorbs their engine noise when they are bow on. Besides, we had a real strong shallow layer and I guess when the scope broke water all he could see was wall-to-wall ship. He almost shit."

"We didn't go deep?"

"Naw, we were across his bow, fifteen hundred yards or so out and pulling clear so we just put on turns and let him pass astern."

The Exec stepped out of Sonar and, supporting himself with his arms, slid in one motion to the foot of the stairs. He made his way quickly to his seat in the wardroom and was standing behind his chair when, seconds later, the Captain entered. Sweat still hung in beads on the Captain's forehead and his poopysuit was blotched with perspiration. His hair was still wet, though he obviously had run a comb through it. He took his seat, and the Exec, along with the rest of the group, followed suit.

The stewards hovered watchfully in the pantry as the officers withdrew their napkins from the plastic rings. By ancient tradition…politics, religion and the ship's business were not to be discussed during meals.

The salads were small. The fresh lettuce the cooks had loaded on board at the last minute before the ship departed Rota was almost gone; the little that remained was already mostly brown and wilted. The carrots would last a few weeks longer, as would the fresh potatoes. After that, the only thing on the menu not canned, frozen or freeze-dried, would be eggs. By the time the crew returned to port, fresh produce would have a more urgent appeal than drink.

The hockey pucks arrived. The Captain had two, consumed them with obvious relish, then ordered seconds, all the while exclaiming about the marvels of the Navy's ration-dense foods. The other officers said little, chewed hard, and left the table early.

After the near ritual cup of coffee, the Captain and Exec walked together toward their staterooms. Halting just outside the doors, Craig announced, "Captain, I'm ready to relieve you."

"All right, XO."

"How did it go back aft?"

It was more than a courteous enquiry. Coupled with his growing concern about the PDC's, the Exec had other training issues on his mind. The last thing he wanted to deal with was a demand for more engineering training time than was already being scheduled.

"Terrible! Somehow we've got to figure out a way to do more training or we're not going to be ready for the ORSE."

"Captain, I don't know how we can schedule any more drills. We're making more noise now than we should."

Agitation crept into the Captain's voice, "XO, you just don't understand. Have you ever failed an ORSE?"

"No, sir."

"It's a terrible experience. I won't let that happen to this crew. If I let that happen, I'll have failed the trust placed in me."

Unable to think of an appropriate rejoinder, the Exec remained silent.

After a moment, the Captain continued. "Remember, I told you that when I was an Engineer I almost failed a Naval Reactors Precritical Inspection?"

"Yes, sir."

"And, remember, I told you then, when it was over, Admiral Rickover came over and talked directly to me. He said I was never to let him down again. He gave me another chance then, and I don't intend to break my word to him. Do you understand?"

"Captain, I do understand, but I don't think you should worry so much. The troops have probably slumped a little since the ORSE was canceled. Besides, rupturing the boot got us another full patrol of training we wouldn't have had otherwise."

"I think God knew we weren't ready for that ORSE, and this is His way of giving me another chance."

Craig hoped the flicker of surprise in his eyes went unnoticed in the semidarkness of the passageway. *The God and Rickover thing again.* It made him uncomfortable and he changed the subject quickly. "What do you have for turnover, sir?"

"Oh, no contacts of any concern. Our last NAVSAT pass was about three and a half hours ago. The Navigator said it checked with LORAN. You write the night orders tonight...pick out whatever satellite passes you think we need. We need a battery charge. Also, the bilges in the condensate bay are filthy. I want the watch section to get those cleaned up before tomorrow's drill period."

"Captain, I was going to suggest a WSRT for tomorrow morning. We also need to do some weapons casualty drills for the front end of the boat. We have the NTPI coming up next refit, too." The Nuclear Weapons Technical Proficiency Inspection bore the same relationship to the nuclear weapons that the ORSE did to the propulsion plant. Failing either would keep the crew from taking the ship on patrol.

Holcomb reluctantly agreed. "I guess we'd better do the WSRT since we haven't done one this week, but I want to hold off on the other weapons drills."

"Aye, aye, sir, but we have a long way to go to be ready for the NTPI."

"XO, first things first. What is Admiral Rickover going to say if we have a bad ORSE? Will it be that we haven't done enough training on this patrol? I'd have to be honest with him and tell him in my letter that I don't think our Engineers are as good as they should be. Then I'd have to tell him I didn't do enough about it. Now, I don't want anything to interfere with Engineering training until I'm satisfied we can do what's expected of us. Of me! Do you understand?"

"Aye, aye, Captain."

There was no point in continuing. The Captain's emotions were rising and the Exec had no relish for a useless confrontation. Weapons drills were a major pain in the ass, anyway.

"Captain, you didn't mention the PDC's. What do you think about them?"

"Nothing. Hydrographic operations. There's nothing unusual about PDC's. Every boat hears them on patrol in here. Why do you ask?"

"Before now, what's the most you have ever heard at one time, sir?"

"I don't know. A few. A few dozen, I guess."

"At what interval?"

The Captain was now plainly exasperated. "How do I know? Sometimes close together, sometimes spread out. What difference does it make?"

"We've had them continuously for nearly nine hours at precise fourteen second intervals. I just wondered if you had ever encountered anything like that before?"

Holcomb stared at his Exec, but made no reply for almost a full minute. "No."

Nothing more to be gained, the Exec broke off the conversation by formally completing their change of the watch.

"I relieve you of the Command Duty, sir. Goodnight."

Craig left and returned to the Wardroom for his coffee mug. Now chipped and battered, it had been a present from his young daughter three patrols earlier. He filled it, savoring a twinge of slightly malicious satisfaction. Something had flared in the Old Man's expression when he had poked him about the PDC's. Alarm? Certainly. The Old Man was no ship driver. He was not self confident in the operational world of tactics, sensors and intelligence. A little fear of the unknown was bound to creep in, like a child's fear of night noises. *He's scared shitless of HGR and the ORSE, so let him sweat the PDC's too for a while.*

In fact, the Exec couldn't suppress his own malaise regarding the PDC's. Unlike things that go bang in the night when you are a child, noises in the sea that you don't understand are best avoided by the prudent submariner. They were probably nothing more than seismic hydrographic operations somewhere near the African coast. The sea plays strange tricks with sound and, due to its curving propagation paths, one could only be sure that the sounds were NOT emanating from their apparent point of origin. They could be bouncing in from anywhere. Still, he was wary and curious about their persistence and regularity, particularly the fixed fourteen-second intervals. As of now, he was fretful, but not yet alarmed.

* * * * *

The next few days passed in a deepening routine of daily engineering drills and nightly housekeeping chores with, at all times, a background of distant PDC's. Like an aimlessly grazing pachyderm, the *Marion* wandered to and fro within her assigned operating areas, randomness of direction and behavior enforced by a pair of dice rolled by the Officer of the Deck. The routine achieved the essence of tranquility despite the alarms and shrill 1MC announcements that accompanied each day's ration of pseudo catastrophes.

Reactor scrams, major steam leaks, fire and flooding, radioactive spills and a host of other casualties, large and small, but all aft, became the fabric of habit. As they are want to do, a few things broke. Most notably, a hydraulic leak on the lead accumulator visited great frustration upon the upper level engine room watch. Less than an hour after the Captain had finally pronounced his satisfaction with the area's cleanliness, the accumulator's tail rod seal let go and deluged one side of the shaft alley with hydraulic oil.

On another occasion, a small electrical fire in the controller to number one main feed pump interrupted one of the innumerable "Low Level in the Steam Generator" drills and earned the gratitude of the entire ship's company by securing drills for the day. Even the electricians called out to replace the welded contacts did not grumble.

Placidly though the patrol was progressing, not everyone was content. The Weapons Officer kept pestering the Exec to schedule weapon casualty drills. The Exec, in turn, kept referring him to the Captain, who kept vetoing weapons drills in favor of Engineering training. Joe Wolfman, an ambitious young man, was rapidly becoming very frustrated. He correctly believed they were not doing enough to prepare for the next refit's NTPI and foresaw a most unenviable experience at the hands of the inspectors. Joe was a meticulous administrator, who knew he had nothing to fear from the inspector's perfectionist standards, except the simulated casualties that would surely test the crew's training. And, he knew the Exec was well aware of his training needs. He also knew the Captain knew it. He couldn't understand why his pleas for training were being shunted aside. The Exec knew why, but there seemed to be little he could do to change the Old Man's position.

More often than not the damned PDC's were still there, always distant and at fourteen second intervals. By now, the Exec and the Sonarmen acknowledged that they didn't understand the source of the explosions. They had gone on far too long and Craig was, by now, distinctly uneasy. Tactically, the Captain should also have been increasingly wary, but he apparently remained indifferent to the world outside the ship, remaining focused on engineering training.

Daily, the Exec fretted and, daily Holcomb refused to give up his training schedule for the NUCS. In the Exec's opinion, the *Marion* was simply settled into too fixed a routine. They were making too much noise, creating too many "observables," and always at the same time every day. It raised Craig's hackles more than a little. He had always been a hunter and, knowing how he would go about stalking a Russian SSBN, he didn't like indulging in the same habit dominated behavior that he would seek to exploit in his quarry. Joe would have to wait. The Exec wasn't about to piggyback any more noisy drills on top of the ones they were already conducting.

Craig wasn't alone in wondering about the PDC's. The Sonarmen, of course, listened to them watch in, watch out. They and the other members of the ship control party, for whom the Control Room sonar speakers provided a background drumbeat, were beginning to wonder aloud and compare notes off watch. As a result, most of the crew was also now aware of them. To most of the sailors they were a curiosity. To a few, they were already slightly sinister. There was continuous speculation from one end of the ship to the other as to their source.

One afternoon, the Exec was up earlier than usual, and came up unseen behind the Navigator and Chief Brown. The two were chatting in the front end of the Navigation Center, the Chief sitting on the Type 11 periscope platform. Brown was a grizzled old wise-ass, who had spent three years as a Border Patrolman between his first and second hitches in the Navy. Nights and a gunfight or two on the West Texas Border had made him more mature than most of his peers in many ways. He was asking the Navigator about the PDC's because he was slightly spooked.

"What do you think about all those PDC's, sir?"

"I dunno, Chief. We've heard a bunch of 'em."

"I was talking to the Chief Sonarman. He says the oil companies use explosives for seismographic exploration. I don't think that's what these are though. Too many."

"You may be right, Chief, what do you think they are?"

"I don't know. What do the Captain and the XO think?"

The Navigator waited while the Navigation Control Console printer chattered out a short printout.

"The Captain doesn't think they are anything to be concerned about. The XO seems to be pretty interested in them."

"You know what I think?"

"No, Chief. What do you think?"

"I think I don't know who's setting those fuckers off, or even if they really are explosions. I think we ought to knock off these damn drills and go find us another patch of ocean."

The Navigator laughed. "I'll pass your tactical advice on to the Captain."

Brown snorted. They both laughed, then spotted the Exec. The Chief jumped up and took great interest in the recent printout.

Brown's right. And, if he's affected, how many others in the crew are getting worried and a little scared?

24
The Poker Game

Saturday brought Field Day, as it would every week of the patrol. It was also the fifteenth day of the patrol and from 0800Z to 1600Z, all hands were turned out for a full day of deep cleaning, followed by the Captain's inspection of a selected area of the ship. With good reason, cleanliness is a fetish of the American submariner, and the Field Day is the traditional supplement to routine daily cleaning. The end of Field Day marked the beginning of the "weekend" with ship's work to recommence on the Monday morning watch.

A group of officers had gathered in the wardroom. There was not enough time between the end of Field Day, during which they were expected to be about the ship policing their assigned spaces, and evening meal to allow for any real activity. One by one, they had drifted to the wardroom for a few minutes of idle gossip. The Exec came in just as Morales started rattling pots and pans in the pantry, a not so subtle signal that he wanted to set the table for dinner.

Stone looked up from the cover-less, ancient girlie magazine he was studying. "Hey, XO, Rak wants to get up a wardroom poker game tonight, what do you think?"

"I thought the Captain wanted to see that spaghetti western he was talking about at lunch."

"We could run that as soon as the stewards clear the table and have the game going by 2100."

"I dunno, Stone, you and Rak got five?"

Rakowski chipped in, "We got the Navigator, Joe, Doc and me. If you play, that's five. Maybe the Captain would like to play too. If he does, we can skip the flick."

The Exec paused. He didn't want to appear too eager. Although he relished the game above all others, after the remarks about God and the ORSE, he wondered just what the Captain's religious feelings were about a game of chance. Some questions were best avoided, he thought. But, temptation won. "Sounds good to me. I'm not very good, but if you'll go slow, I'll play. We'll sound the Captain out at dinner. Now, all you guys haul ass so Morales will stop playing his Goddamned kettle drums."

A few minutes later, as he was washing up at the pullman sink in his stateroom, the Exec heard the Captain's voice. Holcomb was halfway down the short passageway to the wardroom, leaning against the doorway to the Engineer's room. The Engineer, a chronically fatigued and congenitally demoralized chain smoker, had nodded off to sleep at his desk, cigarette still smoldering in his ashtray. The Captain had chosen to inspect the Auxiliary Machinery Space this day and was obviously certain of the Engineer's urgent interest in his verdict. As the Engineer struggled to focus his eyes and mind, the exchange deteriorated rapidly. While the Exec watched, the Captain stiffened, turned abruptly and strode toward his stateroom, mustache aquiver.

Seeing him, the Captain stopped and snapped. "See that the Engineer gets more rest. He's of no use in his present condition."

By then the Exec had managed a blank expression. "What's the matter, Captain? Eng is getting as much rest as anybody, at least he has as much opportunity as anyone else."

"He can't be!"

"Captain, what happened?"

"I just stopped and told him I had inspected the Auxiliary Machinery Space and that there was verdigris behind the Number One MG set, that the riggers had left a snatch block in the bilge and some screws were missing from the feed pump nameplates." Voice rising, "Do you know what he said to me?"

"No, sir." Craig was struggling now to maintain his composure.

"He said he would see that all the greasy snatches got screwed at once!"

Hysteria threatened to overwhelm Craig. "Captain, I wouldn't get so upset. Sometimes Eng is kinda drifty when he first wakes up. I'll bet that right now he doesn't know what either of you said. Besides, you know he wouldn't talk that way to you. He was the Protestant Lay Leader before you got here."

The Captain's color began returning to normal.

"You're right, XO, it wasn't very Christian of me to make a snap judgment about that young man. He works awfully hard, doesn't he?"

"Yes, sir, he sure does."

With that, the Captain was gone.

The Exec waited until he heard the Old Man's sink clank down, then walked to the Engineer's stateroom.

The Engineer still sat staring at the doorway with an expression of mild shock as he fumbled for a fresh cigarette.

"Reveille, Eng!"

"What the hell happened, XO?"

"I'd say the inner man spoke, in a not altogether unknown tongue."

"What the hell do you mean?"

"Tain't nice to get obscene with the Old Man face to face."

Color drained from the Engineer's face.

"Pump name plates! I bet that's the only one you missed. Are you sure you didn't tell him to get pumped, too? You're a Goddamned wonder of interpersonal communications when you first wake up, you know!"

"Fuck you, XO!"

Craig withdrew and walked to the wardroom chuckling. The Eng was a good man who tried to do too much himself and was far too serious, but still a good man. The teasing had let him know what had happened and that his Exec didn't take it too seriously. Craig was sure it wouldn't happen again.

The evening meal passed quickly. It was a New England boiled dinner, corned beef and cabbage done to a Navy recipe guaranteed to eliminate all identifiable flavor. Fortunately, enough real vanilla ice cream was left in the frozen stores to dress the cook's apple pie. Dessert rescued the meal.

Over coffee, the Captain called for the movie list. Stone, whose traditional seat as Supply Officer was at the end of the table opposite the Captain, extracted the sheet from the projector locker behind his head and passed it down the table.

Handing the movie list to the Captain, Craig ventured, "Captain, several of us enjoy a game of cards now and then, and we wondered if you'd like to skip the movie this evening and join us in a game?"

Rearing back in his chair, the Captain tossed the movie list onto the nearby counter. "Great!" he exclaimed. "Some of these movies aren't worth watching anyway. What are we going to play?"

"Well, we all kinda wanted to get a wardroom poker game going. You know, play once a week or so and keep track of wins and losses in a book. Settle up at the end of patrol."

The Captain stiffened, his face reddening as he slammed forward in his chair. He said nothing for several moments, obviously controlling his emotions.

The rest of the officers waited silently.

Finally, Craig decided that he had better break the silence. "Captain, if you want to play something else…"

"XO, gambling is a sin! God has forbidden it since lots were cast for Christ's garments. I'll have no part of it."

Oh, shit! Now how do I recover? Keep it calm. "I understand, sir. We don't all share your religious convictions, but this is your war canoe and we'll respect your wishes." *I hope to hell he doesn't find out about the crew's game!* The troops would be less compliant and more resentful.

"No, it is my duty to help you see the right way, God's way, but I have no right to force it on you. You may have your game, but I'll have no part in it, and you are definitely not to play on the Sabbath!"

With all the sincerity he could muster, Craig went on. "I appreciate your letting us play, Captain. I also appreciate the difficulty you had in making your decision. I hate to press the point, but could we settle for not playing during church services instead of all day Sunday?"

"Why?" Sweat began to bead on the Captain's forehead. He was looking at Craig as though he might have beheld the devil. This was now very serious. A real schism threatened between Holcomb and his officers. It was time for diplomacy.

As had happened before, the Exec grasped for a face-saving argument. "Because Sunday is whenever we set our clocks. By what time zone do we reckon the Sabbath? In another couple of weeks we'll be so far east that local Sunday will be here at our dinner time on Saturday."

Craig's real motivation now was to secure a longer game. He was, unknown to the others, a dedicated and experienced poker player. He was patient at the table and distrusted short games. Given enough time to play, he knew skill inevitably won over luck. Short games were for gamblers, and he was not a gambler.

Cynically, Craig wondered to himself what Holcomb would think if he knew why he attached such importance to the game. Craig, in his most fundamental being, was a hunter, a predator and needed exercise. The poker table was his field. He maintained an earnest, innocent expression and waited for the Captain's reply.

It came quickly. "All right, the wardroom is yours from dinner on Saturday until breakfast on Sunday. Keep your games out of my sight." With that, he jerked himself erect and left the small room.

The Navigator was the first to break the uneasy silence. "Do you think you should have gone that far, XO?" he asked.

In retrospect, Craig regretted that he hadn't sounded the Captain out in private. The exchange had been an embarrassing one for the Old Man, and he had kept after him when he should have eased off. Yet, there had been no way to foresee his reaction. All he replied to the waiting players was, "In for a penny, in for a pound. Let's clear the table and get the green tablecloth on."

A few moments later, as the cards and chips were being found and brought out, the Exec turned to the Navigator, who was searching for a notebook in which to record the "bank."

"Gator, I'm going up and write the Night Orders while you finish setting up. I'm going to direct that we log everything we can observe about those damned PDC's, how many, when they start, stop, bearings if we can get them, whether other contacts interfere, what we're doing when we hear them—in short, everything. Next time you go up, make sure the Quartermasters and Sonarmen have the picture, okay?"

"Yes, sir. How much do you want to start with?"

"Count me out fifty, okay?"

The poker game lasted until 0230Z, with a half hour break for mid-rations. The Exec bumbled along, hand after hand, and Rak caught him twice in poorly executed bluffs. It came as a surprise to all when the chips were counted and he had, on balance, won a few dollars. Rak considered the game's future with a good deal of secret satisfaction. Tonight he had been the big winner and he saw no real competitor. The Exec was satisfied as well. He liked to think of the clumsy bluffs as an investment in the future.

The next day passed quietly. On Monday, the Captain was up at 0600Z, as usual, and waited over his coffee for the Exec to brief him on the events of the night's watch.

When Craig came into the wardroom, he was still wearing a foul weather jacket he had donned during the early morning hours. In the quiet of the midwatch, the crew's activity was nil and the air-conditioning always got a little ahead of the heat load. At such times, he slipped into his foul weather jacket in preference to the generally more popular G.I. sweater.

Usually, the Captain's interest in the operational events of the previous twelve hours was perfunctory, his mind already on his day's plan for training and inspecting the NUCS. But today was different. He didn't smile when he said, "Good morning, XO." Maybe it had been a real bad drill session. Maybe he was having a rash of "imperfect thoughts" and needed to catch up on his sleep. Maybe the PDC's were beginning to bug him too.

The Exec soon found out. It was the PDC's.

"Good morning, Captain. Ready for the new week?"

"XO, never mind the usual stuff. Saturday night you put a long entry in my night orders about PDC's. Yesterday, during my watch, they were there all day. I've been up and looked at our track over the last twelve hours and you moved nearly a hundred miles. You did several radical baffle-clearing maneuvers. The PDC's were there all the time. They still are. What's going on?"

"Captain, I honestly don't know. What I don't understand, I worry about. I don't even know that these noises are explosives. All I know is, they've been with us while we've moved this canoe over six hundred miles. They're always the same and there's never a platform we can correlate to them. They always seem to be to the South, but the beach has only been fifty to one hundred fifty miles away in that direction. That means, at least I think it means, that they have to be moving with us. Last night I tried to determine if they are really an external noise and if so, are they moving with us. Both seem to be the case. Maybe it's coincidence. I don't know, but I also don't like it. There's absolutely nothing in the intelligence summaries to help sort it out either."

The Captain shivered. "Do you think it's some kind of new sensor Ivan is using against us? Is he trailing us?"

"I don't know. But, there's no reason to overreact, we just have to collect all the data we can and keep trying to figure it out. Anyway, the PDC's are so weak they couldn't possibly return a usable echo off of us."

The Captain relaxed slightly. "That's right. Okay, I want to move up to the northeastern corner of our area today and get closer to the shipping lanes. The shipping noise will help mask our snorkeling during drills."

"Yes, sir. The only other thing for the day is a couple of messages in radio. Somebody must have screwed up. There are a couple of early supercessions of crypto material that the Communicator should take care of today. Also, I'd like to run a WSRT right after dinner. HOV1 was a little sticky last night, so I think we should confirm satisfactory hovering. We don't want to accumulate unnecessary down time."

"Right. Goodnight, XO."

The Weapon System Readiness Test did not go particularly well. The valve, HOV1, cycled satisfactorily, opening and closing as the hovering system sighed water in and out, neutralizing the accelerations that would have carried the ship away from its ordered depth. Missile number eleven, however, stubbornly failed to spin up properly and required a change out of its guidance electronics.

* * * * *

On Wednesday, Morales gave the Exec his usual wake-up call. As consciousness dawned on Craig, so did the realization that he had slept without interruption since turning in that morning.

"Morales," he asked, "didn't we have any drills today?"

"No, sir."

"How come? Where's the CO?"

"Dunno. He's been in his stateroom all day with the door shut."

Craig swung out of bed, dressed hurriedly, and trotted to the Engineer's stateroom. The Engineer sat at his desk reviewing the ever-present stack of logs and records.

"Eng, how come no drills? Something broke?"

The Engineer looked up and shrugged. "No, the Captain called back aft and told Rak to tell me he was canceling all training until further notice. I came up forward and the Captain's door was shut. Joe had the deck. He said the CO called and told him the same thing."

"No explanation?"

"Nothing!"

Whatever his reasons, Craig was relieved that the Captain had finally stopped the damned noisy drills. As much as he was relieved at Holcomb's decision to restrict training, the Engineers were even more ferverently grateful for the respite.

But, why the withdrawal to his stateroom? The Old Man was not normally reclusive. If he were ill, the Exec needed to know about it, though he had no idea how he would deal with that scenario, given Holcomb's Christian Science beliefs.

He didn't have long to wait for the answers.

25
Strange Encounter

When the curious Exec knocked on the Captain's door at 1745Z and reported that he was ready to relieve him of the Command Duty, the Old Man was slow to respond. To Craig's surprise, when the door opened, Holcomb seemed wide-awake, but agitated.

"XO, come in and close the door."

"Yes, sir. What's up?"

"The PDC's. We're being tracked somehow, and I have been playing right into their hands. Don't you see?"

I can't tell if he's about to cry or throw up. It's obvious he has been agonizing all night over our tactical blunders. "Captain, you know I have been worried about that for days now, but you didn't want to scale back the training."

"What do you think we should do? Can we lose him? If we can't break contact, should we transmit a SITREP?"

He's more scared than I thought. Christ, he wants to break radio silence and send a situation report to CINCLANT!

Apparently, when he finally recognized that the PDC's were not something to ignore, fear and self-recrimination had begun to overcome Holcomb. The Exec's immediate goal was to calm him. "Captain, I don't think we should jump to any conclusions. As you know, I agree that it looks like the PDC's are staying with us somehow. But we don't know that conclusively. This may be nothing at all but some weird coincidence."

The Captain was not mollified. "I don't believe that, and neither do you."

Craig replied. "Look. Whoever it is, if they are holding contact on us, they don't seem to want to hurt us anymore than one of our SSN's would, for no reason, shoot one of their SSBN's. The real threat is to our mission. If they can detect and trail us, the whole FBM force is vulnerable to preemption. I think we should just go ahead and make our patrol, but do it the way a good stealthy submarine does. We shouldn't alarm the crew or anyone else. Let's just be cool and collect all the intelligence data we can."

Holcomb visibly relaxed. "All right, XO. I guess that makes sense." Then, something in his eyes flared again. "But what if every FBM on patrol is hearing PDC's right now? Maybe we should go up and transmit a warning to CINCLANT."

Craig was adamant. "I don't think so, Captain. We don't even know for sure that we have a problem. It could be just a weird combination of sonar conditions, innocent survey ops and our own imaginations getting out of hand. I don't think we should panic either. We would look pretty stupid if we started a full blown fire drill at CINCLANT over what in reality may be nothing."

Holcomb wasn't completely reassured, but to the Exec's immense relief, he left it at that. After formally assuming the command duty, Craig went off to the Control Room, took a seat on the periscope stand and began to try to figure out his next move. Step number one had to be simply to do nothing foolish.

By now, all hands were aware of the PDC's and, although no explanation was offered, to a man they assumed the increased caution to be a reaction to their threatening presence. They were right. The Captain had always let the Exec do whatever he pleased tactically, but now he demanded some clever evasive maneuver every day. Most of the time the Exec's response didn't include anything drastic. He just started operating like a wily submarine should.

For the next twenty-four hours the Exec directed the *Marion* to do nothing markedly different from her previous behavior other than to become even more predictable. She continued to move east at four knots. The Exec made sure that course changes looked random, but, in fact, never took them very far from a predictably eastern movement. They took a few extra NAVSAT passes and flushed the Trash Disposal Unit once a watch. In general they tried to act like a moderately cautious, unsuspecting FBM intent on going from Point A to Point B. At the end of twenty-four hours, the Exec ordered the ship rigged for ULTRA QUIET and took them off to the northwest at six knots for eighteen hours. During that time, he eliminated all observables that he could. No NAVSAT passes, no housekeeping, no fathometer. At the end of the run he reversed course, ran fast down his back track for thirty minutes, then came to all stop, drifting and listening. Nothing. Absolutely nothing except some distant merchant traffic. Not even one PDC.

An hour or so later, having detected nothing suspicious, the Exec acceded to the Navigator's request for a NAVSAT pass to verify the loran data feeding the SINS, then set a wandering track back to the east. He believed there was little possibility that a trailer could have followed them through his de-lousing maneuvers without being counter detected.

The Captain was ecstatic to be rid of the PDC's, but agreed with Craig's caution not to resume training for a few days. Both felt, at that point, that somehow the PDC's were tactically connected with the *Marion*. At the end of the day, when he turned over the watch to the Captain and turned in, Craig was looking forward to the good rest that accompanies relaxed tension.

It was a short respite. On the patrol's nineteenth day, a little before 1400Z, the messenger woke him. "XO, the Captain wants you on the Conn. Right away!"

As he came awake, Craig could hear a strange reedy, warbling electronic tone. He jumped up and grabbed for his poopysuit. The tones sounded like frequency modulated echo ranging and he was hearing it directly through the hull. Whatever it was, the source had to be right on top of them to produce such a high sound level.

He ran into the Control Room, still buckling his belt. The Captain, the Navigator and the Weapons Officer stood in a circle around the MK 19 Plotter. Rak had the Officer of the Deck watch. He was on the periscope stand, looking at the group, waiting for instructions. Craig could see that the Captain was shaken to the point of trembling.

"This started about five minutes ago, XO. Do you know what kind of echo ranging this is?"

"No, sir. It sounds like its frequency modulated. I've heard some research and development FM stuff a little like it, but nobody I know has anything in service like this. Do you hold any contact on the platform?"

The Navigator spoke, "No, nothing. Do you think this is British?"

"No, they use frequency shift keying in long pulses. This sounds like a continuous frequency modulated tone. How much bearing change since initial detection?"

The Captain spoke up, "None. Zero bearing rate."

That meant to Craig that the source was on a collision course with the *Marion*. No time for niceties. In a loud firm voice he said, "Captain, let's maneuver. NOW!"

"Take the Conn, XO."

"Yes, sir. Rak, come right with full rudder and point the source of this noise."

Rak repeated back the Exec's order and the ship started to swing.

"Rak, get a radioman into the trunk and haul the wire in to short stay." The floating wire antenna would break off at around eight knots if it were left fully extended. One had already been lost and, with only three remaining, the Exec didn't want to risk another if he had to maneuver radically.

The Captain jerked around at that.

"XO, that'll make too much noise!"

"Captain, if this thing has us, it's an active contact. He couldn't give a shit about our signature. He's deafening us and himself. We've lost one wire already. We can't afford to throw this one away."

The ship had come around now so it was pointing toward the sound source.

After a long two minutes, Craig pushed the 31MC press-to-talk switch and asked. "Sonar—Conn, What's the bearing rate now?"

The answer came back after a short delay.

"Zero bearing rate."

"Rak, station the Fire Control and Sonar Tracking Party." If this was going to be a full dress melee, Craig wanted all the plots manned. Word had already flashed through the ship that something was happening, so the 1MC announcement was still in the air as the first of the troops rushed in to the Control Room and started manning phones and otherwise rigging their stations.

"Rak, come right 90 degrees and get a new bearing rate. Our last course change should have changed the geometry and the bearing rate should have changed…a lot…if he's close."

Nothing happened. Is this guy maneuvering with us?

After the course change, bearing rate again stayed zero.

Once more to be sure.

"Rak, go back to the left 180 degrees. Increase speed to eight knots." The wire was in to short stay now. No worry about breaking it if they increased speed. Craig knew it was in because the grinding of the hydraulic line wiper had stopped. When the ship had come around and steadied on the new course, if bearing rate was still zero, his growing suspicion would be confirmed. Sure enough, the answer after the course change was, "Zero bearing rate."

"Secure the Fire Control Party. This guy is way the hell out."

"Aye, aye, XO."

Craig turned to the Captain. "Captain, I don't know what the hell this is, but it isn't close. If we calculated a range from the bearing rate change through these maneuvers it would be infinite. This is an incredible signal strength for a long range contact."

"What do you think we should do, XO? I think we should transmit a situation report."

"No, sir. We have no reason to feel threatened. We don't know he has made contact. I'm sure you can hear this Goddamned thing from Malta to Gibraltar. Let's just tape it and make tracks east to see if we can triangulate the source."

"Well, I think..." He was wavering.

"Captain, we can't afford to break radio silence without a good reason. We'd look panicky if we transmitted over this. What would we say other than that we hear a loud noise?"

"Okay."

Craig went into Sonar. The wavering tone from the speaker drowned out everything else. The Chief was already annotating an intelligence tape recording of the sound.

"Chief, what's the signal to noise ratio of this thing?"

"XO, it's unbelievable. It came on at ninety db above background just like somebody turned on a light. That's what it still is."

"Any intelligence spots that correspond to the bearing?"

"No, sir. Nothing. This ain't like any sonar I ever heard of either."

"Keep looking for a platform. Power output like that ain't coming from a pair of dry cells. Cut two or three backup tapes on this thing. I want one we can listen to later and at least one other to make sure it's a clear recording for NISC to evaluate. Somebody has got to know what the hell this is."

The Naval Intelligence Scientific Center had the best-equipped and most talented sonar analysts in the world. If they couldn't identify the mysterious signal, the whole U.S. intelligence community would be baffled.

With that, he went back to Conn.

"Rak, I want you to keep on this course, 105 degrees. Run as fast as you can at one hundred feet without losing the communications signal. I want to cover as much ground as we can before that emitter shuts down."

"Right, XO."

An hour and seven minutes later, the tone abruptly stopped. By that time the bearings had crossed repeatedly through an area forty-five to fifty nautical miles southeast of the *Marion* on a center bearing of 163 degrees true.

What the hell kind of a sound source could produce a sound pressure level of 90 db forty-five miles away?

One thing was sure. As soon as the emitter shut down, the Exec was going to change what *Marion* was doing. "Rak, come right to 180 degrees true-due south. Slow to one third. Put the wire back out and get as deep as you can."

"Aye, aye, XO, but won't that take us right down on him?"

"If he's harmless, it won't make any difference. If it's Ivan and he had active contact, he should be coming up to intercept us. If that's true, let's sneak down that way and maybe we'll hear him go by."

"Going after him, huh?"

"Nope, just doing the thing I think he'll least expect. Run south for three hours, then turn east to 080 and slow to minimum turns. No housekeeping. No trips to periscope depth, okay?"

Craig went down and briefed the Captain on the instructions he had given the OOD. Holcomb had regained his composure, but had nothing to add to the tactical plan.

"Captain, this is a hell of a coincidence. I didn't like those PDC's and I like this less."

"I know, XO, I know. I don't know how they are doing it, but we're being tracked. Don't you agree?"

"I don't think we have enough evidence to conclude anything except that something is going on and we have to be damned careful. I don't like these things, but they may be harmless. We don't know anything for sure yet and we shouldn't let ourselves get spooked."

Excusing himself from the Captain, Craig went back up to Sonar and listened to the tapes again with Franzei and the Chief. The tapes were of excellent quality, but they couldn't dig anything out of them except the incredible FM signal. There was absolutely no platform noise, either narrow band or broadband, that they could detect. At least they knew that the tapes were good enough data for the spooks to analyze. Everyone present in Sonar that day would have felt a lot better if there had been something, anything, in the background that might have correlated to a platform.

Satisfied that he had done all he could for the moment and that the Captain was well briefed on the tactical plan, Craig went back to bed. Sleep came, but not easily, as the adrenalin slowly washed out of his system. Four hours and a bit later the messenger rousted him out again. Echo ranging to the northeast.

As a precaution, he hadn't undressed and so got to Conn pretty quickly. The Weapons Officer had relieved Rak as Officer of the Deck.

"Joe, where's the echo ranging?"

"We don't hold it any longer. Sonar picked up a half dozen seven kilohertz pings up the northeast. They were very weak. We don't hold any platform noise up there either."

Craig exultantly slapped the OOD's desk with his fist. "The son of a bitch! The only thing that carries seven KHZ is an Echo-II Russian SSGN. We finally out-foxed the bastard."

"The intelligence summaries do put an Echo-II in the Med."

"Yeah, I know. Go up to six knots. Let's move out of here. Report everything to the CO. I'm going to Radio."

The second message he flipped over in the stack of recently received traffic brought him up short. It was an intelligence spot, inexplicably delayed for several hours. A P-3-C out of Sigonella, on the daily nose count flight around the Med, had spotted two Russian AGORs, ocean research ships. One was reportedly towing an unidentified cable astern. He hurried out to the chart table to plot the reported location. Rak had finished his routine post watch tour of the ship and was passing through the Control Room on his way to his stateroom. Craig called to him as he came through the door.

"Look here."

Rak raised his eyebrows and whistled. "Well, I'll be fucked!"

"Yeah. At 1008 the *LEBEDEV* and the *VAVILOV* were within five nautical miles of where, about two hours later, at 1215, we triangulated that noise source."

"So they were the emitter?"

"Sure as hell looks like it. They were operating together, but only one appeared to be towing some kind of array."

"Could they have detected us, XO?"

"Beats the hell out of me. Let's don't spook though, because it seems a lot more likely that we just blundered into hearing range of some sort of oceanographic research experiment."

"Then what about the ECHO-II?"

"More coincidence? Maybe he was working with the AGORs, providing services to them. We're probably the peeping Tom at their party."

Rak grunted in an unconvinced tone and turned back to the periscope stand to report to the OOD "Conditions Normal" on his tour of the ship. Craig went below to show the Captain the Intell Spot. As he expected, the Captain was intensely interested and, as they talked, Holcomb homed in on the AGORs characteristics.

"XO, what type hulls do the *LEBEDEV* and *VAVILOV* have?"

"I'd characterize them as extraordinarily big trawlers. They gross about three thousand tons, but they look like trawlers and have single screw diesel propulsion like trawlers."

"So they sound like trawlers?"

"Probably can't tell the difference." *A true statement, but a bad answer given the Captain's state of mind.*

There was a definite note of despair in Holcomb's voice as he responded. "We've had an awful lot of sonar contacts reported as trawlers."

"Yes, sir. That's typical in here." *I know what he's thinking.*

"We're reconstructing the *LEBEDEV* and *VAVILOV's* movements from INTSUM's since they entered the Med. They came in a few days after we did. They were in that group of INCHOPPERS west of the UK when we left Rota. I doubt that we'll find any correlation between their movement and ours."

Craig was right. The plot showed no apparent correlation between the movements of the *Marion* and the two Soviet ships.

* * * * *

The next day the officers had just sat down to evening meal when the messenger came into the Wardroom.

"Captain. XO. Sirs, the OOD sends his respects and reports we hold distant PDC's to the north this time."

The Captain's fork froze over his plate. "Very well," he said, then quickly put his fork down and left the table.

The Exec muttered, "Oh shit," and reached for his napkin ring.

A murmur of comment ran around the table before the stewards interrupted with the serving trays. No one had much to say. It was like the return of a nagging headache after the aspirin wears off.

After dinner Craig found the COB and he reported a similar reaction from the crew. Everyone, officers and crew alike, were getting Goddamned tired of the PDC's.

* * * * *

The weather worsened. The Med showed its fickle ability to raise a high sea in no time flat. All night and into the next day, seas ran State Four and Five from the northeast. State Four was like a typical northeaster during the winter, State Five more severe and so on. It took seven tries to get the three BRN passes the Navigator needed to maintain the SINS reset calculation. For some reason, Loran C seemed a little unstable and, when they finally got the NAVSAT fixes, they confirmed that Loran C was showing a slightly varying offset of a quarter of a mile or so. Every time the ship came up to periscope depth they were thrown around by the high seas. Twice, the *Marion* broached briefly as the crew cursed and lunged to grab hold of loose gear.

The BRN was still quirky, as it had been all patrol. Over the patrol to date, they were only averaging a bit over seventy per cent success rate on attempted NAVSAT passes. Although everything in the system repeatedly checked out perfectly, the BRN just wasn't performing satisfactorily. The Exec and the Navigator both suspected the problem to be the preamplifier mounted outside the hull in the antenna's hydraulic mast, but there was no way to verify that at sea or, for that matter, to effect repairs.

All the time, even during the worst hours, when seas raged to the State Six of a full storm, the PDC's kept banging away, faint to the northeast, every fourteen seconds.

The Exec was left mystified. *What the fuck? Who the hell could be throwing hand grenades over the side every fourteen seconds in this kind of weather?*

26
Murphy's Second Law

Contrary to Murphy's Second Law, the Number One oxygen generator displayed unusual consideration by waiting for the seas to abate before lending its moment of excitement to the patrol. Basically an oxygen generator is a number of closely packed vertical chambers in which seawater under great pressure is electrolyticly decomposed into gaseous hydrogen and oxygen. The mixture of the two gasses is, of course, highly explosive. After separation, a leakage of the hydrogen gas can quickly lead to a hydrogen concentration in and around the machines' enclosure that turns it into a devastating bomb, needing only a single spark to trigger it. Sparks are readily available from any electrical fault in the "Rube Goldberg" complex of pumps and electrodes that comprise the machine. Of all the equipment on board a submarine, O2 generators are probably the scariest examples of an accident waiting to happen.

It was the twentieth patrol day and the Engineer was on watch as OOD. At 0940Z the Exec was awakened by the General Alarm, followed immediately by the announcement that the smoking lamp was out throughout the ship. As he struggled to get dressed, he felt the deck tilt as the ship started up toward the surface. Shortly, there came the announcement "All hands stand clear of AMR-1. There is a hydrogen leak on the Number One 02 generator."

By the time Craig got to the Control Room, the crisis was just about over. The Captain was already there. The ship was at one hundred twenty feet keel depth and the reports from Sonar were coming in that the baffles were clear, no noise contacts. On the way up to periscope depth the Engineer passed the word to "Prepare to Emergency Ventilate AMR Number One" as he and the Captain took stock of the situation. The Auxiliaryman on watch had been alert and quick to shut down the 02 generator.

So far, so good.

The ships' installed atmosphere analyzer system showed normally low hydrogen levels in all compartments, so the Captain and the Engineer chose to be deliberate in their next steps. Backing up the installed atmosphere monitoring system with portable sniffer readings, to insure that the high hydrogen concentration was trapped within the oxygen generator's enclosing cover, they raised the snorkel mask while deep enough to avoid breaking the surface. Then they completed all preparations to force ventilate the area around the threatening machine. When all was in readiness, the Engineer ordered the ship up a few feet and, when the snorkel head valve was clear of the water, commenced ventilating with the ship's huge main ventilation blower.

As soon as the airflow was established in AMR Number One, the Auxiliaryman, accompanied by an electrician with a portable sniffer entered AMR Number One and removed the inspection covers from the oxygen generator so air could flow freely through the machine. A few minutes later the report came back to Conn that the sniffer readings inside the inspection covers were less than one per cent hydrogen.

Surrounded by collective sighs of relief, the Engineer secured ventilating. Two minutes later the ship was back down at a comfortable depth and the Exec was on his way back to his bunk. Thankfully, he thought, everyone had done a good job. The Auxiliaryman, the Engineer, and the Captain had all been quick and correct in their assessments and actions. That's what keeps small problems on submarines from turning into major catastrophes.

The Captain had been competent and decisive dealing with an equipment casualty. Craig knew he would be back aft now, peering over the shoulders of the Auxiliarymen as they tore into the oxygen generator to find the leaking seal. He also knew that arena was where Holcomb was most comfortable.

The next couple of days were routine as they worked their way toward the southern tip of Sardinia. The PDC's stayed to the north and became intermittent. Sometimes several hours went by without hearing one. Invariably though, they would resume. Sometimes for only a series of a half dozen muffled crashes, sometimes for an hour, sometimes for several hours.

The weather moderated into a flat calm as the Med showed her other face. Just as they worked their way into the choke point of the Mediterranean, that triangle of sea stretching from Cap Blanc north of Tunis to the southern tip of Sardinia, then to Marsala on Sicily, the sea sorted itself into the stable thermal structure of a strongly negative, shallow thermo cline. The "afternoon effect" established itself and became more severe with every passing day of hot, calm weather. With it came ship traffic like a New York City street at rush hour.

At times, while sonar held contact on a dozen, or even twenty contacts ranging from trawlers to three hundred thousand ton crude oil carriers, the thrash of screws passing directly overhead would be the first warning that the perverse acoustic conditions had bent the sound rays of some target away from the sonar arrays. The unpredictable blind spots thrown up by the afternoon effect made every ascent to periscope depth a nerve-wracking experience. Even when the ship was deep and safe from collision, the occasional arrival overhead of an unsuspected contact rattled the watch standers. Tension rose as their sense of security waned.

VLCC's, the Very Large Crude Carriers, were the worst. Bow on, their hundreds of thousands of tons of cargo effectively absorbed their machinery noise when the *Marion* was in or nearly in their path. It was damned disconcerting to be run over by the bow of a three hundred thousand ton tanker before its screw could be heard beating less than a thousand feet away.

Whoever was dropping the PDC's didn't seem to be bothered by sonar conditions. They kept banging away, always to the North of the *Marion*, sometimes for hours at a time.

By the end of the third day, Craig had had enough. The Captain was turning over the watch at 1800Z and, as usual, they were focusing on the PDC's and the tactical difficulties of the afternoon effect.

He said, "Captain, let's get the hell out of here." Both knew the operating areas in the Tyrrhennian Sea had been released to *Marion* as of midnight that day.

"I'm moving us up to the Tyrrhennian as fast as we can for two reasons. One, it'll get us out of this crossroads where everybody in the world is trying to run over us."

"Okay, XO, I agree. What's your second reason though?"

"The PDC's are generally to the northwest of us. If we move up along the east coast of Sardinia, close in to the twelve-mile limit, we put Sardinia between the western Mediterranean and us. If we keep hearing them all the way north of Corsica, the source has to have come into the Tyrrhennian with us. There just ain't no way I can see that a fixed source could be northwest of us now, having been south of us early in the patrol and still be with us up between Corsica and Italy. If we don't lose the PDC's, then the SOB is definitely traveling with us. Sardinia will be a great big curtain between us and every place else that damned noise has been for the last three weeks."

The Captain looked intently at his coffee cup. When he looked up he was a little pale. "What if we don't lose the PDC's when we get up into the Tyrrhennian?"

"I don't know. We'll keep recording them. Build all the case we can for the analysts when we get back. So far we can't really say they have threatened us in any way. They're just there. For all I know, it could be some Black Project we're doing."

Two days later, when they were twelve and a half miles due east of Aliria, Corsica, the explosions were still there, faint as always and due west of them.

Distant, my ass!

27

The Shadower

Satisfied now that the *Marion* did, indeed, have a mysterious companion traveling with her, the Exec chose to turn and amble back south to the wider reaches of the Tyrrhennian.

After a lengthy council of war during which Craig had barely managed to dissuade the Captain from breaking radio silence and reporting their situation, both had finally agreed to take no action that would alert the unwelcome companion shadowing them. It was the twenty-ninth day of the patrol and, in Craig's view, which Holcomb reluctantly accepted, little would be gained by going home with a bundle of suspicions and no hard evidence of a source platform.

Always the hunter, Craig suspected that whoever was driving the platform source of the explosions would, sooner or later, make a tactical blunder that would offer a breach in his cloak of invisibility. When that moment came, he had no intention of missing the opportunity to expose the pursuer.

As the ship moved south, the area remained heavily traveled, mostly by trawlers and general cargo ships shuttling back and forth between the islands and the Italian mainland. The afternoon effect was there, too, but at least the crew was spared the VLCC's. The shipping and ferry lanes were pretty well defined, so, by choosing the ship's track carefully, they were able to operate in reasonable comfort.

Whoever was dropping the PDC's seemed to relax a bit as well. For the better part of a week, the Exec had the ship loiter east of Sardinia. For much of that time the PDC's were quiet with just a few daily bursts to remind the annoyed crew of their continued presence. Because they now came in shorter trains, the Sonarmen were often hard put to determine their direction. Conclusively, though, the shadower moved around the *Marion*, sometimes east, sometimes west, sometimes to port, sometimes to starboard.

The Captain spent much of his time trying to correlate the PDC's to passing trawler contacts. Success eluded him. Several times he rushed to periscope depth to visually scan the area when a train of PDC's started. A couple of times he saw fishing boats, and once a small black hulled merchant ship, but none ever correlated to the sonar bearing of the PDC's.

Several times, the Exec also tried popping up for a look and an electronic countermeasures sweep. His luck was no better than the Captain's. The *LEBEDEV* and *VAVILOV* were reported on the daily INTSUM to be at anchor in the Gulf of Hammamet, several hundred miles away to the west, so they clearly now didn't seem to be part of the puzzle.

28

Non Qualified Pukes

At the end of the fourth week of patrol, McJimsey and Kane were rotated off their mess cooking duties and onto the ship control party watch as helmsman, planesman or messenger. Another pair of seamen, on their first patrol, replaced them in the galley and the cooks' eternal cycle of tribulations began anew.

For McJimsey and Kane the exhilaration of escape from mess cooking was brief. They now fell into the grasp of the Chief Interior Communications Electrician. Chief Gordon was a short, bald, scrawny, evil-tempered scold. The COB and the Exec had decided that Gordon already had the essential qualities of a fine Qualification Petty Officer in that he loved to nag the "Dinks," as non-qualified sailors delinquent in their progress were universally called. Hence, he should have the title. With that, they had assigned him the responsibility of monitoring and reporting weekly on the progress of all the NQP's struggling toward completion of the myriad oral and written checkouts that comprise "Qualification in Submarines." To be an NQP, or Non Qualified Puke, was a lowly and ego buffeting place on the submariners social ladder. To be a Dink under the eye of Chief Gordon was nothing short of purgatory.

McJimsey and Kane, being placed in Chief Gordon's watch section, immediately attracted his special attention. Only Hermasota, a new Steward's Mate, whose imperfect English had raised Chief Gordon's bile, seemed equally blessed. Kane especially, suffered. More given to literature than to science, electrical circuitry was baffling to him, particularly interior communications circuits. By the end of their third day of watches, Chief Gordon's searing sarcasm had begun to raise emotional blisters.

Late one night, having just come off the mid watch, McJimsey sat in the ship's library blearily perusing a TAB, the ship's Training Aid Booklet. Kane came in and, with more than a little feeling, slammed his TAB and the clipboard he was carrying on the table.

McJimsey looked up. "You red-assed again?"

"You fuckin-A I'm red-assed. That shithead. All I did was go into the crew's mess to make myself a fuckin' wedge. The movie was on. He jumped up and gave me a ration of shit for going to the fuckin' movie when I'm Dink on Quals. If he calls me a non-qual puke one more time I'm gonna bust his ass."

McJimsey thought he ought to check to be sure. "Gordon?"

"Yeah. Course I'm Dink. I can't get by his fuckin checkout on IC."

"The little fucker is a flamin' asshole," McJimsey agreed.

Hermasota had come in just in time to catch the gist of the conversation. He too had his TAB and a clipboard. He gesticulated with the oldest salute known to man.

"Yeah," he said. "He call me Monkey Eater all a time. Sometime he call me Monkey Fucker. I like to find monkey to fuck him."

Slowly, as they sat and remonstrated, an alliance emerged. The plan was born when McJimsey suddenly sat upright from his sprawled position and snapped his fingers at Kane. "Do you know what monkey shit is?"

Kane looked at him in disgust. "You get it off the cage floor in a zoo?"

"No, you dumb ass. That's the traditional name for that non-hardening sealer the Auxiliarymen use. It looks like shit and has about the same consistency. That's how it got its name."

"So?"

"So how about we get a tube?"

Ten minutes later three thoroughly cheerful NQP's were off to continue their study of the ship.

A day later, near breakfast time, the Exec was just putting away the section of the patrol report he had been working on when his door flew open. Gordon stood there framed in the light. He was bedraggled, almost demented looking.

"XO," he hissed, "I'm putting McJimsey and Kane on report. I want…I demand you court martial their asses!"

He did look like an enraged man.

"What the hell did they do?"

Gordon was so mad he was barely coherent, but slowly the story emerged. Shortly after he had finished his watch at midnight, he had gone aft to check a reported faulty Dial-X phone. As he passed through the darkened and deserted upper level missile compartment, unknown assailants in the shadows had thrown a fart sack, a mattress cover, over his head and overpowered him.

He had been gagged, trussed up, stuffed into the fart sack and gently laid out in the space between the two rows of missile tubes. It had taken him five hours to struggle out of his bonds, and to get out of the fart sack. He was about as angry a man as Craig had ever seen.

"Okay, Chief, I certainly don't blame you for being pissed, but how do you know it was McJimsey and Kane? Did you get a look at them or hear their voices?"

The Chief was literally jigging from one foot to the other. "No! Goddammit, No! But I know it was those two!"

"Chief, go get cleaned up and get some rest. I certainly agree this is intolerable. When you get to Chief's Quarters, wake the COB and tell him to come up here."

"You gonna court martial them?"

"We're going to find out who is guilty first."

He turned to leave. The rear of his pants was disgusting.

"Gordon, what the hell is all over your pants?"

He whirled around. "MONKEY SHIT!" he screamed. "They packed my fuckin' pants full of monkey shit. I've been rollin' around for five hours in a pile of fuckin MONKEY SHIT!" He whirled around again and raced off.

All Craig could think of to say was, "Oh?"

The case was never "broken" because not a soul ever came forward to admit knowing anything. Gordon's obvious lack of popularity with the crew, as a whole, clearly served the miscreants well. Neither the Exec nor the COB was able to contain a private chuckle when they agreed to have Gordon swap watch sections.

Coincidentally, the sobriquet "Monkey Eater" was not heard again in the *Marion* Gold crew.

29

The Hump

A few days later the *Marion* eased her way south through the Straits of Sicily past the Gulf of Hammamet with its Soviet Navy anchorage, then on past Pantelleria. They were now in the Eastern Mediterranean. To all hand's surprise, the PDC's didn't seem to follow. The occasional trains of explosions drifted further and further astern and faded until they were gone completely. As the ship passed to the north of the Gulf of Sirte and into the open seas west of Crete, the crew began to relax. No PDC's, good Loran coverage and smooth seas. Even the Captain loosened up a little.

They were almost to the Hump, the thirty-first day of the patrol, and it seemed their vexing nemesis had given up the chase. The troops began to plot their hijinks for Hump Night celebration. The Captain wondered about resuming engineering drills, but decided to wait a few more days.

Jim Brown, the Chief NAVET, and the Exec shared a chuckle over a cup of coffee. Brown said he believed they had spooked themselves over the PDC's. The Exec replied that he might be right as they laughed. In truth, both were relieved that whatever was responsible for the explosions hadn't followed them through the Straits of Sicily.

In keeping with tradition, Hump Night dinner was a lavish affair. The cooks laid on a huge meal with steak, lobster and Baked Alaska. Instead of being served in the wardroom, the Officers ate in the Crew's mess with the troops. After dinner, the troops put on a few skits and several of the musically inclined entertained all with a good country western music hour.

Somehow, though, it lacked the spontaneity and exuberance of other Hump nights Craig had experienced. It was slightly too polite, too decorous for a normal crew of submarine sailors. It was a pleasant, even charming evening, but something was definitely holding the crew's morale in check. There was not a single good-natured insult to an officer in any of the skits. Proof enough that the crew's confidence in the wardroom was not unconditional.

After the entertainment finished and the audience dispersed, Craig sought out the COB and Chief Brown. "Okay, nobody took the usual free shots at the wardroom tonight. How come so nice?"

Both Chiefs squirmed around a bit. Neither was anxious to reply.

Finally, the COB said, "I think the guys are a little jumpy from all those damned PDC's. They're still just a little nervous, that's all."

"COB, that's horse shit. We're all in this canoe together, and we both know that when sailors get jumpy they don't dummy up. That's when they turn into wise asses. Try again."

The COB didn't want to try again. He passed the buck to Chief Brown. "What do you think, Brownie?"

Brown squinted and stroked his beard a couple of times before he spoke. "The crew doesn't know where they stand with the Captain. He goes through the ship and makes them take down all the beaver shots, but he doesn't ever seem to talk much to anybody. He doesn't even know my watch supervisors' names. They don't know him—and they're wary of how he'll take things."

"Is that it, COB?"

"Yes, sir. Mostly. Also, it doesn't help the way the Captain stands on the sidelines in Conn whenever there's something going on. The sailors just aren't real comfortable with him. It seems to them that he's a lot more interested in cleaning up their minds than in running the ship."

Craig felt a knot tightening in his gut. Cold fear and a little guilt found its way into his thought process. He was being told that the crew's loss of confidence in the Captain was widespread and cancerous. That kind of cancer is terminal to a crew's efficiency as a fighting unit unless it is checked immediately. He was exasperated and a little unnerved.

In a voice tinged with anger, he told them, "You both know none of that is true. The Captain runs this ship and nobody has yet lost any hide because of foul language or a dirty picture. He has a right to say "no" to anything that offends him. It's his Goddamned war canoe. He's a gentle, pretty shy individual who would go to the mat for any one of you. Do you mean to tell me the troops can't see that?"

It was very clear to Craig, at that moment, that his initial concern about the wisdom of sharing the command role had been well founded.

I should have paid more attention to my misgivings and less to my own ego's urging to take charge. Maybe if I hadn't been so quick at times to push the Old Man aside, and if I had been more supportive in the background as a good XO should be, he would still have the crew's confidence.

Craig didn't share the thoughts that spun through his mind with the two Chief Petty Officers. Instead, he told them to start talking the Captain up with their men and to come down hard on any fretting or bad mouthing. He knew that, to really turn the situation around, the Captain would have to do something visible and confidence inspiring to the watching crew.

With thirty-two days left in the patrol that's going to be a tough one to arrange.

30

Another Strange Encounter

A few days later, the Submarine Operational Commander in the Med, Commander Task Force 64, advised the *Marion* by message that intelligence indicated a large Soviet fleet exercise was going to begin in her assigned areas within a day or two. A dozen or so surface combatants, half as many submarines and several support ships were converging on the eastern Mediterranean. Their old friends the *Lebedev* and the *Vavilov* were part of the fleet.

Based on the projected tracks of the assembling ships and the Notice to Mariners put out by the Russians, CTF-64 expected the exercise area to be over a hundred miles south of the *Marion*. To give the Soviets as wide a berth as possible, the Exec had the ship move up as far north as *Marion*'s area boundaries allowed and there, squeezed up alongside the island of Crete to wait out Ivan's play. For a couple of days it looked like the *Marion* was successfully skirting even the most distant or tenuous contact with the Soviet exercise. Except for a few sweeps of a distant, feeble Soviet air search radar on day one of their exercise, there was no sniff of their presence.

On the patrol's thirty-sixth day, just before daylight at 0515Z, Craig stepped into Sonar to check that the intelligence chart had been properly updated with the summaries and intelligence spots received on the radio broadcast during the night. Intelligence summaries, or INTSUMS, were just that, summaries of all intelligence collected during the day that might be of operational interest to U.S. Navy ships in the Med. Intelligence spots, or SPOTS, were individual reports that were considered time sensitive enough to warrant their immediate distribution.

This was their third day off Crete and there was nothing much of interest to the *Marion* in the intelligence picture. The watch was quiet, with only one active contact, a trawler working a few miles to the south of the ship. Sonar had held contact on him for several hours and, as the ship beat slowly westward, it had approached and was now passing north of the area in which the fisherman was working.

All normal, all peaceful.

Suddenly, as he stood studying the messages and the chart, Craig was startled by the crash of a PDC, not very close, but stronger than any they had heard before. The watchstanders jerked to alert as he spun around. "Where's that coming from?"

On the fourth explosion in the train, Franzei, who had almost miraculously appeared, turned from where he stood behind the BQS-4 operator. Earphone clamped to his ear in one hand, unlit cigarette in the other, he said, "XO, the PDC's are coming from the same sector the trawler is working in."

"Any change in the trawler's behavior?"

Before Franzei could answer, they all froze. Loud and clear, they heard five pings of medium frequency echo ranging and the rush of high speed screws starting up.

All Craig got out was "What the fuck…"

Franzei came back immediately, "Two screws. Turn count two hundred plus. Definitely a warship."

The PDC's had quit after four. The warship had been lying to. Five pings and then no more.

What the hell is going on?

Craig hit the AN/WIC press to talk and yelled at the OOD, "Conn—Sonar. This is the Exec. Drop coverage. Go deep, put on five degrees right rudder. Build up turns to standard. Rig for deep. Call the Captain and report your actions."

No more than five seconds had elapsed since the final ping. Where had the Goddamned destroyer come from? Why was he lying to just off their track? He had to have been there for hours or sonar would have heard his approach. What was his connection with the PDC's? Why only five pings and haul ass? The whole thing was extremely bizarre, and Craig intended to get the hell out of there. Fast. No apologies for dropping coverage of communications and targets. It was time to evade.

"Conn—Sonar. This is the Exec again. Get a radioman into the trunk and haul the wire into short stay. While he's doing that, run southeast. As soon as the wire is in and you are rigged for deep, go down to two hundred feet above test depth, increase speed to Flank and make a gradual course change to 077 degrees true."

Conn repeated back his instructions. *Marion* was already clearing datum at a good clip, but Craig knew they were a long way from being out of the trap.

Why the hell had the destroyer made no effort to prosecute his contact?

Just then the Captain came bursting into Sonar. Craig briefed him on what had happened and explained his actions and intentions. Holcomb didn't ask a single question. He just stood up, his hands clenching and unclenching, and said with great intensity, "I knew it. I knew it. I knew he was there. He knows what we're going to do." The Captain then spun about quickly and left Sonar, not bothering to close the door behind him.

When Craig found him an hour or so later in his stateroom, the ship was humming along at flank speed, still getting the hell away from where they had left the trawler. It was time for the Exec to turn the Command Duty over to the Captain.

When Craig went in, Holcomb just looked at him and said, "Oh, hi, XO, can you keep the watch for a few more hours? I want to think about all this for a while."

Craig replied, "Aye, aye, sir," and backed out of the stateroom. He wasn't in the mood to sleep anyway. He was beginning to feel like the mouse in a losing game with the cat, and this cat was taking on some very spooky dimensions. There was simply no sensor technology Craig knew of that could support what they had experienced, so he kept coming back to coincidence as an explanation. There was still a ship to run, so he headed back up to Conn. As Craig expected, when they slowed down several hours later, a careful sonar search found no sign of anyone trailing them.

The ship went back to normal patrol operations…very carefully!

31
The Wardroom Dinner

A couple of uneventful days later, with more PDC's again in the background, the officers sat down to Sunday dinner in the Wardroom. It was the patrol's thirty-eighth day. The Captain had been very quiet, mostly withdrawn since the brush with the destroyer, but tonight he came to the table in a more amiable, chatty mood. Somehow, as the meal was served and the group relaxed into light chatter, the conversation drifted around to recollections of Christmas seasons.

The Captain joined in with an animated description of his family's traditions in observing the day and the reverence they attached to it in recognition of "Christ's gift to the world." Struck by an intruding thought, the Captain shifted in his seat toward the Weapons Officer and asked, with apparent innocence, "Joe, we all know Christmas should be a celebration of Christ's love for us, but what do you Jews do on Christmas day?"

Caught off guard, Joe laughed a bit uneasily and passed the question off. "Nothing much. We have our own special religious days, such as Hanukkah."

Apparently satisfied not to pursue the point, the Captain sat back for a moment. Suddenly he swung his gaze to Craig and, with a perplexed frown studied him for a moment. "I can understand Joe, but XO, what do you do on Christmas? How can a Godless man find any significance in any day?

Craig felt his bile rising. *I respect other people's right to practice their religion, but I also expect them to respect my right to do without it.* Before the acid could collect in his reply, the warning flags flew up in Craig's mind. *He's going out of bounds. He's a fanatic on religion, so sidestep this issue.*

The best the angry Exec could do was restrain himself to a perceptibly deliberate return look and with level cadence reply, "We do what any normal American family does."

"But what about God?"

"Who needs a God to teach us to love and respect each other?" Craig shot back.

Perhaps sensing the magnitude of his gaffe, Holborn backed off and dropped it, retreating into a silent preoccupation with his plate. He had violated a cardinal rule of wardroom etiquette that religion was never to be a topic of conversation. Tension around the table was so thick it could have been cut with a knife. All the junior officers clammed up and focused unprecedented attention on finishing their meals as quickly as possible.

After a while, the Captain spoke again. "I almost achieved perfect purity of thought last night."

It was obvious that no one else at the table was going to be drawn into a reply.

Craig couldn't imagine what Holcomb was talking about, but felt that he should make an effort to put aside the earlier confrontation, so he feigned interest and asked, "I'm sorry, Captain, but what do you mean? What is 'perfect purity of thought?'"

Holcomb looked at Craig as if he was surprised at the question. Maybe he figured only a heathen could be so ignorant. If so, he decided to pity the poor savage and enlighten him. "Perfect purity of thought. If I can achieve perfect purity of thought in my communion with God, I can be free of every bond of my physical existence."

Craig was stunned into momentary silence as were the other officers. The tension at the wardroom table already palpable, became suffocating. High before, thanks to the clash between the Captain and the Exec over religion, it was intolerable now.

Craig finally found his voice and replied, "Oh. I don't think I understand. In fact, I don't think I can understand."

Several of the officers made a barely dignified bolt for the door. The doctor, the Navigator, the Weapons Officer, Stone, Rakowski and the Exec remained, all by now mesmerized by the Captain's revelations.

Holcomb seemed unaware of the reaction his remarks had caused. After a long pause, he went on. "I'm going to spend next Christmas at home with my family."

By now nothing should have surprised him, but Craig had to ask. "Captain, we'll be on patrol next Christmas. You're not expecting to be relieved at the end of this patrol, are you?"

"Oh, no. I have at least three more patrols with this crew."

"Then do you know something I don't about our schedule?"

"No, no. The ship, with this crew, will be on patrol next Christmas and I will be in command."

"Oh, then you mean you'll be with your family in spirit."

"No. I mean I will be with them in body and in spirit."

That was what Craig had thought Holcomb had meant. The Exec didn't pretend to understand the powers of the mind, but this sounded, to him, more like a mind that was failing to deal with reality than one that could overcome the barriers of transposition between the physical and the spiritual worlds. Foolishly, he gently tried to dissuade him. "Captain, I don't want to take issue with your religious beliefs, but do I understand that you are convinced that upon achieving this 'perfect purity of thought,' you can become a sort of free floating soul existing beyond the constraints of our physical world?"

Holcomb was emphatic now. "That's right. The physical world exists only in our imagination. The soul exists independently of the physical world which is a prison for souls who haven't become pure enough in their love of God."

Craig tried again. "Captain, there's a couple of inches of HY-80 steel, a few hundred feet of sea water and thousands of miles between you and your family. I don't know about your soul, but I have to believe floating your body through all that will result in some serious bruises."

"It doesn't go through anything. It just ceases to exist here and comes to exist there."

"You really believe that?"

"Absolutely!"

Craig looked around. Even Rak and Stone had deserted him and fled. Only the doctor seemed unperturbed as he forked his dessert down. "Captain, how can you believe in a premise such as this without proof? Have you ever known anyone who could do what you just described?"

Holcomb was impatient, frustrated. "The world is full of proof, but you have to believe…you have to have faith to see it. There's no way YOU could see it!"

Holy shit, the Old Man really has lost it! He's denying reality now. Craig couldn't take any more. He got up and politely excused himself, trying to exit with a bit of good humor, lame though it was. "Well, we'll miss you next Christmas when we're all sitting here at dinner."

It was a lame joke. If it turns out to be prophetic, then we're all in real trouble.

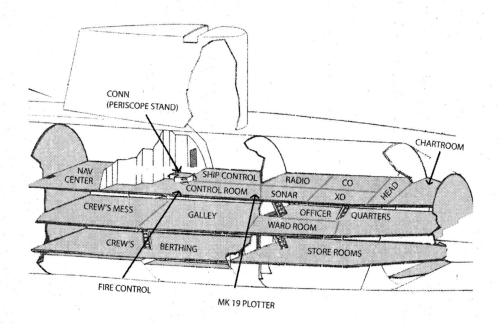

Marion's Interior Arrangement

32
The Breakdown

Ivan finished his exercise and retired to his anchorage at Hammamet off Tunisia, North Africa. It was no wonder that the Russians drank a lot. They certainly didn't give their sailors a chance to do much else, stranded as they were in such a barren and desolate area for six months at a time.

With the way clear, the Exec headed the *Marion* back to the West. It was time to start the slow march home. Life was placid for a while, with the occasional burst of PDC's now assuming a natural, familiar role in the crew's daily awareness. They had become almost companionable, something like a wide-ranging dog on a giant field barely in sight of his master, but always present.

The fortieth patrol day had arrived and the Captain had become even more withdrawn since his revelations some nights ago at the dinner table. The other officers were content to keep themselves as remote as possible from the risk of another embarrassingly naked exposure of conflicting religious beliefs. The result of the uncomfortable relationship between Holcomb and his officers was to virtually limit his direct interface with the ship to a single person—the Exec. Daily, when they were alone together, the Captain rehashed the events of the patrol and the PDC's with the Exec. Never anything new, just an endless repetition of "Who can they be? What can it be? How can this be?" Never any answers.

In Craig's view, they had exhausted themselves and their imaginations without forming even a reasonable hypothesis for all the tactical phenomena of the patrol. There still seemed to be nothing out there that intended to physically harm them, so he was inclined to avoid overreaction and continue watching for a tactical opening that he could exploit.

There remained only twenty-three days of patrol to be gotten through, and then the Naval Intelligence Scientific Center could go to work on their recordings and other data and perhaps discover what had been going on. With the analytical tools and special intelligence available to them, NISC scientists could often extract far more information from submarine data packages than the crew could derive on board. Craig hoped for the best.

* * * * *

Late that evening, the Captain called the Exec to his stateroom. Craig was mildly surprised at the call. Holcomb had become very reclusive and he rarely saw or heard from him after evening meal until he reappeared to assume the Command Duty in the mornings. When Craig knocked and entered the stateroom, he found Holcomb in a state of obvious agitation. The Captain was pacing to and fro, so far as the eight-foot dimensions of the room allowed, carrying a folded sheet of bond paper. While Craig waited, Holcomb paced back and forth slapping the folded piece of paper against the palm of his left hand. Whatever agitated him so was on that sheet of paper.

Craig waited and wondered. After a few minutes, Holcomb stopped in front of him, now an apparition with wildly dancing eyes. He was breathing hard and his right hand, holding the paper, was shaking. *He's more than agitated. He's scared shitless.*

When Holcomb spoke, it was in a low whisper. He held the piece of paper like a death warrant. "XO," he whispered, "I've decided I have to confide in you, so that if something happens to me, this information isn't lost. First, you have to swear you will not divulge it to anyone except the Squadron Commander or other proper authority. It's too sensitive for anyone else on board to be trusted with. I shouldn't even release it to you, but it has to be safeguarded against loss. I don't even dare write it down. Do you give me your word?"

Craig was baffled. *What the hell could he have?* "Yes, sir. You have my word."

"All right. Here, look at this." Holcomb handed over the paper. It seemed to take great willpower for him to lay it in his Exec's hand.

Craig didn't know what to expect, but when he opened the sheet, it was a list of the twenty or so equipment failures the ship had experienced since entering the Med. Craig read it, re-read it, then turned it over looking for something else. There was nothing. In that instant, Craig knew with stark certainty that he was facing a nightmare. It had been obvious to him for days, but he had been refusing to confront the unthinkable. *I should have understood the symptoms for what they were before we ever left Rota.* Holcomb was breaking down mentally and there were still three weeks of patrol left. The question now was how to handle him. "Captain, all I see here is a list of out-of-commission items since the beginning of patrol. What's so sensitive about it?"

Again the conspiratorial whisper. "Don't you see? Don't you understand what this means?"

"No, sir. I don't see any connection between any of the things on this list."

His answer was excited. "There isn't. That's the point! It took me days to understand it all."

"I still don't follow you."

"The only way to explain all these unrelated failures is that there's an external cause. See all of those unexplained NAVSAT problems! The Russian who has been trailing us with the PDC's has some kind of a ray thing that he uses to cause our equipment to fail or, if he wants, just malfunction. Don't you see? He can interfere with us or control us at will. That list is the proof!"

Craig fought down his own panic. Holcomb was farther gone than he could have ever imagined. *"He's paranoid. Deluded. Don't take a chance of affronting him. Get away. Get time to think!* Straining to stay calm, Craig tried to sound reassuring. "Captain, I think this is a pretty normal list for a patrol. Are you sure of your conclusion?"

"You think I'm imagining things, XO?"

"No, sir. There have been a lot of strange things on this patrol. I just don't see any of the items on this list as one of them."

"You'll see, XO. Remember. If I don't get back, you have to make COMSUBLANT understand this."

"Yes, sir, I will. Now get some sleep and I'll see you in the morning."

"Goodnight, XO. You're the only one I can trust with this."

"Thanks, Captain." Craig backed out of the Captain's stateroom and went off to find the doctor. It was immediately obvious to him that he had to retain the Captain's confidence and try to control the situation without risking an open confrontation. If at all possible, Holcomb had to be eased through the rest of patrol and back into port. If, however, a showdown came, the Exec would need support and, in a case like this, making sure it was there was going to be a very delicate task.

Craig's knew without need for reflection that his most immediate concern was to make sure no one could accuse him of inciting distrust of the Captain. Assuming he got Holcomb and the *Marion* back in one piece, the Chain of Command would instantly and instinctively attack his own credibility and motives when he reported the Captain's condition. Craig knew the Naval institution enough to know damned well that he would have to win the fight for his own professional life first, otherwise, the Chain of Command would not take any allegations of the Captain's incompetence seriously. *They'll always shoot the messenger, but I gotta make sure they hear me first.*

Craig found the doctor snoring away in his bunk. For once, he didn't even feel like waking him with a good natured "quack." The last day for highjinks was behind them.

"Doc. Doc."

The Doctor stirred and sat up. "What's up, XO?"

"Get up and come have a cup of coffee with me in the wardroom, okay?"

"Now? It's two fucking thirty in the morning."

"I know. I'm sorry to disturb you, but we need to talk." The Exec pointed to the upper and lower bunks where Rak and the Engineer were sleeping. "We can't do it here."

"Okay. I'll be right in." As the doctor swung his legs out of his bunk, Craig went ahead to the Wardroom and sat down. He didn't give a damn about the coffee. The invitation to the doctor had been purely euphemistic.

A few minutes later Doc appeared, sleepy-looking. "What's up, XO? What's wrong?"

"Look, Doc, I can't explain what I'm about to tell you to do. Furthermore, you have to understand that no one on board this ship is to ever know about this conversation. Okay? That's why I got you up in the middle of the night to have it. Got it, so far?"

The doctor was puzzled and still a little fuzzy with sleep, but he said, "Okay. Don't worry. I'll keep it between us."

"Thanks, Doc. I want you to commence immediately to quietly, but specifically and clinically, observe the Captain's behavior and mine. I want you to keep a log of your observations of both of us and I want it to be absolutely fair, honest and objective. No favors to either of us. No one else is to know what you are doing, although you can use anything you pick up of their observations. The log may get burned without anyone but you ever seeing it, but you have to be ready to acknowledge its existence as a statement of your professional observations and opinions, if it is necessary to make it public."

"XO, I understand and I'll do it. Do you want me to go back to events that have already transpired?"

"Do as you see fit."

"Okay."

"One last thing, Doc. No one, including me, is to see that file unless you have to use it. If you have to come forward with it, you'll know what to do without my telling you."

"Right."

"Goodnight, Doc, and thanks."

"Goodnight, XO…and good luck."

He didn't have to add the last phrase. Much as he teased the doctor, Craig knew he was a sincere, sensitive person and that he had a strong personal commitment to his high moral principles. Craig was counting on that. He knew as they left the wardroom that the doctor had seen enough already to understand the problem. Doc would do what was right.

33

Him!

Two days later, with the Straits of Sicily well astern, the Exec got up, as usual, just before evening meal and, after a shower, began his routine tour of the ship. At 1620Z, as he stepped through the door into the Control Room, he found the Navigator sitting on the Quartermaster's stool behind the MK-19 plotter. Gator looked grim, and when their eyes met, he frowned and shook his head. Something was wrong. Craig walked over to look down at the chart. Without a word, the Navigator stabbed his finger at a spot fifteen miles outside the *Marion*'s assigned operating area.

Craig was aghast. They were in another submarine's assigned area. With boats as quiet as American FBM's, safety from submerged collision rested primarily on scrupulous observation of area boundaries. Just like air traffic control, safe separation depends on strict adherence to procedure.

Craig exploded. "What in the hell are we doing here? Why wasn't I called before we violated our boundaries? What the hell is the reason for this?"

The Navigator held up both hands in protest. "We're here because the captain ordered it."

"Did you warn him that he was getting out of area?"

"Of course. He was deep, running flank and he said it was his judgment that the tactical situation warranted it. We've been headed back toward our own water for over an hour."

"Well, for Christ's sake, get up shallow and speed up. Let's get back as fast as we can!" *I must have been sleeping like the dead. Going deep and fast normally would wake me up.* "Why did he run out of area?"

"I don't know. We had a trawler contact on sonar. He went up to periscope depth for a look, came down and ran like hell. He wouldn't explain why to anyone."

Recognizing the futility of it, Craig was still furious. "Gator, if we ever do anything like this again without my being called, I will have your ass, the OD's and the Quartermaster's. You make Goddamned sure they all know it because I'll come after you first, regardless. Do you understand me?"

"Yeah, XO, but I asked the captain if we should call you and he said 'No.'"

"I don't care what he says. Next time you call or you'll wish you had never met me!"

The navigator was pale as the irate and shaken Exec stormed off back to his stateroom. Craig had to cool down before he dared ask the captain about the incident.

* * * * *

Later, when it was time to change the watch, Craig waited for the captain to volunteer an explanation of his actions. It wasn't long coming. Holcomb signaled the Exec into his stateroom and carefully closed the door. Speaking in low tones, he recounted how, after holding sonar contact on a trawler, he had gone up to see if he could get a look at what he suspected was "HIM."

When he got to periscope depth, on the same bearing as the trawler's noise, he had seen a medium-sized general cargo ship with a gray hull and red superstructure. The merchant was closing rapidly, nearly bow on. With a mixture of apprehension and satisfaction, Holcomb told Craig how he had eluded the trap by going deep and running out of our area, something the Russian would never expect us to do. He couldn't explain his actions to our watch section or they might guess something of what he now knew.

Play the game, but try to bring him around. "Captain, we talked about your suspicion that some external force was interfering with our equipment, but how would the watch section guess that? I sure as hell would never have guessed it!"

"No, no, XO. Today's encounter revealed something else to me. Somehow HE can change his appearance. We were tracking a trawler, but when I looked, HE had made himself look like a ten thousand-ton general cargo ship. Don't you see? HE's been with us all patrol. HE keeps changing his appearance. HE's not going to let us get back to port now that he knows we've seen through his ability to disguise himself. We wouldn't have gotten away if I hadn't run out of our area. HE never expected that."

Christ, we're in Never Never Land! "Captain, that doesn't make sense. HE couldn't have known where our area boundaries are or which areas we're assigned."

"Oh, no, XO. HE can tell. HE can somehow tell what's going on inside this ship. I haven't figured out how yet, but HE can!"

Craig was appalled. As long as the Old Man stayed hell bent on confiding his absurd notions only to him, how could the rest of the world possibly know his condition, recognize his lunacy? Outside his stateroom, Holcomb was certainly beginning to appear haggard, but he was invariably alert and coherent. In humoring him, Craig realized that he probably looked equally crazy to the crew.

For the first time in many years, Craig was genuinely, deeply frightened. How far would Holcomb go in a deluded attempt to protect his precious "intelligence?" *Stay calm. Stay laid back.* "Captain, there's a lot of risk in running into someone else's area. Next time, give me a call so I can give you a hand, okay?"

"Sure, XO. I didn't want to disturb you. You and I are going to have to be very alert for us to have any hope of getting back to Rota. I have conquered my need for sleep, but you haven't. Without God, you can't. I have to make sure you have a chance to rest."

"Captain, I'll hold up. Just call me next time, please."

"Okay, XO."

Craig relieved him of the Command Duty and headed for the Control Room to make sure they were back in their own area. He was in turmoil. Holcomb was deteriorating far too fast. Rota seemed a million miles and years away. *He's deluded and already dangerous, and I'm not yet in a position to control him.*

34
Thunder in the Sea

In perfect consistency with the pattern the patrol had taken since the day the *Marion* had entered the Med, Craig was granted a few days grace to build up his hopes that they just might get back with no further trouble. When the next incident happened, it dissipated any such notion.

Craig had changed his sleeping routine to be up and awake whenever the Captain had the Command Duty. Assuming Holcomb could only do harm when he was up and about, he napped, fully dressed, when he knew the Captain was shut away, indulging in one of his frequent lengthy withdrawals to his stateroom. To stave off exhaustion, he would have to steal much of his own rest when the Captain believed him to be on duty. Craig glumly hoped his stamina and nerves would stretch long enough to get them home.

It was mid-afternoon on the patrol's forty-sixth day. There were only seventeen days left to go as Craig sat relaxed, on the periscope stand, staying awake by watching the ship control party go about their routine. The Captain had been up for lunch and was back in his stateroom, but the Exec wasn't sure he was settled in to stay, so he intended to wait a few more minutes before turning in for a nap. The ship was well up in the western Med basin, above and east of the Balearics. It was a quiet area. Beautiful weather and no contacts other than a sporadic few of the usual distant PDC's.

Without warning, at 1504Z, the ship suddenly lurched and reeled under the impact of three closely spaced heavy explosions. The noise was deafening. Craig had heard many underwater explosions, including depth charges and war shot torpedoes at ranges of a half-mile or less. Nothing approximated this.

He bolted out of his seat, yelling to the Diving Officer, "Ahead Flank. Right full rudder. EMERGENCY DEEP!" No time to include the OOD in the chain of orders. Seconds later the *Marion* was corkscrewing away from the spot in the ocean where the explosions had gone off. A shocked Franzei stood in the door between Sonar and Control, earphones dangling around his neck.

223

"What the hell, XO?"

"I don't know, but it was awful damn big and close. Did you get it on tape?"

"Yes, sir. We had just put in a new work tape. Got it good."

"Okay. Make sure it goes straight in the safe and is protected. I want a good package to put in on this." Then to the OOD, "Pass the word for all compartments to inspect for damage and report."

The Captain came up behind Franzei. He was shaking again. "What's going on, XO?"

"I don't know. Three heavy explosions close alongside. I'm evading."

"You've gone to Flank. What about the wire? We only have one spare left."

Diplomacy failed the Exec. "Fuck the wire, Captain. We're getting the hell out of here!"

Craig was amazed at the inconsistency in Holcomb's concern about losing the trailing wire antenna. *He goes off the deep end over the PDC's then, for the first time, something is out there that actually could hurt us and he frets about the fucking wire!*

Without another word, the Captain shrugged and went back to his stateroom, leaving the Exec in charge.

Below decks, in crew's berthing, the jolt of the explosions had resulted in near pandemonium until the Chief of the Boat snuffed it out. Rattled and thrown about in their bunks by the explosions, the sailors raced for the ladder in confusion and fear. Most had only one thought; get to their Battle Station as quickly as possible. They found their way blocked by a towering, implacable COB, backed by a scowling Chief Brown.

The COB threw the first man back down the ladder with a scornful, "Settle down. If they need you on station, they'll pass the word. Otherwise, stay put and don't get in the fuckin' way!"

The COB's words and action had a powerful calming effect. Another example of how indispensable professionals like the COB and Brownie are in times of stress.

As soon as the ship was deep enough to suppress cavitation from the churning screw, the Exec dodged through the ocean at Flank speed like a broken field runner until they were halfway across the *Marion*'s assigned areas. It cost over three hours of down time, out of communications, and not covering targets, but Craig wanted to put plenty of room between them and the source of that heavy ordinance. In what had become a predictable frustration, when he did slow down, their cautious searches on sonar, ECM and periscope revealed nothing.

Along with the Exec, the Navigator, the Chief Sonarman, and Franzei went back over every scrap of data they had recorded or could remember during the four hours before the three heavy explosions. Nowhere could they find a hint of a delivery platform. There were no weapon noises in the water either.

Maybe it was some French bomber jockey salvoing bombs into the ocean and we just happened to be underneath? Coincidence again!

They didn't know, but no one took comfort in their ignorance. Torpedoes as a source were quickly ruled out because they are contact weapons and sonar would have heard them running. Everything else was a possibility.

Whatever was out there, the way home lay through the Straits of Gibralter so, after due consideration, the Exec headed the ship in that direction. They proceeded rather gingerly, picking their way back west, with a lot of baffle clearing maneuvers to look over their shoulder.

Whatever it was that spontaneously jolted the ship so badly seemed to have impressed their invisible friend with the inexhaustible supply of PDC's as well. Sonar never heard them after that.

When the ship was settled back into normal operations, Craig stopped by to report the known facts to the Captain. Holcomb was apparently deep in thought, preoccupied. He half listened, said "Thanks" and that was all.

35
Communications Panic

The next morning the Captain was up on time, at 0745Z,, and seemed to be energized as he announced to the waiting Exec that he was ready to relieve him of the Command Duty. The subject of yesterday's excitement never came up.

After hearing the magic words, "I relieve you," Craig went to his stateroom to shuffle paper while he waited for the Captain to settle back into seclusion. When he heard the Captain's stateroom door close, he would visit the Control Room, find out what instructions had been left with the OOD, then, if all was quiet, try to catch a short nap.

Shortly, perhaps a half-hour later, he felt the deck tilt. The ship was going up to periscope depth. Wondering why the OOD was going up, Craig started putting away the personnel files he had started working on. He knew there were no NAVSAT passes scheduled until nearly noon. The only other reason for going up would be for the Captain to look at a nearby sonar contact. Apprehension rising, he hurried, threw the stack of files in a locker, pulled his shoes on and headed for the Control Room.

Halfway up the ladder to Control, Craig heard the OOD pass the word, "Radio-Conn. The BRA-9 is raised."

What the hell is going on now?

The BRA-9 was the ship's primary radio transmission antenna. Like the periscope, it could be raised while submerged to put the active length of the antenna above the surface of the water. But the question was, why? FBM's never risk compromising their position by transmitting except in extreme emergency or when ordered to do so by their operational commander. Craig broke into a run. As he topped the ladder, he met the Captain rushing from the Control Room to Radio.

"What's happening, Captain?"

"We can't risk waiting any longer. I'm notifying National Command Authority that we're being trailed, have been attacked and are in immediate danger of another attack!"

He had the sliding door to Radio halfway open. Craig threw his weight against it and forced it shut. Holcomb started to resist, for a moment teetering on the brink of frenzy. Craig got his back to the door and held the Captain away from it, straining hard. Holcomb was, by far, the larger man, and Craig knew he couldn't hold him for very long. His only hope was to talk.

The words poured out. "Captain, hang on. Let's talk this over first. You trust me, don't you? Let's be sure this is the right thing to do. It'll only take a couple of minutes to talk it over, make sure we haven't overlooked something. We're okay for now, let's be deliberate..." and on it went.

Gradually Holcomb gave a little. Craig could feel some of the will going out of him. Finally he stopped trying to wrestle the Exec out of the way.

"Captain, this is too sensitive to talk about here. Let's go down to your room for a couple of minutes."

He agreed. Craig yelled through the Control Room door to the OOD to lower the BRA-9 and stay at periscope depth until he received further instructions, then hustled off after the departing Captain, who had already disappeared below. Craig's mind was racing. He couldn't let that message go out. If it went out and then something happened to them, God only knows what the result would be. War before anyone could pull back? Bells would ring all the way to the White House, then probably on to the Kremlin via the Hotline. *How the hell am I going to talk him out of transmitting?*

Craig followed Holcomb into his stateroom and shut the door. "Captain, I'm not trying to obstruct you. I just think this is so important we have to make sure we get it right."

"You're right, XO. I was hasty, but I believe now's the time when we have to tell our boss what's going on. Any moment it may be too late!"

"Has something happened in the last hour? When I left Conn an hour ago we didn't hold a single contact."

"That's why we have to send a message while we can. HE's not there right now. If we hurry, we can transmit before HE can get back and attack us. Don't you see, XO? HE's just playing with us!"

Craig was desperate, grasping for straws. He spotted the list of equipment failures still lying on the Captain's desk. An idea was born.

"Captain. If you are right about HIM, HE knows what we're doing on board and HE can interfere with our equipment at will. Right?"

"That's right."

"Then we can't transmit. HE'll stop it or jam it. If HE knows we're on to HIM, HE'll be certain to attack. Right?"

A look of panic flashed across Holcomb's face. "Oh, Merciful Lord. I never thought about it that way."

"Our best bet is to keep a low profile and keep working our way back to Rota. Maybe HE doesn't suspect you're onto HIM. If so, maybe HE doesn't want to reveal HIS capability. If HE did attack and miss, HE'd really be revealed. Maybe HE doesn't want to risk that."

"That makes sense, XO. You're right, we won't transmit."

"I'll go up and tell the OOD to get a NAVSAT pass while we're up here, then go down and continue moving west. Okay?"

"Right. I want to rest for a few minutes."

As the Captain slumped into his chair, Craig let himself out. After briefing the OOD, he went down to his room locked the door and sagged into his chair. The Captain bore watching every minute and he still couldn't ask anyone else for help.

Christ, I'm scared!

36
Sink Him!

Luck was with the Exec for most of the next four days as a strained normalcy returned to the *Marion*'s operations. But, the sense that something was ominously abnormal had been palpable throughout the ship ever since the incident with the heavy explosions. By the patrol's fifty-first day, the troops were jumpy, and so were the officers. Too much of the argument outside Radio must have been overheard. Whatever the troops thought about the strange events and odd behavior of the Captain and the Exec, one thing was obvious. Morale was at rock bottom. Good-natured banter and the usual gleeful anticipation of homecoming were conspicuously absent from the Crew's Mess. The most common expression was a sullen wish to be "through with this fuckin' patrol."

As for Craig, there was surely nothing on his personal horizon to be cheerful about. If ship and crew got back in one piece, he then had to tackle the problem of convincing the NUC's that one of their own was defective. Single-handedly, he would have to refute the cultivated myth of the God-like infallibility of NUC submarine CO's. That, he realized, meant taking on Rickover and all his sycophants in SUBLANT.

During the infrequent quiet moments when his growing exhaustion permitted a few minutes relaxation before sleep overcame him, he brooded. Getting the ship home without having to relieve Holcomb of command seemed to be almost possible. As far as Craig's tired mind could see, dealing with the aftermath of the patrol would be impossible. He forced the thought aside. He had to concentrate on getting everyone back first. Worry about getting the Old Man relieved had to wait for later. Still, it crept into his conscious whenever he let his guard down.

Craig's luck ran out again at about 1531Z on the fourth day after the captain's impulse to transmit. This time he was caught in the shower. Standing,

229

lathered head to toe, he heard the word passed, "MAN BATTLE STATIONS, TORPEDO," followed by the General Alarm. He jumped out of the shower, half toweled the soap off, pulled on his poopysuit and ran for the Control Room. Fear clutched at him as he ran, wondering what magnitude of insanity the Captain was truly capable of. *God, I hope this is a drill!*

It was no drill. As Craig fought his way through the crowded Control Room toward the periscope stand, he heard the Weapons Officer, already on the phone to the Torpedo Room, give the order, "Flood Tube Number One. Open the Outer Door. Make Tube Number One Ready in All Respects."

No! You fucking maniac!

The Exec had every reason to be desperate. Tube Number One housed a fully armed MK-37 war shot. The Captain was actually getting ready to shoot someone.

Craig screamed, "Weapon's Officer! Do NOT open the outer door on Tube One!"

Joe looked at the Exec, perplexed at the counter-order, but he repeated it to the Torpedo Room.

Finally pulling himself up onto the periscope stand, Craig turned to Holcomb. "Captain! What's your target?"

Holcomb pointed a shaking finger at the BQS-4 Azimuth Indicator. A spoke indicated the presence of a fairly strong contact. "There. It's HIM."

"What's the classification of that contact?"

The Navigator spoke up from behind the Captain, fright evident in his voice. "It's a trawler. We've been tracking him for almost an hour."

Craig was beyond shock. "A trawler?"

"HE was going by on a steady course and speed. Now HE has stopped and is maneuvering down to the south of us."

"That's perfectly normal for a fisherman, Captain. Why do you want to shoot this guy?"

The Captain's eyes were wild now, darting around. "XO, it's HIM! I can tell by HIS behavior. Besides, HE dropped a PDC."

In the background, the crew had gotten to their Battle Stations. They probably figured the Captain knew much that they did not, and somehow this contact must be a real threat. They would trust the Captain right down to pulling the trigger. Even Rak was falling into line. Stone looked at Craig from his seat at the Target Motion Analyzer. He alone, looked like he might rebel. The Exec was frantic. They were on the cliff edge of a horrible mistake. Somehow, he had to wrest control away from the Captain.

Grab the initiative. Get the Old Man sidelined. Craig raised his voice to a confident firm shout, making sure he could be heard throughout the Control Room when he hit the 31MC press-to-talk switch and asked, "Sonar-Conn. The Captain says this trawler dropped a PDC. Did you record it?" *Plant doubt! Derail the momentum to shoot!*

He was stalling, and had purposely avoided the word "target." The whole fire control party was now obviously uneasy, but the captain was continuing his approach.

The Chief Sonarman came back on the 31MC with a hell of a note of urgency in his voice. "Conn-Sonar. We do not, repeat, DO NOT believe the trawler dropped a PDC. We heard a thump, probably from his otter-boards. I believe this is a working fisherman."

Craig swung to the Captain, now practically pleading. "Captain, I think this is an innocent fisherman. For God's sake, let's go up and take a look at him before we go any farther with this approach!"

"It's HIM, XO!"

It was time to gamble. If the Captain didn't back down, the only choice left to Craig would be to attempt to relieve him from command and hope for the crew's support. An actor now, giving the performance of his life, Craig backed off from the Captain and laughed. Then he told the Weapon's Officer to secure the tube. Joe looked perplexed and frightened, but quickly complied with the order.

"Captain, we've spooked ourselves. I just heard his winches and another clunk from his otter-boards. Please! Let's go up to periscope depth and I'll show you." *I'm so damned scared all I can hear is my own heart pounding!*

The Exec was lying, but the gamble worked. Indecision flickered in the Captain.

"Okay," he said, "Let's go up and look."

They went up and, sure enough, the contact was clearly visible through the periscope. It was a small Spanish trawler, fishing innocently. Craig pointed out his small size, his nets, and the flock of gulls astern. He did everything but hum the Spanish National Anthem. Finally, the Captain was convinced and secured Battle Stations.

The Old Man went straight to his stateroom and closed the door while most of the other officers wandered off to the wardroom. Craig went below and locked himself in his own stateroom. There, in private, as his stress ebbed, he surrendered to the nervous tremors. He shook like he had never shaken before. Real fear invaded every inch of his body and spirit.

For the first time, he wondered if his nerves would hold out. He could handle physical danger, but this was something else. They had come within a minute or less of killing a boatload of innocent fishermen. Again, he weighed the risks of locking the Captain up. If he succeeded, he could deal with his own fate. If he failed, and the Captain managed to keep the support of the crew, he would be the one locked up and Holcomb would be completely unrestrained. That risk was simply too great to accept. *In spite of all this, I gotta hang on. Locking him up has to stay as a last resort. Submariners just don't mutiny.*

About fifteen minutes later there was a knock on the Exec's door. Recovered now, he opened it to let the COB in. The Chief carefully closed the door behind him.

"Mr. Craig…"

"Yeah, COB. What is it?" The COB would normally have called him "XO." The formality and the drawn look on the Chief's face clearly told Craig that he, too, was rattled.

"What the hell is going on? That scene just now scared the shit out of me. Chief Brown and Franzei had to physically stop the Chief Sonarman from coming down here to go after the Captain."

"COB, it scared me too."

"XO, we gotta do something about the crew. They are gonna come apart if someone doesn't tell them something. They don't know whether some son-of-a-bitch is trying to kill us or the Old Man has gone round the bend."

Craig didn't answer. He sat there, at a loss for words, trying to think of a safe way to answer.

The COB broke the silence. "Most of us in Chiefs' Quarters aren't sure about the son-of-a-bitch out there, but we think the Captain has a problem. Brownie and I think you need backup."

"Look, Chief. I really do not think anything out there wants to kill us and I don't want you speculating about the Captain. He made a mistake today. That's all."

The COB shook his head. "The other day outside Radio, too?"

"COB, you and the other Chiefs have got to settle the crew down. There's only twelve days left in the patrol and the important thing now is to get us all back to Rota in good order."

"So what do we tell the crew?"

"Tell them that the drill today was the Captain testing me to see if I'm ready to go to command. Tell them he was just testing my judgment."

"XO, we're not a ship of fools."

"I know that. A lot of the troops will grab anything you give them to hang some peace of mind onto. The best and smartest ones, you, the other Chiefs and the First Class like Franzei—the leaders—will see through the story before you're finished putting it out, but they'll be solid."

The COB nodded his agreement, but his concern for the Exec was not allayed. "You still need backup."

"YOU need to stay as far from this thing as you can. Just keep the crew in line doing their job till we get back. The Captain is the Captain and you have been a good sailor all your life. Keep it that way."

The COB didn't like the Exec's words, but he understood. Leaving, he turned for a last question.

"So what do I do if we have a replay of today's fiasco? You're on one side and the CO is on the other."

"You're a professional. Do what is right."

He nodded.

"And, COB…thanks."

While the COB and Craig were having their conversation, another, equally intense, discussion had been taking place in the wardroom. Stone had berated Rak, Joe and the Navigator for not acting to avert the crisis before the Exec had arrived on the scene. All of them realized how close they had come to killing innocent fishermen. Rak quickly sided with Stone. He had come to the same conclusions before he had even gotten his sound powered phones put away at his Battle Station.

Rak was angry, mostly at himself. Joe, ever the clinical thinker, internalized their abuse, considered it and decided he agreed. In fact, the situation had been saved by Joe's characteristic response when events began to move faster than his logic circuits. When his understanding got behind events, he typically "failed safe," that is, moved to slow events down until he caught up. That "fail safe" instinct had been what caused him to shut the torpedo tube outer door when Craig had countermanded the CO's order.

"So what are you fucking heroes going to do?" Stone asked.

Rak was the first to reply. "I dunno. We can't take a friggin vote on every tactical decision. Me, I'm not lifting any more safety catches unless the XO gives the order."

Joe nodded his agreement. "Take all routine orders from the CO, but where weapons are concerned, we'll only act on orders from the XO."

Stone nodded.

The Navigator stood up to leave the table. The disbelief in his expression registered on the others.

"I don't want any part of this conversation. By Navy Regs, you could all be court-martialed right now for mutiny and sedition. Listen to yourselves. You are plotting against the Captain and his authority! For Christ's sake, knock this kind of talk off, and whatever you do, don't let the crew hear any of it!"

Stone's words followed him out the door. "I'd rather be court-martialed for mutiny than convicted of manslaughter, and I know some fishermen that would agree with me."

Joe stood up next to go. "Gator is right, you know. That's why the XO isn't talking to us. He doesn't want to get forced into relieving the CO. Didn't either of you guys ever read Herman Wouk's *The Caine Mutiny*? If it comes to the point where he has to do it, he knows the Navy Establishment will come after him with a vengeance. If he tried to relieve the Old Man and failed, he would lose all control of our situation. If he succeeded and we could be shown to be complicit, we would all wind up in Portsmouth Naval Prison as soon as we get home. We have to keep quiet."

Leave it to Joe, the thinker, COB, the professional, and warriors like Stone and Rak to get things right. When Craig was feeling totally alone in one of the worst moments of his life, a bunch of good men were standing by, keeping a silent watch just in case their XO needed their help. If they were forced out of the shadows, it would be professional suicide for all of them, but, they would be with him if they were needed.

And, that is the definition of true courage.

37
A Perilous Course

When the excitement from the aborted torpedo attack had died down, the Exec found himself with a couple of hours of privacy before it was time to relieve the Captain of the Command Duty. He was shaken and needed the time alone to do some serious thinking. Craig considered that he might have been the only one on board who knew the Old Man wasn't holding a drill and had meant to use the weapon! Holcomb's madness had become a threat to the ship, to other vessels, and, in reality, to all the world.

Craig couldn't wait any longer in hopes the patrol would run out before the Captain became even more dangerous. He was very dangerous now and the Exec had to make a decision. No one could do it for him and he couldn't avoid it. He had to find a way to cope with the unthinkable; a dangerously deluded, paranoid Commanding Officer who could bring the world to the brink of World War III. He wouldn't even have to touch the sixteen missiles he controlled. All that had to happen was for him to lose the ship in a scenario that made it look like the *Marion* had been the victim of hostile action.

If National Command Authority had reason to believe the nation's strategic weapons were under pre-emptive attack, the whole U. S. strategic force would be at the Soviet's throat in a flash with all their nuclear teeth bared. After that, one miscalculation, one blink on either side and the world as we knew it would be gone. The very existence of a mad Captain at sea with the most devastating assembly of weaponry ever placed in the hands of one man stripped away all but the last few layers of protection that stood between Cold War detente and Armageddon. And, the remaining layers of safeguards for the human race were all too fragile. Craig had every reason to find the situation appalling and terrifying.

What if he had shot that Goddamned torpedo, then something had happened to us? Even if we had gotten off a message, it would have been in his report that we were defending ourselves while under attack.

Craig thought the problem statement was simple—control Holcomb over the remaining eleven days of the patrol and get the ship safely back to port. He had no idea what the explanation was for all the PDC's and strange encounters and, for the moment could have cared less. The Captain's condition was obviously now the immediate and predominant threat.

Success, ultimately, hinged on controlling the CO. *Relieve him and abort the patrol? The Captain would surely resist given his state of paranoia. How violently would he resist? What if I couldn't wrest command away from him? Who would control the situation if he locked me up? Who would the crew follow? Submarine crews don't mutiny. How could any of them be sure which of us was the crazy one?*

The questions ricocheted over and over in Craig's mind. Finally, he got up and rummaged in the locker above his desk until he found his copy of NAVY REGS. The index led him to Article 0867 "Relief of a Commanding Officer by a Subordinate." He read and reread the three relatively short paragraphs.

The first paragraph didn't help. Paragraph Two read in part, "In order that a subordinate officer, acting upon his own initiative, may be vindicated for relieving a commanding officer from duty, the situation must be obvious and clear, and must admit of the single conclusion that the retention of command by such commanding officer will seriously and irretrievably prejudice the public interest…"

It became clear from the third paragraph that if he relieved the Captain, the burden would be on him to prove his actions were justified. Craig was willing to worry about justifying his actions later, but that second paragraph was a stickler. He knew that, if he forced the issue, half the people on board would turn to it to see what they should do.

Without an opportunity to observe the Captain as intimately as Craig had been forced to do, very few would consider the situation "obvious and clear," let alone admissive of only a "single conclusion." The stark reality of what that paragraph said was that, if the Exec relieved the Captain in time to avoid catastrophe, he would certainly be found guilty of mutiny. If he waited until its provisions were satisfied, a catastrophe beyond the conception of the document's drafters might result. It was a classic conundrum.

Clearly, as a way to proceed, relieving Holcomb was definitely not an option. The risk of failure was too great and the personal ramifications suicidal. As he was the only one with any hope of controlling the Captain, and knowing how far the stakes extended beyond even their own survival, Craig had to avoid the gamble.

Craig sat and tried to force some alternative plan to materialize, some clever solution. None came. He kept coming back to the conclusion that all he could do was try to keep the Captain's trust so he could influence him, meanwhile, watching his every movement. He would save "Relief" for the last ditch when they or some other poor bastard was "in extremis." Unaware that they had already settled on their own course of action, the Exec considered that it was too risky to take the other officers into his confidence.

If the Captain overhears a single careless conversation or word, he might cut me off, or worse yet, decide I'm part of the threat. If that happens, we'll be ass deep in the Rubicon.

Craig never much liked the isolation of patrol, but never before had he felt so much alone as he did now. Alone in thought, he would surely be alone in deed if he was forced to challenge Holcomb.

Having decided what had to be done, the Exec waited until the wee hours of the morning and caught Stone coming off the OOD watch at 0400. Stone was on one of the teams that had the combination to the outer door of the safe in the Radio room that held the authentication materials for Emergency Action Messages and the ACIP Key that closed the last link in the missile firing circuit. Together, they were the key to releasing the *Marion*'s nuclear weapons. He needed Stone, no one else.

Craig approached Stone casually. "Hey, Stone. How about taking twenty minutes to do me a favor?"

Stone obviously preferred going straight to his bunk, but he didn't argue. "Sure, XO. What do you need?"

"We're due to change the inner EAM safe door combination. How about giving me a hand?"

That meant he had to open the outer safe, then wait while Craig opened the inner door and changed the combination. Lastly, as a two-man team, they had to inventory the contents and log their signatures.

Stone dozed while Craig fiddled with the lock. It was one of the older varieties and he had to disassemble the lock work to change the settings on the tumblers. Finally they were through. The inventory had been taken and they left the Radio Room.

Outside the door, Craig said, "Thanks, Stone."

Stone smiled back with a slightly curious flick of his eyebrows. "Okay, XO. No problem. I didn't realize we were due to change combinations."

"We weren't. I like to do an extra change now and then just so the Squadron Communicator will be impressed."

Stone laughed and went below. *The XO did that so the Old Man can't get to the ACIP keys without going through him first.*

Craig saw no need to mention to Stone that he had no intention of telling his designated alternate, the Engineer, about the new combination. Stone was the one officer he could count on to understand what had just transpired without explanation. He would be discrete.

With the ACIP keys in the inner safe and no one else in possession of the combination, there was now at least one thing the Old Man couldn't get to. The missiles with their one hundred forty eight warheads couldn't be launched unless someone was able to get the combination out of him. And nothing short of a valid Emergency Action Message from the National Command Authority was going to make that happen.

The next morning the Captain did not show up on time for the regular exchange of the Command Duty. After waiting a half hour and knowing that the Captain was in his stateroom, the Exec decided to investigate and knocked on his door. When Holcomb answered his second knock, Craig went in and found him fully dressed, lying on his bunk.

"Captain, are you feeling all right?"

No answer. Holcomb just stared as if he was looking at an intruding stranger. *He looks gaunt as hell.* Craig tried again. "Captain, are you okay?" *Hell no, he's not OKAY! He's going downhill physically, as well as mentally.*

"XO, I'd like you to keep the watch. I've been thinking all night about the things that have happened on this patrol. I don't want to be disturbed for a while." His voice became very conspiratorial. "You and I are the only ones who really know what's going on. One of us has to survive and get back. We must make sure CINCLANT knows what we've learned."

In spite of his better judgment, Craig had to ask. "Captain, what's your view of what we've learned?"

"The PDC's. The equipment failures. That fishing boat. They're all tied together. When we get back and show CINCLANT all our logs, they'll understand."

"What do you think the connection is?"

"I don't know. That's what I'm trying to work out, to understand."

He then said decisively, almost with vigor, "XO, you keep the watch. You're a good tactician. HE'S trailing us, but you can get us back."

He's taking another step back from the world that's terrifying him. His condition is worsening and he needs some reassurance. "Captain," Craig said, "I don't think anyone is behind us just now. Look, I'll go up in an hour or so and pull a Kamikaze. I'll fade right with slowly increasing rudder and speed, then shift rudder, do a 270-degree to the left and charge back down our track for half an hour. If there's anyone there, we should hear him hauling ass to get out of our way. After a half-hour sprint, we'll go ultra quiet and drift for a while, listening. That'll be hard for any trailer to deal with."

He brightened up. "Good, good, XO. Do that."

"Goodnight or morning, Captain. Get some rest, okay?"

The Captain called Craig three times in the next five hours to see if he had developed any contacts. About 1430Z he suddenly appeared in the Exec's stateroom.

"Captain?"

"Just checking, XO. I was afraid you might have dozed off. We're in too much danger to let our guard down." Then he was gone, back to the sanctuary of his stateroom.

Craig could see the handwriting on the wall and wondered again if he would have the stamina to see the patrol through. *God help us all if he catches me asleep.* Never mind that the elaborate baffle-clearing maneuver hadn't detected anything at all.

That night, when he was reasonably certain that the Captain was asleep, Craig locked his door and, sitting up in his chair, caught a few hours of fitful sleep. Even that was more than he would get later.

The next day was the patrol's fifty-third and the Captain didn't come out of his stateroom. He didn't offer to take the Command Duty and Craig didn't bother to ask. Every now and then Holcomb would call the Exec to come to his stateroom to brief him on the tactical situation. Each visit found him more delusional and closer to physical collapse than the last.

Craig had headed the ship continually west with ten days left in the patrol, pressing against the western boundary of *Marion*'s assigned op areas. He wanted to be as close to the barn as he could get. At midnight they would pick up the Alboran areas, which would cover them all the way to the Straits. Passage out of the Med couldn't come too soon for the exhausted Craig.

After evening meal, the Captain called the Exec into his stateroom again. This time, with great care, Holcomb closed the door and, motioning to Craig to keep his voice low with his index finger over his lips, took an agitated step toward his bunk.

"XO, we've got to go up and communicate."

"Why, Captain?"

"HE's not going to let us get out of the Med! HE can't afford to let us get back to port with all the information we've recorded!"

"Captain, I don't think we're in any danger now."

"XO! You're the last person I would expect to be so non-believing. You're the one who made me realize the PDC's were his sensors. We have to let CINCLANT know what's going on before it's too late. What happens if HE sinks us before we can get word back? CINCLANT won't know the whole FBM force is vulnerable. HE can't afford to let us get back!"

Holy Christ! Did I create this monster? The Captain was beginning to look pretty wild. The last thing the Exec wanted to do was transmit and set alarm bells off all over the Atlantic Fleet. If and when they got back to port, the whole chain of command would sooner or later be on top of both of them. *If he doesn't get a placebo, how far will he work himself up? Think! Talk!* "Captain, I don't think we should transmit."

"Why not?"

"If we transmit, we're located. Maybe HE doesn't hold contact now. Besides, a message won't tell CINCLANT much. They have to have our data package, all of our recordings of the PDC's, and the strange echo ranging, et cetera. That's what we have to get back. We have gone to a lot of trouble to be sure we have a first class intelligence package for them."

That much was true. The Chief Sonarman and Franzei were among the best operators in the Fleet and they were as determined as the Exec to get good tapes back to NISC.

"Yeah, XO. I guess you're right. But how are we going to get back? I know HE's back there. I feel HIM. I know!"

What the hell am I going to do to calm him down? Inspiration struck. "Captain, let's run our track right down the two hundred fathom curve between here and the Straits. That'll make contact an absolute bitch for HIM to maintain and, if we do get hit, we can drive the ship aground in salvageable water."

He actually looked overjoyed. "Excellent! Excellent! HE'll never expect that! Do it! How soon can we be on the two hundred fathom curve?"

"In about ten to twelve hours."

"Great! Great! Lay out the track with the Navigator. I'm going to rest for a while now."

"Aye, aye, Captain. You do realize this will take us inside Spain's Twelve Mile Limit."

He turned back from his bunk. "Of course I do. It's my decision that the tactical threat warrants disregarding international boundaries!"

"Goodnight, Captain."

"XO, do another one of those fancy baffle clearing maneuvers of yours before we move in toward the beach. I don't want to underestimate HIM!"

"Yes, sir. Goodnight, sir."

Craig smothered a sigh of relief. With the right precautions and an alert watch, the track he had proposed was not a difficult, nor particularly hazardous one. If it kept the Old Man quiet until they were out of the Med, it was well worth the risk. He went to officers' country and rousted out the sleeping Navigator. After some well-justified argument, Gator accepted the track and they laid it out on the Quartermaster's chart. Craig told him the Captain felt it was necessary and was surprised to find that the Navigator had been more observant than he had realized. Gator said he reckoned anything that made the Skipper feel better was worth doing.

After the new track was laid down on the chart and they had both checked and re-checked the plot, the Exec turned to the Navigator. "Gator. I don't want any questions. Just listen to me. This is an order. For the rest of the patrol, if I have to rest, you are to be up and about. Should the Captain give ANY direction to you or the OOD, I am to be informed immediately. I repeat, if he changes any instructions I have left for the watch, I am to be called immediately! As Fire Control Coordinator, you will not order a tube made ready if I am not in Conn. Call me if in doubt. Do you understand?"

Gator looked less than happy. "I do understand. You don't have to explain. We've all been talking about it."

"I'm not telling you what to think. It's important you all form your own opinions. Just call me with anything the CO does."

"Aye, aye, XO."

That was that. Now it should be a simple test of stamina.

38
Night Orders

For some three days and four hours after agreeing to the transit tactics, the CO did not leave his stateroom except for infrequent calls of nature. He did not, when forced out of the darkened cubicle, speak nor acknowledge the voices of others. Haggard, but erect and clear-eyed, he simply emerged from his cabin, relieved himself and returned.

All communications and directives from him came through the Exec, who was seen by the Steward's Mates—and sometimes by junior officers—to occasionally slip, for brief periods, into the CO's quarters. The Stewards also observed, and discussed in their native Tagalog, that the Exec's bunk had not been used during this period. They probably found that curious, but no more so than the many other examples of strange behavior they had seen on this patrol.

* * * * *

To Craig, the CO's behavior was a mixed blessing. It was the patrol's fifty-sixth day, with only seven to go. The CO didn't interfere with the Exec's running of the ship, but he demanded constant reassurance. Craig was having trouble finding any opportunity for rest. For the fourth time in six hours, his stateroom phone had buzzed and the quivering voice had spoken.

The request was always the same. "XO, can you come here for a minute?"

For the hundredth time since starting the transit, Craig had risen and taken the single pace from his stateroom to the CO's, pushed through the door and said, "Yes, sir?"

For the hundredth time, the scene was the same. Huddled in his chair, as if blinded by the radiance of the single eight-watt bulb in his desk light, the Captain slowly turned and lifted his gaze toward the door.

God, he looks another hour and half more bedraggled every time he pushes the damned buzzer.

The huddled figure trembled, maybe a little more than before, but made no other move.

At least, he wasn't crying this time. Craig was too tired and too annoyed to feel any compassion for Holcomb. The last call had been a ten-minute whimper session. This call, like all the others, was to allow the Captain to reassure himself that the Exec was awake and vigilant. For an instant, Craig felt contempt flare up and was angry with the cringing mass before him, but the stakes were too high to permit himself any flicker of betraying expression. *This is a real Goddamned monument to Rickover. A real poster boy for the Nuclear Power Program.*

Finally the CO spoke, barely a whisper. "Is HE there?"

"No, sir. We've had no sonar contacts for over two hours."

"Have we cleared baffles? Maybe HE's got a way to know what we're going to do and can just stay in our baffles."

"No, sir. I don't think so."

The answer agitated him. His voice rose. "No sonar contacts for two hours? That isn't possible. HE's done something to interfere with sonar! XO, why didn't you see that?" The Captain's shaking took over in spasms. "HE's probably right behind us this very minute and you let HIM get there!"

The figure collapsed back in the chair, whimpering softly, hands clutching spasmodically at the chair's arms.

Craig stood for a moment, expressionless, looking at the Old Man's shirtfront. *When did he start drooling on himself?* "Captain, the sonar is working fine. The Seven and Four are both fine. We can hear occasional biologics in all quadrants and normal background sea noise. This area is a quiet one. We chose it, remember? Sir, I'd really like you to get some sleep." *What I really mean is that I want to get some sleep. I'd kill for four solid hours in the bunk right now.*

"Okay XO, I guess you're right."

With that Craig withdrew. As long as the CO stayed put and pacified he was confident that he could get through the transit. If he was caught off guard and sleeping, Holcomb's fragile trust might snap. God only knew what would happen in that case. He simply had to stay up and alert and keep the Old Man soothed until the ship was safe. If there was another way, he was far too tired to think of it.

Since he had already been disturbed by the Captain's call, Craig decided to interrupt his work on the patrol report and swing through Control, checking traffic in Radio and contacts in Sonar. It was about time to write the Night Orders and, particularly, he wanted to satisfy himself with the navigational situation. The whole track for the last three days had been risky enough, but the next six and one-half hours would be the most critical. The two hundred fathom curve they were following converged with the coastline until, at their closest point of approach, the ship would pass within five miles of the beach.

Turning time to the next leg was also critical, as they were following the inside curve of a large bay and a turn to the south, seaward, was necessary to avoid a jutting point ahead. They had to skirt south before continuing on a westward track. It was six and a half-hours that the professional seaman in Craig viewed with extreme caution, yet he was confident that two well-settled SINS and meticulous attention to the fathometer would see them safely through.

The Exec stopped first in Radio and skimmed rapidly through the messages that had accumulated since his last visit. None were addressed to the ship. If so, those would have been sent down to him immediately via the Messenger of the Watch. The messages left to be reviewed were routine general administrative traffic. He initialed one after another, hung the clipboard back in its place and pocketed his pen.

"What's up, Deshong?" he said to the Radioman, who sat nearby banging away at a decrepit typewriter. "Those the turnover inventories?"

"Yeah, Mr. Singleton wants to get them done before we go Mod-Alert. Guess he wants to audit them on the way through the Straits after we break coms."

"Aims to make a quick sale to the Bluies, huh?"

With that, Craig moved on to Sonar. One operator was changing the work tape on the UNQ-7 recorder, the other was sitting at the BQR-7, one leg thrown over the arm of his chair, slowly training the ship's biggest ears in an advancing sector search. Nothing showed on the recorder's paper trail except the grey hash of random noise and an occasional short curving punctuation mark when some passing biologic had raised its voice to another of its kind. Absolutely nothing of tactical interest. The Sonar Supervisor looked up from the log sheet that he was filling out.

"Evening, XO."

"Evening, Yancy. Pretty quiet, huh?"

"Aye, sir. Not a thing."

"You did pretty good in the crew's poker game the other night. You gonna buy Momma a 'pretty' or stash it?"

"Aw, XO, you can't believe everything you hear. I'm barely even for the patrol."

"That ain't what the losers say! Better watch your ass if the lights go out."

Both chuckled. Yancy was well over a thousand dollars ahead in the game and they both knew it.

In Control, Craig stopped at the MK-19 plotter and eyed the chart taped to its glass surface. "Where are we, Quartermaster?" His over riding concern was that the ships actual position not be too far ahead of or to the right of the position intended, the "PIM."

The Quartermaster of the Watch came over from where he stood near the periscope stand, sipped from the cup of coffee he was carrying, and answered, "About three miles ahead and a half a mile left of PIM, sir."

So far, so good... "When was your last sounding?"

"About fifteen minutes ago."

"How did it compare with the charted depth for our SINS position?"

"Right on, sir. The SINS are flat walkin' the line, I guess, because with the bottom gradient we got here, right or left a hair would show right up."

"Okay, round up the Night Order book. I'm going to the Nav Center for a few minutes, then I'll be back to write them."

The Nav Center was quiet, with the attendant technicians watching their charges, the SINS, work their subtle sensing magic. The Engineer on watch in Control as OOD, had been engrossed in a discussion with the leading Engineering Laboratory Technician and had not seen the Exec pass. Eng, by nature a harried man, was never able to distribute his attention among multiple tasks. Craig shook his head, resigned to what he was seeing. The ship was running at high speed, within a stone's throw of shoal water, and the Engineer's main concern was his input to the Old Man's end of patrol HGR letter. They had taken some heat on Secondary Chemistry on the last ORSE, so Eng had been sitting on the ELT's shoulders all patrol. Now it was almost time to report to "God" how good they had been.

As Craig walked into the Nav Center, past the Central Navigation Center computer stack, the SINS Technician on watch looked up from the Navigation Center Control console.

"Hi, XO."

"What kind of Hula Dance are these unstable platforms of yours doing?"

"Walkin' the line."

The SINS Tech and Craig stood before the monitor plots where the SINS performance was graphically portrayed. Craig, having once been an FBM Navigator, knew what he was looking at and was comforted. The last fix had been taken from a navigation satellite less than two hours before, and it confirmed very small errors in both SINS, as had every fix taken for several days. To his practiced eye, the SINS were exceptionally well settled and differences between number one and number two were small. He could, he decided, rely on those SINS as long as they didn't begin to diverge from one another. That would signal an error creeping in.

"Keep 'em truckin'!"

"You got it, sir."

From the Nav Center, Craig returned to the Control Room, took the Captain's Night Order book from the Quartermaster and commenced writing. By now, the crew was accustomed to the Exec writing the Night Orders for the Captain. Few noticed that, increasingly, no signature or initials gave evidence that the Captain even saw them.

Finished with his writing, Craig pocketed his pen and, open night orders in hand, approached the periscope stand. The Engineer had temporarily exhausted his angst with the ELT and, this time, noted the Exec's approach. Swinging himself up beside number one periscope, Craig handed the Night Orders to the Engineer.

"Eng, here are the Night Orders for tonight. Read them, and when you get relieved, make sure the Weapons Officer fully understands them."

"Aye, aye, sir."

"Now, listen to what I'm about to tell you. The next six hours or so have the least margin for error of any track you're ever likely to run. To make sure we're safe, I want you to: A. Stay to the left of the plotted track. B. Allow yourself to get no more than one mile ahead of our intended position. C. Clear baffles only to the left. And, D. Take soundings every half hour unless you get one that is less than two hundred fathoms. If that happens, take soundings every five minutes and call me. If less than one hundred fathoms, turn south, slow to one third, take continuous soundings and call me. Do you understand?"

"Aye, sir."

"That last is most important. There's no place on our track where we can go from soundings greater than two hundred fathoms to shoal water in less than forty-five minutes or from one hundred fathoms to shoal water in less than fifteen. If you take soundings every thirty minutes and if, for some reason, we get a sounding you don't like, we have enough time to stay safe. The SINS are well settled, but, understand, the soundings are our insurance!"

"Aye, sir, I understand."

"Make sure Joe understands all of what I have just said when he relieves you."

"Aye, sir, I will."

"Okay, I'm going down and have at the patrol report for a while. It won't write itself. Notice that I've put a call in for thirty minutes before the next turn. Make sure I get it."

As he paused before leaving the compartment, Craig's eye caught the Chief of the Watch turning from his Ballast Control Panel to the Engineer who was now sitting in the Captain's chair on the periscope stand.

The Chief said, "Ain't this kinda hairy, sir?"

The Engineer replied with a noncommittal shrug. "Twelve knots for forty-five minutes takes us nine miles. If that puts us on the beach, we must be running inside somebody's Twelve Mile Limit."

Another shrug.

The quiet routine of the ship's control party settled in and, elsewhere, the mess cooks commenced setting up for the coming watch's evening meal.

39

Twelve Mile Limit

There is a degree of fatigue beyond which the impulse to sleep no longer asserts itself. Just as a starving man's nervous system tires of sending futile signals of hunger and eventually stops doing so, beyond a certain threshold of fatigue, the body ceases to demand the sustenance of needed sleep. Craig had passed that point sometime during the previous day. Now he was running on dwindling reserves of nervous energy and he knew it. He remembered reading theories and thoughts about such things long ago in a book by Viktor Frank, *Man's Search for Meaning.* He never dreamed that he would experience what Frank had so eloquently described.

He stood, stiff and awkward from sitting too long in the steel desk chair, glanced at the clock and began to jog in place. 2350Z. One hour and thirty-five minutes until the next course change. If the Old Man kept still, he would have time to work up a sweat, take a shower to clear his head and grab a snack from the Wardroom before checking the ship's track again. His legs were now pumping a methodical eighty times a minute.

Another hour and a half and we'll have pulled this stunt off. If the son-of-a-bitch just stays dormant, I'll have eight hours to get some rest before we have to run the Straits.

Ten minutes later he was in the shower letting the near scalding water beat on his head and shoulders, wasting water. Water conservation could wait for a time when he wasn't so damned tired. Toweling down, the track flashed through Craig's mind. The point of land off the southeast coast of Spain hooked down before them, just outside his planned turning point. Two or three miles late turning would be dangerous, five would be disastrous. The ship was making twelve knots and he planned to be in the Control Room thirty minutes before the turn, six miles early. Both SINS were tracking well with small differences between them and no abnormal soundings had been reported. Safe enough for the patrol's fifty-seventh day, he reassured himself. Only six days remained.

Craig went to the wardroom, where Rak was having a better night than usual in the poker game. He was up a little over twenty dollars real money and the cards were still falling his way. He had taken every player at the table, at one time or another, except for the Exec. Somehow Craig always eluded him, and, most times, bit hard into Rak's winnings in the process.

Rak had been stalking the Exec at the poker table in every game so far. It had nothing to do with the money. It was purely and simply the friendliest of rivalries. Craig had hit him pretty hard a couple of times and, unless Rak could return a heavier blow, he would stay number two overall in the game. Rak didn't like being second best at anything.

Tonight was not the night to call Rak. He was on a roll and the Exec was, for the first time of the patrol, not in his customary seat at the head of the table. Given the Captain's outspoken disapproval of the game, it would be notable to a careful observer that, during the weekly poker game, Craig invariably used the Old Man's chair. Rak was the kind of observer that would pick up on that.

As the Navigator called the next hand "Five Card Stud" and began to deal, Rak looked up. Craig was standing at the head of the table spooning soup into his mouth from a coffee mug.

"Hey, XO, come on in."

Craig grunted. He didn't like short games. Still, he had another twenty minutes before he needed to be in CONN and the game would keep his mind active.

"Okay, give me fifty out of the bank and watch your ass!" As he took a seat in the nearest open chair, he thought to himself, *Rak's pretty eager. Gotta watch the bluffs.*

The rumble began as the doctor dealt the third card in the next hand. It started abruptly at 0020Z and sounded like the gods shaking a great sheet of tin. The doctor froze in mid deal. Before he could drop the cards and stand, Craig was out of his seat and had cleared the wardroom, rattling up the ladder to the Control Room.

In Crew's berthing, the off watch came awake and waited in a clutch of apprehension. No shock, no vibration, just the deafening rumble.

Craig topped the ladder to the Control Room and burst past the MK 19 to the periscope stand. Blind, coming from the white lights of the Wardroom to the red tinted darkness of Control, only his ears told him of the threat.

"Conn—Nav: Sounding is six feet under the keel and decreasing."

That's what the rumble was! The ship was so close to the bottom that it was creating a venturi as it sped along. The noise came from the turbulent water flow and cavitation between the hull and the bottom they were about to hit. Any second now, the rumble was going to end in an impact. *God help us if it this isn't a flat bottom.*

Submarines are built to be incredibly strong in resisting compressive stresses. Like an egg, though, once the hull cracks or distorts, it can fail catastrophically. The last SSN to drag its stern on the bottom at high speed had left its whole cruciform structure of rudder and stern planes behind, that portion of the hull broken cleanly off. That ship was saved purely by good fortune. One of the early boats, it was a twin-screw design and the failure had been aft of the exit point of the shafts and aft of the rear pressure bulkhead of the engine room.

In *Marion*'s case, with one massive centerline screw, all that was required was to suffer enough distortion to cause the failure of the shaft seal. From that point, death of the ship would be brutally sudden. Craig knew, without thinking, that habitual ship control practices were to angle the ship up and down when changing depth, much like flying an airplane. In the present situation, a two-degree up bubble would put the stern on the bottom. With the stern two hundred feet aft of the center of buoyancy, every degree of up angle would instantly put the stern over three feet lower before the ship could rise. He was terrified and didn't trust Joe to instinctively recognize the terrible danger they were in.

"Conn—Nav: We're losing the sounding in our bottom trace."

The Weapon's Officer stood on the portside of the periscope stand, mouth agape, frozen.

The Chief of the Watch was standing before his Ballast Control Panel looking over his shoulder, desperate for an order.

Without breaking stride in his race from the wardroom, Craig plunged across the periscope stand, screaming now. "Blow all main ballast!"

"Blow the forward group, aye, sir!"

"Blow All Main Ballast, All Main Ballast! Goddammit! We gotta bring her up LEVEL!"

His plunge carried Craig to the Ballast Control Panel and his hand closed over the Chief's just as the After Group Blow Switch rammed home to "Blow!"

Craig's next concern was the inclinometer.

Christ, we've got to bring this SOB up level. Any angle and we'll put the stern in the mud. At twelve knots, we'll leave it there!

There was no time now to waste on giving instructions to Joe. Craig continued to pour out a stream of orders to the ship control party.

"Diving Officer—Zero Bubble!"

"Helm—All Stop!"

Slowly, ever so slowly, the ship began to lift. The rumble had stopped. Craig knew that once she started to rise, a broach was sure to come, but, still he tried to catch her before she popped to the surface.

"Secure the Blow."

"Left full rudder." That would take them south away from the looming shore and into deeper water.

"Open the vents. Ahead Full."

"Maneuvering. Conn. Build turns right up."

Unless directed otherwise, the Throttleman would build turns up slowly to avoid cavitating. Craig needed power now in his attempt to overcome the excess buoyancy with hydrodynamic lift.

"Ten degree down bubble. Diving Officer, make your depth eighty feet."

The depth order was wishful thinking. Eight thousand tons were rising, accelerating upwards faster than the small vents could dump air. Craig knew he couldn't stop it and fervently hoped there was nothing in the area that sonar hadn't heard before this mess started. Too late to worry about what might be above them. They had now traded one opportunity for calamity for another. If there was anything above them, the *Marion*'s HY 80 steel sail that was designed to surface through ten feet of ice would cleave through it like a meat axe. *Marion* would survive, but no ship on the surface above them would.

"Weaps, raise number two periscope and get on it. Check us clear when it breaks."

"Helm, Ahead two thirds. Steer course 180 degrees."

"Goddammit, Weaps, get up here and take this scope! You are night adjusted. I can't see shit!"

The Weapon's Officer pulled himself up to the periscope stand from where he had crouched since the Exec had hurtled past him. He turned to the periscope that was already slithering up.

"Low power, Weaps, just make sure we aren't going to get hit."

"Aye, sir."

From the Diving Officer came, "Broached, sir!"

"Make your depth sixty-two feet. What do you see, Weaps?"

"Jesus, I see a Goddamned four story building and it's a half division in low power!"

The Weapon's Officer had stopped his sweep with the periscope trained astern.

Craig swiftly calculated to himself.

One half division low power, guess fifty feet high. That means we came within a mile of causing one hell of a Saturday night stir in that town!

"Never mind that." Craig snapped. "Is there anyone out there to hit us? Finish your look around."

"Aye, sir. No ship contacts, sir."

"Aye. NAV—CONN, Sounding?"

"CONN—NAV, one hundred eighty feet and increasing."

"Fine. Diving Officer, make your depth one hundred feet. Weaps, take continuous soundings and report to me when we're outside the hundred fathom curve. Maintain this course and speed until I tell you otherwise. Get all compartments to inspect for damage and report the results to me."

Next, Craig turned to the Navigator. "When's the next NAVSAT pass? I want to know where those Goddamned SINS think they are."

Done for the moment, he turned. There, like a ghostly apparition, in the door to the Control Room stood the Captain, dressed only in his skivvies. All five officers and the twenty-two enlisted men in the area went silent, watching and waiting for the apparition to speak.

Finally, through trembling lips, it did. "What happened, XO?"

"We grazed the bottom. We have recovered and are continuing the transit in safe water. I don't know yet how it happened."

"Oh." With that, the apparition disappeared.

After a moment, Craig broke the silence. "Stone," he said, addressing the Supply Officer who was watching from the bench seat at the MK 113.

"Yes, sir."

"I want you to collect all navigational records and plots in use since noon today. Be sure to get the Night Orders, the Engineering Bell Book and the Quartermaster's notebook. Lock everything up in your safe. If you take them out, do so only on my direct order. They are not to leave your view if they are out of your safe. You are responsible for insuring that no one, including me, has an opportunity to tamper with anything before the records are turned over to the Squadron Commander!

"Quartermaster, log my instructions to Mr. Stone."

The Quartermaster answered quickly, "Aye, aye, sir."

"Stone, did you understand me?"

"Yes, sir, aye, aye, sir!" The question still showed in his eyes.

"In a few days, when we get this mother back alongside, a lot of us are going to be in very serious trouble. The only thing that can make it worse is if they can find some way to accuse us of both incompetence and chicanery. You're not a party to this event, so you're appointed 'Conscience.'"

Stone stood a moment longer staring at the Exec. He knew the direction he had just received was prudent and correct and he understood the other dimensions of Craig's angst. There was no way now to keep the outside world from asking the question that dominated the secretive conversations in the wardroom. Even the mess cooks were beginning to wonder aloud about the strangeness that hovered over the central will of the ship.

Finally, with the casual way of a cowhand reaching for his Bull Durham, Stone fished two toothpicks from his breast pocket, offered one to Craig and stuck the other in his mouth. "Right, Boss!" He rolled the toothpick on his tongue. Craig turned and headed for the Nav Center.

They liked and understood each other with an uncommon rapport, and they both knew Craig was in a hell of a mess.

40

Meaghan

It had been a fairly typical fifty-seventh patrol day back in Gales Ferry, Connecticut, for Meaghan. Up at 0600. Kids dressed and at the bus stop by 0730. Struggle to get the balky old Buick running, then off to work at her thirty hour per week job at 0745. Off work at 1400, then an hour's appearance at a "coffee" with the enlisted wives, where she watched Mrs. Holcomb sail through the wives of lesser rank like the Queen Mary parting a fleet of native canoes.

Next, on to her son's school to try to calm his near hysterical teacher with assurances that he would be made to understand that his pet snake was not a welcome guest at "Show and Tell." From there, home, wheeling the old Buick into the driveway just ahead of the approaching school bus. Capture the kids, feed them a snack and shoo them out to play. Clean up the patio where the dog had pooped again. Call Frank down at the corner gas station and tell him to get the new battery that wouldn't fit in last month's budget and fix the damned Buick. Cook dinner. Get the kids through their baths and into bed.

How come the damned car always runs and our son never terrorizes his teachers when Mike is home? There must be some rule Murphy hasn't written yet that applies to submarine wives.

It was not yet 10:00 p.m., and Meaghan was too tired to stay up for the eleven o'clock news. When the kids were finally asleep and she had finished cleaning the kitchen, she had treated herself to a self-prescribed session of therapy for her flagging morale. Pouring herself a sizeable glass of sherry, she had put on a Neil Diamond tape, turned the volume in the headphones up to something just short of the threshold of pain, and immersed herself in the music for an hour.

Just another couple of weeks. Mike will be home and life will be normal again. Bad dream number eleven will be over.

Later, Meaghan stood in front of the mirror in their bathroom, taking her makeup off in preparation for going to bed. She had just put down the face cloth and was reaching for her night cream when an avalanche of fear struck her.

Without warning, she was engulfed in a wave of formless terror. Pale and heart racing, she ran to each of the children's rooms. Both were sleeping peacefully. Accompanied by their curious and watchful dog, she inspected the house room by room. Nothing was amiss. Nothing she had seen or heard in the house had spawned her fear, but it would not subside.

Oh, my God! It's Mike! Something has happened to the Marion!

Until that moment, Meaghan had never worried about Mike when he was at sea. Privately, she had always been sure that she would know telepathically if he were in real danger. Afraid of ridicule, she had never shared her conviction with anyone, not even Mike. Tonight, lacking any rational explanation for her emotion, she decided she was sensing his deep distress and she was frantic. Still, there was literally nothing she could do but agonize. At that hour, there was no one she could call, no help to turn to. *God! All I can do is wait. I can't even call anyone. They'll just think I'm another wife having a breakdown while hubby is on patrol. Oh, shit. Maybe I am!*

The night was hell for Meaghan. Sleep, when it finally came, was filled with nightmares that left her clutching her pillow and sobbing. Finally, daylight came. Steeling herself to maintain her composure, she got the kids up and sent them off to school, then called her office and announced that she would be in late. She then watched the clock make its glacially slow way to 0800 and called the COMSUB Group TWO Chief of Staff. The duty yeoman answered on the second ring and put her through immediately to Captain Bill Davis. Davis' wife Margie and Meaghan were best friends, as were he and Mike. If anything had happened to the *Marion*, Bill would know and he was the one person she felt she could trust with her inquiry.

Bill Davis answered his phone with a jovial "Hi, Meg!"

"Bill, I don't want to sound like some silly spooked wife, but I'm worried about Mike. Have you heard anything from the *Marion*?"

Davis concealed his surprise at the question. They had been close friends for years and the Meaghan Craig he knew was not an easy woman to rattle. "No, Meg. We haven't heard anything from her. She's due into Rota in about a week. Why do you ask? Is something wrong?"

In spite of her fear, Meaghan was already regretting the call. "No. I just had some bad dreams and got myself worked up, I guess."

"Don't worry about it, sweetheart, I'll call Margie and she'll come over and harass you till you feel better. Look, everything is okay. If there is one guy out there that can handle anything that comes along, it's Mike."

"Thanks, Bill. You're right. I don't know what got into me, but don't call Margie. I'm going on in to work. I'll talk to her later." Meaghan hung up the phone and pulled herself together. Bill was right. *But that damn feeling is so terribly strong and it won't go away!.*

After dressing for work, Meaghan went out to the Buick and, with a deftness born of much practice, removed the portable battery charger that she had hooked up the night before, slammed the hood with a muttered blasphemy and started the car. As she backed out of the driveway, the fear and depression suddenly lifted. The change was so palpable, she stopped the car for a few moments, stunned.

It's gone! I actually felt the fear leaving! Whatever was happening must be over and Mike's okay.

Meaghan was still smiling when she walked into the Pfizer lab and sat down at her desk to start her workday.

41
End of Patrol in the Med

"You what?"

The words came out so loud and hard, filled with anger, that every head in Control snapped around. Craig was stunned! Furious.

"After all the precautions I put in the Night Order book you secured the fathometer?"

The Exec was on the verge of going for Joe physically. The COB, who had just come up from the crew's berthing, took the scene in and started to edge between them.

The Weapons Officer was white-faced, trembling, still absorbing how close he had brought himself, along with the ship and its one hundred and forty men, to instant death. Now he was face to face with a man angry beyond all words. His hands flew up in protest.

"XO," he pleaded, "the Captain came up and changed the Night Orders." Craig was incredulous. "He what?"

"He came up and told me to secure the fathometer. He was afraid it would be detected by somebody."

Craig's fury reduced him to hissing through clenched teeth. *The son of a bitch got past me! I thought he was holed up in his room all this time. Damn him! I was a fucking idiot for assuming anything about him while we were on this stretch of the track!* "When was that?"

Knowing he was pleading guilty to a major transgression, Joe responded weakly. "A couple of hours before the grounding."

After seething in silence for a brief moment, the Exec turned back to Joe. "Why didn't you immediately call and tell me that the Captain had changed the night orders?"

"They are his night orders, XO. Besides, we were sending them around again. The messenger just hadn't gotten to you. We all know you're pushing yourself too hard, so I told Kane not to disturb you if your door was closed, because you might be resting."

Craig backed off, struggling with his emotions. He was bewildered that, in spite of all that had happened on the patrol and his repeated instructions to the officers to immediately report any tactical instructions from the Captain, Joe had apparently felt no sense of urgency in this critical instance. *Absolutely no fucking common sense! Has he been asleep for the last month and just woke up like some Goddammed Rip Van Winkle? What the hell should I have expected of him? He's a junior officer and I made the decision not to confide in him about the Old Man. Maybe it's more my fault than his. Damn me, I let myself get careless.* "Okay, Joe, I'm sorry I blew up. My nerves are a little ragged right now. Let's all settle down and get back on our planned track."

After the excitement had drained away and the atmosphere in the Control Room had lost most of its tension, the Exec made a final check of the ship's navigation to be sure they were on a clear safe track. He then went to the wardroom and more or less collapsed into the Captain's chair. After the torpedo incident he had had the shakes. This time he was too tired and defeated to even shake. *The Captain is completely out of touch with reality now and I failed to get us home without an incident. I've lost mightily.*

Since he was the Command Duty Officer at the time of the grounding, Craig knew he would probably be finished professionally. The Old Man might get off if they hung his Exec high enough, but, for the CDO, there would be no escape. Craig was physically exhausted and very depressed. With nothing more to lose, he figured he would take the ship back to port and to hell with appearances. *One peep out of the Old Man and I'll lock him up. If the crew doesn't go along, they can lock me up instead and to hell with the whole fucking mess.*

Brooding for fifteen minutes seemed to relieve the Exec's stress a bit. He got up to go in search of the Navigator. All the other officers were up, chattering about what had happened, but most didn't want to get in Craig's way right then. Two of them had come into the Wardroom during his disconsolate reverie. The Doc had come in, fidgeted a bit, then said, "Thanks for being here, XO. Are you alright?" Satisfied with a slight nod in response, he had left immediately.

Rak had come sidling in a few minutes later. He hadn't said a word, just held out his hand. After a wordless handshake, he shrugged, pulled a face and left.

Craig stared after him as Rak left the room. *Those guys and Stone are keeping my fire from going out tonight.*

At the Navigator's stateroom door, the Exec knocked once and went in without pausing. The Navigator was there, seated at his desk with a troubled stare that he slowly fixed on the intruder. Under normal circumstances, Craig would have felt sorry for the man. Today, sympathy was very far down on his list of priorities. "Gator, I'm going to bed for three hours. You stay up and keep us safe. Get every NAVSAT pass available. I want to find out what happened to those bloody SINS of yours. When I wake up, I'll want to see you and Joe immediately. Right now, I'm too tired to give a shit, but in three hours I intend to find out how we got five miles off track without knowing it."

"Aye, aye, XO. Continue west?"

"Hell, yes! Just keep us headed for the barn. Call me if the Captain leaves his stateroom for any reason. Otherwise, I won't answer anything but the General Alarm."

* * * * *

Craig died for three hours. When Morales finally got him awake, he felt worse than when he had first turned in. He had rested just enough to stop feeling numb.

"Morales," Craig mumbled, "go get the Navigator and the Weapons Officer and tell them to meet me in the wardroom. Then come back and check that I'm up and around."

"Aye, sir, XO. I'll be right back." He started to leave, and then turned around, "Mr. Craig…"

"Yeah."

"There's some hot pie in the pantry. If you look in the refrigerator there's a can of Coke. Lotta sugar and a lotta caffeine helps when you're real tired. Couple of aspirin will help too."

A wave of affection swept over Craig. He knew he was tired enough to be maudlin, but it touched him that Morales and some unknown benefactor cared enough to want to help. Somebody had been hoarding that damned Coke all patrol. Craig knew well that by Hump Night, trolling the ship with a fistful of twenty dollar bills would not have enticed a precious can of Coke out of hiding.

"Where in the world did you turn up a Coke?"

Morales answered with a shy, evasive smile. "Oh, one of the guys had some stashed."

"Guess you wouldn't care to say who." Craig shook his head and couldn't help grinning. "Morales, thanks for fretting. You can tell Mr. Stone his hard ass image is safe. I'll get even with him later."

Morales laughed and went on his way. By now, the conversation had gone on long enough so that Craig was thoroughly awake. He got up and dressed. A glance in the mirror was revolting, but reassuring. The bloodshot eyes were buried in a visage that puffed here, sagged there and looked like hell everywhere, but they were at least focusing.

As he stepped out of his stateroom, Craig looked at the Captain's closed door. The door's unremarkable Formica surface was like a hatch in a spaceship, part of an insensate boundary between two worlds. How many times had he been through that portal during this patrol? How many times had he visited the increasingly self-contained and alien world bottled up there…*How much have I been a party to creating the world that now exists on the other side of that door? At least now I can stay on this side of the wall between our two worlds, mine real, the captain's…*

Craig went into the wardroom and dug the pie out of the pantry and found the chilled can of Coke in the refrigerator. They were food for his body and strength for his spirit, made more delicious than usual because of his need. He wolfed both down, and when the Navigator arrived a few minutes later, Craig already felt better, almost normal.

The Weapons Officer arrived right behind the Navigator. Joe looked haggard, but no more so than everyone else. All three sat down at the wardroom table after pouring a ritual cup of coffee. The Navigator had a roll of SINS monitoring plots with him.

After a brief and polite exchange of inquiries into each other's state of rest, the Exec plunged in. "Look, guys, we almost lost the ship last night. The three of us can expect that we will most probably lose our respective asses when we get back to Rota. We ran an Alert SSBN aground in a friendly nation's territorial waters. Why we chose to be on that track is my problem to answer for. Why we got off that track is a question that we have to answer. Any questions so far?"

Both men nodded, without comment, and the Exec went on. "I want to be sure that we get that answer while everything is fresh in people's minds. No cop-outs. We have to know and be ready to present the true facts. Otherwise, when we get back, the facts will be determined retrospectively by an investigating officer who will have less to work with than we have."

Gator and Weaps exchanged uncomfortable looks.

The Navigator asked, "Okay, where do we start?"

The Exec continued. "For starters, there are three or four basic questions that have to be answered. One is why we chose a track that was contrary to good navigation and seamanship. As I said, that's not your problem, it's mine. Second is the question of prudence and proper watch standing. We have to re-create in detail everything that has any bearing upon the way that watch was stood, in proper sequence and timing. Third, is the technical question of why we were not where we thought we were. How did the navigational error happen? Fourth is our individual performance before, during, and after the incident. That'll take care of itself one way or the other. So, number two and number three are why we're here."

After a couple of hours the three had thoroughly re-created the watch. They stretched a role of chart paper over the length of the Wardroom table and drew a time-line down the middle of it. They then listed all the watchstanders, as well as the Navigator, the Captain and the Exec, and marked, to the best of their ability, everyone's activities from four hours before to fifteen minutes after the grounding. By interviewing all the watchstanders and cross-checking with other observers such as the COB and the cooks, they were able to create a surprisingly accurate and consistent chart of the watch stander's activities during the critical period.

As a final step, the Exec overlaid, in red ink, the schedule of navigational and ship control events that should have been followed. The resultant picture was a clear one. Joe had run his usual tight watch. The only place the critical red chain of events broke down was where the soundings stopped, at the Captain's orders. The Exec and the Navigator, and maybe Joe, could be criticized for lack of prudence, but the watch standing itself was above reproach.

That was small relief. None of the sailors could in any way be indicted. Joe would take some heat but, with enough cover from the XO, he would probably not get burned. They had the proof that he had stood his watch diligently. Only the Captain's orders and the ship's position were at fault.

Satisfied that Joe and the crew could be protected, Craig was ready to move on to the critical technical issue of the SINS position error.

"Okay, Gator. That's about all we can do on the watch standing question. Now let's see what we can figure out about those SINS of yours. Joe, you go on to bed. I think you'll be okay when we get home. The rest of this is for the Navigator, the NAVET's and me to figure out."

Joe didn't look all that reassured, but he nodded and headed for his stateroom. He was such a driven overachiever that Craig could only guess at the torment Joe would suffer from his own id until he was sure of official exoneration.

The Navigator waited until Joe had gone, then picked up the roll of SINS monitoring plots. He tapped the roll across the palm of his left hand a couple of times, and then threw them down on the table. "We don't have to look for what happened. Chief Brown spotted it as soon as the reset calculations came up from our first NAVSAT fix after the grounding. The last two have confirmed it."

The Exec's voice reflected his mild surprise. "Confirmed what?"

"We had a near simultaneous Z axis gyro break on both SINS. Incredibly, it was about the same magnitude as well, so they both followed the same propagation path. The error is there, but it was the same for both SINS, so we never suspected it."

A "gyro break" was an abrupt change in the normally very stable precession rate of the gyroscopes that stabilized the SINS inertial platforms. Individually, they were not uncommon, but to have gyros in the same position on two SINS break the same amount, at the same time, was a mind-boggling million to one coincidence.

"So number one lied and number two swore to it." It was a statement, not a question. Having been an SSBN navigator, the Exec was as knowledgeable as any man on board in the workings of the inertial navigation system.

"Yes."

Knowing in advance what the answer to his question would almost certainly be, Craig said, ruefully. "That's nearly impossible. Are you sure nothing got in from the Nav Center Central keyboard? A partial reset entered manually by mistake or something like that?"

"Brown has been over the data logging tape. No one ever did a reset calculation and the gates were never opened to either SINS."

That was the answer the Exec had expected. "Okay, APL will prove it when they do their normal review of our digital data package after patrol, but I believe you."

Every patrol's data package was reviewed in detail by the scientists at Johns Hopkins University Applied Physics Laboratory, but, the Exec knew, this time the scrutiny would be exceptionally intense.

Craig went on. "So we rule out personnel error in the Nav Center. Did we have any power supply transients during that period?"

The Navigator was ready with his answer. "The Engineers say no. Anyway, Number One was on the 400 KC bus and Number Two was on its independent 12 KVA static power supply."

So, that line of investigation had been explored and went nowhere. Craig was running out of ideas. "Well, no connection there. One of those is supplied with 60-cycle ac straight from the turbine generators, the other's off the battery. What about a gravitational anomaly?"

The Navigator shrugged. "That wouldn't cause a gyro break."

That brought the Exec to the conclusion he had suspected from the beginning. Pushing himself back from the table, he said, "You're right. I must be tired. There's not much left to consider, Gator, except that we must be two of the unluckiest sons a bitches in the world."

"You got it, XO."

"Document everything you've told me." Craig got up and stretched. "Go on to bed, Gator. I'm going up to the Control Room for a while."

Before allowing himself to sleep again, Craig meant to be damned sure there was nothing but deep water ahead of them.

* * * * *

The rest of the trip home was pretty uneventful. The Sonarmen had heard the last PDC before the ship turned in along Costa del Sol off the eastern coast of Spain. The PDC's had never reappeared after the incident of the three heavy explosions. The *Marion* skulked through the Straits of Gibraltar, riding the outbound current. Her crew felt like free men as the navigation party, watching through the periscope, reported the lights of Gibraltar drifting astern.

Through it all, the Old Man never reappeared. Morales took a plate to him at every mealtime. Usually they came back untouched. The Exec never went into his cabin, nor spoke to him. With the enduring forward tilt of sailors everywhere, the crew lost interest in the events of yesterday, or even the last watch, and swung into cleaning up the ship for entering port.

Returning to port was amnesty for the confined hearts and minds of every man on board, and to most it was an undiluted joy. Some knew they had yet to deal with the events of this patrol, but, even for Craig, the dread was lessened by knowing that the confrontation with his soon to be accusers would be in the real world of fresh air and sunshine.

The ship would normally have been met at the sea buoy by one of the harbor tugs, where the Blue Crew party would have boarded to observe the operation of the ship's systems. Under the circumstances, the Exec thought it wiser to go straight in and not have to explain the Captain's absence from view. Thank God the NPEB had decided to revisit the Gold Crew during their next refit rather than at the end of this patrol. The crew had enough on their plate without having to deal with an ORSE.

The night before arrival on the patrol's sixty-second day, the Exec sent out the required end-of-patrol "Quick Look" message to which he added the request to come straight in without embarking the Blue Crew party. He finished the message with "Craig sends," a sure tipoff to the Squadron staff that, for some reason, the Captain was incommunicado. Squadron Operations immediately granted the request and held back their questions.

As he maneuvered the *Marion* into her mooring position alongside the tender on the patrol's last day, Craig had the eerie sensation that the past two months had been a hallucination. The same glaring sun beat down on the same blue harbor and squat white buildings of Rota. Nothing had changed. One instant he had been here departing. The next instant he was here mooring. It was like stopping a movie and restarting it months later at the same frame. *Am I part of the movie or the audience?*

The sensation of lost orientation only lasted a moment before Craig was firmly returned to the reality of present day events as he caught sight of the Squadron Chief of Staff. Hard to believe, but it was Buzz Atkins, an old friend from Craig's early days on diesel boats. While the *Marion* was on patrol, Atkins had relieved the previous twit. Atkins looked serious as hell, but Craig was overjoyed to see him. Buzz could be relied upon to look, listen and understand. He was a good man, never accepted for Nuclear Power training, but now he was a Four Striper and Chief of Staff of a squadron of nuclear submarines. He waved as Craig maneuvered the ship into her berth.

Captain Atkins was the first man across the brow after the *Marion* finished tying up. Craig hurried down from the sail and met him there, leaving the OOD to finish securing the Maneuvering Watch, getting shore power onboard and ordering the reactor plant shut down.

Craig saluted. "Buzz, I'm sure as hell glad to see you."

"What happened? Where's the Captain? Why isn't he topside?"

With a soft downward motion of his hand, the universal hand signal for discretion, Craig answered. "Buzz, hold up the Blue Crew until we've had a chance to talk."

Buzz Atkins turned to the group behind him on the brow, including the Blue Crew Captain. "Wait here. No one is to board until I order the brow open. Pat, keep your crew standing by. I'll be just a few minutes."

Craig and Atkins walked forward along the deck together thirty feet or so to just aft of the sail, far enough to avoid being overheard.

"Mike, what's going on?"

"Buzz, we touched bottom a few days ago. No damage probably, but if it gets out where and how there'll be hell to pay. As for the Captain, I do not want to comment just now. I further request that you not talk to anyone on board until you have spoken to him. He's in his stateroom. I shouldn't talk any more now either. After you have spoken to the Captain, I'll talk to you all you want."

Buzz frowned. All he said was, "I knew something was screwed up from the way you signed off your message last night. Wait here. I'll be back as soon as I've seen your Skipper."

He headed below. The Exec busied himself with a casual inspection of the ship topside. She had come through in pretty good shape. Except for a few peeling patches of paint and the usual slimy stink of marine things already rotting, there was nothing to remark upon.

Occasionally an acquaintance from the Squadron Staff or the Blue Crew yelled a greeting from across the deck of the tender. For all the foreboding worry about the official reaction to what had happened, Craig felt good. They were back alongside, the sun and fresh air were a wonderful tonic. *Whatever else, in a few days, we'll go home and leave this pig iron piss pot of a world behind.*

Craig was content to putter about and wait for Buzz to re-appear. Mentally, he had laid down the burden of getting the ship home without starting World War III. Explaining to the waiting, undoubtedly hostile Chain of Command, seemed an entirely different level of problem. In the days ahead he would realize that the aftermath of these events would be as disturbing to any thinking man as the events themselves. For the moment, it was near bliss to soak up fresh air and let his tired mind idle.

Buzz re-appeared after fifteen minutes or so and promptly forced Craig out of his momentary indolence.

Buzz was obviously shaken by what he had just seen. "Christ-all-mighty! How long has he been this way?"

"Almost three weeks. The symptoms were there well before that."

"What's all this horse shit about someone being out to kill you with ray guns?"

Craig replied, resignation heavy in his voice. "Mostly bullshit from a disordered mind. There is something of real concern there, though, and I'm afraid the Old Man's condition will mask it."

"What's that?"

"Thousands of PDC's trailing us and a couple of tactical encounters that I can't explain. I'll go over it with you later. It's all in the patrol report anyway."

"But you didn't feel threatened?"

Craig was very deliberate in his reply. "Of being sunk? No, we got shaken up pretty good once, but that may well have been a total coincidence. I don't KNOW how much is coincidence, but there's something sinister out there, irrespective of whether or not the Captain is paranoid, and we've got to keep the two issues separate."

Buzz held up his hands. "Okay. No more talk now. Let the Blue Crew on board, but keep your Skipper locked up. I'm going up to get the CO of the Tender and the Squadron doctor. I want them to see what I saw before we move him. As of now, you are to consider yourself acting as Commanding Officer of this ship for purposes of completing turnover to the Bluies. Your skipper is on the sick list. The ship will have to move to the other side of the tender tomorrow. You make the move. Your Captain is not to be on the bridge."

"Aye, aye, sir."

He turned to go, then abruptly spun around and stepped close. "Mike, you're in a hell of a mess. From now on, anytime you open your mouth, it'll be used against you. Unless you take the fall, the Submarine Force has to admit its command and control system is fallible."

Craig didn't try to suppress a wry grin. "Yeah. As W.C. Fields once said, 'All things considered, I'd rather be in Philadelphia.'"

Atkins didn't laugh. He had real concern written on his face for his old friend as he partially turned to go. "Worse for you, Rickover has to admit he fucked up selecting your Skipper and carrying him along. It's you against the entire NUC image. Good luck, but I wouldn't want to be in your shoes."

With that, Atkins left the ship.

Craig watched him go. *So, what else is new? I pretty much figured that out by myself as soon as I started considering relieving the Old Man.*

42
Homeward Bound

The Stretch Eight carrying the Gold crew left Rota precisely on schedule with a Squadron courier accompanying them with the sole duty to securely carry the package of evidence and depositions on the grounding. The forty or so extra seats that remained unfilled after the *Marion* crew had boarded the aircraft were quickly taken, as usual, with families being rotated home after a tour of foreign duty.

Having been sequestered by order of the Squadron Commander throughout the turnover period, the Captain had arrived in a staff car just as the last of the sailors were hurrying up the boarding stairs to the aircraft. It was the first time Holcomb had been seen in the nearly four days since the ship had moored. He walked aboard without speaking and took a seat in the front row of the aircraft. Craig had already taken a seat well back over the wing and made no effort to go forward to greet or sit with the Captain. Normally, they would have sat together up front, but not this time. Craig needed and wanted to be alone.

Craig had motioned the Yeoman First Class into the seat beside him. He had the usual stack of service record entries for the Exec to sign during the flight and was too hung over to talk while Craig scribbled his signature two or three hundred times. It was a mindless task and the Yeoman's condition would make him a mindless companion. Together, the Yeoman and the service records formed a privacy fence between Craig and the rest of the crew.

Craig had plenty to think about. Since tying the ship up at the end of the patrol, he had been too busy with turnover to spend much time or energy thinking about the patrol aftermath.

Turnover to the Bluies had gone smoothly. Even the typical small hitches had been absent. Whatever speculation had gone on within the Blue crew about the Gold Captain and the patrol was kept carefully submerged. In his depressed and anxious state of mind, it had seemed eerily like the behavior of neighbors before a funeral. No one in either crew wanted to be contentious, concerned only to get turnover done so the Gold crew could leave.

Although Buzz had immediately notified COMSUBLANT and CINCLANFLEET of the *Marion* "incident" and the Squadron Commodore had rushed back from his visit to the Holy Loch Squadron and commenced his inquiry, the Exec had been virtually ignored. One evening, over a bottle of excellent Spanish brandy he had had a long, off the record, session with Buzz. Craig described the events of the patrol and Atkins commiserated. Still, no one had even approached any of the crew's officers for a formal briefing. Except for the obvious total absence of the Captain and the unusual preparations for an unscheduled dry docking to check the hull for damage, the turnover routine was undisturbed by any reflection of the crisis that marked the patrol.

The Exec had waited, expecting to be asked about the *Marion*'s strange tactical experiences. When no call for a briefing had come by the third afternoon, his curiosity prompted him to ask Buzz what was going on. Buzz had shrugged and said, "I don't know because I'm out of the loop. The Commodore is dealing directly with COMSUBLANT and his Deputy. I don't even get to see their message traffic."

Craig considered it strange that Atkins was being excluded. Hell, he was the Squadron Chief of Staff, the Deputy Squadron Commander. In any case, Buzz wouldn't be drawn further into the subject. It was as if nothing unusual had taken place on the patrol. After the patrol report and Stone's package of records and statements had been delivered to the Squadron Staff, nothing more was said or heard about tactical operations during the patrol.

Now, as he thought about it, Craig began to suspect an answer. The need for secrecy about any suspected vulnerability of the SSBN fleet was obvious, but concern about that should have made the whole chain of command demand immediate briefings. *If that were the real issue, they would have been anxious to debrief us. It must be the Old Man freaking out that they're afraid will get out.*

COMSUBLANT undoubtedly wanted to suppress the story of the Holborn's breakdown, keep it in house. Craig reckoned that the Captain's situation and the story of the patrol would be politically embarrassing to COMSUBLANT and Rickover. Particularly, neither would want the Air Force or Congress and, especially, the Appropriations Committee to know of it. In the eternal competition for funds, that would amount to their racehorse throwing a shoe.

One thing, at least, was clear enough. Whether or not COMSUBLANT was interested in the tactical threat, he intended to prosecute the miscreants who had run the *Marion* aground. On the morning they were to depart for home, immediately after the token Change of Command ceremony, the Squadron Legal Officer had given the Weapons Officer, the Navigator, and the Exec sealed letters. Each was made to sign a form acknowledging their individual receipt.

The letters served legal notice that they and the Captain were named "parties to an investigation" into the events surrounding the grounding of the USS Francis *Marion,* on or about July 6, 1970. Being a "party" to an "investigation" was tantamount to being the accused at a criminal trial or court-martial. But there was a significant difference. Since an investigation was an administrative proceeding, "parties" had virtually no protective legal rights as would an "accused."

Additionally, the letter warned each man that all aspects of the incident and events surrounding it were "TOP SECRET" and forbade discussion with anyone except their "duly appointed Navy Counsel," or while giving testimony. They, the "parties," were not even to discuss the investigation among themselves. There was going to be a full-blown, career threatening, formal investigation, but COMSUBLANT apparently wanted it kept quiet…very quiet.

* * * * *

After Craig had finished signing the service record entries that no one would ever read nor care about, he sat back and tried to sleep. Sleep was slow to come. Now that the patrol and turnover was done, his mind kept turning to what would come next. If COMSUBLANT wanted to do a cover-up and they all escaped unscathed, then, so be it. However, if they were looking for a scapegoat, Craig suspected that he would be the target. If that happened, he would have to find some way to fight it. The alternative, no doubt expected by the chain of command, would be for him to sacrifice himself professionally to protect the image of the Nuclear Submarine Force.

A half-hour later Craig was still awake. He fervently hoped for the benign "cover-up" option. Whatever profound issues the patrol raised could pass without his challenge if he wasn't threatened professionally, but he knew that if he was made the target, he would fight. *I guess it takes awhile to adjust your thinking to accept something you don't like, to rationalize self-interest into something respectable; but, I won't be made a sacrificial lamb.*

On that decision, he finally fell asleep on a wave of righteous indignation.

43

Arrival Home

Seven hours after departing Rota, the Stretch Eight landed at Quonset Point, Rhode Island, with its load of jubilant inmates about to spring free from three months of incarceration.

In earlier times, before Craig had become an XO, the crew flights he traveled on had sometimes flown into Hartford, Connecticut. On those occasions, he had been able to take leave of the crew at the terminal and go his separate way with Meaghan. Often on those halcyon days, Meaghan had arranged an overnight babysitter and booked a nearby hotel room so that they could concentrate on each other with no distractions. Those few hours had always been immensely effective therapy as they put the stress of the patrol behind them. Those nights of holding, talking, touching and feeling their way back from the isolation and loneliness of the patrol were wonderful.

Coming home off patrol was such an abrupt change of one world for another that it always took Craig a little time to adjust. With three loved ones to embrace and three months of their lives to catch up on, it was hard to concentrate enough time on any one of them during the first day. He also had an almost compulsive need to simply look around their home, to see and touch the familiar things he had left behind three months earlier. In some sense, Craig needed to reassure himself that he really was home and that nothing had changed. Having a few private hours with Meaghan at the outset had always brought some serenity to the excited kaleidoscope of reunions during his first days at home.

This time there would be no gentle reentry. As the Exec, it was his responsibility to see the crew all the way back to the Sub base, so he would ride the bus with the crew. Craig didn't know if the official greeters, sure to be waiting at Building 439, would pull him aside because of the materials the courier carried. He fervently hoped not. Everything else could wait until he had seen Meaghan and the kids.

Especially Meaghan. She was Craig's refuge. Meaghan had a way, when he needed help, of standing firmly beside him to face the world, keeping and sharing a clear and commonsense perspective on unfolding events. She saw the little shams and hypocrisy of Navy society and inter-service politics too clearly to be the perfect "Navy Wife." She managed to be something better, a free and independent spirit.

Craig jumped down off the lead bus as it rolled to a stop and there stood Meaghan. His old friend, Captain Bill Davis, the COMSUBFLOT Two Chief of Staff, was there as well, obviously sent by the Admiral to meet the returning crew. Meaghan stepped quickly around the Chief of Staff and Craig grabbed her, his right hand halfway to his forehead in an awkward salute. Davis smiled as Craig gave up the distraction of military courtesy and held Meaghan in a fierce embrace. As they held each other, she whispered, "Bill's here to grab you. The Admiral wants to see you right away. Are you okay?"

Without relaxing his hold on Meaghan, Craig caught Davis' eye, "Captain, should I be sick or insubordinate until tomorrow morning?"

Still smiling, Bill Davis said, "Neither. The Admiral just wanted you to know he was available if you wanted to see him. Go on home and come in tomorrow around 1000. Margie said she would shoot me if I let you get shanghaied today."

"Thanks, Bill. I need a little time with the family to get my head screwed on."

Serious now, Davis touched Craig on the shoulder. Speaking softly, he said, "By the way, when we first heard you'd had a problem, the Admiral asked me about you. I told him that if the damn ship got back, it was because of you. I called Meaghan as soon as we saw your Quick Look message to let her know that you were okay, but I haven't been able to share anything else with her."

"Thanks for that, too, Bill."

Craig and Meaghan hurried off to their old Buick for the short ride home to where the kids were waiting. Meaghan would usually have brought them with her to meet the buses. This time, knowing only that some undefined problem existed, she had opted to leave them at home with a sitter. It was always a wonder to Craig, how over the course of the patrol, Meaghan changed so little, while the kids changed so much. He was never quite prepared for their quantum leaps in size and maturity.

Children are immensely gratifying to a father coming home from the sea. Even the most incompetent of clowns in this world can still be a hero in his kids' eyes. Craig's family never let him down. The pretty, shy little girl and her bumptious younger brother were waiting at the door when he pulled the Buick into the driveway. Their welcome was a rush of hugs and squeals, a babble of competing show and tell that went on until Meaghan, hovering in the background, shoved them out for an hour's play before dinner. Meaghan then made both she and Mike a gin and tonic and they moved out onto the patio. Both sat quietly, simply relaxing—beginning to recuperate from the emotional ordeal of the patrol. For Craig, the sensation of having put down a heavy load was almost physical. The patio, with Meaghan at his side and the children chattering in the background, was incomprehensibly serene and far removed from the world of the ship that he had just left.

Several hours later, dinner was over, and the kids were long since in bed. Craig watched Meaghan in the bathroom taking off the last traces of her makeup. The sight of her was sheer pleasure. The mirror reflected her petite figure, medium length black hair and her dark snapping eyes. At thirty-five and after twelve years of marriage and two children, her figure was still tight and slim. She could have been a Playboy centerfold. A remarkable woman. Beautiful, bright and strong.

Neither Mike nor Meaghan had yet mentioned the patrol. Now, without turning from the mirror, she asked in a casual voice, "What happened? Bill called me three days ago. He wouldn't tell me anything, but said if I heard any rumors, I should know you were okay."

Mike swung his feet over and sat on the edge of the bed, facing the door and her back. "The Old Man went round the bend. We brushed the bottom."

She turned, still holding a washcloth to her face. "So that's what it was! Did it happen on the sixth of July?"

Mike looked at Meaghan in shock. "Yes. But how in the hell did you know?"

"I don't know how I knew. I just knew something was terribly wrong. I made a fool of myself and called Bill."

Craig was speechless. *My God. She is telepathic!*

Meaghan was calm now. "Could you have lost the ship?"

"Yes, it was very close."

"Was anyone hurt?"

"No."

Meaghan slowly turned back around, finished her nightly ritual of face creams, then came and sat beside Mike. "Was it your fault?"

"Partly, at least."

"Why?"

"Mostly because I may have contributed to the Old Man's breakdown. Maybe I could have done more to head it off."

She settled back against the pillows. "Tell me about it."

So he did. For two and a half hours Craig talked his way through that bloody patrol. Every detail. After he was through, they sat quietly for a few minutes.

Meaghan finally spoke. "We all have to live with being afraid of what might happen when you are out there." She shivered a little. "Now I know one more scenario to have nightmares about."

There was a prolonged spell of silence, both lost in their own thoughts. Meaghan moved from the pillows and sat up a little straighter. "What is this likely to mean to us, to you?"

"End of one career, I expect. So far as I know, I haven't done anything I can be thrown in jail for."

"What are you going to do?"

"If I'm lucky, nothing. People at the Squadron in Rota know what happened, so COMSUBLANT must understand what went on. If he does what's right, he'll make sure the investigation gets to the bottom of what happened, both internally and tactically, and try to fix it. Maybe they'll just try to keep the whole thing quiet. That would be sad for the Submarine Force, but if we all get off without getting hurt, I won't try to be a hero."

"And if you don't get off without being penalized in some way?"

"Fight it, if I have to. I did the best I could and I'm not going to lie down and get kicked out of a career just to keep the fucking NUC image from getting tarnished."

Meaghan leaned forward, put her hand on Mike's arm and became very intense. "Well, if you want to pull out now, it's okay. Whatever happens, you know I'm with you. It's about time for me to go back to work full time anyway. At least, if you get out of the Navy, I don't have to spend half of my life living alone with nightmares."

"And if I stay?"

"That's okay, too, so long as we're together."

As always, her common sense was invaluable to Mike. When he was in danger of thinking that the loss of his submarine career was something akin to the end of life, Meaghan saw a bigger picture. As she had so often done in their life together, she shared her perspective and kept Mike from losing his. *No wonder I love and need her so much.*

275

44
Back to Work

Early the next morning, Craig reluctantly suited up in his uniform and drove to the Submarine Base. Some of his apprehension was back, gnawing away at the bliss of homecoming. Instead of going to the SSBN Off-Crew office in Building 439, he headed directly for Building 138, the Submarine Flotilla Two Headquarters building. He wanted to try to catch Bill Davis before calling on the Admiral. Davis was at his desk and called Craig into his office before his secretary, a Yeoman Third Class, had a chance to speak. As Craig walked in, Davis waved to a chair.

In spite of their close relationship and easy informality when they were off duty, this visit was official. The formality of military courtesy came automatically in Craig's greeting to his friend.

"Thanks, Captain."

Davis signaled to the Yeoman to shut the door on the way out. That done, he turned to Craig. "How are you holding up, Mike?"

"Okay. Got a couple of questions."

Davis waited. "And?"

"Philosophically, you ought to check out the wives' eye view of us and our world. It's revealing."

Davis half grinned, half grimaced. "I don't have to. Margie volunteers it every so often. She and Meaghan are like soul sisters, you know."

"So how about a couple of questions off the record?"

"Okay. If I can't answer, I won't."

Fair enough. Craig knew any answer would be straight. Davis would be loyal to his profession and to his boss, but anything he was free to say, he would say with complete candor.

"Relief for Cause. Does that phrase appear in any correspondence to my CO…relative to this investigation, that is?"

Bill raised an eyebrow. "No."

"When and how will he be relieved?"

"As soon as the investigation is complete, he will be given an early "normal relief.""

"Whose decision was that?"

"It came from COMSUBLANT."

"But whose decision—I should say, recommendation, is it?"

"Deputy COMSUBLANT is the action officer for this."

"Wee Willie?" Craig couldn't keep the exasperation out of his voice.

Bill knew exactly why. Rear Admiral William Joseph Johnson, or "Wee Willie," was one of the first of the early NUCS to reach Flag Rank. He was short in stature, long on ego and, generally, a source of sound and fury calculated to insure the world noted his passing.

Shit! That will spell grief one way or another! "One last question, Bill, then I'll get out of here. Does the Admiral have any background on this, or will he be acting solely on the information he develops during the investigation?"

Bill thought for a moment. "I think he understands what went on and the investigation will be a formality to clear the air. Try you and find you all innocent, so to speak. I wouldn't bet my own career on it, though."

In spite of the news about Wee Willie, Craig felt a bit reassured. "I hope you're right, but I'm also afraid he won't pick up on the fact that there was something very real to worry about in the tactical picture. We're all fools if that gets buried to avoid political embarrassment."

Davis nodded his agreement. "I agree, but I don't know what his guidance is."

"One more favor?"

"Maybe. What?"

"Call my Detailer and find out if I can absorb a bad Fitness Report without getting passed over for Commander."

"Okay, Mike. The Admiral's free now."

"Thanks. Give my love to Margie."

* * * * *

It was thirty feet from Davis' office to that of Rear Admiral Forrest Kincaid. Kincaid was one of the few remaining submarine Admirals that had never been part of the Nuclear Navy. In spite of his two Navy Crosses from World War Two, he was finishing his career in what amounted to a rear echelon command. Revered by those who had served under him, he was, nonetheless, not a man who tolerated fools gladly.

By the time Craig had crossed the short distance between the two offices, the Admiral's secretary was motioning him through the open door to Kincaid's walnut paneled, flag draped inner sanctum. The Admiral was neither hostile nor particularly cordial, and the meeting was short and to the point. After a minimum of polite greetings, Kincaid advised Craig that the investigation would convene at 0800 one week from that day and that a Navy lawyer had been appointed to assist him. Craig should expect a call from the lawyer to arrange a preliminary meeting. The Admiral paused, then continued with a barely perceptible increase in emphasis. He was going to be assisted by the COMSUBLANT Legal Officer rather than his own.

Craig thanked Kincaid for his time and the information, and left the building, all the while wondering why the Admiral had called him in for such a short meeting with no content that Bill could not have passed on. *Curious. Why did he take his time for that? And why make a point of telling me that last bit about the COMSUBLANT Legal Officer?*

45
Lincoln Julius Mann

Lieutenant Lincoln Julius Mann, U. S. Navy (Reserve), arrived at Craig's office that afternoon. Mann had called earlier in the day and left a message to expect him "after lunch." Craig had waited and fidgeted, halfheartedly unpacking his cruise boxes until the lawyer made his appearance. Craig wanted to be at home, or almost anyplace other than in the office, but meeting his lawyer was not an appointment he could afford to delay. Six days was damned little time to prepare to defend himself in the coming investigation.

When the lawyer walked through the office door, Craig's first reaction to Mann was mild astonishment. Having grown up in a traditionally white Navy wherein Blacks and Philippinos generally appeared only as Steward's Mates, he had encountered few Black officers and never a non-white NUC or Legal Officer. Craig didn't harbor any prejudice himself, but like most of his peers, he had never really questioned or taken much note of Navy demographics.

If Mann noticed the flicker of surprise across his prospective client's face, he gave no indication. "Michael Craig?"

"Yeah."

"I'm Lincoln Mann. I've been assigned as your counsel in an investigation that is convening next Monday."

The two men shook hands. Mann was a foot taller than Craig and had a hand the size of a baseball mitt. He was a big, tall, strong man wearing a well-fitted uniform. Craig took it all in and hoped he was an intelligent man as well. Time would tell.

Mann didn't waste much time in coming to the point. "Craig…"

Craig interrupted. "Call me Mike."

"Okay, 'Linc' works for me. I have been assigned to assist you during the forthcoming investigation about the *Marion*'s last patrol. If you prefer, you are entitled to get your own civilian council. I'll tell you right now that I have never had a case like this."

"Why should I go to a civilian?"

Linc calmly replied, "I don't think you should, but I'm required to advise you of your choices. You should do whatever you are most comfortable with, be represented by whoever you think will give you the best legal advice."

Right answer, wrong question. Craig tried again. "Why shouldn't I hire a civilian attorney?"

Linc answered without hesitation. "Because this investigation is going to be highly classified. Either you find someone with a Top Secret clearance, which is probably impossible, or accept the fact that your private counsel won't have access to crucial evidence. Secondly, you may find a lawyer smarter than I am, but I doubt if they will have more expertise in Navy Regulations or the Uniform Code of Military Justice. Third, I'm free."

He's right. Besides, I can't afford to pay for a civilian counsel even if I wanted to. More important, I'm already beginning to like this guy. "Okay. That's your first good advice to me, but, before I take it, what about you? Do you want to help me? Are you interested in this case, and do you want to take this on? How well do you think we can work together?"

Linc thought for a moment before he answered. His answer was quiet and deliberate. "Yes, I want to be on this case."

"Why? You don't know me from Adam."

"Look, Mike, for me it isn't about you. Not yet, anyway. There are about five hundred Legal Officers in the U.S. Navy. Less than five of those are black. My boss never let me take on anything but AWOL cases before today. I may not be God's gift to the legal profession, but I know I'm a pretty decent lawyer. Something tells me this investigation is important. Much more important than a simple grounding episode. I want to be on it."

Good. He's honest, but he hasn't answered the rest of my question. "How about the second part of my question? I'm a pretty opinionated Irishman. Can we work together?"

Linc cracked a small grin. "I can handle you being Irish. Do you have a problem with me being Black?"

"Not that I know of. I'll only have a problem with you if you're dumb."

At that point, both men grinned, maybe a little ruefully on Craig's part. They had sized each other up and, apparently, both found something to his liking.

Craig had long since learned to trust his instinct about other men, and had already decided that, if the investigation turned into a fight, this was the man he would want at his side. But, Linc had dropped something else on the table that he wanted to know more about.

"Okay. We're a team. Now, tell me why you think this is more important to the Chain of Command than a simple grounding."

Linc gave Craig a look that said his patience had been tried in about thirty seconds flat. He then ticked off his reasons. "Your Captain is not being threatened with 'Relief for Cause,' but he has been assigned a hotshot lawyer from the Judge Advocate General's staff. The COMSUBLANT Legal Officer usually doesn't have much use for me, but he specifically requested that I represent you. The whole thing has been over-classified. No routine grounding needs to be classified 'Top Secret,' particularly when, as in this case, there was no apparent damage to the ship. Want me to go on?"

He's good. But, now, he had raised another question that left Craig uneasy. "You're right, so far. But, what is the bit about the COMSUBLANT Legal Officer lining us up together? The Admiral made a point this morning of telling me that his own Legal Officer had been pushed aside and that the COMSUBLANT Legal Officer would be his counsel, the prosecuting attorney, so to speak. I have been wondering ever since why the Admiral made it a point to tell me that."

Again, that mildly scornful look. "Mike, the NUC community in the Submarine Force makes the Augusta National in Georgia look like a hotbed of Affirmative Action. As of this date, there isn't one black officer in the Submarine Nuclear Power Program. Like I said, there are only five of us in the whole JAG corps. So, how come, in this case, which must be a pretty sensitive one to Rickover and the NUC's, did you beat hundred to one odds and get me?"

Craig sat back, stunned. Linc was right. Craig had never met a black NUC. He found himself profoundly disturbed by the realization that he had been blind to such an obvious fact until Linc pointed it out. Beyond that, Craig still didn't understand what Linc was driving at. "So? What are you telling me?"

"Mike, you had better wake up to the fact that there is some reason this establishment doesn't want you to win, or else I wouldn't have been sent here. They think I'm an inferior lawyer and that, consequently, you'll loose for sure. We're both black sheep on this farm."

At that, Craig's shock deepened, then began to transmute into a controlled, hard anger. Linc had touched on a suspicion that had been growing in the back of Craig's mind ever since the *Marion*'s return to Rota. So far, he had mentally pushed it aside, but now his mind was racing.

After a few minutes of desultory conversation about Linc's temporary accommodation at the Sub-base, they agreed to meet the next morning at 0800, and the lawyer headed back to Newport. In spite of the urgency of preparing for an investigation that was now less than a week away, Craig was glad to quit for the day. He wanted time to think through Linc's remarks before he had to start briefing the lawyer in detail about the patrol.

On his drive home, Craig decided not to jump to any conclusions. Maybe Linc was overreacting. In spite of his private, cynical fears and suspicions, Craig still had a guarded faith in his Chain of Command.

Maybe Linc's own experience as a black confronting an unwelcoming establishment has distorted his perception. It was not comforting though to realize that, in their first meeting, Linc had summoned the very demons that were keeping Craig awake at night.

* * * * *

That night, after dinner, Mike and Meaghan sat on the raised deck outside their dining room, sharing a quiet time with drinks and catching up on conversation against a background of pyrotechnics from the nearby bug zapper. It was a warm evening and the zapper was busy. As insects were drawn to the ultraviolet light in the center, the high voltage screens fried them with spectacular electrical arcs. It was the sound of summer in Connecticut. It wasn't long before Mike told her about the day's events.

When he concluded, Meaghan asked, "So, you think from what Bill and the Admiral said that this will be a 'show trial' sort of thing?"

"I think so. But, I also think there is something going on in the background that I'm not privy to."

Meaghan arched a brow and changed the subject. "Did you meet your lawyer?"

"Uh huh."

"What do you think of him?"

Pausing to swat a mosquito that had eluded the zapper, Mike thought for a moment. "I like him. He's Black and hasn't had much of an opportunity to show his ability in Newport, but I think he is damned smart."

Meaghan wanted to know more. "Why do you think that?"

Mike grinned before going on. Meaghan was always quick to question unsubstantiated opinions. It was typical of her that she wanted facts upon which she would make her own judgments. *Sweetheart, you do keep me honest!* Matter of factly, Mike replied, "Mann graduated Magna Cum Laude from some law school in Chicago and came directly out of school into the Navy to do his obligated service for his ROTC scholarship. The closest he's been to the sea-going Navy is three continuous years at the brig in Newport trying AWOL sailors. He only has one more year to do to complete his obligated service. I'll tell you this. He came up with a lot of right answers about this investigation based on very little information."

Meaghan's interest was now intense. "Such as?"

"He's worried that COMSUBLANT is up to something. I think maybe he's overreacting."

Meaghan's expression changed to one of mild horror. Mike was unsure whether it was his description of his lawyer, or the light and sound show of a huge moth that was frying itself into cinders in the bug zapper.

Meaghan set her drink down and muttered, "Wonderful."

"The lawyer or the bug?" Mike really didn't know which was the target of her sarcasm.

"So the lawyer's black with no real experience!"

"Yes."

Meaghan threw up her hands in exasperation. "What are they trying to do? Get rid of a black sheep and a black lawyer with one shot?"

Gotta hand it to her. She sure can be counted on to go straight to the heart of an issue! Mike's voice was calm. "First of all, Meaghan, that's the second time today I've heard those words. Linc said the same thing. He even used the black sheep bit. I like him because he's quick and very bright. Also, I think he's going to be very aggressive because he's not in awe of the Navy Establishment."

Somewhat mollified, Meaghan smiled and shook her head.

Mike continued. "Also, I sense a tough side to him. This kid has fought very hard to get where he is, and in a year he'll be out of the Navy. I don't think his principles are stifled by any reverence for the 'Establishment.' We need that."

She still looked doubtful.

Mike spoke reassuringly now. "Look, Hon. You know I have a pretty quick sense in judging people. This guy is solid. He may have been educated as a lawyer, but he's a warrior at heart. I can feel that in him. In a way, he is a lot like Stone. No bullshit, but a guy that will be there when you need him."

With a level look, Meaghan said, "I admit you are usually right about people. I hope this time isn't the exception."

I hope so, too! Mike continued. "Anyway, if it's going to be a cover-up, they surely won't punish any of us. In that case, I could have Yogi Bear as my counsel. But, if I'm going to be the fall guy, this is probably part of the setup. They figure a dumb lawyer wouldn't be a knowing accomplice. I'm telling you though, this guy isn't nearly as dumb as they may think."

Meaghan didn't look overly convinced. "What kind of lawyers did Joe and the Navigator get?"

"Both white, but with more of the same AWOL and drunk case experiences. Career types with about twice my guy's length of service."

"And the Captain?"

"A three striper from the JAG staff."

"What's your lawyer's name?"

"Lincoln Julius Mann. He likes to be called 'Linc.'"

Meaghan said, "Well, I hope Linc is as good as you think. He's always welcome here, but you should be aware that there are a lot of very backward people in this Submarine Force of yours."

That's the second time today that I've heard that, too. How come she's aware and I didn't wake up to that fact until today!

Meaghan got up to go settle a bedtime altercation between the kids and the dogs. The Craigs now had two of each. As she pushed the sliding door aside, she paused. "I think you're being set up. I don't know why they're doing it, but I think they are."

Mike called after her. "Time will tell."

"Please fix us another drink while I go in and settle the kids down. Your son has his sister and the damned dogs all going crazy!"

As he was pouring the Tanqueray and tonic, Craig thought about what Meaghan had said. He didn't see a motive for a setup. A coverup, yes. He honestly believed there was no reason for penalizing any of the Gold crew officers and he still had a vestigial faith in the Chain of Command. *The only thing we should be facing is a legitimate effort to bring out the true and accurate facts of our patrol. That would be fair enough, though I would have to answer for any mistake I might have made.*

Meaghan and Linc, he decided, were too cynical.

46
Preparing the Defense

The next afternoon, Craig met Linc at Craig's office in Building 439 for their first working session. Cruise boxes full of paper and paraphernalia, the submarine crew's baggage train, littered the outer office. Two such boxes were stacked in the Exec's small cubicle, alongside his desk. The only person in the office besides Linc and Craig was a bored sailor that Craig had never seen before. The sailor was one of the replacements that had been waiting in the barracks for the crew to return from patrol. He had been immediately assigned as the office security and telephone watch.

Craig was sitting at his desk when Linc appeared, first as a head, followed by part of a torso as he leaned over a cruise box to peer into the Exec's office cubical.

He seemed relatively cheerful, but tired. "Hi," he said.

"Hello, Linc."

He looked around. "Where can we work?"

"Here?"

Linc was emphatic. "Nope. No walls. No door. From now on I want cinder blocks between us and anyone who might be interested in our conversation."

Craig thought his concern was a little excessive, but didn't say so. Instead, he offered, "How about the conference room?"

All the off crew offices were laid out exactly the same, three small rooms at the end of a large open floor plan office. A storeroom, a conference room and the CO's office were the only spaces affording privacy.

Craig and Linc moved into the conference room, stopping to fill mugs with steaming, but stale coffee. Navy coffee always goes stale as soon as it is brewed. In thirty minutes it turns to shellac. Theirs was several hours old and was passing through the bitumen stage. Both took an obligatory sip, then shoved the mugs away in an automatic response.

Craig noticed Linc had bags under his eyes and idly wondered if they were permanent. Linc flopped back in his chair and put both feet on the conference table. Craig followed suit and waited.

"I've been up reading half the damned night."

"You look like it."

Linc's face reflected mild distaste. "Yeah, great stuff. The Bureau of Personnel Manual, U.S. Navy Regs, Uniform Code of Military Justice, Judge Advocate General's Manual, various CINCLANT, CINCLANFLEET and COMSUBLANT Instructions and Notices. I can tell you now that there is nothing particularly complicated about our legal situation, and that so far, nothing irregular has been done."

After a long drink of the awful coffee, he went on. "What we have here is an investigation, not a trial. Since there doesn't seem to be a violation of the UCMJ at issue, that may work to your disadvantage. You don't have to be proven guilty of anything and, this being an administrative procedure, you have none of the legal rights that attach to an "accused" in a trial. Keep in mind, that if the investigation shows that you are 'guilty' of something, such as dereliction of duty, you can subsequently be charged and tried. You, Bubba, get to enjoy two or three levels of jeopardy."

Craig, knowing that from the beginning, was not surprised. "It may not be legally complex, but it is more complicated than you think."

Linc squirmed into a more comfortable position. "Why? What's really at stake here? You gotta know I'm just a lawyer. That means I know process. You have to help me understand the underlying issues. Where's everybody coming from and why? You're about to be the accused in an adversarial proceeding designed to kick your indefensible ass. I don't know anything about you, COMSUBLANT, H.G. Rickover or ships with the pointy end on the back. I do know something here ain't what it seems. To reiterate from yesterday, in case you have forgotten, they aren't using the Flot Two Legal Officer, who is a good head, and they've classified the proceedings 'Top Secret.' They picked me to represent you because COMSUBLANT's mouthpiece thinks I'm a dumb shit." He paused. "So start talking. We got today, Saturday and Sunday before you take your seat in front of the long green table. We gotta figure out what COMSUBLANT wants out of this and why."

Bingo! I was right. Linc is okay! Craig hoped COMSUBLANT and his staff weenies had underestimated both of them. To ensure clarity, Craig restated Linc's remarks. "So you want to figure out the other side's motives and objectives, then build a strategy to counter them?"

"Right."

"Then let's take the obvious ones first. The Convening Authority, COMSUBLANT, wants to establish the facts of what happened on this patrol for all the right reasons, find out what happened and why, so he can prevent a reoccurrence. Throw in maintenance of discipline."

Linc barely moved. Again, his body language suggested Craig was stretching his patience. He erupted. "Bullshit! If that were it, he would have been all over you the day you got back. He's more interested in controlling information than getting it. Maintain discipline? How come the CO's not being relieved 'for cause?'"

Craig raised his hand, signaling his intent to continue. "Okay. But, it is a possibility. Otherwise, I can only see one objective. I'm not considering national security interests or disclosure of secrets vis a vis our enemies since nothing of tactical value needs to be discussed to investigate the grounding. The one real objective has to be to avoid exposure of the incident where it could do political harm."

Linc perked up and asked, "Political harm to whom?"

Craig was lecturing now. "To whom or to what? If some of the things that happened on this patrol were known, some reasonably intelligent Air Force General or Congressman might wonder if our submarines are as invulnerable as the Submarine Force claims. Someone might also question the reliability and safeguards in a weapons system that puts the keys to sixteen megatons of strategic missiles in the hands of a disturbed personality. Either one of these could seriously threaten Congressional appropriations and the ever expanding influence of the Submarine Force Senior Officers. The linchpin terms are 'inter-service' rivalry and 'intra-service' rivalry."

There was bemusement in Mann's voice as he questioned. "So the possible fallout from this is big time funding and power politics?"

"Yes, I believe so."

Linc wanted the next shoe to drop. He said pointedly, "But you haven't answered the 'who.'"

"Look, Linc, the senior officers now in positions of influence are all early NUCS, Rickover's disciples. There are a few good ones left…but only a very few. COMSUBFLOTTWO and COMSUBLANT, themselves, are good men. They both have a chest full of real medals from World War II. Most of the others are a different breed though. They may march for Caesar, but they worship Rickover. Admiral Johnson, COMSUBLANT's deputy, is a prime example of the NUC bunch."

Linc quickly filled in the picture for himself. "So Rickover gets off on power and this could threaten the foundation of his influence?"

Craig sat back in his chair. "That's how I see it. 'God's' chosen few can't admit he's really a twisted little egomaniac who chose them exactly because they had something he needed and were weak enough to follow him as a messiah. A neat arrangement. He promises them their ambitions and they guarantee his."

Linc stood up and stretched his long arms. He shook a foot that had gone numb during Craig's diatribe and sat back down. "That doesn't fit the public image."

"Any insider will tell you that Rickover manages his press image just as well as any movie star and is a big time politician."

Linc came back to the point. "So you think Rickover and the Submarine Force Admirals want this covered up because it might cost them appropriations, political influence, their face, or all three."

Craig didn't try to hide the hostility in his remark when he replied, "There's not enough guts and integrity in the command structure or the administrative process to make all that secondary. The real focus should be on finding out what was chasing us out there, and even more importantly, determine if we are misguided in believing that the Submarine Launched Ballistic Missile System is invulnerable."

It was Linc's turn to be shocked. "Christ! Are you saying they would suppress something like that just for personal ambition?"

Craig returned Linc's penetrating stare. "Or misguided values. I don't know what they will do, but we have to be very damned careful."

Linc closed his notepad and slowly, with exaggerated deliberation, capped his pen and returned it to his blouse pocket.

Lunchtime was approaching. Craig got up and retrieved his cap. As he prepared to leave the room, Linc's next question was the same one that had kept Craig awake on the crew flight from Rota.

"And what are you going to do?"

The answer to that was now easy. Craig had already made his decision and saw no reason to revisit it. One discredited Lt. Commander couldn't make a dent in the wall of denial and disinformation that could be forthcoming. Jail was even possible. "I'm going to try to survive professionally, but if I'm cornered, I'll fight."

"Why even be concerned about trying to survive professionally, let's just fight the bastards! If what you're telling me about the patrols' unexplained events is accurate…and, even worse, that you suspect our subs are vulnerable…the American public has a right to know. Why should we be bit players in Rickover's charade?"

"To keep one dinosaur alive."

"Sounds dumb to me."

"Not if you're the dinosaur!"

47
The Long Green Table

The number of secrets stolen over the years by spies lurking outside the windows of a military conference room is, if known, not a matter of public record. Presumably more than one, since every Navy headquarters building has a number of windowless catacombs. Almost always, at least one of these most inner of sanctums is decorated with flags and long green felt covered tables to provide a proper atmosphere for the conduct of solemn and secure affairs of naval business. The room at COMSUBFLOT TWO headquarters, deep in the basement of Building 138 on the Submarine Base, Groton, wherein the *Marion* investigation convened, complied with all requirements of tradition and security.

COMSUBFLOT TWO, having inherited the building that, during World War II had housed COMSUBLANT, enjoyed an even more imposing conference room than most commands could boast. The room itself was a great square with two matching doors, one on the right wall and the other on the left. The door on the right provided public access to the room, while the one on the left led to a private stairway to the Admiral's office.

In the middle of the room, in front of the ubiquitous flags, sat a horseshoe of three ten-foot long tables topped with the required rich green felt-cloth. Bright, but soft lighting, accentuated the room's sterile off-white colored walls. Behind the partially opened dark blue drapes that covered the wall behind the flags one could see a huge multi-colored chart of the Atlantic Ocean that once provided a summary view of World War II naval operations. A lush, wall to wall, navy blue carpet gave the room a false appearance of warmth, though it hushed the footsteps of Craig and the others as the parties and their attorneys filed in and, with a muted scuffling of chairs, took their seats. Neither the carpet, nor the somber elegance of the room dispelled the atmosphere of the place. It felt like a crypt.

The investigating Admiral's seat was, fittingly, directly in front of the flags. COMSUBLANT's Legal Counsel and the Yeoman court recorder sat at the table to the Admiral's right, facing the *Marion* officers across the horseshoe. The designated parties being investigated sat to the Admiral's left in order of rank; the Captain, then the Exec, the Navigator, and the Weapons Officer. Each man's counsel sat slightly to his left and behind him.

The artificial lights and the hum of ventilation blowers in the background created an atmosphere not unlike sitting in the belly of a submarine. The bright sun and rich green of a New England mid summer were carefully shut out. Craig again felt the momentary sensation of being tossed across the boundary between two worlds. A moment earlier he had been in the world of home and family. Now, he was back in a surreal world of artificial light and air.

Craig and the others were a pretty subdued lot. An eerie somberness filled the officers' blank stares as they sat, motionless, immersed in a quiet apprehension that was marked by neither hope nor despair.

As he waited, Craig was lost in thought. *It must have been something like this for participants waiting for the games to commence in ancient Rome. Only, here there are no screaming crowds. The Old Man and I share no particular animus, but these proceedings are probably going to set us against each other like a pair of reluctant gladiators. I don't see a way for both of us to survive this investigation. One of us will have to be carried out on his shield for the other to survive.*

* * * * *

Linc had spent most of the weekend as an overnight guest in Craig's home, asking questions, listening, taking notes and eating everything Meaghan put before him. Craig was skeptically unsure of how much he could absorb of submarine force politics, technicalities and tactics in two days, but he had to acknowledge that the lawyer damn well tried. Linc was clearly a quick study, and both Meaghan and Mike were impressed with his intellect.

Craig had talked until he was hoarse on Saturday, then, on Sunday did the same, covering every detail he could think of about the patrol and the Captain's behavior. He and Linc had agreed, early on, that there was no obvious brilliant defensive strategy at this stage of the proceedings. They simply had to wait and see how the other side was going to play the game. Another point of early agreement was that they could not afford to let their guard down with the Captain or his counsel. Craig thought Holcomb's paranoia was the snake in the grass he had to fear. Linc agreed. Once COMSUBLANT had tipped his hand, both men figured they could formulate a defensive plan to meet that threat. Holcomb, on the other hand, might be more dangerous because of his unpredictability.

* * * * *

Rousing a bit from his reverie, Craig looked around the room. *So here we are. We're all scared shitless. The four of us trying to prove that real men don't show anxiety!*

Admiral Kincaid opened the proceedings by reading the order from COMSUBLANT appointing him to conduct a One Officer Formal Investigation into events surrounding the grounding of the *USS Marion* (SSBN 623) on or about 6 June, 1970. He was to ascertain the causes and responsibility, including culpability, if any, and recommend appropriate actions to COMSUBLANT. It was straight by the book, exactly as Craig and Linc had expected.

The COMSUBLANT Legal Officer then spent a couple of hours instructing the "accused" on procedures, the rights of parties, and the provisions of every applicable reference known to man starting with the New Testament. With all that, he offered no substantive clue as to the direction the investigation would take for each man personally. Such were the opening ceremonies.

Finally, it was the Admiral's turn again. "Gentlemen," he said, "I am here to ascertain the facts surrounding the near grounding and risk to your ship and crew, including your individual performances as they may have influenced that event—nothing more and nothing less."

Linc and Craig exchanged glances. Okay, so they were going to try to limit the focus and any possible disclosure to only the grounding. Avoid raising and recognizing the more dangerous political issues of how we got there. Fair enough. During their weekend planning session, Craig and Linc had considered that opening and had already decided they would play along. Craig was as anxious as anyone to avoid a public spectacle and, Linc, with some reservations, had agreed.

Surely, they thought, this meant COMSUBLANT and CINCLANFLEET understood the implications of the PDC's, the close encounters and the Old

Man's condition. All of it. COMSUBLANT was going to clear the air, then later come to grips with the real issues. Still, proforma in this situation, the CO should have been under investigation for "Possible Relief for Cause." But he wasn't, and both Craig and Linc thought that to be both intentional and suspicious.

The Admiral was speaking again. "As it is now 1145, we will adjourn for lunch until 1330. When we reconvene, I will commence hearing evidence with Commander Holcomb, the first witness to be called. You are all reminded of the classified nature of these proceedings and the limits of authorized discussion outside this room."

He stood and turned to leave as the others all rose raggedly from their chairs.

Craig turned to Linc. "Let's go for a walk."

The Navigator turned toward them and started to say something, but Craig didn't want company and preempted the question. "You other guys go on to the club if you want. Linc and I are going to stretch our legs first."

Once outside, the others quickly piled into their cars and departed toward the Officers' Club.

Linc looked around. "Where do you want to walk?"

Craig gestured toward the old Buick. "To the car. Let's run down to Groton and get a Big Mac. I just wanted to get away from the group."

"Great!"

Once in the car, Craig drove out the nearby main gate. He took the winding river road instead of going via Route 12, the main thoroughfare from the Sub Base to Groton.

As they rode along, Linc opened the discussion. "What do you think is going on?"

Craig thought for a minute before he answered. "They want to treat the whole incident as a simple grounding. There are so many rumors circulating all over the Force about something happening on our patrol that COMSUBLANT can't be sure of keeping it under wraps. His best approach is to create a certifiable red herring that can be trotted out when required, to keep the curious satisfied. Answer questions, but not the real ones."

By now, they were passing under the Gold Star Memorial Bridge that crossed the wide expanse of the Thames River just before it meets the Atlantic Ocean. At Bridge Street, Craig turned left toward Groton's fast-food strip on Route 1.

"Watch your ass," Linc said seriously. "There is some reason why the Old Man is not facing 'Relief for Cause.'"

"I've been curious about that ever since we got back. I have had a nasty suspicion almost from the beginning."

Linc's response was a dour, "Well, I've got one now."

"What's yours?" Craig asked.

Linc grinned, not like he saw anything really funny in what he was about to say. "The captain is a loose bullet. They know that. If he feels threatened, he might do or say anything. Somebody has to be to blame if the cover story is simple negligence. It can't be him, so that leaves you. By not threatening the captain with 'Relief for Cause,' they avoid exciting him." Linc continued. "They're counting on you to be a tame witness. Even under these circumstances, the captain still will get to write a final fitness report on you. If "Relief for Cause" had been cited, that prerogative would have been taken away from him by Navy Regs. I think their reasoning is that you won't be able to explain yourself. If you do—and alienate him—he'll kill you professionally and there is no appeal process for that. You know that. They're also counting on your allegiance to the 'Silent Service.' They think you'll take a hit rather than violate the NUC Club's code of conduct, particularly when it's explained to you how much harm you might do the Submarine Force."

Mike slammed the steering wheel with the flat of his hand. "Spot on! That's how I see it, too. I figured out the final Fitness Report bit as soon as I got back and talked to the Chief of Staff here. Still, they may let us all off rather than risk a fight."

Linc looked less than convinced. "Maybe, but to make 'negligence' look good, they need to rap somebody."

They had arrived at McDonalds. As they got out of the car, Craig asked Linc, "So what do we do?"

"Wait and see which way they jump. For now, answer the questions asked and nothing but the questions asked. Don't volunteer anything."

Craig agreed, but was still troubled. "Okay, but let's try to avoid sandbagging the Old Man. He is actually a very decent human being and none of this is really his fault. The poor bastard has been intimidated his whole life. First his father, then by his religion, and now by Rickover and the peer pressure of the NUC club. Watching he and his wife interact socially, I would guess that he might be even somewhat dominated by her. All he knows in life is trying to live up to other peoples' expectations. He did the best he could. He was just the wrong horse for this course. He's a victim already, and I don't want to hurt him any more if we can help it."

They had reached the counter now and were greeted by an excessively cheerful teenager who welcomed them to McDonalds and asked for their order.

"Counselor, what do you want?"

"Nothing. I hate burgers."

"Well, why the hell didn't you say so?"

"You didn't ask."

"If you're going to be a tongue-tied mouthpiece, I'm a hurtin frog!"

Linc grinned, then broke into a laugh. "Drag me off for burgers again and you can find another lily pad to keep your speckled ass out of the deep water! Get your Big Mac and a large order of fries for me. Let's get back. I can't wait to see what your Old Man has to say."

48

A Loose Bullet

Craig and Linc didn't have to wait long after court reconvened to find out what Holcomb was going to do. Immediately after the Admiral sat down, the COMSUBLANT counsel called the Captain to the stand.

"Captain," the Admiral began, "will you please state for this court of inquiry, your full name, rank, service number and present duty station?"

Holcomb replied, his voice shaky, clearing his throat a couple of times. He appeared to have lost more weight since returning to Groton, and was even gaunter than he had been on the ship. He was obviously tense and near exhaustion. Craig felt a twinge of sympathy.

The Admiral spoke again. "Captain, where were you and what were your duties on 6 June, 1970?"

Holcomb answered in a hushed voice. "I was on board the *USS Marion*, underway on patrol in the Mediterranean. I was the Commanding Officer."

"And did anything unusual happen on that day?"

Something abruptly changed in Holcomb. His eyes sparked and in a suddenly strong voice, he answered. "Yes, we almost hit the bottom, but that's not important. We got away from HIM! That was the important thing. Now, you've got to listen to what happened before that!"

The Admiral and the COMSUBLANT counsel exchanged startled glances.

"Captain," the Admiral said, "please confine yourself to my questions. We're here to investigate the grounding, nothing else."

Holcomb wasn't about to be denied. His voice rose. "You've got to listen to how HE followed us around. How HE interfered with our equipment. How HE was going to kill us! Nobody wants to hear this, but here in this place you have to listen and put it in the record of proceedings!" He looked craftily at the Admiral and went on. "You have to, because you have to make a determination as to why we were in shallow water to begin with!"

Consternation appeared on the faces of both Admiral Kincaid and the COMSUBLANT legal officer. Craig and the others were virtually holding their breath.

The Admiral broke in. "Captain! Stop there! Have you discussed this statement with your counsel?"

"No, sir. He doesn't need to know all this. It's too sensitive. I want you to get these other lawyers out of here, too."

Admiral Kincaid jumped to his feet. "This Court of Inquiry is recessed!" he snapped. "You talk to your counsel before we resume in one hour."

Turning to the COMSUBLANT counsel, he said simply, "Come with me," and stalked out of the room.

All the officers and their counsels broke into a babble of conversation. Linc, laughing hard, punched Craig on the shoulder. When he could control his laughter, Linc said to Craig, "They just got a ricochet from the 'loose bullet' that they never expected!"

Lincoln Julius Mann was greatly amused. Craig was less so. The Captain was beckoning to him from across the room.

Full of apprehension, Craig went over to him. *Oh, shit!*

Holcomb's stood in an aggressive posture. He was suspicious and excited. "XO, you're still with me, aren't you? You're not going to fail our duty, are you? You're going to help me make them listen, aren't you?"

How the hell do I answer him? He's ready to trip off... Parsing his words very carefully, Craig replied, "Yes, sir, I will tell the facts about the PDC's as I know them."

More suspicion flickered in Holcomb's eyes. "Facts as you know them? Are you going to weasel out on me, XO? You're not turning against me, are you?"

Can't afford to lie, but I've got to give him something or he's going to blow! "No, sir," Craig said, "I just mean that we must be very careful to be precisely accurate in what we say."

Not wanting to remain exposed to Holcomb any longer than necessary, Craig hurriedly excused himself and moved back to where Linc was standing. Trying not to be obvious, they moved as quickly as they could across the room to a far corner out of earshot from the Captain.

Standing with his back to Holcomb and his counsel, and keeping his voice low, Linc said, "They can't stop him from talking. He might try to go to CINCLANT, or even the Secretary of Defense if they get him excited enough. This is a whole new ball game."

Craig nodded. "That's how I see it, too. Now I have to back him up or he'll get me for turning against him. He's suspicious of me already. If I keep him pacified, then COMSUBLANT gets me. Classic 'no win,' huh?"

A few minutes later, as he and Linc lounged outside the building, waiting for the recess to be over, a thought struck Craig. "Linc," he said, "we agree that COMSUBLANT has really fucked up. This is the last thing they wanted the Old Man to do. But, do you know where they went wrong?"

Linc's head snapped around. "No, tell me."

Craig was no psychiatrist, but he was sure he knew his man. "The Captain can only deal with one overwhelming paranoid fear at a time. By not threatening him with 'Relief for Cause,' they've left him still hung up on the notion that something on this patrol was out to destroy the ship. By trying to avoid threatening him with that procedure, they just about guaranteed that he would go off the way he has."

Linc understood as soon as Craig started talking. "You're right, Mike! If they had threatened him with a 'Relief for Cause,' a court-martial, anything, he would have zeroed in on that and the grounding, and probably wouldn't have said a word about the PDC's, or the people he thought were out to kill him."

Craig waved toward the headquarters building. "They knew they were dealing with a cocked cannon, but they let it go off because they didn't understand how the safety catch worked, so to speak! Now we've really got a 'loose bullet!'"

Linc asked, "So what now?"

"They'll have to let him talk and try to keep it bottled up here in the record of proceedings. Somehow, they'll have to discredit his allegations."

"How will they do that if, as you say, some of his facts are true?"

Craig had no answer for that. "I don't know. Let's go back in and see what happens. There may yet be a way to keep my ass from becoming a sacrificial anode."

49
The Game Unfolds

When the hearing resumed, the Admiral's manner was perceptibly different.

"Captain," he said softly, "please resume your testimony. Start wherever you like, but please concentrate on the events that led to the grounding or near grounding of your ship."

The Captain looked triumphant. "Yes, sir!" he said and began. "Early on in the patrol we started hearing thousands of PDC's. Wherever we went, they followed us..."

He went on for nearly an hour and laid out the whole nine yards. Craig winced when he pulled that damned 'out-of-commission' list from his pocket as proof of his theory that the *Marion* had been subject to some sort of malignant interference.

"Our track into shallow water," Holcomb concluded, "was a brilliant tactical move without which we would not have escaped."

To Craig's dismay, the Captain generously credited him with being the expert tactician without whom, he assured the Court, the ship would not have returned from patrol.

Concluding his testimony, he said, "The XO will verify everything when he's called to testify."

By the time the Captain had finished speaking, Craig and the other *Marion* officers were thoroughly disconsolate. The silence in the room was oppressive. The Navigator and the Weapons Officer were almost in shock, having seen, for the first time, the full depth of the Captain's dementia. Holcomb had taken them into the sadly distorted world of his mind, the world the Exec had tried to keep shut away behind a stateroom door for nearly half of the patrol.

In addition to the Captain's embarrassment, Craig felt a good deal of pity for the Old Man, sitting under the flags with his frailties and fears exposed for all to see. *Damn the people who put him there to be broken! It is really their failure, not his.*

Without calling anyone else to the stand, the Admiral adjourned the proceedings for the day and quietly walked to the door that opened into the private stairway that led from the conference room to his office. Before pushing his way through the door, he paused for a moment, leveling a penetrating look at each of the *Marion* officers in turn, then left.

Linc and Craig left quickly, avoiding the others, and went directly home. Without bothering to change out of their white summer uniforms, they went into the patio and sat down. Meaghan appeared almost instantly with a quiet greeting and a round of gin and tonic.

Linc was still absorbing the Captain's performance. "That man has totally lost his grip on reality," he said.

"Tell me about it," Mike replied.

"The Submarine Force Chain of Command has to know that. So why this charade?"

"I told you," Mike said. "They have to because they cannot, and will not, deal with the alternative."

"That being?"

"Conceding that a NUC CO was weak and failed. That we put enough firepower to devastate Europe and Russia under the command of a man demented by paranoia. That our SSBN's might be vulnerable. That Rickover is fallible and his followers are not supermen."

"Yeah." Linc grunted. "Well, you get to be the next crazy in the box tomorrow."

50
The Setup

Linc was prophetic. Craig's was, indeed, the next witness called and it was a harrowing experience. The Captain's narrative from the previous day provided the point of departure and the Admiral bombarded the Exec with questions. After the routine questions to document Craig's presence and role on the *Marion*, Kincaid went immediately to the question of the PDC's.

"What is your opinion of the alleged PDC's?" he asked.

Craig answered carefully. "We heard a great many noises that can best be described as distant PDC's. I do not know how they were generated."

"State only facts. Don't get lead into anything that can be labeled 'supposition.' Did they follow you around?"

It was going to be a long day. Craig intended to select every word with great precision. "They appeared to do so and, I believe, their source moved in a pattern similar to our own."

"How can you say that?"

And on it went. All morning and into the afternoon. Craig composed every answer to be meticulously accurate without obviously undermining the Captain. It was a fine line to walk. Tough and nerve racking. The worst moment was when the Admiral finally got around to asking Craig his opinion of the 'out-of-commission' list Holcomb had flourished during his testimony. The damned list was now entered into the investigation as a full exhibit.

"Did the Captain discuss with you his belief that equipment failures were being externally stimulated?"

Craig answered. "Yes, sir."

"Did you see and discuss this list?"

"Yes, sir."

"Did you agree with his assessment?"

Craig had no choice. He couldn't afford to portray himself as demented as Holcomb. "No, sir."

"Why not?"

"I didn't know of any mechanism by which it could happen."

"Did you tell the Captain your opinion?"

"Yes, sir."

"When you recommended the inshore track that led to your nearly losing the ship, did you believe you were under threat of destruction by some hostile force?"

Shit! There it is. The one inescapable question I knew I would have to answer sooner or later.

Holcomb's face told Craig that the Captain was on the brink of turning against him. He quickly glanced at the Admiral, and knew that he was one answer away from the abyss there as well.

Taking a deep breath, Craig plunged in. "No. I did not share the Captain's conviction on that."

He saw the Captain pull himself up in his chair. Holcomb's moustache was trembling slightly. Craig quickly continued. "The Captain knew I felt less physically threatened than he, but, I emphatically state that I shared his conclusion that the anomalous tactical experiences and observations on this patrol dictated extraordinary caution and must be investigated." *Double talk, but I hope the Admiral understands why I'm trying to baffle him with bullshit!* Craig stole a glance at the Captain. He was relaxing. A look at the Admiral was less reassuring. *Did I get across the tightrope?*

Kincaid was ready to change the subject. "Your Captain described an incident in which, as Command Duty Officer, you dropped Alert coverage and evaded at high speed after hearing what you claim were heavy explosions close aboard. You even cut the trailing wire antenna in your haste. What made you think those were explosions?"

Craig was incredulous. *What is he insinuating?* "Admiral, sir, with all due respect, I do not understand your question."

"Why do you think you were subjected to close heavy explosive charges?"

Craig was still off balance. He couldn't keep an edge out of his voice when he answered. "Because I heard them and felt them. I've heard everything from PDC's to depth charges and war shot torpedoes at one time or another. I know a heavy underwater explosion when I hear one, particularly when it throws people out of their bunks!"

The Admiral's non-verbals were clear. He was skeptical to the point of being dismissive. "You are sure? Do you have any evidence?"

Something is beginning to stink here like a dead mouse in the wall of an old house! Craig was wary now and, glancing at Linc, he could see his lawyer sensed danger as well. Turning to squarely face the Admiral, he said, resignedly, "Yes, sir. The explosions in question are recorded on a sonar work tape and were submitted for analysis with the rest of our patrol package. Check with NISC."

"I have, Mr. Craig. They'll be here tomorrow to report their findings."

Craig left the stand and returned to his seat. As he sat down, Craig turned and hissed to Linc through clenched teeth, "Setup! Fuckin' setup!" Linc and Meaghan had been right. Craig had refused until now to give in completely to their suspicions. *Christ, I knew from the beginning that I would have to pay the piper when the dance was over, but I assumed that they would use facts to prosecute me. I never considered the possibility that anyone would falsify data from the patrol.*

The one article of faith he had clung to had turned out to be an illusion. Craig was too furious to be disappointed.

51
Sonar Tapes

As the investigation convened on its third morning, an additional seat was filled on the Admiral's right hand. Master Chief Petty Officer Mark Buckley, leading Sonar Analyst from the Naval Intelligence Scientific Center was there to present the results of his team's analysis of the tape recordings from the *Marion*'s patrol.

Buckley and Craig exchanged a brief nod across the room. They knew each other from an SSN "Spec Ops" years before. Craig was pleased, as he knew Buckley was a good Sonarman and a fine sailor and was, almost certainly, incorruptible.

The Master Chief Sonarman took the stand first, called by the Admiral. His testimony didn't take long.

After establishing Buckley's identity and credentials, the Admiral launched right in. "Master Chief Buckley, have you and your team completed analysis of the sonar tape recordings included in this crew's latest patrol report package?"

"Yes, sir."

"The crew claims to have heard and recorded thousands of PDC's during the patrol. Can you identify those or associate them with any platform?"

Buckley looked uncomfortable as he replied. "No, sir. Actually, sir, I'm not sure what you're talking about. We didn't find any 'thousands' of PDC's on the tapes. A few, but that's real common in the Med. Someone is always conducting seismic ops in there."

The Admiral didn't show a flicker of expression. "Then you found no evidence on the tapes you analyzed of an unusual number of PDC's—for a Med patrol, that is?"

The Master Chief glanced at Craig, pausing almost imperceptibly before answering. "No, sir. If anything, fewer. Another thing, those tapes, on the whole, were of pretty poor quality. If I were to judge by them, I'd say the whole sonar gang needs training."

By now, Craig was seething, choking back his anger. Having listened to the tapes before they left the *Marion*, he knew the package that had been submitted to Squadron had contained nothing but top quality, professionally annotated recordings.

Is this son of a bitch lying or what? I can't wait to talk to Franzi and the Chief.

The Admiral went on. "Did you find any evidence of an incident involving heavy explosions close aboard?"

"None, sir."

"None at all? Did you find a tape so labeled?"

Buckley's discomfort was now obvious, but there was no ambivalence in his reply. "Yes, sir, but there weren't any explosions. Somebody had just cranked the gain way up and saturated the tape. Operator error, but no explosions."

Craig forced himself to stay calm. Glancing over at Holcomb, he could see that the Old Man was a hair's breadth away from catatonic shock. *I figured on a cover-up of some kind, but nothing this fucking corrupt!*

Admiral Kincaid continued boring in.

"What about a reported incident of very strong FM sonar signals?"

"Nothing, sir. There was a little bit of distant British 2000 series, but that was all."

That ended the testimony and Kincaid called a recess for the morning break.

Craig jumped up and followed Buckley out of the conference room door, catching up with him in the men's room. Furious and out of earshot of the other participants, he wasted no time on niceties. "Buckley! What in the hell is going on? Don't bullshit me now, because you know I listened to those tapes before I let them leave the ship!"

The Master Chief gave Craig a pained, bemused look. "Look, Mr. Craig, all I can do is report what I find. Your tapes didn't have a damn thing on them." He paused for a minute. "Except your labels. They were so bad I couldn't believe they were from an operational crew. They sounded like junk work tapes from sonar school."

The anger he had been suppressing, as his suspicions rose, was suddenly threatening to take over in Craig's reaction. Then, in an instant, he realized what had really happened to the tapes and that Buckley would not have been a party to it. As clearly as he dared, the Master Chief had told him that he suspected the tapes weren't the *Marion*'s originals. Now is not the time to lose control. Craig stood looking at Buckley, then slowly nodded his head. "Thanks, Chief."

Later, during the break, he and Linc went to "their" conference room, the parking lot, and Craig told him what Buckley had said.

"Pretty obvious to me," Linc said. "Somebody is more concerned about politics than he is about your ass getting blown off."

52
Wrapping Up

The rest of that day and the next were taken up with testimony from all the junior officers. Each filed up to the stand, recited the details as they recalled them, of the brush with the bottom and sat down. There were few questions and, at 1600 on the fourth day, the Admiral announced the proceedings complete, subject, of course, to reconvening if he found a need for more information during the preparation of his report. Kincaid then set off to draft a statement of his findings and recommendations.

There was nothing for Craig to do now but wait to see what action the convening authority COMSUBLANT would take. Linc stayed for the dinner that Meaghan had made, then headed back to Newport.

The kids had come to adore Linc and loudly protested his departure. To distract them from their disappointment, Meaghan proposed a family vote on what to do for the weekend. The kids thought a picnic was in order, so on Saturday they set off for Green Falls Reservoir, deep in the nearby Pachaug state forest. There Mike and Meaghan filled their canoe with kids, dogs, lobsters and jug wine and sailed off to a quiet spot of beach well away from the public landing.

Early in the sun-filled afternoon, Meaghan and Mike lay resting against a shaded boulder, watching the kids and the dogs harass each other at the water's edge. Mike was worried about the outcome of the investigation and it showed. He was preoccupied, short with the kids and had twice threatened one of the dogs.

Meaghan had had it. "Give us a break," she said.

Mike didn't answer, exercising what he considered to be his right to sullen silence.

Meaghan tried again. "What do you think is going to happen?"

"I don't know."

She turned on him, her exasperation boiling over. "Well, you might have to go to work for a living, but they can't take us away from you, so loosen up for an hour or so. The kids and I need to know you're home!"

There it is again, that damned common sense of hers! Right, as usual!

"Right!" Mike said. "Pass me the jug. I hope you and the dogs can paddle us back."

Meaghan didn't have to paddle, but an awful headache made Mike's Sunday pass with hardly a thought to the investigation. When he woke Monday morning, he felt a hell of a lot looser than he had for weeks.

There's something to be said for old folk remedies.

53
Life Goes On

Arriving at the *Marion*'s "Off Crew" office a little before 0800, Craig found the Chief of the Boat already there happily unpacking a cruise box. The COB dropped the lid on the box and headed immediately toward the Exec. The look on his face was a familiar one, half amusement, half annoyance. "XO!"

"COB, I have a lot on my mind already. Do I want to hear this?"

"Yes, sir...maybe no, sir."

Craig resigned himself to a coming irritation. "What happened?"

"Last night, sir. Somebody flushed a cherry bomb down a third deck shitter in the barracks. It blew out a foot and a half of drain pipe and a big fuckin' hole in the wall on the first deck. There's shit, water and plaster all over the place."

The third deck was the *Marion*'s barracks area. Craig sighed and shook his head. Life with sailors always had a certain schizophrenic quality. They could perpetrate juvenile high jinks at the most inopportune time, then, in some other moment show astonishing insight, dedication or courage. Submarine sailors rattle back and forth between mischief and magnificence. Somehow, the magnificence is always there when it is needed. Unfortunately, sometimes, the mischief is there at precisely the most inopportune time.

Here I am, fighting for my professional life, and I have to deal with some God-damned sailor with arrested development and a cherry bomb! Craig exploded. "I really need this. Were McJimsey and Kane in the barracks?"

The COB replied, "No, sir. They're both on leave."

Christ, that means I have a new prankster on board. Maybe getting sacked would be a relief.

54

Deputy COMSUBLANT

While Craig and the COB were discussing cherry bombs, Rear Admiral "Wee Willie" Johnson arrived at COMSUBLANT Headquarters in Norfolk, Virginia. He preened his five foot two inches as he summoned the Staff Legal Officer to appear. He considered that kicking a little ass first thing in the morning limbered him up for the day.

The investigation that COMSUBFLOT Two had just finished in Groton would be fine exercise material. He was, as he thought to himself, *pissed off* at COMSUBFLOT Two. Those guys had damned near grounded an SSBN and Old Paleface, Admiral Kincaid, was going to let them off scot-free.

"Wee Willie" was indignant, particularly about the XO who had the Command Duty at the time of the incident. He had to be guilty of something, by God! He couldn't criticize the Captain, so the XO had to take the fall. Somebody had to get dropped in the shit or it wouldn't look like a simple grounding incident. Willie, self righteously, saw nothing but his brand of justice. *The bastard had almost let the ship go down. Hell, something had to be done to keep all those rumors from getting out about the captain. Let the guilty pay the way for the greater good,* he thought. "A small price. One guilty Lieutenant Commander to keep the Air Force at bay and the NUC image unblemished."

"Christ Almighty!"

He'd been in COMSUBLANT's office when Rickover had gotten the word. Rickover had gone ballistic. He'd screamed and raged about the damage this incident could do if it got out. In fact, he had screamed and raged until he either threw the phone down or had a seizure. He'd been known to do both. Rickover had made it plain he didn't want any of that crap to get out about something stalking the ship around the Med or a NUC CO mentally breaking down. Let the world know the rumors were started by a real brush with the bottom, caused by lax watch standing, and that COMSUBLANT had already dealt with it."

The Legal Officer's arrival interrupted Admiral Wee Willie's reverie. "Good Morning, Admiral."

Willie pranced to his desk, jerky and quick like a gold braided James Cagney, and growled, "Morning. Brief me on COMSUBFLOT Two's investigation."

"As you know, I acted as Admiral Kincaid's counsel during the investigation. He, however, drafted the 'Conclusions and Recommendations' section of the report."

"Yeah, yeah, go on."

"He concludes that no evidence exists of dereliction of duty, nor improper performance of duty by any party. He limits his recommendations to technical follow-up actions within the navigation system."

Willie exploded. "Goddammit! Doesn't he know what he's doing—what he was supposed to do? I want that Goddamned Exec nailed. You can't have a screwup like this without the Command Duty Officer being guilty of something!"

The Legal Officer attempted to explain. "The Exec was able to show, and the Captain supported him, that he acted on the Captain's orders and, having done so, took all reasonable available precautions. Of course, we CAN make a case against the Captain."

Willie lost it. "NO! Goddammit! Not the Captain! I want a letter of reprimand for that Exec, what's his name? Craig? He's a damned attitude case anyway. Never did fit in the Nuclear Power program."

The Legal Officer remained unruffled. He had borne the brunt of Wee Willie's tantrums before and would again. "What shall I charge him with, sir?"

"Well, dammit, he let the Captain give those orders. He accepted improper orders, didn't he?"

The lawyer shrugged. "He could have refused to obey the Captain's orders, but that would have been mutinous. He could have relieved the Captain."

Willie's eyes sparkled. "Wish he had. I'd have court-martialed the son of a bitch!"

"So what do you want me to charge him with?"

"You're the Goddamned lawyer. Give me some Goddamned completed staff work for a change."

The Legal Officer's expression and voice never changed. "Suppose we charge him with acquiescing to the orders of his Commanding Officer?"

"All right. Do it. Today."

"He might appeal."

"No, he won't Goddamn appeal. He knows we've got him. Besides, you are to give him only three days to reply. He can't say a damn thing as long as his CO is waiting to mail his last Fitness Report."

"Admiral, do you think we ought to bounce this off COMSUBLANT before you sign it out?"

Willie was withering. "No! I'm acting COMSUBLANT until he gets back!"

With a very respectful, "Aye, aye, sir," the Legal Officer withdrew.

Back in his own office, his Yeoman wondered for a moment at the Legal Officer's obvious good humor. Visits to Admiral Johnson generally produced quite another reaction. A half hour later, the Legal Officer handed the Yeoman a handwritten draft of a letter to be typed.

The Yeoman's expression became increasingly perplexed as he read the draft. "Sir, is this the charge you want to cite?"

"Yes. Why?"

"Sir, 'Acquiescing' is what Navy Regs require you to do when in receipt of a lawful order! This doesn't make any sense."

The Legal Officer studied the Yeoman for a moment then broke a hint of a smile. "You know, Yeo, in most Navies of the world you are absolutely right. But, at the moment, you and I are in Admiral Johnson's Navy. I think we should diligently support his decision." With that he retreated to his inner office, closed the door and lit a cigar. He happily contemplated the smoke as it curled upward. He had no interest in or sympathy for the XO, but it had been a very long eighteen months working for that prick Johnson.

55
A Way Out

That same afternoon, right after lunch, the Chief of Staff, Bill Davis, called Craig. There were no preambles. "Mike, the Admiral wants to see you right away."

"What's up, Bill?"

"I don't know. He was on the phone to COMSUBLANT. It must have something to do with the investigation."

Apprehension crawled up Craig's gut like a lizard. It must have showed in his voice when he said, "I'll be right down."

Before he hung up, Bill said, "You don't know this unless he tells you, but he's in your corner. He recommended that no action be taken against any of you. Come down right away and see what he wants."

"Thanks, Bill."

Craig hustled down the hill past the barracks and the commissary to Building 138. When he got to the Admiral's outer office, Bill was standing there.

"Good timing," he observed. "Go on in."

The Admiral sat at his desk, a huge mahogany cube completely devoid of paper. He was expressionless, just as he had been throughout the investigation. He looked somewhat ghost-like with his pale blue eyes and pasty white skin protruding from a short-sleeved white uniform. His light brown hair was mostly white now. Only his service ribbons and shoulder boards relieved the Admiral of his clinical pallor. Appearances can, however, be misleading. Craig knew Kincaid was even more of an anomaly among NUCS than he. The Admiral's family had served as Naval officers in an unbroken line since 1808. His three-inch high swath of ribbons included many that Craig respected.

Kincaid didn't stand for any tin sailor nonsense. As Craig came through the door, the Admiral stood up and started around his desk with a vague wave in the direction of a couple of chairs arranged around a low table.

313

"Come in, Craig. Sit down."

"Thank you, Admiral."

Craig took a chair and waited while Kincaid settled himself in the other one and lit a cigar.

The Admiral puffed his cigar a half dozen times while openly studying Craig before speaking. "Did you help him...or did you help push him over the edge?"

Craig answered thoughtfully. "I think I may have helped push him over, Admiral. My conscience has been grinding on that precise question since the last days of patrol." *There's no other answer I could give.*

"Why?"

"Because I never realized how vulnerable he was until it was too late."

Admiral Kincaid was not a man to dance around a question. "You mean, how weak?"

"Yes, sir."

The Admiral mildly replied, "He wasn't supposed to be weak, was he?"

A little heat began to rise in Craig. "No, sir. He was not supposed to be weak. He did not have the RIGHT to be weak."

The two men sat in silence while the Admiral puffed another half inch of his cigar. He seemed to be working over a decision. Finally, he spoke. "COMSUBLANT is out of pocket for the next ten days. He's at a Type Commander's conference in Pearl. His Deputy is acting for him."

Craig waited.

"He's going to bust your ass."

Still, Craig remained silent. What was there to say?

The Admiral went on. "What are you going to do when you get the Letter of Reprimand they're drafting? It'll kill you professionally. No promotions. No command of your own...ever."

"I don't know, Admiral. I'll decide that when I see the letter."

"They don't think you'll fight it because it would be a disservice to the Submarine Force if you do."

Craig gave the Admiral a straight look and asked, "Maybe. What do you think I should do?"

For the first time, a flicker of a smile showed in those pale blue eyes. "I think," Kincaid said, "that putting you and the Captain together was like putting a Boston Nanny in charge of Sitting Bull. I wonder if Admiral Johnson has thought this through?" Admiral Kincaid changed the subject abruptly. The hint of humor was gone. "Acting for COMSUBLANT, Admiral Johnson has directed me, at my discretion, to relieve your Captain of his duties as Commanding Officer of the *Marion* Gold crew. I see no reason to delay his departure to his next assignment. In fact, I assume he would prefer to get away as soon as possible for some well earned R & R."

Kincaid leaned forward to emphasize his remarks. "I am directing my Chief of Staff to assume temporary command of your crew. Change of command is to be not later than 1000 hours on Friday, four days from now. I want all administrative matters, including final fitness reports, to be completed and so reported to me by 1600 Thursday. No point in having unfinished business following the Captain around on leave, right?"

It clicked in Craig's mind immediately. Kincaid was giving him a shot at beating "Wee Willie" and the whole NUC establishment. If COMSUBLANT was drafting a Letter of Reprimand today, they would get it signed out and in the mail tomorrow. It would reach Craig on Wednesday at the earliest. He had to be allowed at least three working days to prepare an appeal. The JAG manual and BuPers Manual's required that. That made it Monday before he had to answer. By that time, the Old Man's final fitness report would be irretrievably mailed. Holcomb would be relieved and Bill, in his capacity as Chief of Staff, would be the one to endorse and forward the appeal to COMSUBFLOT Two.

I'll bet that Kincaid already has his Legal Officer drafting an endorsement. He doesn't like those bastards any better than I do!

Craig jumped up. "Thank you, Admiral. I'd better haul ass...excuse me...get back to the office. This means I have a hell of a lot of paper to move in the next two days."

Kincaid held up his hand. "Remember the fitness report. One bad one can ruin a career, and you have no right of appeal on the report like you do on the Letter of Reprimand.

Craig just grinned and took his leave. *Hell, he didn't have to remind me of that.*

56
The Letter

The Letter of Reprimand arrived right on schedule in the Wednesday morning mail. Linc had come down from Newport in anticipation of the letter and was lounging in the COMSUBFLOT Two legal office waiting for Craig's call. As is customary in the Navy, the letter was addressed to Craig via his Commanding Officer. It was, therefore, not officially in his hands until he had the yeoman type the endorsement "delivered" on it and got the Captain to sign it. Not wishing to disturb Holcomb from his more urgent task of completing the all important Fitness Report, it seemed proper that it be placed in his "IN" box, along with a stack of Change of Command paperwork. Craig was fairly sure it would not emerge until the next day. Meanwhile, he pocketed a copy of the letter to go over with Linc at lunchtime.

Holcomb had evidenced no surprise, or, for that matter, interest when Craig called to tell him the schedule for his Change of Command. Both arrived at the office that Wednesday at 0800 sharp and they immediately started through the prescribed checklists. Craig recalled all the Department Heads that were on leave to complete their portions of the paperwork, but in reality, there was little to do. All the significant custody items except a few engineering publications had been turned over to the Blue Crew as part of the Change of Command on the ship. Therefore, an off crew change of Commanding Officer required very little more than a final set of Fitness Reports and a ceremony.

The real panic was to organize the ceremony that naval tradition dictates. Craig put Stone in charge of that and focused his effort on drafting Fitness Reports for all the officers junior to himself and helping the Old Man empty his office. Craig found it a sad scene. Holcomb was almost completely apathetic. He gave the Captain a blank Fitness Report form with the name blocks filled in "Craig, Michael" and reminded Holcomb of COMSUBFLOT Two's deadline. Holcomb nodded and put it on his blotter. Craig watched and wondered if he would have to prod him to complete it. Holcomb seemed so drained and detached, Craig wondered if he could even fill the form out.

The most painful part of all was the personal side. "Captain," Craig asked him, "the wardroom officers would like to have a farewell party for you and your wife Friday night. Can you make it?"

"No," Holcomb said quietly. "It isn't that we can't. We just don't want a party. This is not an occasion for joy or celebration."

Not sure how to proceed, Craig tried to reach out to the despondent soul before him. "I understand how you feel, but that's not why your officers want to do it. They're your friends. They want to show that friendship and their respect for you."

"They can't have any respect now, XO. It would just be hypocritical."

Craig gave up. Further argument wouldn't move Holcomb and would have been patronizing. "I don't agree, sir. They know that you and Nancy are good people. But I won't argue if you'd prefer not to have the party."

"I'd prefer not." That was it. Holcomb turned back to the cruise box he was packing.

Craig called Meaghan with the verdict on the party. She said she would try to organize something with just the wives in the hope that would be a little comfort to the Holcombs. Meaghan observed, and Mike agreed, that one had to feel a special sympathy for the Captain's wife. She suffered with and for her man, and there was nothing she could do to soften the blow of present events.

But, Nancy also declined to get together with the wives.

* * * * *

When Mike found Linc at lunchtime, he handed him the Letter of Reprimand without comment. Linc took the document with a raised eyebrow, then sat reading for a few moments. As he read, his expression became increasingly incredulous. He started laughing. Finally containing himself, he blurted out, "Acquiescing to the orders of your Commanding Officer?"

Mike nodded.

"That's the dumbest charge I ever heard. They're saying you should have relieved him or mutinied."

"Yes."

"And they wouldn't relieve him for cause."

"That's right. So I'm reprimanded for not disobeying an order."

"And if you appeal and they deny it, they have to forward the appeal to CINCLANT Fleet. Boy, are they going to look dumb."

"Linc, I couldn't believe my eyes when I saw the reprimand. Notice, it's signed out by Wee Willie, but, even for him, this is a surprising gaffe. Is this just poor staff work or did his Legal Officer help him get his crank under his foot?"

"Who cares? What do you want to do?" asked Linc.

"Have a change of command, then submit our appeal. If I give you a rough draft of some thoughts by late tomorrow, can you have a final draft here by Friday at 0800? Then, provided we don't have to change anything, I can submit it before close of business."

"Sure, but what have you got to back the appeal up with?"

Mike grinned and surrendered to the urge to tweak him a bit. "Wait and see!"

* * * * *

The rest of that day and Thursday raced by. Craig delivered the package of notes and an outline of the appeal to Linc mid-afternoon on Thursday. Linc reviewed it, physically staggered Mike with an unexpected exuberant slap on the shoulder and sped off to his office.

Linc was back in the *Marion* office at 0815 the next morning. He looked like he had been up all night, but the appeal was in his hand. It was in the form of a basic letter, running to a little over three pages with several attached enclosures. Craig carefully reviewed the appeal while Linc nursed a cup of the perpetually stale coffee.

After a half hour's intense study that failed to find a single word to be changed, Mike dropped it on his desk and grinned at Linc. "This is just fucking beautiful! You are one hell of a wordsmith!"

Linc returned the grin. "Of course. Now get your ass down the hill and drop that on the Chief of Staff's desk."

Mike required no urging. He handcarried the appeal down to Bill in his office. Bill took it and disappeared into Admiral Kincaid's office. When he reappeared a few minutes later, all he said aloud was, "The Admiral said to leave it with him. He has no questions at this time."

Craig thanked him and started to leave, but, before he could turn, Bill grabbed his right shoulder and stepped close to whisper. "The endorsement is already written. All we were waiting for was your original appeal so we could get the reference line right and make sure our draft fits your letter. The Admiral wants this out today so COMSUBLANT sees it on Monday." He broke into a big grin. "Admiral Kincaid thinks COMSUBLANT is going to find all this pretty entertaining."

So there it is. Linc, Bill, the Admiral. Just like Stone, Rakowski, the COB and Chief Brown on the boat, I'm getting help from good men when I need it the most.

Change of Command went smoothly and on schedule at 1000. The Admiral attended and made a brief formal address. When it was his turn to speak, the Old Man mumbled a few halting, almost inaudible words. Craig winced as Holcomb tried to find his way through a few simple "thank you's" to the crew for their support. The Old Man did not break down, though, and Craig was grateful for that. No doubt, Nancy Holcomb was grateful, too. She sat stony-faced throughout the proceedings and led her husband away as quickly as possible when the short ceremony was over. As the Captain and Nancy made for the door, Craig intercepted them. Her look was cold. To her, he was a blue suited Brutus.

She understands better than he does. Craig extended his hand to Holcomb. "Good luck, sir. I hope your next tour is easier than this has been."

Holcomb grasped Craig's hand. Slowly, with a hard look, he said, "XO, I mailed your Fitness Report yesterday. You won't suffer any grief from it."

"Thank you, Captain." He wasn't the Captain anymore, but Craig would call him that until he left the premises—crossed the Rubicon, so to speak.

Holcomb started to walk away, then seeming to have forgotten something, returned. To the politely quizzical Craig, he said, "XO, you're free now. From here on in you're free to say whatever you believe to be the truth about me and what happened on the patrol."

Craig couldn't hide his consternation. *The son of a bitch. He has been fully aware of the box I've been in and had been content to keep me there!*

After that exchange, Craig felt considerably less morose about Holcomb's fate.

57
Wee Willie Johnson

Commander, Submarine Force Atlantic had returned from the Type Commander's conference in Pearl Harbor on Saturday. After a quiet day at his home, relaxing with his wife and visiting grandchildren, he was rested and ready to plunge back into his headquarters routine. So far, it had been a typical Monday's round of staff briefings, a long day of catch up briefings and status reports, aggravated by his absence the previous week. The Legal Officer had the last slot on the day's agenda and his briefing had turned the day from a routine aggravation into a major exasperation for the old warrior. After eight World War II war patrols, minor problems rarely exercised him, but he did not suffer fools gladly.

When the Legal Officer had finished speaking, the meeting adjourned and COMSUBLANT motioned to his Deputy to remain behind. When they were alone, he asked, almost conversationally, "Willie, you were the action officer on the incident with the *Marion* Gold crew?"

Rear Admiral Willie Johnson prided himself on being decisive. He had missed the Legal Officer's briefing in order to complete a lengthy telephone conversation with Naval Reactors about the training implications of a recent Reactor Safeguards Exam. *Damn! He had put that one to bed!*

"Yes, sir. COMSUBFLOT Two reported out last week and I've already signed out the Letter of Reprimand to the Exec. Craig is his name."

Wee Willie didn't like the acid in COMSUBLANT's voice when he heard, "I was just told that."

Willie began to worry slightly. *What was the boss leading up to?*

"Willie, you're a great one for action, but do you ever use your Goddammed head for anything but a battering ram?"

"Sir?"

"Have you seen this?" COMSUBLANT tossed a sheaf of papers across his desk.

Willie caught them in a scramble. COMSUBLANT had made no gesture towards a seat, so his Deputy stood and read, scarlet creeping up his neck as he passed from page to page.

COMSUBLANT was never too far from his pipe. It was commonly observed that the longer he tamped it, the greater the force of the coming explosion. "Willie, I find some remarkable words in there. Starting with your, 'Acquiescing to the orders of.' That may be the most ludicrous charge I have ever heard of. Next, let me read you something, in case you missed it!" He grabbed the letter back and began reading from it. "I assumed in good faith that the background circumstances of the Captain's mental condition were known to the Investigating Officer. In the interest of the welfare of the Submarine Force and the Nuclear Power Program, I chose to remain silent. Receipt of this Punitive Letter of Reprimand leaves me no choice but to assume these circumstances were either unknown or disregarded. I, therefore, request this investigation be reopened, so that a full disclosure of the true facts may be made. Specific information and facts essential to a full understanding of my actions are as follows…"

As Johnson started to sputter a response, COMSUBLANT cut him short. "Shut up, Willie. Craig goes on for three pages proving the Captain was incompetent and came within a hair of starting World War III. He's appended enough documentary evidence, starting with a sworn statement from the doctor on board and ending with that dumb-assed OOC list to prove it in any court of law in the land. Finally, he's listed over twenty witnesses, including CONSUBRON SIXTEEN."

"That son of a bitch!" exploded Willie Johnson.

"That son of a bitch can demand we forward this to CINCLANT FLEET if we deny his appeal. He'll have copies, so you can't burn his Goddamned letter. Even if you've already burned the records of the investigation, there's enough here," his voice rose, "to put you in Portsmouth Naval Prison for all the classified material you've had stolen, falsified, misplaced or shit-canned."

He then leaned forward and practically shouted, "That 'acquiesce' bullshit is the final straw! Since we didn't consider Relief for Cause, it wouldn't even take a very bright lawyer to show the world you stupidly put that Exec on report for failure to refuse a lawful order."

Rear Admiral William Johnson was pale and uncharacteristically quiet.

"And there's one more thing!"

"Yes, sir?"

"What did you do with those sonar tapes, and who helped you?" COMSUBLANT stopped for a breath and fumbled on his desk for his pipe, which he had dropped during his outburst. Before Willie could answer, he went on, "No. Don't tell me. I don't want to know."

"What do you want me to do?"

"Retract that letter of reprimand and be damned quick about it...today! Then you sit down and write our friend Rickover and try to explain this mess. If Craig drops his appeal after we issue our letter, wait about two weeks, then strip the files and have a shredding party. After that, you'd better pray nothing ever surfaces."

"Yes, sir. Anything else?"

"Yes. Get the hell out of here, and the next time I'm away, try to use your Goddamned brain!"

58
First Prize

The next evening, Linc, Mike and Meaghan were back on the deck of the Craig's home, scene of so many skull sessions over the last month. This time, they were well into celebrative gin and tonics. Mike had gotten the cryptic letter from COMSUBLANT earlier that afternoon. It was signed by Rear Admiral Willie Johnson, and simply read, "Reference (a) is withdrawn." That was all he needed.

After the whoops and exuberant high fives of relief and mutual congratulations, they were settled into a quiet review of where they had been and what it all meant. Each of the three was left with a cynicism they would never lose, a shaken faith in the ability of institutions to somehow merit trust greater than that conferred upon individuals.

As they turned their thoughts to the future, Mike spoke up. "Linc, considering what you now know about "big men" and how the world operates, what are you going to do?"

Linc said he might find his way into the private practice of law and perhaps politics. He thought that the only real power in the world was political, and there ought to be at least one good man wielding some of it. They all agreed.

Meaghan turned to Mike. "And what are you…we…going to do?"

Craig didn't hesitate. "Go on. Try to get a command. Look for a junior officer that may be a baby dinosaur and a future warrior. Hope that I can leave at least one behind so we don't become extinct."

As always, Meaghan understood her man. She nodded. "Then what are we left with after all of this?"

"First Prize!"

Meaghan and Linc both looked quizzical at that.

Mike turned to Linc. "Here's something I had made up for you to remember this summer's events."

The small brass plaque was engraved with Hyman G. Rickover's first rule of positive leadership:

First Prize is nothing.
Second Prize is a kick in the ass.

St. Petersburg, Russia

July, 2001

59
St. Petersburg

I was already awake at 6:30 a.m. when the phone rang with my wake up call. I was extremely happy that I had packed before going to bed. I had been too "wired" from Mike and Linc's real life naval saga to sleep. My mind and body were both telling me that it had been a very short and restless night.

I quickly showered and dressed in preparation for my flight to Russia. The hotel doorman flagged a taxi to take me to Gatwick International Airport, about an hour outside of London. Normally, from the enormous back seat of my London "black cab," I would admire the timeless grandeur of London's architecture, with its ubiquitous Roman influence. But even my sleepy gaze could not soften the less than attractive architecture of south London. As Mike had once pithily noted, "You're not exactly up to your ass in bucolic beauty traveling through south London." Thankfully, this being an early Saturday morning, there was very little traffic and soon we were in the London countryside.

Despite the thin veil of an early morning mist, I stared at the wide green expanses of a classic rural English landscape. Great pastures, bounded by loosely piled stone walls and towering oaks, were dotted with the summer's array of rainbow colored wildflowers. Monet's masterpieces were not more beautiful. For the hundredth time I marveled at how country landscapes throughout the world were always unique and so beautifully distinct from each other.

Over the years, I had been to Moscow several times, but this would be my first trip to St. Petersburg. For the first time in a very long time, I was traveling alone and intended this trip to be solely for pleasure. Some six months earlier I had planned this mini-vacation of sorts around the London business trip, with the specific purpose of seeing my dear—and now old—friend from another life, Nikolai Pesarik. "Nik," as he preferred to be called, had suggested I stop in St. Petersburg first for a few days sightseeing before going on to Moscow. He had two days of business meetings in St. Petersburg before I was scheduled to arrive, and hoped to meet me at my hotel for a long afternoon lunch before he flew back to Moscow.

I was anxious to see Nik again. Like Mike and Linc, we shared a past as players in a drama greater than most could imagine or appreciate.

The last vestiges of my detached tranquility were swept away by the increase in fast paced cars darting in and out of highway lanes as we approached the airport. Arriving at Gatwick, with its modern British "build it cheap and square" architecture, ended all remaining reverie. I hurriedly made a mental review of my "checklist" for departure to St. Petersburg.

After a routine check-in at British Airways, I meandered to the business class lounge area nearest the St. Petersburg departure gate to relax with the *London Times* and my usual black coffee. The monitor showed my flight departure time on schedule, leaving me about forty-five minutes to wait.

As I sipped my coffee, I couldn't help noticing that I was the only Westerner sitting in the lounge area. It is interesting that differences in mannerisms and dress, sometimes too subtle to describe, at a glance convey that a fellow traveler is not "like you." The feeling of my impending isolation from Western culture was a bit eerie. It wasn't long, though, before the combination of a now bright sun streaming through the lounge's panoramic windows brought a warmth to the lounge area that dispelled my mood.

Foolishly, I got a second cup of coffee despite the fact I knew it would probably keep me awake for most of the flight. I was physically exhausted from staying up till nearly dawn each of the last three nights. I had been working full days, then listening to Mike and Linc detail what I had now come to think of as the "*Marion* incident." I desperately needed sleep. But my mind was still hyperactive. The *Marion* incident and the implications it had on my, heretofore, generally accepted trust in our senior military leadership played and replayed through my mind. A part of me was very troubled.

Prior to the revelation of the *Marion* incident, I had only a vague historical perspective of Rickover. But now, two men who I would trust with the lives of my children had, in my eyes, convincingly shattered his public persona—and also the somewhat blind confidence I had always placed in our senior military command.

To be sure, I was not naïve, nor cynical. Despite my State Department experiences in the early seventies, I still thought of myself as a somewhat typical American, steeped in its traditional values and morals. Yet, I couldn't help wondering as I stood and began the short walk to the boarding gate, how many other times the "fail safe" system of an FBM or some other doomsday creation had come frighteningly close to rendering civilization a nullity.

It was incredible to me that Rickover and his cult were so consumed with the politics of power and stature that, even at the height of the Cold War, they would ignore the *Marion* occurrences that seriously questioned the invincibility of the FBM. Worse yet, that they had had the audacity to cover up the events of the *Marion* patrol purely for political reasons at a time when everyone in America—the public, the government, Congress and a good part of the military—believed that the FBM was, in fact, invincible. Certainly, during the seventies, to a large extent, the reality of our security and our perception of it was based on the belief that the FBM was invincible...and that the might of our power was ultimately superior to that of the Soviet Block.

I also wondered how Rickover and his accomplices kept the *Marion* incident shrouded for over thirty years under the guise of "Top Secret?" I suspected that the passage of time only emboldened them to hold the truth hostage from public scrutiny and the storm of criticism that surely would have ensued.

Where were the consciences of the purported "gate-keepers" during that period of time? Indeed, who are they now and, more to the point, do they still hold sway? Are there still those in our government or military, with a hidden agenda—suppressing, manipulating and misrepresenting material facts that affected the public's knowledge and judgment of major issues involving our nation's military capabilities, missions and strategies?

Throughout history, most Napoleonic figures have believed themselves to be above their society's stated rules, legal or moral. They were blind to their hypocrisy—ostensibly obeying society's traditional standards, but, in practice, adhering to a loosely defined self-serving code by which those standards were bent to suit the exigencies of their moment.

While I had to concede that such figures might be noted for their accomplishments, the real and ultimate issue was—at what price? Clearly a fine line separated such accomplishments from the resulting tragedies wrought on those they touched. And I remembered with fascination that the judgment of history had been unkind to most, if not all, such Napoleonic figures.

* * * * *

I found my aisle seat, stowed my travel-on bags and sat down. In spite of my need for sleep, I was promptly drawn into conversation with the man seated next to me. He was a good-natured Russian who spoke very fluent, if somewhat accented English. He was on his way home to Pskovia, a village outside of St. Petersburg, after visiting family members in London.

As we buckled up for takeoff, my new acquaintance pulled from his bulging tan briefcase an unlabeled glass bottle filled with colorless liquid. Mostly to be friendly and courteous, I obliged his offer to join him in a drink. I wasn't crazy about homemade vodka, but I knew a few long slugs of this white lightening would, in a short time, dull my senses and leave me drowsy. Sleep was not far behind the third shot. I slept through most of the smooth flight and didn't wake until three hours later as the plane touched down in St. Petersburg.

As we rolled out after touchdown, the thought occurred to me that Mike and Linc had plans for dinner tonight. Their relationship was obviously steeped in genuine respect for each other, but there was more to this relationship than respect…much more. Their bond had been forged in one of life's crucibles of daunting experiences. Each, in his own way, had been severely tested and found strength in their friendship. They understood, that over the years, the "Gods" had been kind to them, perhaps beginning with their eventual "triumph" in the *Marion* investigation. I was sure they were now eternally grateful that their paths had crossed.

Once inside the terminal, my new Russian friend and I exchanged a warm goodbye. I then walked to the queue at immigration. I was surprised to discover that St. Petersburg's airport was small, dirty and decrepit, unimpressive for a city that had recently become extremely popular with the world's tourists. The terminal walls were replete with graffiti and exposed electrical wires dangling from portions of open ceilings. The physical condition of Pulkovo Airport astounded me and reminded me of some of New York's older train and subway stations.

The weather was just as bad—cool and dank. A mist hung over the outside taxi area and parking lot, which was half paved, half mud. I quickly realized there was no organized ground transportation outside the airport, as personal cars and taxis were all mixed together.

Acquiring a taxi severely tested my negotiating skills as each driver had a different price and version of the amount of travel time to downtown St.

Petersburg. I knew the ride from the airport to my hotel should be approximately forty-five minutes and persevered until I obtained a reasonable fare.

I wasn't prepared for the scene that unfolded as my taxi sped along the narrow two-lane highway that serviced the airport and surrounding rural area. The roadway was in such a sad state of disrepair that I would have been reluctant to ride a good horse over it, let alone hurtle along at breakneck speed in a decrepit car. In fact, I was somewhat awestruck by the stark nakedness of the countryside and adjacent towns. I had thought the typical Russian's life had vastly improved after the fall of communism. Obviously it had for the rich, but not for the growing middle class and the poor.

Old cars of every make and abandoned heavy construction equipment dating back to the fifties and early sixties covered the landscape with rusty waste. Otherwise, the countryside was virtually barren and devoid of vegetation. The few children and adults I saw were poorly dressed and watched our passing with empty, hopeless stares. It reminded me of the harsh economic and living conditions that existed in so many other places of the world where the multitudes of homeless and the suffering poor resided. Typically, a life not of their own making...just the misfortunes of fate.

As we approached the outskirts of the city of St. Petersburg, we seemed to be abruptly entering a different world. Soon we were traveling on a typical western four-lane highway with large, towering modern apartment complexes dotting the adjoining landscape. Green foliage and flowers slowly became more prominent and abundant. The weather also had changed from the cool drizzle mist at Pulkovo Airport to bright sunshine.

Known in Europe as the "Venice of the North," and Russia's cultural capital, St. Petersburg is a city of haunting and magnificent beauty filled with great squares and palaces. Built by Czar Peter the Great beginning in 1703, on expansive marshlands next to the Neva River Delta and the Gulf of Finland, the city is dissected by hundreds of canals whose waters reflect the imperial city's past and present.

By the time I arrived in the city, it was early afternoon and a noticeable vibrancy marked the bustling crowds thronging the wide sidewalks. A palpable, pervasive sense of urgency seemed to emanate from the people as they went about their affairs in the unusual warmth of a sunny Russian summer day. Young and middle-aged men and women predominated the city's clean, wide streets and bricked sidewalks. It was quickly obvious that the modern St. Petersburg women were youthful, radiant and very chic. Indeed, they seemed at the moment to be the most beautiful I had ever seen anywhere in the world.

I had planned a four-day, three-night stay at the Kapinsky Grand Hotel of Europe in the heart of downtown St. Petersburg. Many of the world's rich and famous had stayed there, including a number of Europe's Premiers and a few American Presidents. It is one of Europe's classic old grand hotels.

In anticipation of my arrival, Nik had arranged a guide for me who spoke fluent English. She was, he had said, "a very special young lady." Katyana had worked for Nik in one capacity or another and he had assured me, with a laugh, that she would be a tour guide without peer.

Nik had left two messages at the hotel's front desk. One requested that the manager call him when I checked in. The other left instructions for me to meet him one hour later in the Kapinsky's bar. Nik was being Nik—allowing me the hour to unpack and freshened up.

The bar was a lounge area located off a grand hallway that began on the right side of the hotel's main lobby. The lounge was expensively and tastefully appointed, with small groupings of chairs and tables well spaced to allow its patrons privacy. Nik spotted me as soon as I walked through the tall arched entrance and stood waving his arm.

"Na sdorovie, my dear friend Patrick. It has been far too long."

After a warm bear hug and the typical Russian exchange of kisses on both cheeks, I replied, "You're right, Nik, it has been far too long. You look fantastic, you old Bolshie."

Nik laughed. "Patrick, allow me the pleasure of introducing you to Katyana Yusopov, the daughter of one of my oldest and closest friends, one that I hope you will meet while you're here in St. Petersburg. Unfortunately, I will not be able to stay with you very long this afternoon."

"Why must you leave so quickly?"

"I have a slight business "emergency" back in Moscow."

Knowing Nik as I did, I could also see in his eyes that he was up to something. Time would tell. "Katyana, I'm pleased to meet you and very grateful that you can be my guide while I'm here in St. Petersburg."

Katyana was quite young, and strikingly pretty, with beautiful long flowing auburn hair.

Oh to be twenty again—or even thirty!

Katyana smiled, a bit shyly I thought. "I am very happy to meet you, Patrick. My father and I have heard much about you from Nik, and we feel honored by your visit."

A little embarrassed, I turned to Nik and again caught that mischievous twinkle behind his hearty laugh. "Come," he said, "you have all day to talk, and I must eat something before I leave. I do not have much time."

The three of us shared a light lunch and some glasses of Chardonnay. Most of the conversation centered on Russia's fast-paced modernization and the recent happenings in Nik's life and mine as we tried to quickly get caught up on the years that had passed all to quickly. Our reunion was short-lived, as Nik's flight back to Moscow permitted a scant hour and a half for lunch. Our desire for more details from each other would have to wait a few days.

Before he left, we confirmed my arrival time in Moscow. As Nik stood to leave, we shook hands and he warmly hugged Katyana goodbye, exiting quickly through a secluded private door in the darkened recesses of the bar area.

60
The Yusopovs

Katyana, who had said little during lunch, while patiently listening to our babble of renewed friendship, now had my full attention. She suggested her view of the essential itinerary for sightseeing in St. Petersburg. A day and a half at the Hermitage Museum, a night at the Mariinsky Opera House, Yusupov Palace where Rasputin was murdered, the Alexander Column Monument honoring the defeat of Napoleon in 1812—with its grandiose stone arch aligned perfectly with the entrance to the Hermitages' Winter Palace, grand Russian Orthodox churches; and, eventually a trip around the Gulf of Finland.

Katyana, took pains to be sure I understood her pride as she explained to me that Russian cities are famous for the beautiful towering spires and multi-colored cupolas that sit on top of many of their historic Russian Orthodox churches. She didn't seem to be particularly religious, just very proud of her heritage.

Lunch finished, our first stop was to the awe-inspiring Church of the Savior on the Spilled Blood, built on the site where Czar Alexander II was assassinated. Alexander II had freed the serfs some years before Lincoln did the same for the slaves. Modeled after St. Basil's in Red Square, the church is considered one of the most beautiful and famous in the world. It is a lively multitude of brightly colored onion domes, glittering spires and a breathtaking detailed multi-colored mosaic interior.

Next was St. Isaac's cathedral, whose large golden dome rises high into the sky, visible throughout all of St. Petersburg and even from a distance out onto the Gulf of Finland.

That first evening, after a long walk along the many canals that run through the scenic city, she steered us to a very up-scale Japanese restaurant. Looking about, the place struck me as emblematic of the changes taking place in Russia.

Expensive, cosmopolitan sections like this were popping up all over its major cities. Russia no longer seemed to be an unknown cold, dark place…baleful in its lair behind foreboding walls.

As we casually sipped warm sake and chatted, Katyana peppered me with questions about my family and our life in America. She had learned English in an exclusive state school, thanks to her father's influence, but was bright enough to question the objectivity of the American image taught by her professors. The more we talked, the more I liked her. In many ways she reminded me of my own daughter. Younger perhaps, but with the same quick mind and insatiable curiosity.

Abruptly and without preamble, Katyana asked me if I would like to join her family the next night for dinner at their summer home. She particularly wanted me to meet her dad, Dmitry. Knowing of Nik's long-standing friendship with the family, I was intrigued by the request and quick to say yes.

* * * * *

The next morning, "Kat" as I had begun to address her, appeared promptly at eight o'clock in the hotel lobby. After a quick breakfast of coffee, bread and fruit, we set off to visit the Hermitage. Whether or not one is an art lover, the Hermitage, featuring the Winter Palace of the Csars, awakens the finest elements in the human spirit and Russian history. The visit was a breathtaking, unforgettable experience. Only the Louvre rivals the Hermitage in size and the quantity of its art collection. The marble floors and walls, with different colors in each room, was as beautiful as anything I had seen anywhere in the world. Kat and I spent a full day in the Hermitage, then went back to the Kapinsky so I could change for dinner. Kat waited for me in the lounge area with a glass of white wine in hand to help pass the time.

The dress for dinner was casual. The Yusopovs family summer home was on one of the small unnamed islands that dot the Gulf of Finland. The shallow gulf waters are fed by the Narva River and the waters from Lake Lagoda and the Saimaa Lakes. Usually frozen from December to March when they could be accessed by sleigh, today we would travel by boat. Dmitry himself drove the launch that met us, precisely at 7:00 p.m., at a pier not far from the Hermitage.

The best way to describe Dmitry was to imagine your favorite jovial Santa Claus, happily plump, wearing a full face of cropped white beard. He exuded an infectious warmth of spirit, and I instinctively took to him.

335

Pulling away from the pier, Dmitry motioned his daughter to open the small wicker basket near his feet. Kat extracted a well-chilled bottle of Moet champagne and three glasses, then passed the bottle to me to open. We shared the champagne, along with small talk and much laughter during the half hour ride over the smooth waters of the Gulf to their island home. By the time we reached their dock, two things were abundantly clear to me. Dmitry's English was as good as his daughter's, and they adored each other.

The Yusopovs were the only inhabitants of the island, and I quickly discerned that this was not by accident. The home, large and quite modern by Russian standards, was very charming. Having been in their family for many years, it marked Dmitry as one of the elite from the old Soviet regime. Kat's mother met us at the door. A slim, elegant woman, she appeared to be about fifty— substantially younger than my host. Charming and gracious, she spoke little English, but by manner and gesture made the warmth of her welcome obvious. Nik had obviously prepared them for my visit with "good press."

Dinner was fabulous. The food and drink were superb, but being embraced by a family such as the Yusopovs placed the experience far beyond the ordinary. I had rarely experienced such kindness and generosity of spirit.

After dinner, Dmitry suggested a walk while we sipped our post-dinner glass of fine Spanish port. It was a warm, star filled night and we strolled quietly for some minutes, each lost in our own thoughts.

Dmitry seemed to come to some sort of decision and broke our contented silence. "Patrick, my daughter tells me that she admires you and thinks Nik's judgment of you is correct. He is the one man in the world that I would trust with her life. Tonight, I have had a glimpse of you firsthand, and now, I also, have come to understand why our mutual friend Nik regards you so highly. Over the years he has often talked about you, the various endeavors you have shared, and his trust in you. Quite honestly, there is probably nothing in your life or background of importance that I do not know about you.

"It was on Nik's suggestion that I let Katyana be your guide. Nik and I have been close friends since we were young children and, thereafter, throughout our respective naval careers. He has often told me, that if not for his covert relationship with you during the SALT negotiations, the treaty in all likelihood would not have been completed. He believes you are a man of great principle."

"Dmitry, your remarks flatter me, but I think they embellish my resume more than they should."

Dmitry roared with laughter. "Nik said that would be your reply! He is right. You are a good man, and now I also believe this to be true. Having said that, I wish to ask a favor of you; but it is one that I would not consider…without first knowing you…the man.

"I am presently making arrangements to send Katyana to the U.S. to study medicine. America is such a large place and so far away…and to me she is still so young. Will you honor me and personally look after her while she is there?"

"Dmitry, you honor me…from this moment on, be assured, she is a member of my family. I promise you I will do all that I can for her in your stead."

"You are most gracious and I will be indebted to you, Patrick. Nik said that I could count on you. He was not mistaken."

As we turned to retrace our steps and rejoin the women, I thought it might be a good time to ask Dmitry about his past. The wine had probably somewhat mellowed Dmitry, so he would be less guarded and more comfortable talking about the time when our countries had been on opposite sides of a great divide.

"Dmitry, if you don't mind my asking, what did you do while you were in the Navy?"

"I had an extended career and rose to the rank of what in your American navy would be equivalent to a Vice Admiral. I was a scientist, not a seaman, specializing in the development of submarine sonar systems in the late sixties and throughout the seventies.

Scientist…sub sonar systems…now that's interesting! No mere technician gets a dacha like yours.

"Where did you do your research?"

"Across the Gulf in a secret area located on the island of Kronstadt, just off St. Petersburg. I will show you where the island is on our way back tonight, as it is near to the course we must take."

"There must have been quite a competition in those days between you and us."

"Da!" Dmitry chuckled. "Sometimes we were ahead, sometimes the Amis were ahead. Sometimes we had our heads up each other's ass."

Patrick laughed too, and said, "The infamous arms race made us both crazy."

"Da. It is now so long ago. The Amis concentrated on passive sonar systems. We were never really able to compete with them in that field. Further, their submarines were too quiet for us to detect by listening and, with one exception, ours were too noisy."

"So we won the race?"

Another chuckle and a sly grin, then Dmitry answered. "Not always!"

I knew a little about the theory of sonar and the evenings with Mike and Linc had taught me just enough to lead me to the next question. "Did you focus on active systems instead?"

"Ah. How interesting…you know something about sonar! To answer your question…yes, of course…I designed active sonar systems."

Again the chuckle. "Even today, I cannot talk about the technical details, but I will tell you that the trick with active sonar is to keep the enemy from detecting it and that, while it may not have the long range of passive systems, once it has acquired a target, it—how do you say—sticks like glue."

Hoping I was concealing my excitement, I couldn't resist one more question. "Did any of your active sonar transmit at a fourteen second interval?"

Dmitry suddenly stopped like he had walked into a wall. All joviality gone now, he simply said, "I told you, I cannot talk about technical details."

Bingo! Dmitry must be curious as hell about where that question came from…Mike, I hope you're listening!

We didn't pursue the subject any further, and, in a few minutes, the earlier "bon homie" had reestablished itself. Old war wounds heal slowly, but they do heal. The rest of the night we talked about our two families and the present day relations between our countries. A wonderful and long lasting friendship was born.

Katyana drove the launch back to the pier near the Hermitage while Dmitry and I shared light banter and the final vestiges of his port wine. The Gulf waters were still calm, but the magic of the evening couldn't drown out a small voice somewhere inside of me that kept echoing the words "active sonar systems." But for now, my curiosity would also have to remain silent.

The third day of sightseeing with Kat was both exhausting and exhilarating. It was highlighted by an early evening gourmet dinner, compliments of Dmitry, served on the top deck of an old restored wooden cruise boat that crawled between the coastlines of Finland and St. Petersburg. A clear star filled night added an unusual background luster to the brilliantly lit sights that filled both coastlines.

My last morning in St. Petersburg was spent at Suryenka Prison located on a windy promontory of the Gulf of Finland. Despite the warm summer day it was quite cool inside the dark, dirt floors of the infamous gulags' cells and torture rooms. Here Stalin had imprisoned dissidents such as Aleksandr Solzhenitsyn, the 1970 Nobel Prize winner for literature. The prison was a macabre place haunted with the history of gruesome experiences.

The rest of the day passed quickly and I realized that to properly visit and tour St. Petersburg, one literally needed weeks. Before I left, I promised Dmitry and Katyana that I would return one day with my children.

61

Moscow

My flight to Moscow left Pulkovo Airport mid afternoon on time. I wasn't thrilled about flying in the smaller, more cramped Aeroflot jets. Based on prior experience, I did not trust Russian aviation, particularly the competency of their maintenance procedures. Thankfully the two-hour flight was uneventful, complete with a soft landing.

The tall, burly and well-dressed shape of Nik approached as I entered Sheremetevo's customs and passport clearance area. Despite the passing years, he always remained in great shape. His short-cropped black hair accentuated piercing hazel eyes.

"Na sdorovie again, Patrick. How was the sightseeing in St. Petersburg?" *You know exactly how it was!* "Fantastic," I replied.

"And how is Katyana and my old friend Dmitry? I understand you had dinner with the Yusopovs at their summer home."

I smiled. "They all send their love. I didn't know news traveled that fast in Russia."

"Patrick, you are in for a lot of surprises."

My friendship with Nik was one of the small wonders born from the tense days before SALT I, signed by the Soviet Union and the United States in Moscow in May of 1972.

At first, our relationship was based on our mutual desires to have our countries seek every avenue to reduce the tensions of the Cold War and pursue peaceful coexistence. But, over time, our trust and respect for each other grew. After a stint in South America as head of KGB operations there, Nik and his family were transferred to New York City in the early eighties, attached to the Soviet U.N. delegation as its Charge d'Affaires for Foreign Policy.

Nik did not return to Russia until late 1990 after the demise of Communism, a process that started with the fall of the Berlin Wall in November of 1989, and ended with the eventual dissolution of the federated territories that then comprised the Soviet Union. Until he left the States, I was occasionally requested by my "friends" in Washington to be a conduit, via Nik, of sensitive information under seal, between the CIA and the KGB.

While Nik was in New York, our personal friendship grew and became an important aspect of each of our lives with frequent family and individual social visits. And Nik, much to my chagrin, became an ardent Yankees fan, adding yet another colorful chapter to our relationship. *Damn, he loved being a "winner."*

After his return to Moscow, he became a very successful entrepreneur as an importer of a wide variety of high-end consumer goods. To my surprise, he also became a devout member of the Russian Orthodox Church, giving new meaning to the expression "coming full circle."

Life had been good to Nik and his family, as evidenced by the fact he now owned a Lincoln Navigator and lived in one of Moscow's most affluent suburbs. Expensive luxury automobiles and good housing were still relatively scarce in Russia, except for the very wealthy.

* * * * *

Nik drove, and as we approached Moscow proper, I had to smile to myself. *God, these drivers are still, by far, the worst the world has ever known. Muscovites redefined the meaning of a "Chinese fire drill."*

As we came to a four way intersection, with a standard three light control signal, Nik turned to me, laughing, and said, "Patrick, I know how much you like to play chicken with my fellow Moscow drivers. Let me pull over and have you drive."

"Are you crazy? You know I can't stand this!"

Suddenly all four lanes of traffic, ignoring the light's signals, converged in the middle of the intersection, with honking horns and animated gestures. It was the Russian version of "chicken"…more absurd than one could imagine! One had to experience this event to believe it.

"Patrick, it's a glorious sunny afternoon and the first place I want to take you is to our reconstructed main cathedral, the Church of Christ the Savior, which was, at last, finished in late 1999. You have never seen it. It has taken the painters and sculptors over five years to complete the interior. Ten thousand people can worship inside at one time, and I'd like you to see this grand work of beauty. I'm sure you will agree with me, as many Russians believe, that it could only have been accomplished by the very hands of the angels themselves."

In no time at all, as we followed the highway along the banks of the Moscow River, the glistening golden dome and exterior white marble walls of the great cathedral came into view. "Magnificent" was all that came to my mind. We parked in the back of the cathedral and walked through one of the four enormous wooden doors, carved with exquisite designs that served as entryways into the main basilica. On this late weekday afternoon, there must have been four to five thousand visitors and worshipers inside the church. The pungent smell of incense wafted through every recess of the cavernous cathedral.

Nik turned to me. "We Russians and all the members of our thousand year old Russian Orthodox Church are extremely proud of this cathedral."

"Nik, I've been to St. Peter's in Rome twice. This is every bit as beautiful, and in many respects, the paintings on the ceiling and the colorful wall frescos are even more striking. I can't believe the number of people worshiping in here. Is it like this every day?"

He replied, "On weekends there are thousands more. The young and old alike come to marvel at the work of their Russian artisans. Even the eyes and hearts of non-believers are filled with pride in their Russian heritage. And, I have another surprise for you. Do you remember that small Russian Orthodox Church, on the far right-hand corner of Red Square, that the Communists closed for so many years? Now, from sun-up to sundown, it is filled with monks and people from all over Moscow singing Gregorian chants. Every day music and incense float over the cobblestones of Red Square and, quite ironically, now Lenin's tomb."

Nik paused and made a long sweeping arm gesture to the scene around us. "You might find some of this hard to believe, but there have been many changes in Russia since your last visit. Unthinkable when the Communists ruled, the Kremlin Museum is now filled with the relics and mementos of the era of the Emperors and Czars. Russian people go to churches in droves. They laugh and dance again in their homes and public places. Of course, everything is not utopian, but in time we will get there."

Nik stepped inside a souvenir shop and returned with a number of religious artifacts as presents for my children. While I waited for him, I studied an exquisitely colored mosaic of the world-renowned black Madonna. I could not help but remember that I had always sensed that this lion of a man, a former stalwart KGB Communist, possessed deep inside his humanity, the warm heart of a fluffy teddy bear. Incredible! Intuitively, I began to believe and understand that the Russian people were poised for greatness.

As we walked to the car, Nik said, "Before we have dinner tonight with my family—who by the way can't wait to see you—let's share a few quiet moments over at Poklonnaya Hill. It's far too nice to spend a late afternoon in my office. Poklonnaya Hill is a good place for us to get caught up on our lives."

"That's fine with me, Nik. You know I love our walks there."

"By the way, Patrick, I've arranged a suite for you at the Hotel National across the street from Red Square. Your room has spectacular views of St. Basil and the Kremlin. The food is quite good, and a number of single ladies often frequent the bar and lounge area." A sly grin, and Nik continued. "I think you'll enjoy your stay there. In the morning we are scheduled to meet some of your old Kremlin friends for prayer at St. Basils, then breakfast."

I couldn't help but burst ou laughing. *The Hotel National was Russia's Ritz Carlton and very exclusive. Nik still had serious friends!*

62
Poklonnaya Hill

It was now close to 4:30 in the afternoon as Nik and I stood under a cloudless blue sky on the consecrated grounds of the Victory Memorial on Poklonnaya Hill, located on high bluffs just outside the outskirts of Moscow. Rays of sunlight streamed everywhere bathing thousands of flowers that were dancing in the light winds on the Memorial's grounds.

The monument's name in Russian is WTBIK or SHTYK and is dedicated to the victory of what is known in Russia as the "Great Patriotic War of World War II, 1941-5." The monument's sword stands 141.8 meters high, in memory of the 1418 days that the Great Patriotic War lasted. No Allied nation suffered more from World War II than Russia. To this day, the memory of that holocaust is a seminal and ghostly presence in virtually every Russian's life.

For a moment, I raised my head in quiet reverence, looking up at this magnificent sword. Gentle winds seemed to stir the very spirits of the souls memorialized by it, who had sacrificed so much for their motherland. The scenes of war and triumph depicted on this sword that rose so majestically into the blue sky seemed to surreally leap off its face. The whispering winds filled my being with a powerful unseen presence.

My face, hands and body are covered with the grimy dirt and blood of the horribly gruesome battles of this war. In time the dirt would be washed away from my body, my wounds would heal, but the blood of this war will stain my soul for as long as I lived in the shadows of its forsaken horror. No light is able to pierce the veil of darkness that hangs over this...my troubled and wondering soul. Peace will only come to me when my ashes are cleansed and scattered by the healing winds of time throughout all eternity.

I turned to speak to Nik and realized that he too, was lost in a labyrinth of his own mystical thoughts.

His eyes fixed on the monument, he said, "Patrick, as you know, this ground is sacred, no less and no more, than similar American monuments such as the one to the GI's who raised your flag over Iowa Jima, or the still waters that serve as a grave for the *Arizona* at Pearl Harbor."

A profound sadness enveloped me, and Nik seemed even more subdued. After a quiet moment, I broke the reverie. "Nik, doesn't it strike you as one of history's greatest ironies that, after standing together against the greatest evil of our time, our countries then spent close to forty-five years in the most dangerous game of brinkmanship humanity has ever known?"

Nik slowly shook his head, as if to clear it of some awful image. "Yes, my friend. Such a waste of both our human and material resources. Especially for Russia. And the terrible fear we had for each other! Literally a shame."

"I never asked you before in detail, but what were your KGB days like in the sixties?"

"My assignment was to the Navy, so I experienced some of that fear first-hand."

I didn't quite grasp the significance of what Nik had just said. I knew that Soviet ships always carried a political officer, but the KGB? "Were you a political officer?"

Nik laughed. "No. I never told you before, because at that time I couldn't, but at one time I was the Captain of a nuclear submarine. Later, I was on the staff of Fleet Admiral Gorshkov."

"As KGB?"

"A quiet minnow in the school, there to watch the other minnows."

Suddenly the coincidence struck me like a thunderbolt. Nik was about the same age as Mike, and they both must have been at sea on submarines at about the same time. Both were my friends, and, though the odds were long, they may have actually faced each other in the Cold War's deadly insane seas of the sixties and seventies. I remembered from Mike's comments that our Navy had always viewed the Soviets with some trepidation and as a formidable threat.

How had the Soviets felt about us? "Nik, how did you feel about the American submarines back then?"

"You mean your FBM's?"

"Yes."

"We feared and distrusted you. Your technology was always ahead of ours. Trying to keep up, we pushed our scientists and ship builders far too hard—and too fast. As a result, we sacrificed many ships and a lot of good men in the race."

I knew from recently disclosed stories that service in the former Soviet submarine force had truly been very hazardous duty. The *Kursk*, the lost Soviet SSN, was fresh evidence of that.

"Were you ever frightened?"

"Of dying in a submarine accident? A little, I suppose. But only once was I truly frightened."

I was fascinated and now my curiosity heightened. "When was that?"

The memory brought a dark frown from Nik. "I will never forget the incident. It was after I had finished going to sea in the late sixties and was assigned to Admiral Gorshkov's staff in the early spring of 1970."

Incident! Coincidences were beginning to pile up. The spring of 1970 was when Mike's saga had taken place.

"Can you tell me what happened that frightened you while you were on the Admiral's staff?"

Nik waved wearily to a nearby bench. "Frightened is not the right word. Scared to death was more like it. Yes, of course, I will tell you, but let us sit. It will take awhile."

After we sat on the bench, Nik produced a cigarette from his sport coat and lit it with an old and very worn Zippo lighter. "Given to my father by an Ami when our armies met on the Rhine in 1945. A cherished memento from a man I admired greatly. The lighter is just like us Russians. Simple and reliable."

He laughed again, in a vain effort to mask the seriousness of the coming conversation. "In 1970, our Severodvinsk shipyard had developed a prototype of what you Americans later called an Alpha class submarine. It embodied all the latest technology we could cram into it, including a propulsion system that was designed and used on only that particular ship. It was also equipped with an experimental suite of active sonars, thanks to the genius of your new friend Dmitry, that we hoped would allow us to track your ballistic missile submarines—and even hunt your attack submarines."

Flicking an ash, Nik looked at me with evident pride. "Although we didn't use it in future ships for reasons I will explain later, the propulsion system in that submarine is only now being discussed by your Navy as a concept. I think they still do not suspect that we actually put her to sea, even deployed her to the Mediterranean in the spring of 1970."

Now my excitement level was fully elevated. *1970! Mediterranean! What could be next, Nik!* "Please go on."

"This propulsion system was revolutionary. It was hydro magnetic. It used the seawater around the ship as a moving conductor in the magnetic field created by the ship's propulsion system. Have you heard of a 'rail gun?' It worked something like that, with the ship itself becoming the 'projectile.' It was extremely quiet since there were no shafts or propellers."

I completely understood. "Very stealthy, then. She must have been almost impossible to detect using passive sonar, right."

"Exactly." *I didn't know Patrick knew about or understood the nuances of submarine sonar.* "She was very quiet and also very fast. The advanced experimental active sonar we placed in her operated at such a high frequency that it was virtually undetectable. We knew you would never figure it out; and also, that you would not be able evade it—or so we thought."

From what I had just learned from Mike, I knew the potential for just such a ship. "Nik, why didn't you build more of those submarines? It sounds like it would have changed the whole strategic balance at that time in your favor."

Nik grimaced. "It would have, if it had worked as we thought it would. Unfortunately, we lost the prototype during its first real operational mission. It took a little time to understand and figure out the details of what had actually happened."

"And, what did happen?"

"Before commencing serial production of the prototype, as a final test, she was sent to the Mediterranean to demonstrate her capability against American ballistic missile submarines. She was to locate one of yours with the help of our other assets already in place, and with her new sonar, trail it until near the end of its patrol. Then she was supposed to make a mock torpedo attack to prove she could have destroyed the enemy. But our submarine blew up during the mock torpedo attack and was lost with all hands. Our intelligence ships in the Western Mediterranean detected the explosions or we would have never known what happened to her."

Holy Christ! Am I hearing the other side of Mike's patrol on the Marion! First Mike, then Dmitry, now Nik. What are the incredible odds of knowing all three and hearing both sides of the story? "Explosions? Were there three?"

"Yes. Three to be exact. All very closely spaced." Over thirty years after the event, Nik still paled as he told me about it. "We later understood that three of her own torpedo warheads had exploded. We eventually discovered that the magnetic field from the propulsion system was sufficient to activate the exploders in one type of rocket-propelled torpedoes if they were in one particular stowage position. At the time, though, all we knew was that the ship had been destroyed by explosions while she was engaged with an American submarine in maneuvers. Initially, the explosions were interpreted as hostile. That was the only time in my life when I was truly scared to death."

"Why Nik? What scared you so much?"

Nik's voice was somewhat strained as he answered. "Don't forget how much we feared you. Gorshkov's entire command wanted to immediately go to a full Red Alert status. However, Gorshkov refused and only he remained calm. His refusal to report the loss of our submarine to the Politiboro was due to the fact he wanted more accurate information as to what had actually happened. If your submarine had made a transmission to report the incident, and we then detected that your military was increasing its readiness posture, Gorshkov would have had no alternative but to report what was happening. But, strangely, and for us quite unexpectedly, your submarine never initiated a transmission. We didn't know why, but after double checking all available sources we were absolutely sure no transmission was made."

I felt the chill of certainty. "And if a transmission had been made?"

Nik's memory of the event still haunted him. "Then we probably would not be sitting here now. It's quite simple. If our military had thought that hostilities were commencing, the Politburo would have ordered the Premiere to launch our nuclear missiles. They would never have risked having them destroyed in their silos. And your President Nixon would have had to respond in kind. Patrick, you are one of the few that truly understands what a "nuclear winter" would have meant for mankind!"

Nik turned on the bench to face me. "Gorshkov also understood, all to well, the consequences of any precipitous action on his part. That's why he was patient for more accurate information. He was a true warrior."

Warrior! My God, it is the chaos theory proven. The nuclear storm that would have resulted from any exchange would have been the end of mankind. Thank God the Russians had warriors back then too. One was just discovered—and he was the Soviets' most famous Admiral...Sergei Gorshkov. A warrior just like the ones Mike kept referring to.

"Nik, the American and Russian people must someday finally come to understand that in the most profound sense, the most 'Merciful of Forces,' literally saved us from ourselves. In the vernacular of spiritualism, there are no coincidences.

"It has long been time for the darkness of fear between our nations to be replaced by the very real light of truth—the truth of our commonality—that we are all one people with the simplest of wants and desires, peace in our hearts, for our families, and for all humanity.

"Thankfully, the warriors of all nations are also truly one. They are not separated from this commonality, ultimately seeking and attempting to ensure these same simple wants and desires for those they protect and love."

Nik started to stand up. "Patrick, that was well said. I think you should run for a Senate seat in your Congress. Both of our countries need politicians with a moral conscience."

Nik then placed his large left hand on my left shoulder as I continued to sit. "The true warriors are imbued with the abiding reality of their responsibility as caretakers for all of humanity. They share only one fear...irrational and politically motivated actions by their governments that would make us all refugees wandering in a desert wasteland."

I stood up now and faced Nik. "You will not believe this, but tonight after dinner I'm going to share with you the American counterpart to your Gorshkov story. It's still classified "Top Secret.""

"Patrick, you must be joking. And if you're not—why after all this time would it still be classified. That's crazy!"

"I know!"

I made a mental note to call an old friend at the American Embassy, here in Moscow, and arrange to see him early the next morning before my "reunion" at the Kremlin. I needed to send a secure cable to a retired Lt. General.

Nik and I walked slowly and quietly through the monument grounds on our way back to his car.

Nik abruptly grabbed my right arm. "Patrick, it just occurred to me. How in hell did you know there was more than one explosion on our prototype submarine?"

63
USA Homebound

The next five days with Nik and his family passed quickly, and before I knew it, it was time to leave. While I was in Russia, Mike had managed to finish our assigned work in London and had left for home. We were scheduled for a meeting at corporate headquarters late the following week.

I had been able to change my Moscow return flight from JFK in New York to Dulles International in Washington, DC with relative ease. With my favored Rusty Nail in hand, I leaned back in my business class seat to relax. The last month had been exceptionally interesting—and busy. My thoughts drifted back to a portion of my last hour in London with Mike and Linc when they discussed what had eventually happened to most of the *Marion*'s crew.

* * * * *

Linc had stood up from the table at which the three of us were sitting. His presence over those last three nights was powerful, almost regal, a presence that was enhanced by his articulated diction and the slow gesturing of his large hands.

"Patrick, our story is almost finished. But I want to leave you with a few lingering personal thoughts—thoughts that over the last three nights have been rekindled.

"The NUCS are still here and, unfortunately, MAD remained the strategic imbecility of the moment until the fall of the Soviet Union. And to this day, politicians' unquenchable thirst for power still outweighs principles.

"Integrity has been generally defined as a firm adherence to a code of incorruptible values and principles of behavioral right or wrong. It is central to the Warrior Code and a fundamental principle of every honorable military officer corps. It is the foundation upon which effective military command and leadership is based. Those who lose sight of this fact sacrifice the legitimacy of command and undermine the very nature of military service."

He looked at Mike and a fusion of shared thoughts silently passed between them. "How does one reconcile the conduct of the Navy's senior chain of command, as it relates to the events of the *Marion* patrol, with the concept of integrity? Unfortunately, one cannot. The true warrior can't live without integrity, and a politicized command structure cannot live with it."

He was right. The paradox was the integrity of the warrior versus the political nature of a senior command structure. A command structure which had become an evolved hierarchy sustained by the exigencies of egos—and institutions that have come to be their alter ego. Irreconcilable!

Linc sat again at the table. "The Soviet Union and the tensions of the Cold War exist no more—both replaced by a daunting confusion of worldwide geopolitical crisis. With every passing year our senior military leadership becomes more political and the few remaining warriors, like the dinosaur, daily hue closer to extinction. I am sad to have been a witness to this bit of history." Linc then took a sip of water and looked at Mike. His turn.

Mike leaned forward and followed in a soft firm voice. "The Gold Crew's 18th Patrol on board the *Marion* broke Commander John Holcomb—and the Submarine Force did its best to break me.

"Our lives were permanently changed by the events of this patrol. Many of us acquired a deeper insight into who we were as individuals; and undoubtedly, also acquired a much more cynical view of institutions we had come to trust."

Interrupting Mike, I asked, "What happened to the captain?"

"After leaving command of the *Marion*, Holcomb was assigned to a Joint Staff position in the Pentagon from which he soon retired. His relief from command was routine and he was never officially criticized. After retirement, he returned to his native Arkansas and, fulfilling his personal destiny, became a minister. I understand he is revered to this day by his congregation for the depth of his kindness."

"What about the others?"

"The doctor did one more patrol on the *Marion*, then returned home to Wisconsin to begin what would become a successful private practice. Surprisingly, he remained in the Naval Reserves until he was eligible for retirement. Since retiring and selling his medical practice, he volunteers his services to the poor and disabled in local outpatient medical centers.

"The Engineer did two more patrols on the *Marion*, and was then assigned to another SSBN as its Executive Officer. Later he had a successful tour as Commander of an SSBN. He then had a series of Staff jobs until his retirement from the Navy as a Four Striper in 1990. He died of lung cancer in 1996.

"Rak went on to a very successful career in the Submarine Force, including command of Submarine Development Group Two, overseeing the development of submarine tactics. A dinosaur who made Admiral, he retired in 1994 as Deputy Chief of Naval Operations—a true warrior.

"Stone left the Navy at the end of his four years of required service. He entered politics in his native Oklahoma and years later, in 1996, returned to the service for a second tour as the Secretary of the Navy. Even in that position, he was subdued by the political resilience of the Naval establishment. He learned that the political culture of the peacetime Navy is imperturbable in its confrontation with any one man. Wartime failures and national peril are, historically, society's only tools for a general cleansing of parochial and self-serving leadership within the military establishment. He and Rak are two of the best men I ever served with.

"Joe Wolfman, the lieutenant who was rejected by Rickover for NUC training, despite being highly competent and conscientious, resigned from the Navy at the end of the crew's next patrol. Unfortunately, he never fully recovered his confidence as an Officer of the Deck, nor his faith in the Navy as an institution. He returned to the family brokerage business and presently enjoys a seat on the New York Stock Exchange.

I couldn't resist, "And that asshole Johnson?"

"Rear Admiral 'Wee Willie' Johnson is still the overbearing and highly ambitious ass he always was, but as you know, he was favored by Rickover. He retired three years after the *Marion* incident, having been promoted to COMSUBLANT where he served his last two years on active duty. He now lives in Connecticut close to numerous other retired NUCS.

"By the way, I'm curious. What happened to the sailors?"

I was startled to see Mike's eyes begin to mist. It was a side of him I seldom had seen.

"You know, regardless of rank, some of us came out of that experience with a bond the average civilian might never experience and find difficult to understand. Over the years, from time to time, I hear from those guys. Most have done very well. Here's what I know about them.

"Franzei was the consummate technician and always steady in a crisis. He made Senior Chief Petty Officer prior to his retirement, then undertook a second career as an Engineer at the Naval Underwater Systems Center in Newport, Rhode Island. He is still active in submarine technology and enjoys a superb reputation for his ability to provide onboard assistance to crews grooming their current generation sonars.

"Kane and McJimsey both qualified in submarines. Kane, two years later, applied for and won an appointment to the U.S. Naval Academy. He went on to an exemplary and highly decorated officer's career, a gregarious and honorable warrior. McJimsey, having been trained on the *Marion* as a diver to meet the ship's quota of two qualified divers, applied for and received a transfer to the elite Navy Seals. Years later in the early eighties, as a Chief Petty Officer, he disappeared on a 'black operation' in Central America.

"Morales completed his service obligation, then used his service benefits to complete a master's degree in clinical psychology. He now has a PhD in psychology and is a tenured professor at UCLA.

"After retirement, Chief Brown, the epitome of an old sea dog, worked for several years in a second career with a Connecticut based support contractor to the Naval Underwater Systems Center. He eventually bought a small ranch in West Texas and returned to his roots.

"Unfortunately, I lost track of the COB. I feel bad about that because he was a damned good man…and I hope life has been good to him."

Mike stood up. "There's not much more to our story that we can tell you. Linc and I have decided to squeeze in one more day in London to rest and relax. We won't be up to see you off in the morning, Patrick. Have a safe trip to St. Petersburg and we'll catch up to you in the States on your return. Rest well and have some fun."

I hated to leave the two of them, but it was late and they were obviously finished reminiscing.

"Linc, it was great to meet you. When I get home, I'll call you and Mike to arrange a reunion at my beach home in Connecticut. Make sure you bring the entire family. You both have safe trips and stay in touch. Goodnight."

* * * * *

My musing, remembering the last evening with Mike and Linc, was interrupted by the beginning of my flight's meal service. I had ordered a split of Australian Cabernet and baked lasagna with extra sauce and cheese. I craved some Italian food. As I took my first sip of wine, my thoughts drifted to my children and the beach. I missed them both dearly. I also looked forward to spending some time with my old friend in Langley.

After dinner, full of good food and wine, my thoughts became cloudy as I soon nodded off into a deep sleep.

64

The Analyst

As I walked up to the entrance to CIA Headquarters, it occurred to me that despite recent expansions, the structure's campus-like area always retained a quiet beauty and detachment as compared to most of the other buildings in nearby Washington, D.C. that were huddled close in clusters next to each other.

The General was waiting for me in the main foyer with my visitor clip-on I.D. tag in hand. We were both punctual men. Once again I admired the portrait of "Wild Bill" Donovan, who seemed to stare back at me with a devilish grin on his face—a grin that I attributed to the reflection of the foyer's bright sunlight.

The General had long ago formally retired his position at the agency. But, due to his stature, he retained special privileges to return whenever he wished. He had confided in me, that before he left, he had groomed two protégées that he could trust.

"Good to see you again, General. The days have been kind to you."

"Patrick, it's always good to see you. It's been awhile since you last visited with us at our summer home. You must plan to come soon. I think my wife misses seeing you. How was your trip to London and Russia?"

"London is London, but I loved every minute of St. Petersburg. It is exceptionally beautiful. Someday I hope to get back there with the kids for a longer stay."

"That's great. Before we move on, I have to say I was quite puzzled by your cable request. I asked one of my protégées, a research analyst named Allyson O'Haire, to gather all the information she could about the *Marion* incident based on the areas you requested me to check. She's expecting us momentarily. I must admit, I'm curious as hell as to what you're onto."

"General," I replied, "a month ago this was the furthest thing from my mind. But now I'm consumed by the *Marion* incident."

We took the elevator to the second floor, walked down a long corridor, passing through a set of double doors, whose entry was secured by a hand print and voice identification decoder. Then we entered the maze of offices dedicated only for analysts.

The General knocked on the door of Allyson O'Haire's office and we entered after hearing a soft, "Please come in, General."

The General then introduced me to a petite, red-haired lady. I surmised she was in her late forties, but she looked much younger.

"Good morning, Allyson. Meet an old friend of mine, Patrick Conley."

We made brief eye contact and exchanged a friendly handshake. Her eyes intrigued me. More green than hazel, there was a hint of steel in them that said, "I'm a woman to be reckoned with."

"Please tell my friend what you have discovered from your exhaustive research."

The tone of her reply, despite the words, conveyed all business, "Happy to, General. Mr. Conley, within three weeks after the close of the *Marion* investigation, all evidence of it was expunged from COMSUBLANT archives. No record of the events that took place on the *Marion*'s 18th Patrol exists, nor is there one of the subsequent Administrative Hearing. Someone must have made sure of that—or so he thought! Admiral Kincaid is still alive and he was very helpful to me. I will fill you in later on Kincaid's feelings about the hearing and its details."

Kincaid's still alive? Now that's interesting! The memories of good men are not so easily erased even with the passage of time.

"Your question about the PDC's the *Marion* crew experienced was quite difficult to solve and takes some explanation. Their existence was never acknowledged by the Navy, probably because at that time they potentially implied a serious threat to the aura of the SSBN's invincibility. Politics apparently overrode any concern for the tactical risk faced by the crews that continued to go to sea on patrols in the strange, near-war environment that existed in the 1970s.

"Further, no explanation for the PDC's was ever provided to the Gold Crew of the *Marion*, and apparently they did not reoccur on their subsequent patrols. Although not reported by the Blue Commanding Officer, probably because he did not want to risk being associated with the issue, his sonar team did report to the Gold sonar team that they had sporadically experienced an unusual number of PDC's throughout the ship's previous patrol in the Mediterranean, though not at any fixed interval. I was able to verify this from retired crew members who still clearly remembered the PDC's issue. This surprised me, so I checked further.

"No other cases are known to have been reported, and neither CINCLANTFLEET nor COMSUBLANT ever acknowledged the PDC issue in intelligence briefings or message summaries. About two years after this incident, however, it was acknowledged by the Submarine Force Chain of Command that Soviet submarines were being outfitted with new, very high frequency active sonars that were so difficult to detect that they required special intercept gear to hear them. The Soviet sonar was also very difficult to shake off once they obtained contact.

"The General and I believe the two-year delay before the new sonar capability of the Soviets was acknowledged, could have been because the Soviets assumed, from the *Marion*'s behavior, that we had counter-detected them and therefore were spooked. In that case, they probably would have taken the experimental sonar system out of service for a period of time for more refinement."

Allyson paused and turned to another folder on her desk.

"I needed the General's help to put into context for me the Administrative Hearing that occurred after the patrol, which in essence was a masquerade for a de facto court-martial of the *Marion*'s senior officers. Normally, I never get emotionally involved with work matters. But the more I dug into the *Marion* situation, the more I found it difficult to maintain an objective detachment.

"At first, I thought the hearing was quite unfair under the circumstances as I knew them. But then I factored in that all of this took place at the height of the Cold War and initially believed that alone might serve as justification. And then I realized, if Rickover didn't want our people and the Russians to know anything about what happened on the *Marion* patrol, issuing a 'gag order' or 'Top Secret' classification would have been more than sufficient. Honorable officers and their crew would have surely obeyed such an order. So, I was still troubled by the hearing and, for me personally, there seemed to be no reasonable justification for it."

Nodding toward the General, she said, "Ultimately, you sir, gave me a motive which confirms your, and now my own, suspicions. Plain and simple, you told me that Rickover was the type of personality who ravaged souls, so to speak, to assure adherence to his personal code of loyalty and his obsession—cultured by his compulsive egotism—to protect the NUC cult.

"At first blush I believed the General over-simplified his answer, but others whose opinions I have high regard for confirmed his scenario. The General knew Rickover and had more than a passing acquaintance with him."

The General interrupted, "Patrick, it's very clear to me now that it was disgraceful that these good men had to endure such an ordeal just to be sacrificial lambs on the altar of politics—to satisfy someone's distorted view of a code of loyalty."

There probably was not a person born that did not have the experience of at least one person or event significantly impacting their lives. I wondered now, in the grand scheme of things, how the "Marion incident" had factored into the vagaries of life's carousel for the other Marion men. "Allyson," I interrupted, "how did you dig up this much information in such a limited time? This happened thirty years ago!"

The General laughed. "I told you she's one of our best, and as such, has her ways. Also, Patrick, I'd be careful if I were you. She also knows all there is to know about you."

I was not sure whether to laugh or play the smug role.

Allyson smiled, obviously relishing the moment. "I have my resources. But there's something else you should know. I was also able to uncover, by pure accident, an old Navy shipyard memo about the *Marion*'s condition after the grounding. The grounding was a closer brush with the submariner's ultimate horror than anyone may have realized at the time. When the *Marion* was dry-docked to check for physical damages within days of coming back to port, nothing significant was found, except that the bottom sixteen inches of the rudder was scoured clean and covered with scars. The *Marion* had actually put a foot and a half of her rudder into the Mediterranean's soft bottom.

"Fortunately, the *Marion* didn't catch a ledge. If it had, your friend Mike wouldn't have been here to tell you his story—and the secrets and memories of good men would have been erased."

Allyson had obviously finished for the time being, and as only a curious woman could, lackadaisically stared at me as she occasionally brushed back the strands of her long red hair.

"Allyson," I asked, "do you know where Wee Willie Johnson is?"

"Groton, Connecticut," she responded.

I wonder if the General agrees with me that the time is appropriate to publicly disclose the Marion incident and ignore its continued ridiculous "Top Secret" classification. I hope Wee Willie is still alive and can read...I'd love to see his reaction!

The General stood to go and said, "While I'm here I have to attend to some other affairs. I've asked Allyson to keep digging for you and answer any other questions you may have. If you're able, I took the liberty of making reservations for us tonight at the Capitol Grill at 8:30. I've been assured a quiet table awaits. Tomorrow I must return home."

"General, I'll look forward to it."

I spent another hour or so listening to Allyson explain the details of the administrative hearing and stood to leave. *Why not? Don't be shy—you're attracted to her and she's very pretty.* "Allyson, would you be free to join the General and me for dinner tonight?"

Her warm smile assured me of her answer.

"How about drinks there at 7:30 p.m."

"See you then."

"Great."

Can she tell how thrilled I am?

* * * * *

The next day's late morning flight to Newark was quick and routine.

I needed to stop at my corporate offices before I went home. I looked forward with great anticipation to a quiet week at the beach. Dan was patiently waiting for me on my arrival.

"Dan, it's good to see you. Looks like you lost some weight. How's the family?"

"Pat...Mr. Conley, everyone's great. Look at this!"

He handed me the *Boston Globe* front page. The headlines screamed, *Red Sox tie Yanks for First.*

"Dan, it's 1986 all over again."

Mr. Conley: "I still can't believe it."

"Dan, you'll have to bring the family down to the beach this weekend. We can cheer the Sox on and I'll cook something special. The water is warm, I heard the surf will be up, and I can teach your kids how to body surf."

"Sounds great to me. My wife will call you tonight or early tomorrow to confirm."

"Hope you can make it. I want you both to meet my new friend, Allyson. She's flying in on the shuttle to Providence from D.C. tomorrow and will join me at the beach for the rest of the week. I think the kids will like her."

"Mr. Conley, we'll look forward to meeting her."

* * * * *

As I rode in the quiet comfort of the limousine toward home, I remembered what Mike had said to me about Rickover's First Rule of Positive Leadership. "First prize is nothing, second prize is a kick in the ass." It occurred to me that relative to the *Marion* incident, First Prize had indeed been nothing. No war, no loss of the *Marion*, no career ending suicide for Mike and no political or public embarrassment for Rickover and the Nucs. Yet, second prize might have truly been a disastrous kick in the ass—particularly for humanity given Nik's assessment on Poklonnaya Hill.

* * * * *

The following morning, promptly at nine o'clock, I called my agent. Gily Wong was a long stemmed Oriental rose. Born to immigrant Chinese parents, she was as American as apple pie, with sparkling hazel eyes that were framed by short black hair. She had come to know her way around the publishing scene where her charm and intelligence had gained her wide access to the inner circle of influential editors. Gily had led me through the frustrations of publishing my first book, *Appolyon's Journal*, a thinly fictionalized account of my three years in the background of strategic arms limitation negotiations. On the market now for just a year, *Appolyon* was selling reasonably well.

She picked up on the second ring. "Gily Wong."

"Gily. Hi. It's Patrick Conley. I just got back from the UK and Russia a few days ago. How's *Appolyon* doing this week?"

"Glad to hear from you, Patrick, and welcome back. We haven't made the *Times*' Best Seller list yet, but, so help me God, I think we may be only a couple of weeks or so away. According to Ken over at the publisher, sales have been accelerating for the last two to three weeks."

That was gratifying news, exciting even, but I had something else I was more anxious to talk about. "Gily, ask Ken if they will take another book from me in about a year."

"Patrick, you know they will. *Appolyon* is already giving you widespread credibility in the marketplace. What will this one be about anyway?"

I could have laughed, but it was not a comedy that I had in mind. "I'll send you a synopsis and short outline within the next week."

Gily had too much experience with excited authors to show too much curiosity.

"What are we going to call this one?"

That's easy…*First Prize is Nothing.*

Glossary

ACIP – Attack Console Indicator Panel. The panel in the ships combat center that displays the status of missiles as they are readied and fired. Also contains the key operated switches that must be separately closed by the Commanding Officer and a second officer to permit missile launch.

AFT – The rear of the ship or towards the stern of the ship. Often used by the crew to mean the Engineering Spaces, all compartments after the Missile Compartment. Collectively, the Reactor Compartment, the Auxiliary Machinery Room, and the Engine Room.

AFTERNOON EFFECT – A condition of the sea arising from the heating of the surface layer by the sun during a period of calm seas that provide little mixing effect. The result is a strongly negative, persistent thermocline near the ocean surface that bends sound rays downward from a surface target. Sonar detection ranges on surface contacts are thereby much reduced.

AN/WIC – The small console box in an MC system containing the speaker and press-to-talk switch.

ATF – Automatic Target Following. An operating mode of many sonars in which the sonar automatically keeps itself trained on the selected noise source. On a target of sufficient signal strength, ATF tends to provide more consistent, accurate bearings than can be obtained from manual steering of the sonar array.

BAFFLES - A sector of about 30 degrees, centered on the stern of the submarine, in which the bow-mounted sonars are deaf. Sound insulation shields the sonars from the noise of its own ship's propulsion machinery. To "clear" baffles is to maneuver the ship to allow the sonar to look into the previously obscured area.

BLACK PROJECT – A project carried on by the government behind a veil of secrecy.

BRN – The Navy Navigation Satellite system receiver. An early version of the present Global Positioning System. Utilized a small number of satellites and derived a position fix from a single satellite, but only when the satellite was passing overhead.

BROW – The walkway placed between ships or between ship and pier to allow access to the ship by foot while it is moored.

COMSUBLANT – Commander Submarine Force, Atlantic Feet. The Submarine type commander. Responsible for the administration, maintenance, and training of Submarines in the Atlantic. Subordinate commands are Submarine Flotillas (SUBFLOT) each of which is comprised of two or more Submarine Squadrons (SUBRON).

COMSUBRON 16 – Commander Submarine Squadron 16. The Squadron based in Rota, Spain. Responsible for refitting assigned SSBN's and their operational control during pre-patrol training at sea.

CTF 64 – Commander Task Force 64. Operational commander of submarines operating on patrol in the Mediterranean.

CUMSHAW – The time-honored practice of unofficially obtaining goods and services for the ship through small bribes of commodities from the ships stores. An under the table barter exchange.

db - Decibel. A relative measure of signal strength, usually sound intensity. One db change represents a change in signal strength by a factor of 2.

ECHO RANGER – A sonar contact from which active sonar transmissions can be heard.

ECM – Electronics Counter Measures. In this case, the passive detection of a radar's emission exactly similar to the radar detector in an automobile to detect a speed trap.

ENGINEERING SPACES – Everything aft of the forward Reactor Compartment bulkhead consisting of the Reactor Compartment, Auxiliary Machinery Room, and Engine Room. (Maneuvering Room is an enclosed space within the Engine Room.)

FORWARD – The front of the ship or ahead of the ship. Often used by the crew to mean all spaces forward of the Reactor Compartment.

INCHOP – Derived from the acronym "CHOP" or Change of Operational command. Term "INCHOPPER" commonly used in reference to deploying Soviet North Fleet units as they enter the Mediterranean.

INTSUM – Intelligence Summary.

"MC" SYSTEMS – Intercom circuits of loud speakers and press-to-talk switches. The "1MC" is the ships general announcing system. The "7MC" connects the stations required to maneuver the ship, others, (21MC, 27MC, 31MC) are dedicated to other functionally related stations, such as Sonar/Conn or Torpedo Room/Missile Control Center/Conn.

NPEB –Nuclear Propulsion Examining Board. An inspection team assigned to the Fleet Commander's staff for administrative purposes, but operating in direct support of and under the direction of Naval Reactors. Charged with insuring the safe and correct operation of all nuclear propulsion plants in the Fleet through detailed annual inspections called the Operational Reactor Safeguards Exam (ORSE).

NTPI – Navy Technical Proficiency Inspection. An annual inspection of the ship's nuclear weapons, their supporting systems and equipment and the crew's proficiency in maintaining, storing, and employing the weapons. Emphasis is on absolute safety, security, and reliability of the nuclear weapons and their handlers.

ORSE – Operational Reactor Safeguards Examination. An intensive inspection of all nuclear powered ships Engineering Departments conducted annually by dedicated inspection teams assigned to the Atlantic and Pacific

Fleet Commands. Satisfactory performance on the ORSE is a prerequisite for the crew to continue conducting critical reactor operations under their own recognizance. Intended to insure nuclear safety of reactor plant operations.

OUTCHOP – Soviet fleet units departing the Mediterranean to return to the Soviet North Fleet.

PDC – Practice Depth Charge. A small explosive charge, usually a hand grenade, used by surface ships to simulate an attack on a submarine. Often used generically to describe any small explosion heard on sonar.

PERT CHART – A planning aid. A Pert Chart is a graphic dependency network of planned activities.

PIM – Position of Intended Movement. The planned track of the ship.

PM's – Preventive Maintenance Actions. Specific maintenance actions prescribed for equipment or systems based on elapsed time, time in service or operating cycles that is done to prevent failure.

POOPY SUIT – A one piece coverall, somewhat similar to an aviator's flight suit that was provided to FBM crews to wear on patrol. The suits were quick drying and fire retardant.

PORT (side) – Left (side).

QUICK LOOK REPORT – A message report transmitted by the SSBN as it returns to port after a Patrol advising the Refit site of known material deficiencies that may affect planning for the forthcoming refit. Also, a message report from Johns Hopkins (APL) sent to the ship in refit following an urgent and preliminary review of the data package from the previous patrol.

RADIAC GEAR – Radiation monitoring equipment. May be either portable or permanently installed.

REFIT – The 28 day period between patrols during which the FBM submarine was repaired as necessary, provisioned, and prepared for return to sea.

RUBE GOLDBERG – A cartoonist of the 1930's and 1940's famous for his sketches of outlandishly complicated contraptions accomplishing nonsensical activities.

SABOT – In this case, an inert concrete cylinder with a non-abrasive coating to protect the missile tube and of the same diameter and weight as a missile. Used to test the missile tube's functioning without expending a missile.

SCRAM – Instantaneous shutdown of the nuclear reactor by unlatching the control rods and allowing them to be driven into the core by spring pressure. Initiated either manually or automatically by the reactor instrumentation and control systems when an approaching unsafe condition is detected. Often done manually for crew training.

SSBN – Submarine (SS), Ballistic Missile (B), Nuclear Powered (N)

STARBOARD (side) – Right (side).

STRATEGIC – In the case of weapons systems, those that are designed or employed to strike at the war making capability or political will of the enemy.

TACTICAL – Those weapons or maneuvers utilized in direct interaction between opposing forces or units.

TEST DEPTH – The maximum depth at which the submarine is certified for operation.

THERMO CLIME – The rate of change of seawater temperature with depth. In a "negative" thermo clime, the water becomes colder with increasing depth. The point at which the rate of change increases or decreases marks a "layer" boundary.

TYPE 11 – The Type Eleven periscope was a stabilized, star-tracking periscope used exclusively to obtain precise celestial position fixes used in determining errors in the Ships Inertial Navigation Systems (SINS).

VENTURI EFFECT – The decrease in pressure associated with the increase in velocity of fluid flowing through a tapering constriction. In the case of the submarine, the surface of the water or the sea bed can combine with the tapering shape of the submarine hull to provide the conditions for a venturi effect. The resultant local decrease in pressure can, under the right conditions, exert enough force to overcome the influence of the ship's control surfaces.

VLCC – Very Large Crude Carrier. In the Mediterranean, typically a tanker of 200,000 to 300,000 tons displacement. A huge ship.

WSRT – Weapon System Readiness Test.

EXHIBIT "A"

USS (SHIP'S NAME)

(Date)

MEMORANDUM

From: Executive Officer
To: All Officers

Subj: Preparation for VADM RICKOVER, USN

The following arrangements will be made by officers indicated to insure the Admiral's comfort during Sea Trial ALPHA:

DONE		ITEM	OFFICER
_____	a.	Two full sets of khakis available in XOSR with sox and belt. Shirt size 14-32; trousers waist 30 length 29.	Supply
_____	b.	Menu – Clear menu with OIC prior to 10/26. Fruit available – grapes/apples/etc. (fresh orange juice). Keep bowl in XOSR full. No milk, eggs, cheese, etc. Have margarine and skimmed milk available.	Supply
_____	c.	Insure RM's check out on Marine operator Procedures. He will want to make ship to shore calls.	Comm.

_____ d.   Have late airlines schedules available to   XC
XOSR desk.

_____ e.   Disconnect MC systems, buzzers, dial-X   Elect.
Ringer in XOSR. DO NOT disconnect pantry
call button. E Div. Officer see XO(G) for details.

_____ f.   Turn all MC speakers in WR Country down   Elect.
to low, pleasant, but discernible level. He
will talk to crew and it should be heard
in Wardroom. 1MC speaker outside XOSR
disconnected.

_____ g.   Ship's force film badge and dosimeter.   Med.
Doctor deliver personally.

_____ h.   Provide plenty of (SHIP'S NAME) stationary,   XO
envelopes, and pen available in XOSR desk.

_____ i.   Do not pull in shore phone connection until   OCD
last minute when getting underway and then
with CO's permission.

_____ j.   Have foul weather jacket (Khaki) available   Supply
in XOSR with jacket patch (leather name
patch) and (SHIP'S NAME) patch. The
jacket must be expendable.

_____ k.   Rig for RED only when required by Standing   ODDs
Orders and with permission of OIC.

_____ l.   Insure toilet articles such as soap, towels,   Supply
etc. are available in XOSR.

_____ m.   Insure at least 500 plain envelopes on board.   YN-XO

_____ n.   Insure latest weather reports are available   OPS
immediately upon request.

_____ o.   Insure stock of message blanks available in   Comm.
the XOSR desk. (Deliver to XO(G)).

_____ p.   Insure Engineer is in Engineering spaces any   Eng/All
time Admiral is there.

_____ q.   Insure bunk ready on barge for Admiral if he   Supply
desires to use it. Be prepared to serve Sat.
evening meal to Admiral and guests on the barge
or boat is he desires.

_____ r.   LT (NAME) should handle arrangements for   XO
departing.

_____ s.   Insure brow hanging on crane on arrival. He may   XO
leave immediately.

_____ t.   Have 2 stop watches available for Admiral in   Eng
Maneuvering and one in XOSR.
Flashlight in XOSR.

_____ u.   Minimize use of 1MC. Emergencies and essential   All
traffic only (and then use in a modulated
unexcited voice).

_____ v.   Have one yeoman available to take care of   XO
stenographic needs. (TICE).

_____ w.   Provide copy of local newspaper and Sunday's New   XO
York Times (if possible) in XOSR. Also provide
recent magazines (Time, U.S. News and
World Report, Harpers, Newsweek, etc.)

_____ x.   On scrams don't fiddle around warming up mains.   Eng
Get back on the line safely but quickly.
Don't forget to order a gravity taken.

_____ y.   Provide dental floss in XOSR medicine cabinet.   Med
(Deliver to XO(G)).

_____ z.   Insure we have equipment for transfer to small boat 1ˢᵗ LT/S.Y.

_____ aa.   Have transportation sedan ready (on one minutes   XO-COB
notice) clean, fueled, driver standing by, etc.
(SO5 sedan).

_____ bb.   Be prepared for full camera coverage (Polaroid,   PIO
35121 and speedgraphic).

_____ cc.   Insure plenty good books and reading material   Med
available in XOSR and Wardroom (Librarian
coordinate with XO(G)).

_____ dd.   Insure embossing machine and at least three   Supply-COB
different colors to tape are available. Provide
plenty of tape.

_____ ee.   Check installation of flexowriters. Yeo, XO(G)   XO-YN-OPS
and one Trial Alpha RM (Crypto Repair Trained)
check out with Tech. Rep. by Friday 10/23.

_____ ff.   Insure barber available on instant call with   Supply
hair cutting equipment.

_____ gg.   Minimize use of dial-X in Maneuvering   All hands

_____ hh.   S.S. Pierce lemon drops   Supply

All officers concerned keep master copy of this memo in WRSR#1 up to
date as items are completed.